Aliens and UFOs

EXTRATERRESTRIAL TALES FROM

Asimov's Science Fiction AND

Analog Science Fiction and Fact

EDITED BY

Cynthia Manson and Charles Ardai

SMITHMARK

This edition published in 1993 by SMITHMARK Publishers Inc., 16 East 32nd Street, New York, NY 10016

SMITHMARK books are available for bulk purchase for sales promotion and premium use. For details write or call the manager of special sales, SMITHMARK Publishers Inc., 16 East 32nd Street, New York, NY 10016; (212) 532-6600.

Library of Congress Cataloging-in-Publication Data

Aliens and UFOs from Asimov's science fiction and Analog / edited by Cynthia Manson and Charles Ardai
    p. cm.
    "A collection of 19 short stories to extraterrestrials and other worlds, taken from the pages of Asimov's science fiction and Analog science fiction and fact"—CIP galley.
    ISBN 0-8317-0436-5
    1. Science fiction, American.   2. Life on other planets—Fiction.
3. Unidentified flying objects—Fiction. I. Manson, Cynthia.
II. Ardai, Charles.   III. Analog science fiction & fact.
IV. Asimov's science fiction.
PS648.S3A475 1993
813'.0876208—dc20
                                    93-20150
                                       CIP

Printed in United States of America

10 9 8 7 6 5 4 3 2 1

Aliens and UFOs

Contents

Introduction

The idea that human beings might be alone in the cosmos is a disturbing one. This is one of two reasons people tell stories about aliens.

But the idea that humans might *not* be alone in the cosmos is perhaps even more disturbing; hence, the second reason people concoct such stories.

There is more to it, of course. Stories about aliens can be touching, as in *E.T. The Extra-Terrestrial*, or frightening, as in *The War of the Worlds* and *Alien*, or thought-provoking, as in *2001: A Space Odyssey* or *Close Encounters of the Third Kind*. They can be as exciting as every pulp paperback that has ever featured a bug-eyed space monster on the cover, as fanciful as the spacefaring adventures of Baron von Munchausen and the Little Prince, or as sobering as the dark, philosophical tales of Philip K. Dick. Yet all these different types of stories share a common origin: They spring from a powerful human desire to know if anyone, or anything, else is "out there."

Why, after all, should Earth be unique among planets? Why should our sun be the only one among billions to cast its light upon living creatures? Is it not more probable, given the size of the universe, that extraterrestrial life exists somewhere and simply hasn't yet crossed our path than that there is no other life to be found?

The answers to these questions, questions that storytellers have been asking for as long as they have been aware of the existence of other planets, are not necessarily obvious. In recent years scientific progress has allowed storytellers, and their storytelling, to become much more sophisticated. Many of today's top science fiction writers, in fact, are scientists themselves—astronomers, biologists, physicists, sociologists—and they bring their professional expertise to the subject. But the questions they ask, and still try to answer, have not changed through the centuries.

The result of so many different voices speaking and speculating on the same subject for so long is a rich, diverse literature about aliens. In the following collection you will find stories that span the entire breadth of this literature, culled from the pages of the single most critically acclaimed science fiction magazine of our time, *Asimov's Science Fiction*, and the prestigious, oldest continuously published science fiction magazine in the world, *Analog Science Fiction and Fact* (born in 1930 as *Astounding*).

Featured authors include such giants in the field as Larry Niven, Frederik Pohl, Poul Anderson, Hal Clement, Gene Wolfe, and Joan Vinge as well as award-winning newer authors such as Lawrence Watt-Evans, Allen Steele, and Thomas M. Disch. There are even stories from the editor of *Analog*, Stanley Schmidt, and the late editorial director of *Asimov's*, Isaac Asimov himself.

Part One of the collection features stories about aliens coming to Earth—or, in the case of Michael Bishop's "Cabinet Meeting," aliens on Pluto making contact with Earth by communicating through a wire coat hanger. Barry B. Longyear describes an ancient race of Earth-dwellers returning after a seventy million year absence to claim our planet as their own in "Homecoming"; Frederik Pohl imagines what the consequences would be if NASA found creatures on Mars and brought them back in "Iriadeska's Martians"; Lawrence Watt-Evans has to figure out how to hide a broken-down UFO from prying eyes in "A Flying Saucer with Minnesota Plates"; and Thomas M. Disch serves up a delicious satire of those kidnapped-by-aliens books in "The Abduction of Bunny Steiner, or A Shameless Lie."

In Part Two, our authors blast off for parts unknown. The space travelers in Isaac Asimov's "Sure Thing" and Larry Niven's "The

Real Thing," and the colonists of hostile worlds in C. R. Faddis's "Caduceus" and Hal Clement's "Seasoning," must deal with aliens on their own turf, far from the comforts of Earth. Sometimes it is not even clear who the real aliens are, as in Poul Anderson's disorienting "Strangers."

Capping things off are two novelettes in which humans and aliens go head to head, in one case with the future of the human race hanging in the balance: "Grimes and the Great Race" by A. Bertram Chandler and "If You Can Fill the Unforgiving Minute" by David Andreissen and D. C. Poyer. Which species, human or alien, will win these grueling contests? Read on—whatever you expect, we think you'll be surprised.

In general, science fiction provides a glimpse of what could be out there, waiting to be discovered. Stories about aliens specifically hold out the hope—and the fear—that we are not alone.

But whether extraterrestrials *actually* exist is almost beside the point. They exist in the minds of writers and readers; they exist in the collective imagination of the human race; and they exist in the stories you are about to read.

As for the rest of it, is is pure speculation—though it is fascinating speculation, all of it. For instance, one wonders whether, if there are extraterrestrials, they resemble the creatures in any of the following stories. And one can only imagine what kinds of stories, millions of light years away, they must be telling about us.

—THE EDITORS

PART ONE

The Aliens Come to Earth

Homecoming

by Barry B. Longyear

Lothas draped his heavy green tail between the seat cushion and backrest. Extending a claw on a scaled, five-fingered hand, he inserted it in a slotswitch and pulled down. The armored shield on the forward view bubble slowly lifted as the control center went to redlight. Lothas felt the strange pain grow in his chest as he looked through the filter at the target star, now no longer a point of light but a tiny, brilliant disc. He leaned against the backrest, his large dark eyes glittering as they drank in the sight of the star. *It has been so long. Even though I have been out of suspension for only a total of six star cycles, yet I still know it has been . . . seventy million star cycles. A third of a galactic cycle.*

Lothas noticed his own reflection in the filter, turned his long neck left, then right, and marveled at the absence of change. The large eyes, occupying a fifth of the image, were clear and glinted with points of red, blue, and yellow light reflected from service and indicator lights. The skin, grey-green and smooth, pressed against and outlined the large veins leading from his eyes down the elongated muzzle, with its rows of thick, white, needle-sharp teeth. His focus returned to the star as he reached and pressed a panel with one of the five clawed fingers of his right hand.

3

"This is Lothas Dim Ir, on regular watch." He paused and examined the navigation readout, then switched to a display of the rest of the cluster formation of ships. "The formation is normal; no course corrections necessary; the homestar Amasaat now at . . ." he examined an instrument, ". . . four degrees of arc."

He pressed another panel, signaling to all the watches on the rest of the ships. The display showed all but three of the two hundred ships answering. Lothas studied the display, slightly confused that he felt nothing about the missing ships. Automatic recording systems had shown the three ships wrecked by the same meteor. *But that was . . . millions of cycles ago. Difficult to feel pain for deaths that old.*

He pressed another panel, and the display began filling with life unit survival-percentage figures transmitted by the watches on the other ships. Automatically an average was made and a total rate of survival and unit count was made. 77.031%; 308,124 life units surviving. Lothas nodded. There had been no change in the figure for . . . over thirty million star cycles. The three wrecked ships, and the others who could not survive the suspension process. *But, the rest of us shall see Nitola.*

Lothas looked around at the empty control center. Moments after he gave the initiate-desuspension command, the center would be a hive of activity. . . . *A hive of activity; I wonder if the little stinging sweetsects have survived?* He looked at the banks of receiving equipment, sensor and analysis piles, and the rest of the tools that the knowing ones would use to see how Nitola had changed. *But, this moment there is still quiet—this wondrous, jeweled loneliness of space. I ache for my home planet, but this, too, has become my home.*

He reached out a claw and closed the shield, cutting off his view of the homestar. As the center returned to yellow light, Lothas pressed the initiate-desuspension command. As the ships answered, he listened to the sounds of life stirring in his own vessel—motors whined, draining the clear suspension fluid from countless lengths of veins and replacing it with warm blood. Lothas looked at the drain set into the skin of his own arm. He pulled it free and watched as the blood pooled slightly, then began clotting. He tossed the drain into a recycler. *We will need them no longer. We are almost home.*

Carl Baxter, garbed in regulation briefs and tee shirt, looked up from under the bed. "Where are my socks?"

The lump on the bed, sheets pulled over her head, mumbled. "I don't wear 'em."

"It's my last pair of clean socks. Now, where are they?"

The lump pulled the sheets down, exposing a sleep-mussed tousle of black curls framing a pretty, if angry, face. "You'd have clean socks if you'd do the laundry more often. We both work. There's no reason why I have to be the—"

"Yeah, yeah, yeah." Baxter pulled out the dresser and looked behind it.

"Yeah, yeah, is it?"

"Yeah." He pushed the dresser back against the wall. "Look, it's not like we had the same kind of job, Deb. I have to be at the base at oh six-thirty six days a week, and sometimes seven. I'm lucky if I can drag it home in time for Johnny Carson. And you want me to pitch in with the laundry, grocery shopping, housecleaning—"

"Look, supersoldier!" Deb pushed the hair from her eyes. "You think keeping the agency going by myself is easy? Just last week that idiot layout man you hired before you were called up totally feebed the Boxman Spring campaign. I've been putting in sixteen hour days to try and have it ready in time! You want laundry on top of that?"

Baxter concluded his third survey of the dresser drawers by slamming the upper right. "Why don't you hire some help? We can afford it."

Deb's eyes widened. "Yawl means dat Massa Baxter gonna let dis nappy ol' head actually hire someone? Me, a *woman*!"

"Oh, knock it off!" Baxter frowned and sat on the bed. He put a hand on Deb's shoulder. "Look. I'm sorry, Deb. I know I said no hiring until I got back, and I know it's been tough on you. Go ahead and hire whatever you need in the way of help. I'll give Boxman a call and try and straighten things out."

Deb put her hand on Baxter's and looked up into his eyes. "Carl, when is the Air Force going to be finished with you? This whole thing is so silly. One day we are running a successful advertising agency and living in a nice condo, and the next we're stuck here in the middle of nowhere in a shack that hasn't been repaired since Billy Mitchell was a P. F. C. Tell me there's a light at the end of the tunnel."

Baxter shrugged. "I don't know." He raised his head and looked at her. "That trip to Santa Barbara every day is getting you down, isn't it? Maybe you'd be happier if you stayed at home?"

"Look, Baxter, I'll stick it out as long as you do, and how much longer can that be? Your six months is almost up, isn't it?"

Baxter stood up and resumed his search for the missing pair of socks. "You think I might have left them in the living room?"

Deb's face developed an instant frown. "Isn't it?"

"Isn't what?"

She shook her head and pounded on the mattress with her fists. "Oh, no! You didn't! Tell me you didn't get extended, Baxter! Tell me you didn't, or I'll brain you with the alarm clock!"

He sighed, shrugged, scratched his head, then held out his hands. "I didn't have any choice, Deb—"

"Ooooooooooo! You . . . you . . . monster!" She threw off the covers, swung her legs to the floor, then stormed off into the bathroom. The door slammed, then clicked.

"Deb?" Baxter walked to the door. "Deb, honey? Don't lock yourself in, honey, I still have to shave."

"Go away."

"Deb, I'm all they have in public relations right now to promote the Air Force's argument for the combined shuttle, not to mention the new bomber, and the—"

The door opened, a pair of socks flew out, and the door slammed shut.

* * *

Wearing one regulation blue and one not-so-regulation yellow and red Argyle sock in addition to his uniform, Captain Carl F. Baxter pulled away in the blue staff car assigned to him. He came to the cross-street stop sign, screeched to a halt, and rummaged through the glove compartment for his electric shaver. A honk came from behind, and Baxter looked over the top of the headrest to check the honker's rank. Seeing only single golden bars, he returned to his search. *Damned thing has got to be in here.* His hand closed on the ancient Remington, a gift from his mother-in-law, and he sat up and removed the cap. The driver behind honked again, and Baxter extended a finger in the Hawaiian good luck tradition, then returned to the shaver. With an angry squeal of tires, the lieutenant pulled around Baxter's car, ignored the stop sign, and pulled out onto the base's main drag. With his shaver humming, Baxter pulled out and turned right.

Baxter caught a flash of a sign, "ODQ-D7," recalling Deb's comment when she first saw it. "This is our new home? Oh, I like the name; it's so much nicer than Hollywood Hills or Sutton Place." He snorted and leaned on the accelerator as he came abreast of the parking ramp for the experimental aircraft. Deb was ready with a comment for that, too. "Oh, what a nice view—Baxter, I want a divorce!" She didn't really, but she was not happy, and neither was Baxter. An experienced test pilot, he had left the Air Force during the testing cutbacks of the late sixties to begin his own advertising agency. As a reserve officer, he had assumed that, if he ever was called up, it would be as a pilot. But the Air Force had found his advertising skills much more desirable, and dropped him in public relations. Baxter glanced out of the side window at the black, needle-pointed craft on the ramp being readied for a test. *Dammit, it is a beautiful view!*

He turned back to his driving and concentrated on missing the larger pieces of traffic. The congressional delegation would show up in two days, and the presentation on the combined shuttle was still in search of a theme—or at least a theme less obvious than "Gimmie bucks!" Then, there was still the planning board in town to deal with.

The proposed recruiting facility violated the town's zoning ordinances, and it was feather-smoothing time. Even though federal departments aren't obligated to be governed by local zoning regulations, bad press is still bad press. The theme: cram the new facility down their throats, but in a manner that makes it look like the Air Force is doing the town a big favor. The Concerned Women from town still had to have a number done on them. In the office, the group was known as the Anti-Slop Chute and Whorehouse League. The dear ladies objected to men from the base supplying a market in town for the growing number of bars and ladies of negotiable virtue. Theme? *Perhaps we could have all the men castrated, ladies. How would that be?* Baxter chuckled, then resumed his sober expression as he remembered the school board *had* to be dealt with. The screams over supporting the educations of the base's dependent children were getting loud, and the charge that a group of Air Force brats had introduced pot to their playmates was no help . . . "Ah, nuts!"

Baxter drove it all from his mind as he pulled up to the guard shack at the security gate. An AP, three times larger than life, with a jaw the size, shape, and color of a cinder block, saluted and bent down to the car's window. "Captain Baxter?"

Baxter nodded. "Yes, I'm Baxter."

"Carl F.?"

"That's right."

The AP opened the door and motioned with his hand. "Please slide over, sir."

"What?"

"I'm supposed to drive you to a security area, Captain. Please, slide over."

Baxter reached for the door and tried to pull it shut. The AP's grip on the door might as well have been a ton of reenforced concrete. Baxter looked into the guard shack and saw Wilson, one of the regular AP's on the gate. "Wilson, will you call off this trained gorilla? I have a lot of work to do today, and no time to fool around."

Wilson stood in the shack's doorway and shrugged. "I'm sorry, Captain, but Inovsky has his orders."

Baxter looked at the gorilla. "Inovsky, huh?"

"Yes sir."

"You sure you got the right Air Force, Inovsky?"

The AP unsnapped the cover on his holster. "Please, Captain Baxter. Slide over."

Baxter shrugged and put the car in park. "Sure. Why not?" He slid over and watched as the huge AP slid in, slammed the door, then squealed off, heading the car in the direction of the experimental parking ramp. "What's this all about?"

The AP shook his head. "I don't know, Captain. I was detailed to get you to the experimental section." The man cracked his first smile. "But with all the brass that's been landed out on the field during the past hour, it looks like you're going to see some important people."

"How important?"

"The secretary of defense, the base commander, and just about everything in between, from what I hear."

Baxter looked out of the window on his side, and tried to inch his right trouser leg down over his Argyle sock.

"A question rests without answer in my mind, Lothas."

Lothas turned away from the side port where he had been drinking in sights of the blue-white planet Nitola—now called Earth. Medp stood next to him. "Medp, have the knowing ones among you time now for idle thoughts?" Both of them looked at Nitola. "What is the question, Medp?"

Medp nodded in the direction of the planet. "How does a race such as that select a representative to treat with us?"

"The hue-muns?" Lothas paused, wondering how his own race would have reacted at the news of seventy-million-cycle-old visitors from the past. "I can not even speculate, Medp." Lothas held out a clawed hand. "All those separate tribes, such confusion—I know not." He turned toward Medp. "How are the surveys progressing?"

Medp looked at a readout strapped to his wrist. "We have over twenty distinct languages, with as yet uncounted dialects, entered in the lingpile, and this from only their radio and television. Many more languages are yet to be entered. However, the tribe who is sending the representative speaks the English, and that we have entered in quantity."

Lothas turned back to the view port. "And the other surveys?"

"Everything is much as predicted. Residual radiation is negligible, vegetable and animal life is reestablished, although the forms are highly mutated. As I said, it is all much as predicted."

Lothas nodded toward Nitola. "All except this hue-muns creature. That we did not predict." He reached up and touched a panel that dropped armor over the view port, then turned to Medp. "I have a question of my own, knowing one."

"Speak."

Lothas lowered himself into a couch and closed his eyes. "How would we choose a representative, Medp, if the positions were reversed?"

"That is easily answered; we would send the wisest of our race. Nothing less could serve such a moment."

Lothas nodded. "Perhaps the hue-muns will do the same."

Baxter looked around the room at the circle of seated high-ranking officers and officials. "What in the ever-loving, four-color-processed Hell are you people *talking* about?"

The secretary of defense looked at the chairman of the joint chiefs of staff, and the chairman and the secretary of the air force both looked at Baxter's base commander, General Stayer. Stayer's glance seemed to lower the room's temperature by twenty degrees. "You don't understand, Captain. You aren't being asked; you're being ordered. You're it."

Baxter found a chair and lowered himself into it. He realized that he was coming across as being a little wild-eyed, and he took several deep breaths before he continued. "Gentlemen, what I do not understand is how I drew the black marble on this one. It's been seven, no, eight years since I flew anything even resembling the Python."

An unnamed colonel seated next to the secretary of the Air Force leaned forward. "Captain, you are familiar with the XK-17 Python, are you not?"

Baxter shrugged and shook his head. "Only for publicity purposes. I never flew it, or even checked out in it. The things I know are things people want to know, like cost figures, performance—"

"And all your tickets are up to date?"

Baxter held out his hands, then dropped them. "Yes."

"And you are in top physical shape?"

Baxter nodded again. "But, Colonel—"

The Colonel held up a hand. "Captain, you will be surprised how fast we can check you out in the XK-17—"

"Colonel!" Baxter was startled by the loudness of his own voice. "Colonel, there must be at least five pilots I can name who are checked out on the Python, and who are on the base right now."

General Stayer gave a curt wave of his hand at the Colonel. "Let's cut through the crap. Baxter, you're it. None of those pilots is trained in public relations. You are."

"What about whatsisface? The astronaut in the senate?"

Stayer shook his head. "Too old, his tickets aren't up to date, and we can't locate him. He's somewhere in Canada right now, fishing." The General leaned forward and pointed a finger at Baxter's throat. "You are the closest thing to a flying diplomat that we can get off the ground within the next twenty-four hours, because the Python is the only vehicle that is ready to go right now."

The secretary of defense moved his head a fraction of an inch, signaling his desire to speak. "If I may, General?"

"Of course, Mr. Secretary."

The secretary, a blown-dry glory in four-hundred-dollar pin stripes, let his gaze wander around the room as he talked. "Captain Baxter, I realize you are being asked to perform a difficult task, but we have little choice. The . . ." he waved a hand up in the air, ". . . aliens, or whatever they are, made a broadband contact. In other words, their invitation was extended to whosoever can make it up there. The Russians, of course, will get there, but," he held up a finger, "it will take them at least three days to get off the ground. Am I making myself clear?"

Baxter folded his hands over his belly and nodded. "Yes, Mr. Secretary."

The Secretary nodded. "Good. While you are there, you will be in constant touch with the Department of State, and with the White House. There will always be someone with whom you can consult on any matter."

Baxter nodded and smiled. "This is what I mean, Mr. Secretary. If all I'm supposed to do is carry a radio for the State Department, why not use another—qualified—pilot? I don't see what particular use my training in public relations will be."

The Secretary nodded. "You must know the value in eyeball-to-eyeball negotiations, Captain. When you deal with groups and committees on behalf of the Air Force, do you telephone or appear in person?"

Baxter nodded, noting the chains being locked in place. "And what am I supposed to attempt to accomplish?"

"Your meaning?"

"Mr. Secretary, the only purpose of public relations, or diplomacy for that matter, is to get people to do things that they would normally not do. If everyone did what we wanted, there would be no need for PR types or diplomats. Now, just what is it that I am supposed to get them to do?"

The Secretary frowned. "I don't know."

"You don't *know?*"

"Captain, if these beings are what they say they are— inhabitants of Earth from seventy million years ago—it is possible that they are thinking of reclaiming the planet for themselves. In such a case, discourage them." The Secretary raised his eyebrows and held out his hands. "However, they may be from another solar system and bent on conquering Earth. Then, perhaps, in either case, they might only want to land and live here. If that is the case, it may prove beneficial to have them on our side. They are obviously more advanced . . . but, then again, it might be better to sic them on the Russians." The Secretary dropped his hands into his lap. "All I can say, Baxter, is look out for the interests of your country, and the interests of your planet and the human race, while you're at it."

An hour later, as two technicians stood waiting to help him into his pressure suit, Baxter remembered that he had forgotten to telephone Boxman about the Boxman Spring account. He sat down on a cold metal bench and untied his shoes. Security on the base was locked up tighter than a million uninflated dollars, and no calls allowed. *Deb! I can't call her! She'll kill me!* He removed his red and yellow Argyle sock and held it in his hand. It had a hole in it. *I guess it's just going to be one of those days.*

Lothas studied the circle of eight faces seated around the polished black table in the half-light of the governor's conference compartment, aft of the control center. Deayl brushed a clawed hand over his muzzle, then let the hand drop to the surface of the table. "Lothas, it is still my mind that we wait no longer. The hue-muns are divided, and they have nothing that can protect them against the power. We can brush them aside."

Lothas examined the other faces. "How many of you have this mind?" Four clawed hands went forward toward the center of the table. "The mind that counsels us to wait, then, still prevails."

Deayl put two fists on the table and turned to the ones who had not voted with him. "After seventy million cycles traveling from and to our home, we are to sit here polishing our claws? We are so close!"

Lothas noted that two who had voted with him were wavering. The desire to go home was strong, and Deayl's argument appealed to that desire. The desire twisted with no less strength in Lothas, but he held out his hands. "Our knowledge of the hue-muns is but pieces—what they are, and what they can do. The hue-muns' knowledge of us is even less—what we are, and what we can do." He lowered his hands to the table. "We must also grant that the sense of right we feel in our cause is shared by the hue-muns in their cause. They grew to dominate and control Nitola, much as we did. By what we acknowledge to be the right—"

"No!" Deayl crossed his wrists. All could hear the angry swishing of his tail across the deck. "We do not know that. What if the hue-muns are from another planet? What if they invaded our home planet, and now simply stand to defend their conquest?"

Lothas nodded. "The hue-muns must have like suspicions about us, Deayl. After all, they are on the planet; we are the ones in space ships." He brought his hands together. "We have much to learn about each other, if we are to avoid error." Lothas looked around the table and stopped on Deayl. "Do you wish another vote?"

Deayl leaned against his back rest. "No. Not at the present."

Medp entered the compartment, bowed toward those seated at the table, then turned toward Lothas. "We have just been told that the hue-muns representative has been launched. Other hue-muns, speaking the Russian, have said that the true representative will be launched in three days, and that we should refuse to see the other."

Lothas looked at the table top, then raised his glance and looked at Deayl. "We do have much to learn. Deayl, I will leave to you the task of instructing our visitor in what we can do. If the hue-muns understand *the* power, they will understand *our* power."

"Yes, Lothas."

Lothas stood and bowed toward the ones seated at the table. The others stood and bowed in return. Lothas turned toward the control center and entered, Medp at his side. "Medp, do you have contact with the representative?"

"Yes. He is called Captaincarlbaxter."

Lothas nodded. "Is everything in readyness?"

"Yes. It will take him approximately a tenth of a cycle to come into safe power range."

Lothas tucked his tail between the seat and back rest of a chair before a monitor and sat down. He lifted his head and looked at Medp. "Deayl will sway some minds before the council sits again."

Medp nodded and pointed at the monitor. Nitola hung blue-white on the blackness of space. "The feeling is very strong, Lothas. All of us can see, and . . . we have been away for a very long time."

Lothas turned toward the monitor, studied once more the beautiful planet, then nodded. "Have you assembled enough information to comprehend this squabble and division among the hue-muns?"

Medp shifted his weight from one clawed foot to the other. "We can see a little. We have determined from their transmissions, and our sensor surveys support this, that there are over four billion hue-muns belonging to the various tribes."

"Four billion?"

"And, they grow in numbers every day. This does not explain all, but it lets us see a little."

Lothas changed the positions on several slotswitches, then energized a panel, causing a tiny dot to appear on the monitor. He pressed another panel, and the dot expanded until the monitor was filled with an image of a sleek, black ship, just separating from a cluster of white acceleration tubes. "Such a tiny craft. Have you come to a determination about the hue-muns rite called humor?"

"It is exasperating. The loud reaction—the laughing, chuckling, and so on—appears to be pleasurable. But, the causes of the reaction—pain, misfortune, shame, misunderstanding—all are causes of grief as well." Medp looked at the monitor. "It needs more information for sense to be made of it. Still, they are fascinating creatures. I could devote my remaining cycles to studying them."

Lothas extended a claw toward the monitor. "Part of your wish approaches now, Medp: your first specimen, Captaincarlbaxter."

Baxter was surprised at how familiar everything was. The wing drop from the mother plane, the slam of the initial and secondary burns, even the attitude correction rockets. He looked out of the tiny canopy windows, little more than a hand's breadth from his faceplate, to see himself floating on the outer limits of Earth's atmosphere. Above, the sky was star-studded black. He searched the space above for a visual sighting, but could see nothing. He looked down, and the cluster of ships were indicated clearly on his readout screen. As he studied the screen, he finally realized what he was about to do. The frustrations of the morning, and the skull-popping briefing by the Python's pilot, plus frantic phone conversations with several Undersecretaries of State, along with a brief inspirational call from the President, faded as the thought of meeting . . . whoever they are, filled his mind.

This is a bigger moment than walking on the moon. This is what generations of movie makers and novelists have speculated about.

"Messenger, this is Mission Contol."

Baxter opened his channel. "This is Messenger. Go ahead."

"Messenger, we're patching you into a line connected with the State Department. Stand by."

Baxter listened to a series of clicks, howls, and crackles. "Captain Baxter, this is Undersecretary Wyman. Can you hear me?"

"Loud and clear, Mr. Wyman."

"Baxter, our most recent information on the Soviet mission indicates that they will have a man up in less than three days. They are sending Lavr Razin. Razin is a former cosmonaut, now attached to the Soviet mission to the U.N. Understand?"

"Affirmative. Can you tell me anything about him?"

The channel went dead for long moments, then came to life. "Baxter, since we don't know, we are assuming that none of our transmissions are secure from the . . . visitors." Another pause. "We can tell you to watch out. Razin is no Fozzie Bear, savvy?"

"Affirmative."

"Goodbye, and good luck, Baxter."

Baxter signed off with Mission Control, wishing that Undersecretary Wyman's goodbye hadn't sounded so final. He gave his instruments a casual sweep, then looked out of the left side canopy window. Green fire danced upon the Python's skin. "Captaincarlbaxter?"

"This is Messenger. Go ahead, Mission Control."

A long pause. "I am called Deayl. Are you Captaincarlbaxter?"

A strange feeling began tugging at Baxter's stomach. The voice sounded . . . ultranormal—the ideal of every midwestern radio announcer. "Yes, this is Baxter."

"Greetings. Our instruments inform us that, unless you remove the force of your engines, you will be destroyed." Baxter turned back to his own instruments. Every dial was either pegged or dead. "We have you in the grip of our power. With it, we shall bring you into our control ship. It will not harm you, unless you fail to turn off your engines."

Baxter raised a gloved hand, hesitated, then began punching and flicking switches according to the Python's shutdown SOP. "The craft is shut down . . . Deayl."

"Sensible. I am curious, Captaincarlbaxter. What were you hue-muns seventy million years ago?"

Baxter swallowed and tried to recall his ten minute high-speed briefing on the lineage of Man. *"After all, Baxter, they may want to establish the authenticity of our claim to this planet."* "At that stage, we were prosimians—the apes hadn't evolved yet. You know what I mean when I say 'apes'?"

"Yes. We have seen them on your transmissions."

Baxter frowned. *What if those guys can pick up every radio and TV transmission on Earth? They could assemble quite a body of information.* "Interesting."

"What did the prosimians look like?"

"Well, I understand that they were small, long-tailed creatures that resembled present-day squirrels. Probably they were adept at securing food by leaping about in the trees, eating fruit, seeds, eggs—"

"Ah, the tree jontyl. I recognize them. That is very curious, Captaincarlbaxter. Tree jontyls were very well known to my race when we occupied this planet. My mouth has been watering for one for over seventy million years. I am looking forward to seeing you."

They called themselves Nitolans—Earthlings in another tongue. As his craft approached the ship in the lead center of the armada of Nitolan vessels, Baxter felt the awe he experienced when, as a boy of ten, he had been taken into St. Patrick's cathedral in New York. One hundred and ninety-seven ships, and any one of them large enough to dwarf a supertanker. The ships were long, cylindrical, and with ridges along the sides that could be retractable wings. As he observed the smooth skin and flowing configuration of the ships, Baxter realized that the vessels were designed for atmospheric flight.

"Captaincarlbaxter?"

"This is Baxter. Deayl?"

A pause. "This is Deayl. This shortening of the name; is this a friendly gesture of you hue-muns?"

"Yes . . . everybody just calls me 'Baxter'—even my wife."

"Your mate?"

Baxter nodded to himself. "Yes."

Another pause. "Very well, Baxter. I will accept this gesture in kind. I am known as Illya . . ." Baxter listened while the Nitolan supervising his approach seemed to be wrestling with a thought. "This gesture, Baxter. Understand that it does not obligate me to anything."

Baxter smiled. *This guy could have come straight from a Middle East peace conference.* "I understand, Illya. Is there anything I should know about being taken into your ship's landing bay?"

"If your craft has surface landing apparatus that is now retracted, you should prepare it. Otherwise, we can suspend your craft in a neutral field. Air will be normal to you."

Baxter noted the existence of artificial gravity. None of the ships were spinning. The Python landed on two fixed rear skids and a nose wheel. He threw the switch and felt the wheel lower and lock as his eyes confirmed the event by observing the dull green glow of the safe/go light for the landing gear. "Landing gear down and locked, Illya."

"Noted."

Baxter watched as a bay on the underside (toward Earth) of the ship opened, much like the iris of a camera. Dull red light came from the bay, and as the Python closed on the iris, Baxter felt a slight panic at the size of the opening, then at the size of the bay. *I feel like a pea rattling around in a fifty-five gallon drum!*

The Python rose just above the opening, and Baxter watched open-mouthed as the enormous iris blinked shut. His craft was gently lowered to the deck, and he let out his breath. He checked his instruments, shut down the works, and waited. In the distance he could see four jumbo-jet-sized ships parked off to the side. The bay switched from red to yellow light, and Baxter's mouth remained open as a hatch opened and a delegation of grey-green long necked, heavy tailed creatures entered. They walked toward him on powerful legs with clawed feet. Although bipedal, they stooped forward, carrying their long, thin arms in front. Baxter's gaze went from the clawed toes to the clawed fingers, then to the gleaming rows of teeth. As he unstrapped, removed his helmet and cracked the Python's canopy, Baxter ran a dry tongue over equally dry lips. He stood, stepped over the side of the cockpit, pushing his toes into the step holes, and climbed down from his craft. He turned as the delegation of creatures came to a halt. Stooped over, the creatures were only a little taller than himself. One of them rotated its body, bringing its neck and head well above the others. Baxter cleared his throat and croaked. "I bring you greetings from the President of the United States."

Deayl watched the scene of the docking bay reception a moment longer, then closed his eyes. *If so long ago we had not abandoned our gods. If I could only lay my burden at the feet of Sisil, or old Fane.* He extended a claw and shut off the monitor. Energizing another monitor, he watched Nitola, and his pain eased. *I do not do it for myself, but for all of us.* He kept his eyes on the image as he pressed the signal to Lothas's quarters.

"Lothas."

"Deayl, Lothas. Baxter has landed safely, and Medp brings him now to the quarters prepared for him."

"Deayl, is 'Baxter' the representative's name of friendship?"

Deayl lowered his muzzle to his chest. "Yes. And I extended mine to him."

"This is good. He shall rest for the remainder of the cycle, then you shall demonstrate to him the power. I shall meet with him after."

"All will be as you wish, Lothas."

"Deayl, with your mind concerning the return to Nitola, exchanging names with the hue-muns was a fine gesture." A pause, as though Lothas expected some sort of comment. "Deayl, I know you disapprove of my direction as governor, but I know you to be a strong and determined champion of our race. I would exchange names with you. I am called 'Dimmis'."

Deayl wiped a shaking hand over his muzzle, then nodded. "I am called 'Illya.'" Deayl reached for the panel. "A home for you, Dimmis."

"A home for you, Illya."

Deayl pressed the panel, extended his fingers, and placed his palms over his eyes. *Ah! Ah, it comes! The pain returns. How many disgraces must I bring upon myself before my task is done? How many?*

In his quarters, Baxter sagged as he tried to get comfortable in the strange chair. As near as he could figure it, he had just completed a three kilometer dead run from the docking bay, trying to keep up with the delegation. He opened his eyes and looked around at the room. The white bulkheads were bare, except for the three iris-like doors. One door led to a closet, another to the corridor, and the third to a bathroom straight from one of Baxter's more imaginative nightmares. He had been literally relieved to find that he could use the equipment, although with some difficulty. On the deck, several thick cushions were arranged for sleeping. His chair had a black metal frame and was upholstered with a soft, green fabric. Baxter sat on one side of the seat, since the center-rear was open to comfortably seat the Nitolan tail. The backrest, tilted forward to accommodate the creatures' stooping backs, dug into Baxter's shoulderblades. His ankles reached to the edge of the seat.

He reached to his belt and pressed the switch to his radio that, through the relay set in the Python, would keep him in touch with Earth. "Mission control, this is Messenger."

"Messenger, report on your situation."

"I'm established in quarters. At the moment, I'm supposed to be resting . . . although that's going to be a little difficult. At about oh four hundred GMT tomorrow, I'll be taken on some kind of demonstration, then meet Lothas. The best their language mechanics can make out of his title is 'governor.' Then whatever negotiations there will be will begin."

"Acknowledged, Messenger. From now on, until you begin preparations for reentry, your communications will be handled by the State Department mission control. Stand by."

Baxter looked down from the chair at the knee-high thick pallet on the deck that would serve him as a bed during his stay. "Baxter, this is Wyman. Do you read?"

"Five by five, Mr. Wyman."

"Good. What have you found out?"

"The Nitolans, first. They look like a cross between a kangaroo, an ostrich and an alligator; general shape for the first, eyes for the second, claws and teeth for the third—lots of teeth. The head is pretty large."

"I understand, Baxter. The ships?"

"Incredible."

"Could you be more specific?"

"The ships are enormous. I can't even tell you how wide they are. Everything seemed to extend out of sight. But I'm pretty sure they are monitering our commercial radio and television broadcasts. The lingpile—the thing they use to convert their language into and out of English—talks like Merv Griffin. They have some sort of force field or tractor beam that pulled me into their lead ship, and I think the same thing allows them to simulate gravity on board. Gravity appears to be Earth normal, and there appears to be no inducement of this by centrifugal force or other physical means. That's it, except that they seem friendly—and curious."

"Baxter, do they appear secretive or evasive about themselves?"

Baxter shook his head. "Not that I could tell. In fact, they provided me with a reader of some kind in case I wanted some diversion when I wasn't sleeping. They prepared something for me that contains a nutshell history of them, their mission, customs, and so on."

"You will begin on it at once, Baxter."

"Mr. Wyman, I'm a little bushed right now—"

"At once, Baxter! Until we know more, all of us are groping in the dark—including you. Now, do your homework."

"Yessir."

"One more thing, Baxter."

"Go ahead."

"We must establish to a certainty from where they came. If they, in fact, have come from Earth's past, we must be sure. Do you have any indications other than their appearance? Things they've said? Answers to your questions?"

"Mr. Wyman, I haven't asked them Babe Ruth's all-time batting average, or the words to 'Yankee Doodle', if that's what you're talking about."

"I understand. I'll see about preparing a suitable list of questions—things based on our knowledge of the period they claim to be from. Is there anything you need?"

Baxter thought a moment. "How is all this striking the public?"

"Officially, we are denying everything, and so are the Soviets, but rumors are spreading fast. Too many people picked up that initial broadband contact, although it hasn't grown serious yet."

"What about the Russian?"

"Launch is still go for the day after tomorrow. We still don't have a line on what they plan to pull. That it?"

"Yes. Baxter out." He released the switch, sighed and slid to the front edge of the seat, then dropped to the floor. The edge of the seat came to his waist. Baxter walked to the door panel, reached up and pressed the platter-sized button with both hands. Part of the wall dilated iris-fashion, exposing a wide corridor and a Nitolan standing guard. The creature walked to the opening, its heavy tail scraping harshly against the deck, and stooped in Baxter's direction.

"May I help you, Captaincarlbaxter? I am Simdna."

Baxter nodded and pointed at the swept-screened contraption attached to a chair by a swinging metal brace. "Yes. Medp said that I could use the reader if I wanted, but I am ignorant of its operation." Baxter walked to the reader chair, climbed up and settled in as the

Nitolan followed, then pushed the reader more closely to the chair. "Now, what do I do?"

Simdna picked up two pancake-sized tabs and held them out to Baxter. "Put one on each side of your head. They will attach themselves."

Baxter held one tab in each hand, then held them to the sides of his head. "What now?"

Simdna pointed toward a panel. "This will begin the record." He pointed at a slotswitch. "The more you pull this toward you, the faster will run the record."

Baxter nodded. "Thank you. I don't think I'll need anything else."

Simdna turned, left the room and the door closed after him. Baxter studied the screen then looked at the panel for starting. He leaned forward and pushed it with the palm of his hand. At once, a feeling of mild intoxication swept him. It stayed as he pulled the switch, and images and narratives attacked his senses at high input levels. He realized this, but realized also that he understood it all, as fast as it was. He pulled again at the slotswitch. . . .

. . . *The Nitolans were a highly evolved race, with self-made imperatives of right and wrong, a structured social system, great cities, long before man thought these even to exist. In the midst of the great reptiles, the Nitolans had science, law, and the creation of wealth, for the Power was theirs. They studied truth. . . .*

. . . And the knowing ones read their instruments and saw the death of every creature that could not hide within the mud, or beneath the waters. The night brightstar would grow in brilliance, until it washed all other stars from the sky, and even paled Amasaat from the day sky. To survive, the Nitolans must leave the planet for as long as the planet took to again become green and alive with creatures.

While the wisest of the knowing ones searched the future for a time that would serve the race, others of the knowing ones spread across Nitola to tell the things that they had learned. "We must leave Nitola, else the race shall die." . . . Many believed, and helped to construct the great ships that would protect precious cargo through the vacuum of space and the emptiness of time. Others did not believe, and the Power was turned against itself as the factions decided the issue through blood.

As the ships were completed, the war concluded, and the victors gathered among the ships to depart Nitola.

The knowing ones looked at their planet and saw the ravaged cities, the gaping wounds of mines and quarries, their own structures for building the ships. They wondered if this evidence, if left behind, would lead an alien visitor or a newly evolved race to find them and destroy them as they crossed the void. The Power was turned against the cities, and the other marks they had made, removing all trace of their existence. Then they swept the planet and removed all traces of the substance of the Power, should they return and find a newly evolved race using the Power and turning it against the homecomers.

When all was done, the ships were filled, the travelers' life processes slowed, and the journey begun. . . .

"There are many of us who share your mind, Deayl."

Deayl looked from Nozn to his companion Suleth, then back to Nozn. "My mind has been voted down by the council. What brings you to my quarters?"

Nozn studied Deayl. "We read the piles and can see what the huemuns do. Many of us would not wait until the creatures render Nitola unfit for habitation."

Deayl turned away and studied a blank wall. "If there are such as you talk about, they would disgrace themselves by acting against the common mind."

Suleth looked from Nozn to Deayl. "We have had enough of these word games, Deayl. Do you plan to take an action?"

"Action?"

Suleth nodded. "Will you lead us?"

Deayl lowered himself to his sleeping pallet, placed his head on his cushion, and looked up at the overhead. "I will speak with you two later."

Nozn placed a clawed hand on Suleth's arm to quiet him, then nodded at Deayl. "It is my mind that this task would be bonded by our exchanging of names. Is this your mind as well, Deayl?"

Deayl rolled over and propped himself up with an elbow. His black eyes fixed Nozn to the deck. "No! Treason to our race is no excuse for friendship!" He lowered himself back to his cushion. "Leave me now. I will call you if I wish to converse further."

Nozn and Suleth bowed and left Deayl's quarters. Deayl rolled to his left side, his eyes tightly shut. *I belittle myself enough by the enterprise I have undertaken. I shall not suck others into the same mire.* He opened his eyes and spoke to a dark corner of the compartment. "You are my governor, Lothas, and you speak for the common mind." Deayl sighed. "But, you stand between us and our home. Isn't yours the greater crime?" Deayl closed his eyes and tossed. The question was yet to be answered in his own mind.

Midway through the next planetary cycle, Baxter bid farewell to his Nitolan friend Illya, then entered his quarters and flopped onto his sleeping pallet. He detached the insulated gloves from his suit, threw them aside and placed his hands against his cheeks. His face felt drained of color. Without rising, Baxter keyed his transceiver. "State, this is Messenger." He opened his eyes and looked at the overhead. "State, this is Messenger. Do you read?"

"Go ahead, Baxter. This is Wyman."

Baxter licked his lips, took a deep breath, then sat up. "Wyman, are there any manned missions on the Moon—secret things that I don't know about?"

"I'm sure there aren't, but I can check it for you. Is it important?"

"It's important. I also want to know if the Soviets have anything on the Lunar surface, and if so, where."

"Understood. What's going on, Baxter?"

Baxter shook his head. *I'm rattled, that's what's going on. Calm down.* "I was taken on a demonstration today. It's a thing they call 'the power'. I saw a quarter of the Lunar surface turned into glass in less time than it's taking me to tell you about it." Baxter licked his lips again. "My guide took me down about two hours later and I walked the surface. The dark side now has a *mare* that makes Imbrium, Serenity, and Tranquillity together look like a wading pool." The radio remained silent. "Did you copy that, Wyman?"

"Baxter, what is your feeling about it?"

Baxter's eyes widened. "My *feeling*? How in the Hell do you think I feel about it? If these lizards want to, they can fry my entire planet in about twenty minutes!"

"What I meant, Baxter, is your feeling about the purpose of the demonstration."

Baxter thought a moment, then flushed. "I suppose its purpose was to produce exactly the kind of hysterical gibbering I've been doing; correct?"

"Correct. Look, Baxter; you are not dealing with an overweight Congressional committee or the local school board. You can't make a mistake, then go back and patch it up later with an apology or some syrup from the White House. You have to keep your head clear and your feelings out of it, while you look for the angles, feel out the edges, find out where to push, and where to back off. You understand?"

Baxter shook his head. "You diplomatic types have all the sensitivity of an oyster."

State paused for a long moment. "It's not lack of feelings, Baxter; it's called 'guts.' Grow some. Wyman out."

Baxter released the key on his transceiver, stood, and began shucking his pressure suit. *At least I wasn't as rattled as Deayl.* The Nitolan had walked the Lunar surface with him, and had been strangely quiet. Deayl's answers to direct questions were brief, shaken, and almost incoherent. *I wonder what my old buddy Illya was nervous about?*

The iris to Baxter's compartment opened and the Nitolan called Simdna entered. "I extend an invitation from Lothas, our governor, to meet with him in private before you meet with the full council."

Baxter nodded. "I am most happy to accept his invitation." *I'm already beginning to talk like a diplomat.* "When does Lothas wish to see me?"

"Is it convenient for you to come now?"

"Yes."

Simdna backed away from the door and held out a clawed hand. "Then, Lothas would see you now."

On the way to his quarters, Deayl sagged against the corridor wall. He turned his head up, then closed his eyes and let his muzzle drop to his chest. The claws on his fingers dug into his palms, the pain almost blotting out the waves of self-condemnation that threatened to drive his mind empty. He heard the sound of someone approaching, and he pushed himself away from the wall and opened his eyes. It was Nozn.

"There you are, Deayl."

"Here I am."

Nozn turned back, and seeing the corridor empty, returned his gaze to Deayl. "The hue-mun still lives, Deayl. If you cannot perform the task, leave it to someone who can."

Deayl hissed, his eyes sparking. "You forget your place, Nozn!"

Nozn closed his eyes and performed a shallow bow. "I meant no disrespect, Deayl."

"I shall do what needs to be done, and with no one's help. That I can keep all others but myself clean from this act is my only claim to honor. Do not take this from me by becoming involved."

Nozn bowed again. "It will be as you wish, Deayl." He stood and half-turned to go. "But, if you should fail, there are others who will not." Nozn nodded once, then moved off down the corridor. Deayl placed a hand against the corridor wall, turned his gaze toward the deck plates, and saw the glassy surface of Naal, the child-moon of Nitola. Baxter had stood on the thin crust of the molten pool, and it would have taken only a slight shove to have removed the creature from existence. The Council would have accepted the event as an accident, while the hue-muns on the planet would have . . . *Are the hue-muns that sensitive that they would attempt retaliation on the basis of one suspicious death? Will they adopt an attitude that will make their removal the only option left to the Council, for just one death?* Deayl wiped his hand over his muzzle, then let it drop to his side. *Or, will the hue-muns' tribes be more reflective, making the murder I will commit a futile gesture?*

Deayl, still supporting himself by moving his hand along the corridor wall, walked the few remaining steps to his quarters. He pressed the panel and the iris opened. Inside, the compartment was black, making the door appear as the dark, slathering maw of some nightmare begotten creature. *If the hue-muns know it is a murder, the Council will as well. But, perhaps this is the only way— exchange my future for the future of my race.* Deayl stepped into the iris, and it closed behind him.

Baxter stared at the upholstered wing-backed chair in disbelief. From its wooden claw-on-ball legs to the garish oranges and yellows of the fabric, the chair appeared to have been cloned from a discount department store's loss leader. He looked over to Lothas. The Nitolan governor reclined on several of the familiar thick cushions. "Where did you get this?" Baxter held out a hand toward the chair.

"Do you like it? I hope it is comfortable."

Baxter lowered himself into it, did one or two experimental bounces, then leaned back and crossed his legs. "It's fine."

"That pleases me, Captaincarlbaxter. It was constructed according to information gleaned from your television transmissions. It was felt that you might find our furniture out of size."

Baxter smiled. "Thank you very much . . . do I call you 'governor'?"

"I am Lothas. If you would exchange names, I am called Dimmis."

Baxter nodded. "Very well, Dimmis. I am called Baxter. I appreciate the chair very much."

"Another like it will be placed in your quarters, and one more in the conference compartment where you will meet with my council."

"Excellent." Baxter wondered if he should mention something about the horrible pattern, but decided against it.

"We can prepare you one of your beds, if you wish."

Baxter held up his hands. "Thank you, but that would be quite unnecessary. I find the cushions in my quarters quite comfortable."

Lothas nodded. "Baxter, you know of us and our mission, do you not?"

"Yes. I watched the record you prepared before I slept."

The governor nodded again. "Still, you know too little of us, and we, too little of you." The Nitolan sat up and pulled a table console to where he could reach it. "The knowing ones have amassed a great deal of information from your radio and television, and from the visual and sensor surveys they have done. Still, we know too little to judge properly what we should do."

Baxter nodded. *These lizards don't know what to do any more than I do.* "I understand. If you will tell me the information you want, perhaps I can arrange to get it for you."

"We understand that your information storage piles can talk to each other, is this not true?"

Baxter nodded. "Yes. Computers."

"The information we need appears to be contained in a number of your . . . computers. I would like to send three of our knowing ones down to a place that can talk to your computers."

"I'll see if I can arrange it."

Lothas sat quietly for a moment, then lifted his head. "There is much, Baxter, that we must learn about each other as well."

Baxter followed the direction of the governor's gaze and saw nothing but an inverted green dome set into the overhead. He looked back at Lothas and shrugged. "I agree, we must . . ."

Baxter's vision blurred as Lothas removed a hand from the console beside his cushion bed.

"It is good you agreed, Baxter. Trust is important." Lothas's hand rose to the console, and Baxter felt himself expanding, whirling up and out, as the compartment went black.

He felt his gorge rise as he realized he was standing off to one side observing while another thumbed and sorted through his memories. From memories to automatized interactions and responses as memories were let to play, mesh, divide, and redivide according to their own dictates . . . *the job; the goddamned job . . . still haven't called Boxman. Deb. That damned Argyle sock . . .* He felt his thoughts pulled from one area, then forced into another . . . *a documentary; stacking them up like cordwood in Auschwitz . . . Eichmann in a little glass booth . . . Korea, Lebanon, Vietnam, Gaza, Suez, South Afr . . .* His thoughts plunged down a dimly lit hole . . . *a little red balsa wood plane with a wind up . . . Christmas, and Grandma's there, so we'll say grace this time . . . high school, college, . . . planes at the grass strip near Evanston . . . testing at Lockheed . . . Air Force . . .* A cesspool of repressed fear yawned before him . . . *The Python, panic . . . what to do, God, what to do? . . . the size of them . . . why me? . . .*

Baxter opened his eyes and saw Lothas removing his hand from the console. The Nitolan stared at him for a long time, then held its hands over its eyes for a moment. Lothas let his hands fall to his knees. "Baxter . . . you, your race . . . you are everything. . . ." He waved a hand toward his compartment's iris. "Please leave. Take no offense, but please leave. I must think."

Baxter stood, a feeling of panic rising in his chest. He watched as Lothas put his head down on the cushions and appeared to sleep.

Back in his quarters, seated in a duplicate of the wing-backed chair, Baxter shook his head at his transceiver. "I don't know, Wyman. After I woke up, Lothas seemed very upset. Then he asked me to leave."

"I don't know what to make of it, Baxter. You think it's some kind of mind reading machine?"

"I'm sure of it. Should I make a break for it? I know the way to the docking bay, and—"

"No. Baxter, get control of yourself. Since we don't have any plans, Lothas couldn't have uncovered any hostile intentions. We just don't know, so sit tight until we do."

"Sit tight."

"You read me correctly."

Baxter listened to the static as he reviewed language forms he had not used since high school. He let out his breath. "Wyman, has anyone gotten in touch with Deb yet?"

"Deb?"

"My wife."

"I'm sure someone has. Is it important?"

Baxter could feel himself becoming wild eyed again, and he took several deep breaths. "You're damn right it's important, Wyman. I want you—you personally—to make sure that my wife is notified."

"Very well. I'll let you know as soon as I can about that visit from your friends. There shouldn't be any problems with letting them down—the slip-stick jockeys down here are as curious about them as they are about us. As far as access to computers, it depends on what they want. We aren't about to hand over classified information to a potential enemy. Do you know what they're interested in?"

"No." Baxter wiped a hand over his face. The hand came away wet. "What about the Russian?"

"No change. Lift off is tomorrow. We still don't have a reading on the approach he's going to use."

Baxter laughed. "I think I do. He'll probably use the same one I'm using: sort of a combination of Alice in Wonderland with Blind Man's Bluff."

"Baxter?"

"Yeah?"

"Hang in there, Baxter. Okay?"

Baxter closed his eyes and nodded. "No sweat. And thanks. Baxter out." He released the key on his transceiver and studied the overhead. It was eggshell white, smooth and seamless. Images from his stay under Lothas's machine flashed through his mind, and he gripped the armrests of the chair to keep his hands from shaking. *I don't believe it! I'm scared. I am finger-shaking, head-sweating, pants-wetting scared.*

The iris to his compartment opened, and he jumped and began backing away from the door. It was Simdna. "Captaincarlbaxter?"

Baxter held his head back as the muscles at the back of his neck knotted. "What is it, Simdna?"

"Lothas wishes to inform you that the council meeting has been postponed."

Baxter studied the guard, then nodded. "Thank you."

Simdna left, the door closing behind him. Baxter lowered himself to the knee-high pallet on the deck and exhaled. "Now what?"

Baxter tossed on his pallet, his fingers clawing at the throats of his mind's monsters. *He saw himself, a fraud in man's clothing. A creature of petty evasion, weak, frightened—above all, frightened. Thin hands reached out to work levers and turn knobs; watery eyes, reflective and darting, sought out lights and dials. Shaking and pain-whipped, the creature operated a machine. Baxter's view faded back, through the wall of the machine, into the light. He stumbled back as his view of the machine reached a point of recognition. With thick painted lips, gleaming cardboard teeth, and dime store flashlight bulbs for eyes, Carl Baxter raised a hand in his direction . . . the machine-Baxter buzzed as the creature inside screamed. . . .*

Baxter bolted upright, looked around the compartment, then wrapped his arms around his body to still the shaking. A low buzzing sound drew his attention to the transceiver on the wing-back chair. Baxter stood, walked over to the chair, and keyed the instrument. "This is Baxter."

"Wyman here."

"What is it, Wyman?"

"Hold on for a moment while we patch you back through Mission Control. Remember, you won't have long."

"Wyman . . ." Baxter could hear the static shifts as Wyman went out and unseen hands fed unseen signals over new routes.

"Baxter?" The voice was clear, husky, yet soft.

Baxter stared at the transceiver. "Deb? Is that you?"

Baxter heard a familiar sniff, and knew she would be nodding her head and crying. "What have you gotten yourself into now?"

He swallowed, picked up the transceiver, and sat in the chair. "This is a fine mess I've gotten us in, Ollie." Baxter felt the tears welling in his eyes. "Has anyone explained . . . you know."

"Yes. I see from your new friends down here that you've become a real social climber." She laughed. "You want to know who sat up and held my hand last night?"

"Who?"

"Her husband lives in a white house." She sniffed again. "And you voted for the other one."

Baxter smiled and shook his head. "This'll teach you to mismatch my socks. Hey, you'd never believe the bathroom in my quarters. There's a machine in there that can clean and dry my uniform and underwear in twenty seconds flat—and you should see my laundress. His name's Simdna . . . cooks too—"

"Baxter, I love you."

He bit his lower lip. "Deb, is there anyone else listening in?"

"Only three or four hundred people that I know of."

Baxter shut his eyes. "Deb . . . there's something I . . . something I want to tell you."

"I know."

"How do you know?"

"I've been holding down my side of your bed for a bunch of years, Baxter. I know. You can handle it. Do you understand that?"

"Sure."

"I know you don't believe it, Baxter, but it's true. You've got what it takes."

"Deb . . ."

"I have to go now, Baxter. Don't forget where you live."

"The house with the view, right?"

"Right." The audio filled with static as the frequency was returned to State. *I love you, Deb. God, do I need you.*

"Baxter, this is Wyman."

"Go ahead."

"It's go on the trip. Mission Control will get in touch with the Nitolan mission directly regarding the landing field and time. Still go on the Russian."

Baxter nodded. "I copy. And Wyman?"

"Yes, Baxter?"

"Thanks."

"You're welcome, but for what?"

"You know. The call to my wife."

Wyman chuckled. "Don't thank me, Baxter. That call was made at the orders of the President because of an urgent request by your friend Lothas. I thought you knew."

"Lothas requested that you put me in touch with my wife?"

"Affirmative. What do you make of it?"

What I make of it is I needed, very badly, to hear from Deb—to have her tell me I can handle it—to prop up my crumbling self-esteem. That, and that Lothas knew that. "I haven't a clue. I'll keep in touch."

"Wyman out."

Baxter released the key, leaned his head back against the chair, and fell into a troubled sleep.

In the control center, Lothas leaned against his chair's backrest while Medp shut down the receiver. "Medp, why would Baxter forget where he lives?"

Medp swung his chair in the governor's direction. "It is a joke, Lothas. It is said as a substitute for 'I want you to come home.'"

Lothas held up a hand toward the receiver. "Baxter did not laugh at the joke."

Medp shook his head. "There are jokes not to be laughed at. It is but another facet to this humor that still eludes me."

Lothas let his hand drop to his knee. "Why did his mate, Deb, not simply say 'I want you to come home'? There would be less confusion."

"Lothas, I am sure Baxter understood. This is what he meant by saying 'the house with the view,' when, from what you said, Baxter believes his mate to detest the view from their house. Another joke."

Lothas hissed, then let his muzzle drop to his chest as he passed a hand over one eye. "The melding showed me Baxter's mind, but it did not give me an understanding of it. On the outside, he functions as you or I; inside he is a warren of screaming agonies." Lothas turned to Medp. "I have never witnessed such confusion . . . such pain." He leaned forward. "Do the creatures use the humor to hide the things they feel from others?"

Medp nodded. "And from themselves as well."

"How can they hide what they are from themselves? It is impossible."

"You saw it for yourself, Lothas. All I have seen shows them to be complex, contradictory, self-deceptive, and even self-destructive."

Lothas leaned back in his chair. "Medp, the melding process not only makes clear to me the workings of Baxter's mind, you know that it will do the same for him. If what you say is true—as improbable as it sounds—then Baxter will have seen himself for the first time."

Medp nodded. "Possible."

"We cannot hide our motives from our own minds; to do so would cause us much pain and confusion. But, if a creature cannot see himself, do we damage it by allowing it to discover its motives?"

Medp leaned back and looked at the overhead. He then lowered his head and turned toward Lothas. "It is outside of my experience to imagine that knowledge of oneself could be damaging. But the hue-muns are also outside of my experience. Perhaps it could be damaging." Medp turned to a monitor displaying but a crescent of night-shrouded Nitola. "A more important question, Lothas, is can we live together with such creatures in peace?" Medp looked at Lothas. "My mind thinks not."

Lothas looked at the monitor and nodded. "Perhaps Deayl is in the right." He turned to Medp. "In any event, we shall know once you obtain the information from their computers. Prepare your mission well, Medp. The future of this curious race may depend upon what you find. Our own futures, as well."

In his private quarters, Lothas reclined on his cushions and studied the human sitting nervously in the wing-backed chair. Baxter would cross his legs, uncross them, then cross them again. His eyes would dart about, then look in one direction for long, unblinking minutes. "Are you well, Baxter?"

The human raised his glance and looked at the Nitolan. "Well?" He nodded, then smiled. "Yes, and you?"

Lothas nodded. "I am well." He watched as the human's appearance altered to become calm, his motions unhurried. *Perhaps this denial of the self is a means of human survival.*

"What did you wish to see me about, Dimmis? Has the new meeting with the council been arranged?"

"No. Baxter, we are very different creatures from each other."

Baxter laughed. "This much even I could see."

Lothas waited for the human to quiet himself, then he sat up. "I do not talk of skin, bones, shape, and size, Baxter." Lothas held up a five fingered hand. "Our bone structures are similar, we are both carbon-based lifeforms—two eyes, two nostrils, two arms, two legs. I believe your race originated on my planet, as you must believe that my race did as well."

Baxter shrugged. "That judgement is for others to make, Dimmis. But, for myself, I believe you are what you say you are."

Lothas nodded. "There is a difference. Your thinking, Baxter; it is *alien*. But I can see it is alien by your own choosing. What I do not see is why. I know of no form of life that acts against its interests by choice, except yours."

Baxter frowned, then wiped a hand over his face. "I'm not sure I know what you mean." His hand came away wet. "Do you mean wars?"

Lothas shook his head. "No. We have had our own wars, Baxter.

Wars can be an expression of self-interest." The Nitolan pointed a clawed finger at the human. "I talk about your thinking, and how your thinking makes you act. During the meld, among your many pains, I saw the need for your mate. Yet, when you talked with her, you make jokes; you hide the things you mean to say."

Baxter flushed. "That's my business. I would like to thank you for making the request."

"Is this what you mean, Baxter, or is this a joke? I do not understand. Understand that, to my mind, there are only a few ways that this situation can be resolved: First, we end human life on Nitola and resume control of our planet. We can do this."

Baxter blanched, then leaned forward, his elbows on the chair's armrests. "That would gain you nothing but a dead planet, Dimmis. To kill us from orbit, you will have to kill everything. If you land to kill us, then we can fight back, and we will."

Lothas nodded. "This is why my mind has not been in favor of this choice, although the minds of many Nitolans do favor it." Lothas waved a hand, dismissing the option. "Of course, I think it impossible that your race could attack and destroy mine. We have the Power. This leaves us with both races living together on Nitola, in some manner."

Baxter nodded as he exhaled a nervous breath. "I would prefer that."

"But the more we examine that course, Baxter, the more impossible it appears. We see you destroying the home planet, and this we could not tolerate. But your tribes are so divided, how could they agree to stop? I find that you do not represent all humans, but only a small number. The Russian also represents only a small number. Yet, even so, you could not agree. I see that your tribes would try to use us each to gain an advantage over the other." Lothas shook his head. "Another way is for the humans to leave Nitola."

"Leave?"

"Yes. Find another planet."

Baxter leaned back in his chair and stared at Lothas. He placed a hand over his chest as he felt his heart beating, threatening to come loose of its supports. "How can we?"

"We have these ships, and we can build you more. Enough to vacate the planet."

Impossible! Baxter shook his head as he remembered that it was not his decision to make. "I don't know, Dimmis. It seems unlikely, but I will talk with my people."

"Such of them as you represent."

Baxter nodded. "Yes." He stood.

"Before you go, Baxter, you should understand that these talks with me and with the council are different in substance to us than they are to you."

"How do you mean?"

"In you I read an attitude . . . a desire to use this experience to gain an advantage for your race. To us, we are learning. When we know enough, the proper choice will become obvious. Such a choice is not something subject to concession or negotiation. We will see where the right is, then we shall pursue it. This right we seek is independent of either my desires—or yours."

Baxter gently rubbed his temples as he reviewed his meeting with Lothas and waited for Wyman to get back to him. State had not been pleased. *The whole damned thing is falling apart.* Baxter leaned back in the chair, thinking. *This whole thing—it's like trying to stop the fall of mountains by stringing spools of rotting thread across the Grand Canyon.*

Lothas had pointed at the dying oceans, the poison air, the sheer number of human mouths. "*Still, Dimmis, we have a right to our future—and, on Earth. It is the future you committed us to. We didn't bail out and take the power with us—you did. If you had left us the power, perhaps things would have been different.*"

Lothas had swept the argument away with a wave of his clawed hand. "*As lifeforms, you are freaks—self-destructive, murdering freaks. And what is your answer? 'We are only human.' You use this phrase to excuse it all. But, Baxter, this defines you as a lifeform; it defines you as flawed, unworthy. And this is how you define your-*

selves." The Nitolan had leaned forward. *"If we had left you the Power, there would be none of you left."*

Baxter leaned forward, placed his elbows on his knees, then lowered his face into his hands. He had reported the talk to Wyman. *"Baxter, are you insane?"*

"Wyman, dammit, we both know I didn't ask for this! I knew I didn't know what I was doing, and so did you people! Now Lothas knows it, too. Wyman, you have got to get someone else up here. When Medp takes down the ship to get at the computers, what about putting a State Department mission—or something from the U.N.—on board?"

There had been a long silence, then Wyman came back on the air. *"I have to talk to some people about all of this Baxter, then I'll get back to you. One thing I can tell you now: if and when you have any more meetings with Lothas or with his council, keep your transceiver keyed and your mouth shut. We shall inform Lothas that State will attempt to deal directly with him. Understood?"*

Baxter let his head fall between his hands, then began kneading the knot of muscles at the back of his neck. Wyman had taken the responsibility off of him, except for working the transceiver— something Baxter felt confident enough to handle. But, still, he felt no relief. He leaned back in the chair and bit his lower lip. He was coming across as a complaining, whining, incompetent loser. "Dammit, Wyman," he said to the overhead, "don't you understand that they're messing with my mind? How would you weather a good look at yourself, you brass-plated diplomat?"

His transceiver buzzed, and he pressed the key. "This is Baxter."

"Wyman. Well, boy, it looks as though you have royally screwed up the works. To tell you the truth, I wouldn't give two cents for the chances your tailfeathers have if you ever set foot in this country again."

"It's nice hearing from you too, Wyman."

"Okay, here is the drill. We have put together a mission, and we're waiting now on Lothas or his council to decide whether or not to take them on board. The communications we've had were not encouraging. Just in case, we're going on full alert, and a spit-and-baling-wire arrangement is being put together to coordinate the military defenses of every nation on Earth. By the way, we've had at least one break. The Russian isn't going to make it. He bought it during the launch—"

"Wyman, you twit! A *break?* You call that a *break?* What brand of bumwad are you using for brains? I need *help* up here, and fast—"

"Grow up, Baxter! Help, from the Soviets?"

Baxter shook his head. "No, Wyman. Help from another human." Baxter felt himself giggling. "You haven't gotten the message yet—you people down there. We're all in this together . . . all of us." He shook his head as his giggles turned into quiet tears. The transceiver clicked, then clicked again. Wyman had keyed in, then keyed out—nothing to say.

The transceiver clicked again. "Remember, Baxter. Do nothing without authorization, and make sure they understand that, from now on, they will be dealing with us directly. Wyman out."

Baxter released the key on the transceiver. He shrugged, released the catch on his belt, and stood, leaving the belt and transceiver in the chair. The iris to his compartment opened and Simdna entered. "Captaincarlbaxter, Deayl would speak with you if it is your desire."

Baxter looked at the transceiver on the chair, then back at Simdna. "Yes. I will see him." Simdna left through the iris and Deayl entered. "It is good to see you again, Illya. Are you feeling better?"

Deayl stared down at the human, the creature's image wavered before his eyes. *Better? Do I feel better?* The iris closed and Deayl took a step toward the human. "Baxter, we have exchanged names."

"Yes, Illya."

Deayl wiped a clawed hand over his muzzle. "Do you remember I said this obligates me to nothing?"

"I remember." Baxter frowned, then looked once again at the transceiver. He turned back and faced the Nitolan. Deayl had come another step closer, his frightful clawed hands were outstretched.

"Still, I must tell you why I do this, Baxter."

Baxter began edging away from the Nitolan. "Do what?"

"Baxter, the knowing ones have left for Nitola to talk with your computers. The humans below struggle with the same problem: how are we to live together in peace—a thing that can never be."

"How do you know? You're upset—"

"The longer we wait to take back our planet, the harder it will be. Even now the humans prepare. But, I must make this clear to the council, and to do this I must provoke the humans. You see, I must murder you."

"Murder . . ." Baxter watched as Deayl came closer, his black, dagger-sized claws glowing softly in the light of the compartment. The hands struck out, and Baxter ducked. He turned, grabbed the wing-backed chair and threw it at the Nitolan. Deayl swatted it away, splintering it, and smashing the transceiver. Before the pieces hit the deck, Baxter reached the panel controlling the iris and slapped it with both hands. "Simdna! For God's sake, Simdna!" As the iris opened, Baxter felt Deayl's hands encircling his chest, the long claws ripping into his lungs. . . .

A week passed, and many of those on Earth marveled at how easily arms and territorial agreements between nations could be reached, now that they—in the face of the power—had become meaningless. The strange Nitolan vessel squatted silently next to the hangar where human technicians maintained the links between the ship and a vast array of computers located in almost every nation of Earth. No one saw the Nitolans, and for a week, there had been no communications from either Lothas or Baxter.

In a motel, near the airbase, a diplomatic mission headed by the secretary of state waited impatiently to board the Nitolan ship. On the other side of the field, a task force of commandos practiced their assault plan on the vessel. In Washington, Moscow, Paris, London, Peking, Cairo . . . haggard faces circled cup- and butt-littered tables, waiting by brand new communication facilities for some kind—any kind—of news.

The base Commander, General Stayer, heard it first. A shaken voice—one of the technicians in the hanger. No warning. The Nitolans had disconnected the links to the hangar, then they rose into the night.

The waiting began in earnest.

Deb Baxter listened to the rain spatter against the window and let her arm fall on the empty side of the bed. She opened her hand, palm down, and caressed the overstuffed quilt. She made a fist, then rolled over and pulled a cigarette from a half-empty pack on her night stand. She had been three years off cigarettes, and she realized as she struck a match that she was already back to two packs a day. In the light of the match, her eyes were puffy, with dark circles. She touched the match to the end of the cigarette, then shook it out. Taking a pillow and propping it up against the headboard, she propped herself up against it and studied the dark surrounding the warm coal that brightened with each drag she took.

She had faced that Baxter wasn't coming back, learned she could survive the fact, then accepted it—almost. Nights without sleeping pills still became vigils. She threw off the covers, swung her legs to the cold floor and walked barefooted to the bedroom window. Holding the dark curtain aside, she stared at the security lights surrounding the experimental parking ramp. Somewhere out there, some poor jerk who had been conned off the farm with promises of becoming an 'Aerospace Technician' was walking guard, rifle muzzle down, head and shoulders hunched under a poncho against the rain. She shook her head. "Stupid. It's not even supposed to rain in the desert."

She heard sirens in the distance, and then red lights streaked down the base's main drag, between her and the lights around the experimental ramp. There were always sirens. Baxter used to roll over and mumble something about the AP's playing cops and robbers, then sink back into sleep. She listened as the sirens grew dim, then gradually increased in volume. *Must be turning into the area.* She smiled and shook her head. *An area. I don't call it a neighbor-*

hood, or even a development, anymore. An area. She felt an ash brush her knuckles as it fell from the cigarette to the carpet. "Damn!" She stooped down to make certain that she had not ignited the cheap pile, then held up her head as she heard the sirens grow very loud, then die amidst a squeal of brakes. Immediately a loud pounding came from her door.

She looked around the dark bedroom, found her robe thrown over a chair, then began putting it on. "Mrs. Baxter! Mrs. Baxter, are you in there?"

She tied the sash with trembling fingers. "Just a minute!" She ran into the living room, then to the front door. Unlocking the door, she pulled it open. In the street before her house was a blue staff car flanked fore and aft by AP jeeps, red lights still flashing. She turned on the outside light and a greying Air Force officer, accompanied by an AP, removed his hat.

"Mrs. Baxter. I am the base commander, General Stayer. I must ask you to come with me."

"I . . . General, is this about my husband? Is it?"

The officer looked down. "I'm sorry. I don't know. Please hurry. We haven't much time."

Deb turned from the door, opened the hall closet and pulled out a raincoat. As she put it on, she found the first thing handy, and slipped Baxter's rubber galoshes over her bare feet. Moments later, she sat by the general in the back of the blue staff car as the procession screamed its way toward the field.

The car stood silently on the edge of the field, the dim blue taxiing lights diffused by the droplets on the windows, illuminating Deb's face with a cold glow. She looked across the back seat through the windshield, but could see nothing but rain. Pulling the raincoat around her, she shivered.

"I'm sorry, Mrs. Baxter." The General turned to the driver. "Bill?"

"Yessir?"

"Turn on the car and let's have some heat."

"Yessir." The driver hit the ignition, the motor caught, and in moments warm air blew against Deb's legs. She turned toward Stayer.

"Thank you. I didn't realize how cold I was."

Stayer nodded, then reached for a microphone attached to the back seat. He keyed the mike. "Tower, this is Stayer. Has GCA got 'em yet?"

"Affirmative, General. Ground con—"

Stayer switched the frequency indicator next to the mike hanger, then keyed the mike. "GCA, this is Stayer. You have an ETA yet?"

"This is GCA. Yes, General. They should be over the field in about a minute, although with this visibility you probably won't be able to see them until they land. The other ship didn't use lights."

"Stayer out." The General hung up the mike, looked at Deb, then turned back to the driver. "Bill, hit the wipers."

"Yessir." The car's electric wipers whined and thumped back and forth, but the field before them, as well as the sky above, remained empty.

Stayer leaned back, keeping his eyes on the deserted runway. "This is the first contact of any kind that we've had with them for three weeks, Mrs. Baxter. I know how difficult this is, but . . . they specifically asked to meet with you. We tried to ask, but they ended the transmission before we could ask about your husband."

Deb nodded, then turned to face Stayer. "I'll do whatever I can. . . ." The entire field grew bright with a blinding, yellow-white glare. Deb put her hands over her eyes, then peered through her fingers. The driver was leaning forward, over the steering wheel, looking up through the windshield. "Jesus!" The driver craned his neck further, trying to get a vertical look. "Jesus, General, the size of it!"

Stayer, his head pressed against the rear window, simply nodded. Deb held her breath as a glittering shape filled the landing field before her. She was startled to realize that the only sound she heard was the car's motor and the patter of the rain on the roof. Without thinking, she reached out a hand and grasped Stayer's forearm.

The area beneath the ship grew bright as it came within a few meters of the ground. Redlight joined the white as the belly opened, and a small, black craft was gently lowered to the runway. "It's the Python, General. And there's something else. Looks like two boxes."

Somewhere on the ship, a blue panel illuminated. The General took a breath, leaned forward and tapped the driver on the shoulder. "That's the signal, Bill. Get going."

Deb saw the driver looking at the controls of the staff car as though it was the first time he had ever seen them. "Damn!" He put the car in gear, the car jumped forward, then died. "I'm sorry, sir . . . I . . ."

"Take it easy, Bill. Just start it up, and take it easy."

"Yessir." The car started, then began approaching the ship. Deb's hand dropped from her eyes as she stared at the vessel, growing larger just at the moment she would have sworn it could grow no larger. The car stopped. Deb watched as an illuminated ramp extended from under the blue panel on the ship, and touched the ground. A moment later, a creature with massive legs for walking, smaller clawed legs held in front, and a thick tail behind, walked down the ramp and took up a position next to it.

"Mrs. Baxter?"

Deb turned toward Stayer, realizing she still held his arm. "What . . . what do I do?"

Stayer nodded at the creature. "Go over to . . . that. It'll tell you what to do. Good luck."

Deb opened the door, stepped out, and stood facing the ship. She could tell it was still raining, but none fell around the vessel. Leaving the door open, she walked toward the ramp, keeping her eyes on the creature. When she was ten feet from it, she stopped. "Well?"

The creature looked down at her. "You are the mate of Captaincarlbaxter?"

"Yes." She looked up the ramp into the ship, and at the top she saw a familiar face. "Baxter!" She ran past the creature, onto the ramp, and then reached the top. Tears streamed down her face as she looked at him, then ran to him and held him tightly.

"Easy, Deb." He kissed her, then held his cheek tight against hers.

She pushed back and held him at arm's length. "Baxter." She sniffed, then laughed. "That's some dynamite entrance you've got there, Baxter!"

Baxter smiled. "Wait until you see the rest of my act." He looked from Deb's wet hair, to his old raincoat, then to his old rubber galoshes. He looked back at her face and shook his head. "That's my Deb. All class. Why didn't you dress up? You're going to meet some important people."

"Oh, you jerk!" She embraced him again, then withdrew her arms as she heard a rasping sound behind her.

Baxter nodded in the direction of the open ramp door, where the creature Deb had seen was now standing. "Deb, I would like you to meet my friend, Deayl. If you would be friends with him, he would be called Illya."

Deb nodded at Deayl. "My name is Deb."

The creature nodded back. "You must call me Illya, then."

Baxter bent down, picked a helmet up from the deck, and turned to Deayl. "Illya, there's something I have to do. Would you keep Deb company for a few minutes?"

Deb frowned. "Baxter!"

He kissed her, then turned and walked down the ramp. Both she and Illya stood at the head of the ramp as Baxter went down, walked to the edge of the concrete runway, and knelt down. She turned to Deayl. "What is he doing?"

"Something that he wishes to do." He turned his head down toward Deb. "I asked Baxter if I could explain to you what has happened, and he consented." Deayl looked back at the human kneeling on the edge of the runway. "I tried to kill Baxter." Deb looked at the creature's clawed hands, then to the coal black eyes. "I hurt him very badly. This was to make you humans angry, and make impossible a settlement between us." Deayl nodded toward Baxter. "Our medicine saved him, then he saved me. I was to be tried by the council for my act, and Baxter interceded. What was said is not important, but he showed us something we had never seen before."

Deayl looked back at Deb. "When we see the right, that is what we accept and follow. But the right says Baxter should have demanded my death. Instead, he pleaded for me. He understood why I had acted the way I did. He . . . showed mercy. You hue-muns are everything evil that we had feared becoming, but you are also greater than we could hope to be. Because of this, and because of the things the knowing ones found, our ships will leave. Earth is yours for as long as you can keep it."

Deb looked down the ramp and saw Baxter at the bottom. In his arms he carried his helmet, and as he came close to the door, she saw that the helmet was filled to the brim with mud. He stopped, held it out toward Deayl, and smiled as the Nitolan took it and bowed. "A home for you, Baxter."

"A home for you, Illya."

Deayl stood up, turned and went through an open iris. It blinked shut behind him. Baxter took Deb's arm and steered her down the ramp. When they reached the runway, the ramp retracted, the ship became dark, then it lifted quietly away from the field. Deb felt the rain on her cheek as she followed Baxter to where the Python stood on the runway next to the two cubical containers. General Stayer got out of his car and stopped next to them.

Baxter patted the nose of the Python and turned toward the General. "There you are, General. I'm returning your property, and I even saved you some fuel."

Stayer placed a hand on Baxter's shoulder. "I'm glad to see you, Baxter. You'll never know how glad."

"The feeling is mutual, General." Baxter looked up as he saw a stampede of siren-screaming, light-flashing vehicles moving toward their location from the tower area. "I guess that'll be all the brass." He turned toward Stayer. "General, I have two favors to ask."

"Shoot."

Baxter went to one of the containers. "General, this is the information the Nitolans pulled out of our computers. It's been put together with their information and processed in ways I don't pretend to understand. It shows, day by day, the human race lasting another hundred and twenty years at the outside. Their predictions are accurate, which is why they left. What they saw told them that they could come back in a few hundred years and pick up where they left off—that humanity will have eliminated itself by then." Baxter nodded, then held Deb around the shoulders. "But, Medp told me that this particular prediction of theirs has one very large, unpredictable variable. That's us: humanity. If I were you, I'd have that container moved to wherever it was the Nitolans linked into those computers, then get to work."

Stayer nodded. "And the other favor?"

"Before all the brass shows up, I'd like to borrow your car and driver. I want to go home."

"Baxter, there are briefings, the Secretary . . ."

"General, I want to go home."

Stayer motioned at his car, it started up, and began rolling in their direction. The car's headlights illuminated the Python and the two containers. "One more thing, Baxter."

"Yessir?"

"What's in the other container?"

Baxter pulled on Deb's arm, stopped next to the car-sized cube, and pressed a panel set into the side of the container. It parted into two sections and swung open, exposing two wing-backed chairs, claw-on-ball feet, yellow and orange floral pattern. "I'd like these sent to my house."

Deb looked at them, then began laughing. "Oh . . . oh, Baxter . . . they're *horrible!*"

Stayer shook Baxter's arm. "Get going, Captain. And expect an early call. You have quite a selling job to do."

"Yessir. Thank you, sir."

The two entered the rear door held by the driver, and after shutting it, the driver ran around the front of the car and entered. In moments, the car moved off. Stayer felt the rain, hunched his shoulders and walked to the container with the chairs. As waves of vehicles pulled up, lighting the area with their headlights, the General took a last look, then pressed the container's panel. The cube closed with a snap. He nodded. "She's right. They are horrible." Shaking his head, General Stayer turned to greet the brass.

Lothas closed his fingers over the handful of dirt, then looked up at the image of receding Nitola in the monitor. He held the closed hand toward the monitor and turned toward Medp. "In suspension, it will be nothing to us. Perhaps a few planetary cycles, then we shall go home."

Medp studied the monitor. "Perhaps not."

Lothas nodded. "I hope you are right, Medp. They are special creatures, aren't they?"

"Indeed. It will take me many star cycles to absorb the information on them that I have acquired."

Lothas turned back toward the monitor. "Have you found an answer to the humor ritual?"

Medp gave an involuntary snort, then shook his head. "Perhaps there is no answer." He giggled.

"You seem to have discovered the cause of the reaction. Please explain."

Medp nodded, then looked up at the overhead. "Very well. Do you know of mice?"

Lothas nodded. "The small rodent."

"Yes." Medp giggled again. "And the mythical being of Santa Claus?"

Lothas leaned against his backrest, half-closed his large, dark eyes, and studied the knowing one. "Yes. You explained that in your report on hue-mun beliefs. Explain this behavior."

Medp held out his hands. "Lothas, why are a little grey mouse and Santa Claus similar?" Medp closed his eyes, shook, and gasped for breath.

"Are you well?"

Medp waved a hand. "Yes, yes. Answer the question."

Lothas thought a moment, then shook his head. "It escapes me, knowing one. Why are a little grey mouse and Santa Claus similar?"

Medp reached out a hand and grasped the back of Lothas's chair, apparently to keep from falling to the deck. "You see, Lothas . . . they both have long white beards . . ." tears began streaming from the knowing one's eyes, ". . . *except for the mouse!*"

The control center rocked with the sounds of Medp's laughter as the knowing one slapped Lothas's back, then staggered through an open iris, leaving Lothas alone with only a puzzled expression for company. Lothas shook his head. "Truly, there is much to learn." He reached out a clawed finger to press the panel for the voice log. His finger stopped short of the panel, he closed his eyes and nodded. Then the dinosaur laughed.

Darktouch

by S.P. Somtow

The terms were not the best.

But these were harsh times, weren't they? A war with aliens that couldn't be seen or heard. Power struggles and civil wars within the heart of the Dispersal of Man itself.

But it wasn't the prospect of the fee. Or the fatal attraction of the overcosm, that space *beyond* and *between*, where light goes wild and tantalizes you and drives you crazy with strange yearnings. Or that promise that it would only be a one-way trip in realtime, with guaranteed return by tachyon bubble, so that he would lose at most two centuries of objective time.

Kail Kirian found these conditions satisfactory. But—for an astrogator of his ability—they were not overly tempting.

No.

It was the woman Darktouch.

The face, soft and proud, the hair jet-black, the eyes dark, the skin snow-pale as though it had never seen suns' light, the single piece of clingfire that hugged her and burned against the frail whiteness—

She was all white and black, a holosculpture of monochrome projected into a colorclashing chamber, a thing from another world.

"You'll take the offer?"

"Offer . . ."

Where am I? This was Lalaparalla, he remembered, the planet of warrior's rest, and he was rising from *fang*-drenched torpor, and tongues of solvent were licking the crusts from his eyes . . . the war ached in his bones still, and the *fang* mist rose once more to succor the deep hurt, to steep him in oblivion.

Ah yes. At the hostel. A message. "Request: for an astrogator of clan Kail, to take party of approximately fifty to destination Earth, terms negotiable. Whereto, Inquestral Seal." Why *request*? If an Inquestral mission were involved, why not just *requisition*?

"You'll take the offer?" A hard voice.

And then he saw her eyes through the parting mist.

"Let me know more," he said, baffled. *Such eyes! There can't be a woman like this. I'm still in a drugged dream.*

And then he saw who stood behind the woman.

Tall. A shimmercloak that glowed, pink and blue, through the dense mist. Sternfaced. *Old.*

Powers of powers! he thought. *An Inquestor!*

"Yours to command," he said automatically. He could hardly believe he was standing so close to one, sitting naked in a *fang* bath. And he one of the rulers of the Dispersal of Man. Practically a God.

"You're mistaken," said the Inquestor, and he laughed. He didn't speak with the deep-voiced authority that Inquestors had. Somehow . . . his voice was *tender.* "I cannot command you. I am no longer *Ton* Davaryush, Kingling of Gallendys, but merely Davaryush without-a-Clan. I am apostate. And all these people here with me . . . are dreamers. Refugees. They want to secede from the Dispersal of Man."

The *fang* . . . it must still be clouding his senses! "You aren't real," Kirian muttered. And he mindflicked for more solvent, to wash his eyes and clear his vision. *Inquestors don't lead groups of crazies on wild-goose chases. Inquestors—*

And then he saw the woman again.

There isn't such a woman.

But the dream stood there, defying him to blink her away.

"The money's good," Davaryush said. "Three thousand in tarn-crystal carat-equivalents."

"That'll sway you, if nothing else!" the woman hissed. "Mercenary!"

What's behind this woman? I feel as if I ought to take her away from this obviously lunatic Inquestor, take her to a deserted planet and—

"I don't suppose you've ever heard of Earth," said the Inquestor. "It's an abandoned place, far beyond the worlds of the Dispersal. Our ancestors came from there once. We dream about it all the time, of building a utopia there, a perfect world."

"We don't want our children to be packed off to war at six," said the woman. "We think civilization is done for."

"The alien war out there . . ." Davaryush said. "Do you know how many planets they've burned? Of course not: the Inquest never reveals anything. . . ."

Kirian did not listen. He couldn't take his eyes off the woman, and her look of contempt never abated. Not once.

"Take this woman Darktouch," Davaryush said. "She is from Gallendys. Do you know of Gallendys?" Mist enveloped his face.

"No."

"You astrogators of the clan of Kail, you who mindlink with the delphinoid shipminds to guide the starships through the overcosm . . . you of all people should know. Do you really know of the delphinoid shipminds, the gigantic brains that are fused into the starships?"

"What is this?" said Kirian, uneasy. "I'm not a historian, not a philosopher. Just tell me the terms and let me decide. I'm a soldier, an overcosm flier, a man of action."

The woman laughed once, a warm laugh. Perhaps she was not solid rock to the core, then, like a dead planet.

"Listen, then," said Davaryush. "On Gallendys there is a gigantic volcanic crater, a hundred kilometers high, a thousand across. Within is a dense atmosphere, a relic from a previous epoch . . . in this dark land, above the Sunless Sound, the delphinoids float. They are creatures who are all brain. They perceive the overcosm directly, without instruments. It is this power that we use to travel between the stars.

"But listen more! These delphinoids sing, Kail Kirian. Their songs are holosculptures ten kilometers across, suspended over the perpetual darkness of the Sunless Sound. They are imagesongs, lightpoems woven out of overcosm visions. And a strange music too, a harmony that makes men weep, even hardened soldiers like you. Even Inquestors. For every starship that flies the overcosm, a song must die."

The mist was dying now. Davaryush's intensity touched Kirian, made him nervous. And he glimpsed other people behind, other crazies. Davaryush continued. "No human who had once seen the light on the sound, and heard the songs of the ones whose minds were turned to the space beyond our space, to the utter beauty of the overcosm . . . no human who had once experienced this could willingly kill a delphinoid. The Inquest understood the need for space travel. They mutated a race that was deaf and blind, and gave them a mythos and a mission, and now they live in the darkness and silence of the crater-wall caverns. And they fly out on their airships and fling their forcenets over the delphinoids and bring them home. They do not know that it is to feed the shipyards, to glorify the Dispersal of Man.

"I was Kingling of Gallendys once. This woman was a girl, a genetic throwback; she could see and hear. At puberty she joined the holy hunt, and what she saw there made her flee, half-crazed, out of the dark country to the City of Effelkang where I held power. And later she took me to see for myself. An old man and a girl, we saw the slaughter of joy. It changed us. . . .

"We have all had these experiences. All of us."

And Kirian saw the others now, behind them: an old man, a couple of child-soldiers with laser-irises, who could have killed him with a glance and a subvocalized command; a matron; a young hermaphrodite in a whore's robe; a princeling clad in lapis and iridium; a slaveboy with a chrysanthemum branded on his forehead; a girl-singer with a whisperlyre. . . .

They're shameless! he thought. *Look how they carry on, without regard for rank. Look how brazenly they flout the principle of degree.* The slaveboy and the princeling held hands and were close. The hermaphrodite leaned on a child-soldier's arm, defying all decency.

"You're shocking."

"Don't criticize," said Darktouch coldly. "Just take the money and help us."

The Inquestor motioned her to be quiet. With such a strange gentleness . . . "We are giving up anger. Remember that." With the same voice he said to Kirian: "We have all been through such experiences as Darktouch has. We have all turned our backs on the Dispersal. I say this so that you may see why I, an Inquestor, a former Kingling, a hunter of utopias once . . . have come begging to you."

Kirian was profoundly shocked. Only once before in his life—

And then he mouthed his deepest fear. "This Earth. Is the route well mapped? Are there any anomalies in spacetime, any tachyon whirlpools?"

"None are known to exist," said Davaryush. "And moreover, I have been able to requisition power enough for one tachyon bubble. When you have delivered us to Earth, you may use it to return to your homeworld."

Powers of powers! "You must have been a very important man," said Kirian, wondering at how low the Inquestor had fallen.

For the tachyon bubble's secret was known only to the Inquest. They were bubbles of realspace, held together by phenomenal power expenditure—the deaths of suns, it was sometimes said— that smashed their way through planes even higher than the overcosm, travelling instantaneously . . . If Davaryush could really supply such a thing, Kirian's travel time would be halved, the problems of time dilation would not be nearly so bad.

Not that he cared about time dilation. Only a loner could be an astrogator: how could a sociable person stand it, coming home after every trip to find his friends grown old, dead?

"If it weren't for travelling with you lunatics," he said, "I wouldn't even hesitate."

The slaveboy and the princeling had moved closer to each other for reassurance, had their arms around each other's shoulders—intolerable!

Darktouch cried, "I told you, Daavye!" and Kirian cringed, that a clanless woman should dare to call an Inquestor by a diminutive. "He's a mercenary, and for what *we* want we'll never be able to pay him. We're trampling on all he believes in. He's a cog in a machine, a rat in a maze, and he'll never know it—"

"Hold it!" Kirian said.

She turned back to look at him. The mist had parted, and she was so *real* that no overdose of *fang* could have created her. He wanted to touch her so badly it hurt him . . . but he could not even reach out. The rift between them was complete. It was not her remoteness (he sensed it was insecurity as much as anything), not her beauty. But the fact that she would not acknowledge him as a person, only as a type. Was there a brittleness behind her scorn?

Davaryush was saying, "It has to be Earth, because it is so far away from people's minds, so that they will not search us out and kill us. And because it is the source, the place of beginning, a potent symbol out of the farthest past there can have been . . ."

"Don't go on talking," said Darktouch. "It's just wind to him, just noise." She was bitter; how many astrogators had they tried?

"I haven't said no yet, have I?" he said, feigning toughness.

They all edged forward like one man—

He heard their unison intake of breath, he saw the woman and the Inquestor exchange a quick look that shut him out of their topsy-turvy world and their crazy philosophy—

And felt naked, suddenly.

It was a routine journey at first.

The passengers had all opted for stasis; they would only awake on Earth. Except for Davaryush: he was an Inquestor, who must always lead, even if dethroned; and also Darktouch. That he couldn't understand. Six months subjective, in the overcosm—but he brushed her from his mind.

Or tried to.

He reclined in the small room. Circular mirror walls gleamed around him. He was shielded. He was at the ship's heart. He closed his eyes and reached out with brain-implanted sensors. It was second nature; he had been doing it since puberty.

The delphinoid shipmind came alive, moving like an ocean in darkness. The sensation was soft, familiar. Endless darkness cushions swam by . . . he knew the ship was easing from its orbital anchor. But he saw nothing. He was alone in the room. It was so still. . . .

(*What's it like, to be born in the dark country of Gallendys, to see the imagesongs of the delphinoids, and not to have words to protest, to understand? And how can something be so beautiful that you can't bring yourself to kill it?* Killing was second nature to him, like touching the delphinoid shipmind. *If commanded to, could I have killed the woman Darktouch?*)

Kirian was no thinker. Thinking was for Inquestors. You couldn't afford to think. . . .

The delphinoid's warmth enveloped him.

Then a voice, tugging at the bottom of his mind—

Do you hear?

(An untried delphinoid. He would have to coax it, firmly, onto the right flight plan.)

I hear you, he mindwhispered. *Are you ready?*

I'm afraid. This route is poorly charted. . . .

Be still, be still, he mindspoke, as though to a pet animal. But he was frightened too.

There was always the split second of blinding terror that would come upon him, seconds before bursting into the *other* space where space and time go mad. A memory would come to him, a nightmare—

On his first war mission. He was seven years old. A newboy. Anyone could have ordered his death. A hundred starships packed into a shieldsphere, charging through the overcosm; and he was alone on a deck with the walls deopaqued and the overcosm light raging, and alarms blaring and sirens screeching and he was so alone, and—

One by one. The ships falling into darkness.

So strangely beautiful. . . .

They flew into gold-tinged scarlet nets of flame, vanished, a ship at a time, like beads of a cut necklace, slipping one by one into water.

And after, in another chamber, stripped and lined up and black mourning cloaks thrust over their shoulders, all the children standing stiff and frightened while the Inquestors paced and raged. Huge reflections of their shimmercloaks flapping, blushing the mirror-silver walls. . . .

What's happened to the other ships?

Not looking at the other children. Obeying or dying.

"It was a tachyon whirlpool."

The Inquestor's voice rasping above his head. And Kirian could almost touch the silence. More pacing, and the floor humming eerily as the Inquestor's fursoles rubbed and whispered. A child burst out crying. He clenched his eyes. The boy would be returned to homeworld in disgrace. Impassive. Make your face impassive.

Another Inquestor's voice: "Never forget this experience until the day you die! Tachyon whirlpools were made by men. During the first experiments in tachyon travel there were foolish errors. A thing that travels faster than light, like a tachyon, must have a negative timeflow relative to our universe! And the first experimenters were hurled into the past, twisting the local continuum, wrenching causality apart. And even now these tachyon whirlpools remain, symbols of their lust for knowledge! Repeat this! It is good that only the Inquest knows the secret of tachyon travel."

Unison chorus: *It is good that only the Inquest knows the secret of tachyon travel.*

"It is evil to question nature. Only the Inquest is wise."

It is evil—

Theirs was the only ship to survive.

And later they burst into realspace in the region of the star

Keima, and they obliterated the planet Zelterkangh. It had been a simple punitive expedition, nothing a single starship couldn't handle. . . .

The terror lived again for a moment in the ship's darkness. Even after twenty years. More vividly this time than the other times. . . .

So it isn't a perfect universe. That much my lunatics have gotten right. But they're wrong to run away from it. They shouldn't question the way things are. Man is a fallen being after all, he thought.

Quickly he returned the memory to its cage.

You can't hurt me, he lied to himself.

The nightmare beat at the cage bars. This time it came mingled with the eyes of the woman Darktouch. He beat it back. And the darkness of the shipmind did take him, eventually, but not before he had gazed into the strange woman's eyes for a long time, puzzling himself. . . .

Some weeks later, he broke free from the shipmind and staggered up to the observatory.

She was alone there. All the walls were deopaqued. They stood on the metallic floordisk, floating in—

The overcosm raged. Oppressing him. No escape from it.

And she was a silhouette gazing out, not moving. Even her clingfire garment was muted by comparison with it. She didn't acknowledge him, only stared out at the—

—vermilion hurricanes spattering whitepeaked wavecrests, the ochre lightpeaks tumbling crumbling over blindingwhite catherinewheel firevolleys—

"You mustn't expose yourself to the overcosm too long." She flinched from the words, startled. "You'll stare your eyes into cinders." He went on, not liking the silence, "People have gone mad, you know, from being unable to cope with the torrent of sensations—"

"It's beautiful." She turned her back on him.

—geysers of green flame gushing through scarlet walls, veils that ripped to reveal more veils—

"It's just nothing, just mass hallucinations, because we can't understand what we perceive." Damn it, why did she ignore him? "You spend all your interstellar trips like this?"

"Always. I am afraid of stasis." She was frail in the colorstorm.

"They're just lights."

"The world the delphinoids see, Kirian. Isn't it strange?" She turned and watched him; he wanted her then, and despised her too, and could think of nothing to say.

Finally he said, "You're so full of words. As though words could save the universe. Like this utopia of yours . . . more words."

"You poor mercenary . . ."

"Don't pity me! You reject reality, you dream hopeless dreams—"

"Of love, brotherhood, things like that . . ." She began to explain it all to him, and it was like a child's wishful thinkings, impractical, destructive. "Oh. I see you're not impressed. How could you be? They've lied to you so much you couldn't recognize a truth to save your own skin."

"To be so sure of something . . ." he said. He saw how her eyes shone, how she seemed to be looking straight through him, to some world she and the others had made up. "You're not perfect either," he said brusquely.

"Of course not! But—"

"Oh, you're so proud. You see not what I am, but what I'm supposed to be like in your eyes, and—"

She turned away sullenly. No, she was no angel.

—volcanohearts twisted inside out, lightfeathers fluffed out of prismpools fracturing into mosaics—

"Why shouldn't I hate your kind?" she burst out. "Don't you know how you make the delphinoids suffer, how every moment of their lives from the moment they are mindsoldered into the ships is spent in excruciating agony, how you force them to live when they can't sing, which is agony beyond your understanding?"

"Intellectually one knows—"

"Every parsec we've advanced across the Dispersal of Man has given unconscionable agony to a sentient creature! How can you live with that? How can we all live with that? If you can live with it you must be—"

It was true. But it had always been the way. There were no alternatives.

In the end he said, "Are the imagesongs even more beautiful than this?"

Not looking at him, she said, "Of course. They are art, and this, though beautiful too, is random lightnoise. . . ."

She's the first woman ever to despise me! I'm not a rôle, I'm a human being! he thought. And she was so still. Like a holosculpture in a museum: untouchable.

You're proud, so proud it goes against all your fine talk about love and brotherhood. You're hypocritical as the rest of us.

Above them, the firestorm stretched to forever. Behind the stormshards, past the colorclouds, pale sinuous snakes of light darted from dark to dark.

And he was jealous of the certainty for which Darktouch had given up the whole galaxy. And jealous of the lunatics who had stolen her from him. . . .

So he fled and sought the comfort of the shipmind's darkness, and drew the darkness over his thoughts as a child retreats into a blanket heavy with familiar smells, retreats from the fear of night.

He even welcomed the recurring nightmare of the tachyon whirlpool . . . that at least was familiar.

Many months later, from out of the darkness—

—he burst blind through terror that didn't belong there at all, his mind screaming burning ANOMALY ANOMALY against the relentless logic of the shipmind, and he was crushed into darkness within darkness screaming falling burning ANOMALY ANOMALY—

(Memory: a hundred ships dropping into the net of flame.)

"Cut the connection!"

(Memory: alone on deck with the sirens bawling.)

The shipmind said, *Kail Kirian, we have navigated safely past the tachyon whirlpool.* A toneless internal whisper.

"Identify the anomaly," he said, "for the last time."

It is a tachyon whirlpool, Kirian. What else can I say?

(A *fang* dream?) "If that's true, we're off course."

No.

"Yes! This should be the vicinity of Earth, and the failed tachyon experiments were millennia after the first Dispersal from Firstworld!"

I understand this. I understand the unlikelihood. Nevertheless, what I sense I sense.

"How can there be whirlpools in this uninhabited, abandoned sector? You're malfunctioning—"

No.

Kirian broke the connection finally. And passed through the forcecurtain to the observatory. She was still there; it was almost as though minutes, not months, had elapsed.

—firebubbles foamed through lacelightcurtains lanced by liquid lightnings—

The old man was there too. His shimmercloak blushed softly against the patches of night.

Darktouch turned around—

He gaped at her. The light from the overcosm haloed over her face, the hair flowed dark and free, the clingfire kissed her slight body. He couldn't speak.

"Well?" Davaryush said. "We felt . . . disturbance."

"Tachyon whirlpool." *Mustn't sound frightened. Mustn't give anything away!*

"That's—" said Darktouch.

"I know! I know it's impossible!"

The Inquestor merely said, "Will it delay us much?"

Is that all they can think about, their fool mission? And Darktouch moved closer to him, and his desire embarrassed him. "Not long."

"Good," she said. Fanatic eyes, shining . . .

"I don't share your dream," he said angrily. "I just want to get to the bottom of this anomaly."

"Mercenary!"

"You should go into stasis!" he shouted. "The strain's getting to you—"

"Darktouch," the Inquestor interrupted, "scorn, hate, all the things we are giving up."

She subsided. Behind her, the lightveils parted—

—kaleidoscoped, dissolved—

Darkness fell without warning.

"WHAT HAVE YOU DONE?" he shouted.

Another whirlpool! said the ship. The mind connections closed all around him, the darkness breathed on him, mathematical figures danced and wavered in his head—

Afterwards, they burst out of the overcosm into a blackness of new stars. One in particular, a yellow dwarf of no importance. Realspace was dull, compared with the overcosm; so Kirian stayed in his wombchamber, assessing the damage. It was bad, very bad.

The utopians didn't have a chance.

The stasis-pod life-support systems had been thrown into dysfunction. They were all dead: the princeling, the slaveboy, the girl with the lyre, the hermaphrodite, all of them with their hope-fired eyes and their false, poignant dreams. . . .

The tachyon bubble system was dead too. He would have to use the delphinoid to return home. He would lose four centuries to time dilation, not two.

Before he went to the observatory he opaqued the walls. He felt more comfortable between the gray walls.

"You have to go back."

They looked blankly at him. They could have been holosculptures of the dead.

"Look, the last tachyon whirlpool   it wiped out all your chances. Even though I still can't believe it was there at all. The dormant passengers are permanently dead. You can't create a viable colony. You can't even propagate the species—you must be over three hundred years old, Davaryush."

"Four hundred and twelve."

He felt a sudden compassion for their shattered dream. But pushed it aside. "The shipmind can think us home readily enough," he said. "It's learned where the two anomalies are. . . ."

"No!" cried Darktouch. "Not while we still have one male left—" And she glared at Kirian, hostile.

Oh no! I desire her, but not like this—

"Now wait!" he said angrily. "I'm no head-in-the-clouds utopian like you and the Inquestor. I *know* where I belong. I've finished my part of the bargain. You've failed, and I'm sorry for you, and I can take you home at no extra charge. I can't leave an old man and a woman to fend for themselves on a dead planet—"

"Never! Not after the agony the delphinoid has been through to bring us here!" cried Darktouch, trembling. "We vowed to let it die, to free it from its shipbonds!"

He saw that she was assessing him now, as genetic material, as a piece of meat, a pawn in her utopia . . . he wanted to help her so badly, in spite of her hate. She couldn't want to stay. It was beyond all reason, even a fanatic's.

"I want to go back to what I know," he said.

"With the war and the civil war," said Davaryush, "I think it's rather an ambiguous question as to whether there will *be* a Dispersal to return to. . . .

I can't accept that! "No!"

"All right," said Darktouch calmly. "We'll land on Earth. Then you can impregnate me and leave. You do desire me, don't you? I am beautiful, aren't I?" And then she began to weep, terribly, hysterically.

But he was afraid to comfort her.

"Delphinoids don't make mistakes. . . ." he said.

"Don't speak of delphinoids again!" she screamed.

"It will pass," said the Inquestor gently. "You will never understand what she has suffered on Gallendys."

"Blank out the walls!" she cried out. "I want to see Earth! I want to see the dream!"

Abruptly the starstream burned in darkness behind her. She turned and stared her eyes out at the tiny yellow disk. He tried to put his arms around her, but she was like a statue.

"Remember the delphinoid's pain," she said quietly. Her eyes said, *Animal!*

Davaryush's voice came from behind them: "You see the desperation that drove us, Kail Kirian. You *must* let us down on Earth; and then, if you choose to go, we will at least die on the ground that made us, on the planet untouched by the Inquest. . . ."

And he was moved, in spite of himself.

The inconvenience of it! He longed to be in battle where he belonged. Here they were as far from the center of things as it was possible to be, as far as the very primordial beginnings of Man. Even the stars were thin here, in this wisp of galactic arm; it was a bleak and desolate sky. Cold touched his spine.

"Very well," he heard himself say. "I'll land you there, then ship back to homeworld. Even though abandoning you goes against my conscience."

"Oh," said Darktouch, mocking him, "do you have one?"

But she thanked him with her eyes.

I cannot touch her he thought, *while she still hates me. But perhaps I can find a way. . . .*

"Look, Earth," said Davaryush.

They smiled, both of them, falling into their dream. *How could they smile, when there was no hope? How could they—*

Earth hung in the blackness: opalescent, white-blue, beautiful, dead.

Desert. Rocky desert, hilly desert, dunedeserts, deserts of blasted glass that might have been cities fused together in some cataclysm . . . harsh polar caps made ice deserts. Millennia before, men had done a good job of killing Earth. . . .

In the north of one the great landmasses they found thin

grassfields, yellow-gray and stubblestrewn, and the lander settled on a hill-fringed plain where a brook ran to merge beyond the horizon with a shallow river. The lander sprouted wheels—Kirian realized with a shock that here they could not travel from place to place by displacement plates—and waited.

The three of them stood by the stream. Why, they didn't even know how to set up a camp or forage for food, thought Kirian, any of the skills that a Kail learned from childhood.

"I'd better help you find food," he said, avoiding their eyes. But they were watching their new planet, enraptured.

Food they found readily enough. On the foothills were fruit-trees with reddish round fruit and soft yellow meat; and curious, fearless fish fairly leapt into their forcenets from the brook.

They'll live an idyllic life, thought Kirian, *without my help.*
Until they die.

He didn't want to admit that he feared the four-hundred-year time dilation and the tachyon whirlpools that didn't belong. . . . *I mustn't leave in unseemly haste,* he thought.

The next day they went exploring. They climbed the hills easily; Davaryush followed on a floater, because of his age and because the gravity was a shade higher than he was used to.

Darktouch was silent the first few hours.

He would look at her when she didn't know he was looking, and see her somehow at peace. She no longer groomed her hair, so it streamed free in the wind; the clingfire garment was worn threadbare. It gave off no fire but a pearly rainbow. She belonged here.

The ground was soft, yielding to his feet. It was a strange sensation, quite unlike the continual disruptions of displacement plates.

It would take days, months, to explore the world. But from what they could see around them it was truly dead. Twenty millennia had rubbed the planet smooth. They saw no sunken cathedrals such as the sand acropolises of war-torn Kellendrang, no mile-high husks of skyscrapers such as bestrode the firesnowed horizons of Ont. . . .

At the summit he said, awkwardly, "I wish there was not this gulf between us."

"I pity you, Kail Kirian," she said, avoiding his eyes. "You belong

to the old things, cruel and senseless. You've no pride in yourself—
otherwise why would you have come here for mere money? If you
could only see things as they are—"

"If only *you* could!" he retorted. "You're just as hypocritical as the
rest of the human race. You took my help, didn't you? Help in
running away. You're cowards. Running away—to die!"

They glared at each other. Her hair blew across her face—

How softly she glows, he thought, *against the strange yellow light
of this sun.*

Davaryush, ahead of them, called out. Kirian eased himself over
the hillcrest and rested his elbows on a flat boulder, and his field of
vision telescoped abruptly to an endless brown plain spattered with
smooth sand-carved rockshapes like sculpted bushes. Half-way to
the horizon was a forest of brown trees . . . trees?

"What are they?" he said.

"Let's go and see," Darktouch answered. He felt an unbecoming
curiosity in himself for a moment. "Well, don't you want to find out?
Why, they look almost like . . . people, those trees."

"It's too far to walk," he said, and summoned two more floaters
with a flick of his mind.

They rode the breeze, the two of them, down through the desert.
It was so far . . . sand stretched until distance meant nothing any
more. And the wind-etched sandstone sculptures . . . they were
huge, bigger even than the delphinoid that orbited above them,
waiting.

They were dwarfed by this one plain. And the thought that the
huge world stretched around them forever. Kirian felt lonely. From
ground level they could not see their objective at all, so they floated
blindly, trusting the floater settings.

And then there were—

People.

Kirian stepped gingerly off his floater. He practically walked into
a man. The man was quite cold and he didn't move.

There were other men standing nearby. Further off, some
women. Many were naked; these had on nothing but a blue strap
around their wrists. Others had clothes: clingfire was one of the

fabrics, but the fire was frozen. Others were in fantastical costumes, headdresses with pointed layers, extravagant codpieces.

They didn't move.

"What *is* this?" Kirian felt panic. "First the tachyon whirlpools, now this—holosculpture museum, on a planet with no people. This is the wrong planet!"

"Delphinoids don't lie," Davaryush mocked him, gently.

"You don't like mysteries, do you, mercenary?" said Darktouch and smiled a hard smile.

"No, I don't," said Kirian. "I like answers! We've got to get back now if we can. Obviously we had a warped shipmind and we're somewhere quite different from where we set out for. Maybe you plan to die here, but *I'm* leaving."

"Coward!" Darktouch shouted.

"I'm no coward! I've killed more men than you've ever seen! But I'm going to go back to what I *do* understand."

The statues never moved. He slammed his fist hard on a woman's shoulder; it was harder than a starship's hull.

"You're all alike," said Darktouch bitterly. "You want no mysteries. You've no pride in being humans. Inside, you hate yourselves!"

Her anger sounded small on the huge plain. Kirian looked around him. Perhaps a thousand humans, frozen hard and seemingly indestructible. Children, too. He touched a child near him; red-haired, the hair tousled but stiff as metal.

Red hair, like mine, he thought. The thought irritated him, obscurely . . . something oddly familiar about the child . . . he stared at the unseeing eyes. He *did* want to know what they were.

Maybe there's no harm in asking one question. . . .

"All right," he said. "I'll stay a few days more, we can run tests on the statues. Maybe this is a hall of fame, an ancient artifact, an Inquestral plot, a cunning mirage . . . when we've found the answer I'll leave."

And he surprised himself, that he was able to wonder . . . Were they humans somehow frozen out of time? Or imitations of humans, bait laid by some alien?

And why do they seem so familiar?

Afterwards he closed his eyes and used the delphinoid—whose orbit matched their position, monitoring them constantly—to move the landing craft to the edge of the forest of statues and set up the shelters.

But he found that the order to the delphinoid was not a simple reflex as it had always been; for the first time, a thought nagged at him:

This ship is in agony, and cannot die.

He woke to the dawn. The sands had shifted; the statues had not moved at all, and some were now knee-deep in little dunes.

The dawn—here it was like pink feathers of a pteratyger, speared and brought down over the gray sea on Keneg, Kirian's homeworld. The image chilled him; he did not think he could still be homesick.

This planet did have a magic then . . . it was the primal home-world.

He shut the shelter door and approached the nearest statue. For they must be statues, if they didn't move—statues from a time of primitive technology that had stood the ravages of twenty millennia. Impossible.

He and Darktouch worked on the statues that morning. They wanted to saw off a piece—part of a garment, they had decided, just in case the statues were real people—and they were trying an old man's white tunic. A pretty tableau watched them, a young woman and two boys all in white. Their metal tools all broke on the cloth. It never gave so much as a micron, from what their instruments could tell them.

In one of the pauses she said to him: "Did you ever figure out why the tachyon whirlpools were there?"

"I suppose our history is wrong. The Dispersal of Man is too large for full records, perhaps. The abortive experiments were so long ago, and—"

"But the whirlpools are anomalies in space and *time*, aren't they? So they could be experimenters in the future?"

"Rather hypothetical, considering your sort think the future is pretty much done for."

"You've no imagination. What could I have expected." But the insult was automatic, not laced with spite as it might have been two days before. They worked on without talking.

It was hard to take his eyes off her. Long crimson-tinged shadows crossed her face . . . *If I don't leave, immediately, I'll . . . fall in love with her.* And the thought was like pain.

After the laser device had failed to chisel off a piece of the man's clothing, they rested, leaning against the hard statues. A light wind sprang up, sprinkling them with sand.

"You've never had any experience," Darktouch said, "to make you doubt the universe you were taught to believe in?"

"No."

—but there were the hundred ships falling into the tachyon whirlpool—

"Not even war?"

"War is necessary! It keeps the children occupied, it purifies the human instincts, it keeps down the population. . . ."

—I blasted one of the revivified corpses over and over and still he came barrelling towards me. I blew off his head and he collapsed a centimeter from my face . . . my first kill—

"You don't believe that."

"The Inquest told me!"

—and the headless torso of the kindled corpse, still groping towards me across the starship's silver floor, struggling without a mind, and me striking it over and over in my nine-year-old passion, yelling hot anger from my heart—

Kirian was in tears, suddenly.

—and the hundred starships falling—

—and after, on leave, going to Alykh the pleasure planet, riding the varigrav coasters until we were drunk with giddiness, and then on to the oblivion of f ang and Lalaparalla . . . and then another war and another—

He didn't want to think of himself. He didn't know who he was, anymore. "Why are you called Darktouch," he said, "in the high-tongue, and not a pretty name from an archaic language?"

"Because," she said, "in the dark crater over the Sunless Sound there are no names. People speak with their hands. I did not know I could have a name, until I went on my first hunt and saw and heard . . .

"They're not delphinoids to us, they're—" She did a fingerdance across his palm then. "Huge, sleek, streamlined creatures that are all brain. They talk by drawing patterns of light in the dark air above the Sound. And they leap and soar and sing, they sing!

"We had netted one and were towing him home in the airship. Their bodies were twined around each other, singing of victory. And then he began to sing. The lightstrands tore the air apart. It was pure tragedy . . . of course you have to be deaf and blind to hunt them! At lightsend I ran away, crawling through the hidden tunnels till I reached the lightworld, struggling across the badlands of Zhnefftikak until I reached the city where men could see and hear, Effelkang. . . ."

Kirian turned his back on her and began to laser the man's tunic again. "I'm not responsible for the sins of the Inquest," he said. "You're just trying to make me feel guilty so I'll stay here and join with you in a loveless breeding plan and make your project come true."

"No!"

But he *was* feeling guilty.

"Look," he said at last, "they all have these blue bracelets in common . . . maybe if we lasered a bracelet."

By noon there was still no result. By then Kirian felt an overpowering need to find the answer to the riddle.

"How about this one?" He indicated a boy standing behind the old man. "His bracelet seems a little askew."

A red-haired boy, that odd familiar look, unnerving somehow . . . Kirian tugged at the bracelet.

The boy sprang to life. "Where is this?" he shrieked, looking wildly around him. "Where's the space station?"

Darktouch was beside him quickly, trying to calm him.

"What?" said Kirian. "He speaks the hightongue?" They took the boy to the shelter, kicking, screaming, and biting all the way.

The shelter: a circular silver wall around them. Like a room on the starship.

The boy: eleven or twelve. The age of a young warrior of the Dispersal. That familiar look—Kirian could almost put his finger on it. But no . . .

"Who are you?" he demanded.

The boy shrank back, still defiant. He tried to break free of the tranquilizer field—

"Let me out of here! This is the wrong planet I guess; there's no space station, and I didn't fasten my stasis bracelet tight enough—"

He stopped. He looked into Kirian's face. And then he said, "I'm dreaming." And then he smiled. The smile made Kirian uneasier than ever.

And then Davaryush smiled too. And Darktouch. They were all smiling, threatening Kirian with some secret knowledge—

"I'm getting out of here!" he said, trapped. "I'm calling the delphinoid now—"

The fear was gone from the boy. He looked at Kirian with a strange reverence . . . almost as if Kirian were some prince, some Inquestor even. "I'm not afraid now," the boy said. "This is the dawn time; I understand that I've accidentally triggered the bracelet thing by tying it wrong on Sirius. What a stroke of luck I've found you!

Now you can do it up properly for me and bundle me off to the station and I can get home. Right?"

Kirian released the tranquilizer field. "Tell me what's happening, someone?" he said desperately.

The boy laughed, a silvery laugh that somehow made his throat catch. "Ha! Well . . . I guess you really wouldn't know. Would you? Davaryush, Darktouch, and Kirian?"

"Now, answers," Kirian said tightly. The boy had known his name. What next?

"Be gentle," said Darktouch. She moved closer to Kirian, and their hands touched and were warm together. "Where are you from?"

"Sirius."

"Where—?" Kirian said.

"It's a colony. My parents sent me back to Earth to go to school."

"To this empty planet?" said Kirian, more and more bewildered.

"Well, it *is* the dawn time. The stasis field—"

"All right," said Davaryush. The boy turned and stared at him, huge-eyed. "You recognize us."

The boy nodded slowly.

"So you must be from the future, from a time when Earth is populated again, with a colony or two even."

He nodded again.

"We're a little simple," Davaryush said, "to sophisticated people from the future like you. So why don't you tell us in easy language, what's happened, what you're doing here . . ."

"Simple!" the boy blurted out, awestruck. "*You* of all people, Davaryush, *you*, how can you possibly say that?" And he seemed moved.

"I'm old," Davaryush said: and Kirian saw that his face was not tired the way old men's faces are; it was aglow with wonder.

"If I tell you everything," said the boy, "will you take me back to the space station and do up my bracelet properly?"

"Of course."

"Well then—"

Kirian could not forget the story.

More than a thousand years ago, the fathers had come, fleeing an intolerable world: Davaryush, Kirian, Darktouch. Men filled the whole galaxy; but great wars decimated them, and broke the web of power that the Inquest had spun over the million worlds of the Dispersal of Man. . . .

Davaryush and Darktouch and Kirian came with their dream of a new humanity. They came and rekindled the Earth.

There were great secrets of science in the old days. Men knew how to compress a fragment of spacetime into a tachyon bubble, and send it flying instantaneously through space . . . it was a lost secret. The children of the utopians did not recover all the knowledge of the past. But they felt a longing for the stars, a longing common to all men. A way was found, without the tremendous energy of tachyon bubbles. Men were sent through space through the tachyon universe, with its negative time-flow, in a time-stasis shield which locked the traveller into the moment of his departure, preventing time paradoxes until reality could recapitulate to the same moment. . . .

The plain of statues was a gigantic space station, a harbor. But its walls and its machinery were not built yet, nor was the huge town of Kirian-Angkar beside the station. One day the domes would come, and the towers of a great city.

How had they known they would succeed? How had they picked the site of the space station? It was easy. For they had grown up seeing the passengers standing in the sand, in their millennial sleep. . . .

And how had the earliest people known who the travellers were? There was a legend of a young boy with his stasis-bracelet askew, who had accidentally awoken in the dawn time and spoken with the ancestors. . . .

"*I'm* the boy!" the boy was shouting. "And to think my parents named me after the boy in the myth. . . ."

Davaryush said, thoughtfully: "Science is strange. We had the technology to do all this in our own civilization. But it never occurred to them to use tachyon travel for mass journeys . . . because above all, the Inquest wanted power, exclusive power, over the Dispersal of Man. We didn't have tachyon travel for everyone because the Inquest could not bear to give up one iota of its terrible power!"

Darktouch added: "The rules of the universe don't change. But the uses to which they're put . . . our children *did* learn—*will* learn—from our dream, Davaryush! To work for the good of all. Our hopeless dreams of freedom and love—are vindicated, Kail Kirian!"

It was too much for Kirian to take. *Got to get home. . . .*

"You'll stay now, Kirian," said Darktouch.

"I can't, I can't!" He blacked out desperately and groped for the shipmind in the sky. *Homeworld! I want homeworld!*

And the three of them were roaring with laughter—"You're staying, Kirian. Not a doubt of it," said Davaryush.

"Of course not! You must have tricked me. . . ."

The silver walls returned to his vision.

"Tricked you, Kirian?" said Darktouch. "Just look at the boy, Kirian, just look at the boy!"

And he did.

The boy. Standing against the wall. A redhead with unkempt hair, a slight, insignificant sort of boy: there were a million boys like him, scrabbling in the ruins of burnt cities, hawking sweets in the bazaars of Alykh, staring wide-eyed at the delphinoid starships that streaked across the night skies of their homeworlds . . . he saw nothing remarkable.

Until he saw his own face, reflected in the wall beside the boy's. Distorted by the wall-curve, and yet so alike . . .

"You're my . . . I mean, I'm your—"

"Forefather," the boy whispered, and knelt down to kiss his hand. As though he were a visiting Inquestor . . .

He trembled with pride. Then he raised the child up and gazed at the face until he could see, behind the features that mimicked his own, traces of Darktouch's face, too.

Darktouch, who had despised him, who had accused him of hating himself, of being without pride, of being senseless and meaningless and cruel . . . but he knew now how to make her love him.

And thought of the delphinoid, orbiting above them, in its terrible pain.

Darkness, a terrible loneliness.

Kirian's mind was blank, joined to the shipmind. The darkness pressed against him, waiting.

"Shipmind," he called softly, "what is it you really feel? Can you not share it with me?"

And he felt pain. Like nails being driven into his head, over and over, into his spine, into his bones, his body rolling in a barrel of nails, pain beating burning blasting bursting him and more nails driving driving into him everywhere and screaming until he could never stop screaming until he screamed himself into silence—

Nails nails nails nails nails—

And behind the pain, a still grief. The grief of the Sunless Sound whispering under the hunters' airships. The grief of lost songs. Of unborn torrents of light in the thick dark sky. And Kirian wept until he was beyond tears—

Nails nails nails—

And pity behind the grief. Pity for a being so pitiless it would torture a sentient creature. Compassion for him.

Kirian's mind whispered, "Shipmind, I'm sorry. I knew, but I tried not to know. Go free now."

He awoke to night. Darktouch was standing by the shelter under the strange thin starlight. He came to her. . . .

"I freed the shipmind," he said. "I think he's going to die now."

Darktouch said, "I tried to hate you so much! Because all soldiers were supposed to be mindless automata, slaves of the Inquest! But you do have compassion after all."

"Glimpsing the future has changed so much."

They were silent. The air was heavy with the tension of beginning relationships.

He said, suddenly, "I can't believe that everything I believe in, out there, is coming to an end!"

"We don't know."

"Maybe our children will burst out into the galaxy again. And find the worlds of the Inquestors. And heal the wounds, maybe."

She smiled at him in the alien moonlight. There was a moment of fierce, burning pride.

Then—

"Look!" she cried suddenly—

His eyes followed the curve of her arm, up into the blackness. A meteor flashed. Fireworks. The sand glittered silver for a moment. The hills glowed and faded.

"It's the ship," he said. "It's the past, burning up as it hits the atmosphere."

"Happy?"

"I suppose so. . . ."

The moon hid in a cloud, and in the darkness the only light was the cold clingfire of her dress. *We'll have to make our own warmth.*

They pressed closer together. Ahead, the plain was full of their unborn children, waiting to be created.

They held each other close, not only for the warmth now. The first step into the future waited to be taken. And then they took it.

The first step was a kiss, an embrace, an act of love.

Panic

by Stanley Schmidt

Qdarok, one might say, was getting cold feet. But you would have to understand that that was purely figurative. You might balk at calling his feet feet, and they did not tend to get cold under stress.

But the stress was building up. He crouched nervously at one of the instrument panels as the invading fleet cruised through the alien night, silent, invisible, guided by autopilots with radar-like senses. Qdarok, on the edge of the fleet, would have liked fewer larqan between ships. But, he kept telling himself, the strategists and autopilots knew what they were doing. . . .

That faith was shattered abruptly by a grating, tortured scream from the ship's vitals. Qdarok and Xorl, the ship's other occupant and senior officer, sprang to alertness. Xorl surveyed glowing indicators and announced, "Number two drive out of control. If it's left running, we're dead."

Qdarok threw a switch. The scream died, but the ship lurched violently. Grabbing manual steering, Qdarok yelped, "This thing wasn't built to run on one drive. We'll have to land. Scanners?"

Xorl's pointed upper lip twitched in distaste, but he flipped them on. "We can't cut across the fleet," he muttered, scanning screens that now showed low, rounded mountains. "Cut to the right. Don't seem to be any towns over there. Aim for a valley."

Qdarok obeyed. The manual steering fought back with a will of its own. Cursing the designers while struggling to interpret the viewscreens, he somehow coaxed the ship toward a minor valley slanting down the side of a major ridge.

Over the nearer rim, the steering quit. Qdarok tried a frantic assortment of pushes and pulls with all four tentacles and ended by throwing them despairingly around his head. He screamed a Kurlin profanity which fortunately has no English equivalent, then added, "Cut the other drive!"

Xorl touched something on his panel and the tiny hum gave way to overwhelming silence. He and Qdarok scrambled for respirators and acceleration tanks.

The crash came. Instruments and furniture shook; some broke. Even the acceleration tanks shattered, spilling Qdarok and Xorl onto the floor in a disgusting puddle of liquid cushion. Qdarok picked shards off his leathery skin, disentangled himself from safety harness and respirator, and stood up with great care.

"Some days. . . ." he growled. "Xorl, you contact the others. I'll check outside."

"Right." Xorl started to fiddle with the communicator. He didn't offer to trade tasks.

Qdarok dragged himself up the spiral "ladder" in the ship's center, passed through the airlock, and twisted the outer door. Motors finished unscrewing it, and it swung back on a metal arm.

He fought off a wave of nausea as a gust of local air caught him full in the face. It was chilly and it stank. "Needs work," the advance expedition had said, with somewhat colossal understatement. But the med branch had assured the conquest planners it would be less than lethal in the meantime. So Qdarok stoically endured it.

The thick crescent of a satellite gave enough light to make out contours, once his eyes adapted. The ship was in a sheltered notch halfway up the mountain, kept from rolling down by the black skeletons of big, branched plants, nearly leafless due to a seasonal change. Qdarok was relieved to see no artificial lights. Such light as there was came only from the satellite and the sky, a sky neither so black nor so starry as on a world not cursed with such an atmosphere. *So dense and so putrid!* he thought. *What a combination!*

He listened. Nothing but chirps and buzzes of small local fauna. So he withdrew, hastily and relieved, to go below. As he sealed the door and started down, he almost fell. He had felt heavy ever since the crash. "Grav generators out too?" he asked as he reached the bottom.

"Afraid so. We'll have to take it easy. See anything?"

"Trees. Hills. No natives or dwellings. We were lucky— population's generally pretty dense in this area. The air's wretched. Any luck with the communicator?"

"Not yet. Transmitter's dead." Qdarok joined his superior in checking it. Xorl found the trouble—a small but very vital and very mangled module—and lumbered off for a replacement.

He came back looking glum. "No spare. How anybody ever—"

"Well, I guess there's nothing to do but set out a radio flare. What frequencies are safe?"

Xorl conjured up a chart on the library viewer and uttered a sound as close to a whistle as his thin, V-shaped mouth could manage. "Not much choice," he said. "The natives use just about every band." The chart showed a few small gaps, but there was also a note that the natives' use of radio was an abnormally recent development and subject to rapid and unpredictable changes.

So they would have to find their own vacancy. Xorl turned on the all-band receiver. It was working fine—which was adding insult to injury, since it could have provided half a dialogue with the Fleet Commander to end this predicament. But without a transmitter, there was no way to initiate that dialogue.

Xorl tuned rapidly through band after noisy band, listening for signals without regard to content. He found a gap in the fourth band he tried, and took a flare from a sealed, heavily protected cabinet. He popped the lid off, and a conical indicator on top glowed to show the distress signal was working.

And that was all they could do. They did take a closer look at the ruined drive and steering, but that just confirmed that neither flight nor repair was feasible. There was nothing to do but wait, and hope another ship of the fleet arrived before curious natives.

"Are we going to listen for them?" Qdarok asked.

"Nothing to listen for. Pre-invasion blackout, remember? Our flare'll be the only transmission in the fleet."

"Oh." Qdarok thought for a moment. "Since we're not contributing anything else to the cause, why don't we put on a translator and see what some of that native gibberish is saying? Maybe we'll learn something we can use later."

Xorl stared as if astonished that even a first-timer could make such an idiotic suggestion. "Fat chance."

"Well," Qdarok said defensively, "it might be amusing, even if it isn't valuable. It might be . . . quaint. We have nothing better to do."

Xorl made an Urling counterpart of a shrug. "Suit yourself."

Qdarok dug out the translator, luckily undamaged, and plugged it in. He rechecked the advance expedition's frequency chart, then ran the viewer to a language map. That one amazed him. How could a world not much bigger than Urlik need so many languages? There were even places where the map showed more than one.

Ridiculous!

He memorized what he needed and turned back to the translator. He set it, picked a frequency band, and leaned back to listen. Noises that might have been native speech issued from the speaker, but the tape that flowed from the translator was blank. Annoyed, Qdarok fiddled, without results. The sounds changed character and immediately the translator began printing. Just as suddenly, the first type of sounds returned and the translator quit again. "Intermittent," he grumbled.

He looked at the translation. "That was [Y1] playing a collection of [Z1]. We continue now with more [Z2] performed by [Y2(1?)]."

With so many untranslated words, it was not very informative. But it did suggest that the fault might not be in the translator. Qdarok tuned slowly through other frequencies, noting a few words of each transmission that showed any and then moving on. He was about to turn away from one—the voice of a male native, he thought—when he noticed the translation and his hand froze on the dial.

". . . directly in front of me, half-buried in a vast pit. Must have struck with terrific force. . . . What I can see of . . . object itself doesn't look very much like a meteor. . . . It looks more like a huge cylinder." (*On its end or its side?* Qdarok wondered.) "It has a diameter of . . . what would you say, [Y5]?"

Another native said, "About twenty-four dohk."

The first, identified as [Y3], repeated, "About twenty-four dohk. . . . The metal on the sheath . . . well, I've never seen anything like it. The color is sort of yellowish-white." Qdarok felt the beginnings of a remote fear. How accurate was that twenty-four-dohk estimate?

The commentators continued without saying much. There were garbled shouts, an interview with an inarticulate witness to the landing of the object, a casual reference to some local scholar talking on the radio about Rokan, a return to [Y3] painting a word picture of the native crowd gathered around the "thing."

And, gradually becoming audible through that, a faint hum that sounded a little too familiar to Qdarok. "Do you hear it?" [Y3] asked his listeners. "It's a curious humming sound that seems to come from inside the object. I'll move the microphone nearer. . . ."

Pause. The hum became louder and was joined by a new sound. [Y3] asked [Y5], "Can you tell us the meaning of that scraping noise?" It was growing more insistent. Qdarok stole a nervous glance at Xorl.

[Y5] replied, "Possibly the unequal cooling of its surface."

"Do you still think it's a meteor?" [Y3] asked.

"I don't know what to think. The metal casing is definitely extraplanetary. . . ."

"Just a hixix. Something's happening. Females and males, this is terrific. The end of the thing is beginning to flake off. The top is beginning to rotate like a screw. The thing must be hollow!"

And this was beginning to strike too close to home for Qdarok's tastes. Xorl looked as if he were beginning to grasp the implications.

The radio gave out a hubbub of many voices; the translator tried to handle them all and sprayed ink all over the tape. There was a clank of falling metal. Qdarok shuddered as he visualized the door-arm on a ship giving away.

[Y3]'s voice rose above the commotion. "Someone's crawling out of the top. I can see . . . two luminous disks . . . are they eyes? It might be a face. . . ." More shouts; then he sounded very excited. "Something's wriggling out of the shadow like a gray [Z10]. Now it's another. . . . They look like tentacles . . . I can see the thing's body. It's large as a [Z11] and it glistens like wet leather. . . . The eyes are black and gleam. . . . The mouth is V-shaped with saliva dripping . . ."

Xorl's face was dark: he had finally got the message. "Great Hkan, they're talking about us! One of our ships is in danger!"

"Yes . . . and we were supposed to be hidden for the entire first phase."

A sharply pulsating squeal joined the din on the radio. "A humped shape," [Y3] said, "is rising out of the pit. I can make out a small beam of light against a mirror. . . . There's a jet of flame springing from that mirror, and it leaps right at the advancing men. It strikes them head on! [Z14], they're turning into flame!"

A multitude screamed. The translator fed blank tape. Xorl and Qdarok cheered wildly.

Abruptly, dead silence. More blank tape. Then another voice, with apologies for inability to continue the field transmission. A series of bulletins, one of them saying that some local astronomer "expressed the opinion that the explosions on Rokan are undoubtedly nothing more than severe volcanic disturbances . . ."

"Do you realize," Qdarok asked, dialing a library reference, "that was the second reference to Rokan since we've had this on? That's the next planet out." Xorl stared but said nothing. "I hate to suggest this, but could we be mistaken? Maybe those things they're talking about are from Rokan. If they are—"

"Not a chance." But a faint twitch of Xorl's pointed upper lip betrayed him. "Rokan is uninhabited. They're talking about us."

The radio proclaimed martial law and returned to descriptions of the "battle" scene and the flames spreading from it. Then another introduction of [Y5], who had witnessed the incident and was evidently considered some sort of authority. "Of the creatures," he said when questioned, "I can give you no authoritative information. . . . Of their destructive instrument, I might venture some conjectural explanation. . . . It's all too evident that these creatures have scientific knowledge far in advance of our own."

A statement of fact, an admission of limitations? No, Qdarok decided, *not on the air. They know we're listening. It's a trap.*

But only moments later, he heard, ". . . inescapable assumption that those strange beings . . . are the vanguard of an invading army from Rokan. The battle which . . ."

"There!" shrieked Qdarok. "As blunt as can be. Are you *sure* it's uninhabited?" He hardly heard, and took little solace from, the announcer's admission of one of the most startling defeats in modern times. "How do we *know*?" he demanded.

Xorl looked annoyed but shaken. "No radio signals, of course."

"Maybe the advance team missed something."

"How could they?"

Qdarok didn't like either of his answers. "Maybe Rokan has natives so advanced we don't even know how to listen for them. Or maybe some other army has taken over Rokan as a base."

"Shut up!" Xorl snarled. "Still, it wouldn't have hurt to make a more thorough study. . . ."

"They should have studied the whole system better!"

"I guess it wasn't practical," Xorl said weakly. "A system's too big. A *planet's* too big."

More fragments of conversations. A bulletin about escape routes, many of them clogged with fleeting natives. More word painting, more bulletins. "Rokang cylinders are falling all over the country. One outside [P180], one in [P2201], [P3003] . . . seem to be timed and spaced. Now—"

And the receiver quit—so Qdarok and Xorl had no time to check the map and be astonished. They cursed and set off in frantic pursuit of the new trouble.

* * *

But they were not alone in their fear. Others were listening, including the Fleet Commander, and his receiver did not quit. He heard the whole bulletin, stared at the new red dots in his viewer, and his gleaming black eyes bulged out even more than usual.

"What?" he bellowed, dashing to the invasion map that covered an entire bulkhead. He located [P180], [P2201], and [P3003] and let out a horrified gasp. "Great Hkan!" he exclaimed, turning to his communications officer. He motioned vaguely at the receiver-translator hookup. "Forget about that thing and get me through to the High Commander. At once."

The com officer looked stunned. "The High Commander, sir? But, sir . . . that's spacewarp."

"You heard me!"

"Yes, sir." The com officer turned off the receiver and unlocked the vault housing the spacewarp transceiver. The Fleet Commander paced impatiently as his underling alternately twiddled gizmos and spoke to a microphone. Finally a connection was established.

The High Commander, light-years away, did not look pleased. He glared. His pointed upper lip twitched unpleasantly. His tentacles, intertwined, writhed restlessly among themselves. "Well," he said disdainfully, "what is it?"

The Fleet Commander went through the required ceremonial forms of reverent groveling. Then he said, "About this Xigalunk project. Third planet of its system, natives of fair-to-middling intelligence, culturally fragmented, some embryonic technology—"

"Yes, yes. Get to the point."

"Well, sir, I was wondering how thoroughly the advance expedition studied this system. We've been monitoring a native newscast. . . ." He summarized what they had heard. The High Commander was obviously shocked, but did not interrupt. The Fleet Commander talked doggedly onward, ending, "And as if the possibility of being discovered isn't enough, the last thing we heard was that ships were dropping all over the continent. 'Timed and spaced,' yet."

"I suppose you have a hypothesis or two?"

The Fleet Commander swallowed. "Possibly, sir. The natives

here believe the invading ships are coming from the fourth planet of this system."

"Bah! Has it occurred to you that the barbarians may be feeding you a clever line to scare you away?"

"Yes, it occurred to me, sir. I have no doubt that they're tricky and brave. According to the reports, they fight back like nothing we've ever seen. Following that line of thought just led to the conclusion that the natives haven't been studied enough. We may have underestimated them. The efforts we've heard are astounding, in view of the relatively infantile level of their technology. It wouldn't surprise me to learn that they have unsuspected resources of both weaponry and character." He paused. "Either way, it looks very bad."

The High Commander pondered with an Urling equivalent of a scowl. "I hate to do this," he muttered finally, "but . . . you're there and I'm here. Commander, what is your personal opinion? Is that planet worth sending in a lot of reinforcements?"

"Well, sir, this is only private opinion, but—"

"Is it or isn't it?"

The Fleet Commander sighed. "No, sir. The gravity's frightful. The resources aren't even as good as several planets we already have plans for. And the atmosphere . . . well, it stinks. Even the advance expedition conceded that it would need extensive modification."

"Hmph. So you don't think much of the place?"

"Well, sir, I think there are a lot better pickings that we can get easier."

"Very well." The High Commander looked pained. "Order the fleet out, pick up your survivors, and hightail it to the next job. Let's try to forget about this one."

Qdarok looked up from the receiver after a hundred hixix of futile effort. "Xorl, listen."

The hum was very faint, but growing. Xorl heard it too. "A ship!"

"Yes. We're rescued, or. . . ." He didn't finish the other possibility. The hum reached a peak and stopped just outside. There was a pause, a scuffling noise, and someone trying to open the door above.

Qdarok dragged himself up the ladder as quickly as he could. But he hesitated at the top. "Who's there?" he called out.

"Mumble-wug-a-mumph," came the reply.

Which was good enough for Qdarok.

"Xorl!" he cried out, overjoyed, as the door swung open. "It's the Fleet Commander!" He turned to the Commander and to the other welcome faces glistening darkly against the stars, and babbled, "Are we ever glad to see you, sir. This hasn't been our day at all. First a drive—"

"Very good," the Commander interrupted. He sounded tired.

Qdarok said anxiously, "Commander, we heard a native newscast. Either they've discovered us, or—"

The Commander cut him off. "I heard it too. I talked to the High Commander and we're leaving—at once and at top speed."

As the Urling fleet sped away from the jinxed system, they did not hear the voice trying to calm the millions of terrified local listeners to that broadcast. Which was just as well, both for those listeners and for the would-be invaders. The Urlin would have understood but little, anyway. There were too many local allusions which their translators were not equipped to handle.

But they might have understood, at least enough to give them second thoughts, the announcer's claim that, ". . . the *War of the Worlds* has no further significance than as the holiday offering it was intended to be. . . ."

The funny thing is, he actually believed that—which must make Orson Welles a classic example of that singular anomaly, a hero unsung even by himself.

Quotations from the radio play, "Invasion from Mars," are included with the kind permission of the play's author, Howard Koch.

Of the Last Kind

P. J. Plauger

"But it just ain't fair!"

John Wellington Parkinson whined into the microphone of his CB transceiver with the practiced whine of a thirteen-year-old misfit. He was not getting his way.

"Explain 'fair,' in this context," the singsong voice came back at him after the customary delay.

John Wellington sniveled, considered terminating the conversation early. The Galactic Overlords always seemed to be more agreeable after a spell of the silent treatment. Unfortunately, he lacked the patience to use that tactic very often.

"Jerry Markleston goes for rides on flying saucers," he blurted out. There, he'd said it. So much for the careful line of reasoning he'd rehearsed all afternoon.

Jerry Markleston was his pen pal from Boulder, Colorado, who always seemed to be able to get one up on John Wellington. When the latter got a catcher's mitt for Christmas, Jerry Markleston talked his dad into a complete baseball uniform. When John Wellington established contact with the Galactic Overlords, Jerry Markleston was quickly doing business with the local UFOs.

Only Jerry Markleston got to fly around the Moon. Twice. And all

John Wellington ever got to do was talk with his stuffy extrater-restrials.

"You know our policy concerning contact with humans," the answer came back after a satisfactorily protracted pause. He had them scared again. Maybe this time they would knuckle under.

"Yaah, I know," his voice dripping scorn. "Maybe I should sign a treaty with Jerry Markleston."

That would scare them good. So far as the Galactic Overlords knew, John Wellington was Emperor of the Pacific Hemisphere, ruling from his palatial estate just outside Honolulu. Jerry Markleston, on the other hand, was the evil Prime Minister who held sway over the shaky Eastern Alliance of Nations, otherwise known as the Commie Ratfinks.

The thought of a united Earth doing business with the sort of riffraff who roamed the stars making illicit contact with young civilizations—that very thought seemed to curdle the green slime that coursed through the veins of the Overlords.

John Wellington didn't know for a certainty that the Galactic Overlords had green slime instead of blood, but he liked to think they did. Just as he liked to think of them as the Galactic Overlords, even though they had a much humbler term for themselves. It made him feel more important.

Still no answer from the transceiver. There must be an intense debate going on at the other end. That was all to the good. John Wellington admired his wall-to-ceiling collection of baseball cards and Star Trek memorabilia. He looked out the small square of window above the humming air conditioner at the eaves of the Dawson house next door. He was blind to the rich blue of the tropical sky, to the lush palms framing the view, to the shelves of gadgets bought for him by adoring parents. None of that mattered to an unhappy adolescent.

The CB transceiver would have been relegated to those selfsame overloaded shelves weeks ago, had it not been for a peculiar flaw. Somewhere in Tokyo lived a Sony research chemist who had falsi-fied some lab results when he couldn't explain the anomalous properties of a new semiconductor doping. He had missed out on a Nobel Prize. Somewhere in nearby Yokohama lived a quality control engineer who had been watching a passing fanny when John Wellington's CB exhibited its peculiar properties under test. The engineer had scored that night, but missed out on becoming a billionaire.

Now John Wellington was the proud and sole owner of the Earth's only interstellar hyperskip jump transceiver, or whatever you call a device that ties granny knots in Maxwell's laws. For five weeks now he had been educating the Galactic Overlords in the peculiarities of human civilization, and doing his level best to con them into a joyride.

"We have been considering," the radio suddenly sang out, "and wish to advise you that it would be extremely unsafe for you to deal with those who have established contact with Jerry Markleston."

John Wellington counted to ten, thumbed the transmit.

"Yeah, maybe, but they seem to be more cooperative than you've been."

"We merely wished to advise you. If you insist on a visit from us, however, we will oblige."

"Hot dawg!" John Wellington cried out, but not to a live mike. He would go around the Moon three times. And make them land him on Venus as well. A part of his mind began drafting his next letter to Jerry Markleston.

"We must warn you," the singsong continued, "that our ship is quite large. Our engineers must confer with you on preparations for our arrival."

John Wellington's dad was a 747 pilot, so John Wellington knew what the Overlords meant. Try to put one of those big babies down in a jerkwater airport and Goodnight Nurse. John Wellington subconsciously mimicked his father's pedantic nod as he mouthed that most favorite of phrases.

"Don't worry," he said into the microphone with easy confidence, "we're right next door to one of the biggest landing fields in the Pacific. We can deal with you."

A sly thought stole into his mind.

"But you may have some problems with the Commies, so be prepared for some interference on your way in."

It is a tribute to John Wellington's groundwork that this pronouncement was accepted without comment. In case you can't accept that, and in case you can't accept the premise that a thirteen-year-old could do business with a superior civilization, read any transcript of the United Nations Security Council. Large nations, at the best of times, behave with the emotional maturity of teenage boys.

"Very well," the Overlords replied. "We are approaching now and will be arriving in three days. Meanwhile, you promised to explain 'nitro burning funny cars,' 'female midget tag team grudge return match,' and 'peace with honor.'"

The Overlords landed, as promised, but not quite as expected. Since their ship was approximately one-sixth the size of the Moon, it would be more accurate to say they docked. The US Air Force did its level best to stop them, as did the Russians, the Chinese, and the Israelis. But the Overlords hardly noticed.

John Wellington was one of the first killed, of course. His body was sucked up by the tremendous gravitational forces that wracked Oahu, then fried in the spouting lava that followed. As for Jerry Markleston, he never saw the gloating letter that was washed out of a Los Angeles postal sorting station. The same tidal wave crested the Rockies an hour or so later and destroyed Boulder, Colorado in seconds.

Cabinet Meeting

by Michael Bishop

Dressed in a pair of sodden fatigues, stooped in a concrete bunker built seven feet beneath the east wing of the New White House in New Washington, U.S.A. (formerly Forgan, Oklahoma), President Henry David Thoreau Montoya y Florit did not realize that the fate of the nation hung from the very essence—the revealing quiddity, to express it philosophically—of a single wire coathanger. Mind you, it was not what hung from the coathanger that was so important to our nation's destiny; it was the coathanger itself. And one can scarcely blame President Montoya for being ignorant of the mind-staggering future developments that depended therefrom. In the last two weeks the bludgeon of History had staggered him so many times that he had come permanently to doubt his own legendary sobriety.

As this story opens, President Montoya was busy trying to unstick the doors on an antique chifforobe in the corner of his private bunker so that he could shed his wet fatigues and put on a velveteen dressing-gown. The chifforobe had been designed and commissioned of master craftsmen by Thomas Jefferson during the third year of his presidency way back in 1803, when no American worried much about visitations from beings not demonstrably human (other than those from the British, of course) and a man was free to hang his clothes in a piece of furniture as elegant as the imported silk in the stockings he wore. This chifforobe, in fact, was the only piece of furniture that President Montoya had ordered salvaged from the wreckage of the Old White House in Old Washington, D.C., as soon as it had become apparent that the combined forces of the Arab-Mediterranean-Israeli Alliance had forsaken that plundered city and were marching toward the great metropolises of New England. After securing the chifforobe, the President—along with several top advisors and his Irish setter, Endgame—retreated westward in a dilapidated U-Haul van that Colonel "Feisty" Phillips had driven away from a caravan of looters while the driver of the vehicle was wrestling with an intransigent television set in the shattered display window of a local appliance store.

The U-Haul truck broke down on the barren, alkaline plains of northern Oklahoma; and President Henry David Thoreau Montoya y Florit, a physical-fitness addict and one-time winner of the Taos Marathon, led his scraggly assemblage of advisors the twelve remaining miles into the tumbleweed-infested environs of Forgan. As they followed the narrow asphalt road toward the bloated eye of the westering sun, Endgame, the Irish setter, trembled with fear at the sight of each disgruntled jackrabbit that lurched out of the roadside ditches and away into the bitter sage of the prairie. Chief Advisor Marvin C. Swearingin had to pull the dog along by its choke collar.

In Forgan the President's party found a number of die-hard Okies who had refused to migrate to Canada during the dust storms of '79, a few whitewashed houses, and a building of impressive solidity that bore the proud trademark of an Enco service station.

"That's it!" President Montoya said with the same tone of astonishment, nicely commingled with gratitude for their deliverance, that had undoubtedly marked Brigham Young's voice upon his discovery of the future site of Salt Lake City. "That's it! Our new headquarters!"

And so it was.

Montoya had intended the station to be only a temporary headquarters, but on their second day in Forgan a messenger from Liberal, Kansas, informed the President and his aides that the Sino-Soviet-Subcontinental Invasion Fleet had sailed into the San Francisco Bay and that the entire West Coast lay prostrate beneath the indifferent feet of Ukrainian, Pakistani, Mongol, and New Kshatriya soldiers, among others. Two fronts now existed, and Montoya saw no reason to leave Forgan.

In less than two weeks' time, with the help of the townspeople and supplies from Liberal, they converted the Enco station into the New White House and built an impregnable bunker under its eastern wing. (The eastern wing was the garage.) These things done, they rechristened the city and held a three-day celebration in honor of the establishment of a new and thriving capital. Then, hoping to see to his own comfort during the trying days ahead, President Montoya dispatched Colonel Phillips, Chief Advisor Swearingin, and Bobby Gilby (the sixteen-year-old boy who had occasionally pumped gas at the Enco station) to go down the road in Bobby's '58 Ford pickup to the derelict U-Haul van and retrieve Thomas Jefferson's invaluable chifforobe for immediate installation in Montoya's otherwise austere bunker.

But as I said earlier, this story truly begins while the President was in the awkward process of trying to unstick the doors on his invaluable antique. Unmindful of both its antiquity and its spiritual congruence with the mind of Thomas Jefferson, Montoya was uttering imprecations of a singularly unpresidential nature and banging the carven facade of the cabinet with his elbow. His fatigues were wet because he had just driven back from Liberal in Bobby's windowless pickup during an especially severe Great Plains thunderstorm, and he desperately wanted his dressing-gown.

". . . . , ... !" The President said, frustrated.

At that precise moment, a dull wooden thumping above the President's head augmented the din of his intemperate elbowing and swearing. A genuinely pious but never sanctimonious man, the President left off his exertions and blushed. He did not move. He asked silent forgiveness of three saints and wondered briefly if his nation's enemies had at last arrived. The dull thumping continued.

"Hank?" a voice called. "Hank, can I talk to you a minute?"

It was Swearingin. Henry David Thoreau Montoya y Florit rolled his eyes heavenward, exhaled a simultaneously relieved and exasperated sigh, and shouted, "Come on down, Marvin. Nobody here but me and Thomas Jefferson's red-eared ghost." After slipping back a heavy iron bolt on the trapdoor overhead, he sat down on his bed. The dampness from his fatigues seeped into his clean linen, but he was beyond caring.

Looking like a stork with an Oliver Cromwell haircut, tight bangs providing a blond fringe over the beak of his nose, Marvin C. Swearingin clambered through the trapdoor and stood in the middle of the President's bunker.

His clothes, like the President's, dripped. A bead of either perspiration, or rainwater hung just beneath the tip of his nose, threatening to elongate and fall. The President noted that in its deliquescent roundness the bead of water contained beautiful emeralds, and blues, and brandywine ambers, another entire universe pendant from Swearingin's nose. Montoya had to concentrate to restore to the man an identity beyond that as a waterbead bearer.

"Oh," he said, by way of concentrating. "It is you, isn't it?"

"Yes, sir." This was an exceptionally astute answer for the Chief Advisor. Although he had been the most brilliant man in the President's inner circle of aides, the retreat from Old Washington had done something to his mind.

"What do you want, Marvin?" the President said more tenderly.

"Our trip to Liberal, sir? I mean, that trip tells us—"

"Wipe your nose, Marvin." Marvin rubbed the back of his hand under his nose and the other universe dissolved into a colorless moistness along the Chief Advisor's knuckles. "Okay, Marvin, get on with it."

"Sir, this afternoon in Liberal we learned that the enemy forces from both the east and the west are closing in on us. For over a week we've seen the vapor trails of their aircraft, and now the foot soldiers are upon us. Their troops ought to converge on Forgan in two days' time. Two days' time, Hank."

Swearingin called the President alternately "Hank" and "sir," unaware of inconsistency.

Absently, President Montoya said, "Well, let's hope that the tracks match up and that somebody brings along a golden spike."

Chief Advisor Swearingin kept a disapproving silence. He stood rigidly at attention, dripping.

"Please relax, Marvin. You're making me nervous." Marvin's shoulders slumped. "All right. All right. Your expression tells me that facetiousness is out of order, and I grant you that. I agree wholeheartedly. But what is it—exactly—that you want of me? I'm tired. You should be tired. Can't we make this brief?"

"Yes, sir. I wanted to know what we're going to do."

"We're going to re-institute the draft, take our missiles out of mothballs, and shoot down the moon so that the fragments from the darkside fall everywhere but the Western hemisphere. Like shrapnel, Marvin."

"That wouldn't work, Hank. I don't think it'd work."

"Well, I'm certain that it's absolutely our best emergency plan— but I'm sure you have reasons for expressing doubts, Marv." Montoya took off his boots. "What would you advise? As Chief Advisor, of course."

"We've pretty much done what we had to, Hank," Swearingin said seriously. "I mean, with the whole world aligned against us we couldn't very well shoot off missiles to all corners of the globe. Impractical and immoral both, Hank. So we withdrew as we had to. You can't kill everybody, you know."

"I know." Montoya looked at the puddle his boots had allowed to form between his stockinged feet. "Nobody likes us anymore, Marv." He said this less as a lament than as a straightforward recitation of the facts.

"Oh," Swearingin said brightly, "I'm sure somebody likes us."

"Who?" The President's face was tight and brown, intent but somehow abstracted away from the question he so perfunctorily spat out. "Who's that, Marv?"

"Well," Swearingin said, his voice dulling appreciably, "somebody . . ."

Montoya got up and slapped the taller man on the arm. "Never mind that, Marvin. We've got today and tomorrow and maybe part of another day before the Huns are upon us, and I suggest that we make ourselves as comfortable as possible in the interval so that we'll be able to think the matter properly through. Okay?"

"Okay."

"Fine. Now do you think you can unstick the doors on my chifforobe?"

"I don't know, sir. What's wrong with it?"

"The doors. They're stuck."

"And you'd like to get them open?"

"That's right, Marv. In order to get inside."

"Well, it was probably the move that did it, the move and all the time it sat out there on Highway 61 in the U-Haul van. Changes in climate frequently affect furniture that way. I mean, we came from Old Washington where the humidity in the summertime can be quite high all the way out here to Forg—I mean, New Washington—where it's a good deal more arid. That's probably what made the doors stick. I'm pretty sure of it. Not to mention the age of the chifforobe, the sensitivity of the wood."

"No, let's not mention those things. Can you open it?"

"I don't know."

"Well, why don't you try while I get undressed and towel myself down?"

"All right, Hank."

President Montoya removed his fatigues, sponged down with a terry-cloth hand towel, and then, dressed only in a pair of tattered boxer shorts, changed the linen on his bed. Swearingin worked diligently at the face of the cabinet, leaning against it and attempting at the same time to pull it open with eight pressure-whitened fingers. Chief Advisor Swearingin grunted. He broke off two fingernails. Unconsciously echoing an earlier sentiment of the President, Chief Advisor Swearingin swore:

". . . . , ... !" he said. He said it louder than he meant to.

The President, sitting cross-legged on the bed, watched his Chief Advisor for several minutes and then offered a bit of arbitrary but well-intentioned advice—even though he, the President, had never been one to think his solutions viable and all other men's suspect.

"Why don't you try to pry open the door you're not leaning against?"

"Right!" Swearingin began pulling at the other door of the cabinet—with considerably more success. he lost no more fingernails in the crevice between the doors. "Say, Hank," he said, while engaged in the struggle, "no kidding. What're we . . . gonna . . . do? I mean, the armies of the . . . A.M.I. Alliance and the S.S.S. Pact Nations . . . they'll torture and hang us . . . if they find out who we are."

"Undoubtedly. And there's no time to grow beards, either."

"No, there isn't," Swearingin said. He stopped struggling with the chifforobe. He turned toward the President, his brow corrugated with the perplexity of latter-day world affairs. "What're we going to do, Hank?"

Montoya looked at his hands. "Well, seeing as how we can't shoot, I'd say negotiations were in order, wouldn't you?" The President immediately regretted the use of the word *negotiations* because it called up a remote, unfocused light in Chief Advisor Swearingin's eyes. The man's brow unwrinkled momentarily, then resolved itself into ridges again.

"Negotiations?" he said.

"In Old Washington we could never arrange them—even though you did your damndest to get everyone around a table. That's why it's come to this, I'm afraid." Montoya sat quietly for a moment, musing. "What I wouldn't give to have old Valerie Podgornitsyn of the Triple-S Nations and cagey little Gamil Yosef Economous of the A.M.I. Powers right here in this room!"

"Why would they come here, Hank? They've got us on the run."

The President looked up, smarting from the sting of his Chief Advisor's innocent directness. "Why indeed?" he said.

"I don't think you can depend on that," Swearingin was saying. "Their coming here to negotiate, I mean."

"You're right, Marv. We can't depend on that."

"Do you want me to try to open the chifforobe again?"

"Please."

Chief Advisor Swearingin approached the Jefferson antique again, but this time he went about the task of opening it a little more methodically. He knelt and put his ear to the cabinet. With the heel of his fist he tapped the seam where the two doors came together. He listened. He was like a man sounding a watermelon or trying to crack a safe. With the heel of his other fist he again tapped the fissure between the chifforobe's doors.

"Umm," he said.

"What is it?"

"It sounds empty," Swearingin reported.

"Well, it *is* almost empty, Marvin. All I've got in there is a dressing-gown. A dressing-gown I'd very much like to put on before my simple paranoia turns into a complicated case of pneumonia."

"It sounds even emptier than that."

"It would be hard to sound emptier than that." Because he was about to go to bed, the President suddenly shifted his line of questioning. "Look, Marv, have you seen Endgame recently? I don't want him down here if he's wet."

"No, sir, he's not wet. He's in the gara—I mean the east wing, chewing on the old tubeless tire Billy gave him. You should've stopped to see ole E. G. when we got back from Liberal. He only chews tires when he feels resentful."

"Poor Endgame." Swearingin glaced over at the President reproachfully. "No, no, I mean that, Marv. I'm sorry I didn't stop to see him. Send him down here when you're through. Okay?"

"Okay." There was a sudden bursting rush of air—inward, it seemed, rather than outward—and the chifforobe stood open. "Through!" Swearingin announced.

President Montoya had looked up just in time to see the doors burst open and the inward-sucking breeze lift the bangs on the left side of the Chief Advisor's head. He put his legs over the edge of his bed and leaned forward.

"My dressing-gown's fallen," he said. He looked at the crumpled yellow garment on the floor of Thomas Jefferson's erstwhile wardrobe and felt the cold seep into the soles of his feet. "Would you hang it back up for me, Marv—so that the wrinkles'll work themselves out? The President of the United States can't go around looking like Shirley Booth in *Come Back, Little Sheba*." He tried to recall the last time he had seen an old movie on television, but Swearingin straightened up with the dressing-gown and faced him.

"There's no coathanger, sir. I can't hang it up."

"What?"

"There's no coathanger."

"But it was hanging on a coathanger, Marvin. Look around."

Chief Advisor Swearingin put his head into the chifforobe and revolved it on his supple, storklike neck. "No, there's no coathanger, Hank."

"Damn it all!" the President said, going across the bunker to see for himself. "Did Phillips, that lousy dog-soldier, come down here and take my coathanger while we were gone? Is that why this thing was stuck?"

"I don't think so, sir. Feisty spent the morning with the Gilby family. He's been trying to talk them out of their storm shelter so he'll have a bunker of his own. A military bunker. He's offered Billy's father a battlefield commission and an option on the motor in the U-Haul van."

"Then where's my coathanger? It was the only one I had."

"Do you want me to go up and see if Mrs. Gilby's got an extra one? When she had me for supper the other night, she said Billy never uses them, anyway."

"All right, Marv. Go see if you can borrow one."

Swearingin clambered awkwardly out through the trapdoor, and the President of the United States stared disconsolately at the enigmatical emptiness of his chifforobe and wondered how many more days he would be able to hold the highest office in the land. Disconsolately, he grinned. Disconsolately, he put on his wrinkled dressing-gown.

"My kingdom for a coathanger," he said.

* * *

At 0330 hours the President of the United States awoke to the
ferocious, jaw-snapping barking of his Irish setter Endgame. A
small night-light burned in the one electric outlet they had built
into the wall of the bunker, and by this dim illumination Montoya
could see Endgame beyond the foot of his bed first snarling and then
grr-woofing at the ominously shadowed bulk of the Jefferson chifforobe. The dog's oafish voice echoed inside the cramped bunker
like a succession of cherry bombs in an empty swimming pool; and
Montoya, shouting, could scarcely make himself heard.

"Endgame! Endgame, get over here!"

The dog finally came to him. It sat beside his bed facing the
cabinet and making guttural canine threats in its sleek throat. The
President stroked the animal's head. He whispered soothing words.

But among the members both of the presidential staff and the Old
Washington press corps Endgame had a reputation for cowardice
that was proverbial, and Montoya himself was more unsettled than
he cared to admit by the dog's bristling hackles and uncharacteristic
ferociousness. (How many times, after all, had the *Washington Post*
run a photograph of Endgame cowering away from his food dish
while a contemptuous blue jay sat alertly on the dish's edge, its beak
closed on a water-logged nugget of Gravy Train?) Montoya was
intimidated—slightly—by the darkness and by the dog's behavior.
He was intimidated—a little—by the chifforobe. The chifforobe
possessed an aura of humble self-satisfaction, an aura of amenable
patience: uncanny attributes in a piece of furniture. In fact, the
President found himself thinking the cabinet a living creature. He
half-expected it to stump toward him on its squat, meticulously
carven Queen Anne legs.

Perhaps both he and Endgame had fallen down a rabbit's hole—a
white rabbit's hole.

The President pulled his dressing-gown about him and put his
feet on the cold floor. Gently taking up the slack in Endgame's choke
collar, he restrained the dog and continued to talk to it, as much for
his own benefit as the animal's.

The chifforobe did not move—but it bulked in the shadows like
something living and now the President believed he could see a

faint bluish light emanating from the seam where the doors came together.

"*Carramba*," he said under his breath, knowing there was nothing for it but to get up and investigate. A chill of an altogether different sort displaced his awareness of the chill seeping up through his feet. He pulled Endgame toward the seemingly humming wardrobe and the otherworldly light. The dog, however, had suffered an acute relapse of its former character; it pulled backward on the chain, whimpering. "Endgame!" the President said. "Endgame!" His voice sounded hollow, and the dog tried desperately to slip the collar over its narrow mahogany-red skull.

If I survive this, Montoya thought, *and if our enemies imprison me, I will ask Podgnornitsyn and Economous to let me keep a parakeet in my cell.*

He opened the doors of the chifforobe.

That a medusa with snaky hair and cinderlike eyes did not turn him at once into a slab of unpolished granite mildly surprised him. But as the doors came open, Endgame broke free and disappeared under the President's rumpled cot. He watched the dog go, then turned back to the cabinet.

Its interior did seem to be suffused with a rarefied illumination of some kind—but more than likely this was simply a function of the night-light's glow and the glossiness of the lacquered oak. But since when did one lacquer the *inside* of a clothes cabinet? And besides, Montoya recalled, the Jefferson antique had been treated and restored, but never subjected to the ignominy of a crude lacquering. Wherefrom, then, this subtle but subtly rich lambency?

He put out his hand and closed it on—a coathanger.

No wonder in that, however; it was one of Mrs. Gilby's coathangers. Chief Advisor Swearingin had brought it into the bunker at the same time he delivered Endgame into the President's care. *A simple explanation for everything*, Montoya thought, forgetting the conundrum of the sheen inside the chifforobe; *no need for alarm.* He threw the coathanger on his bed and winced at Endgame's startled, monosyllabic yap.

Then he found the other coathanger—the one that had been

missing that afternoon when Chief Advisor Swearingin managed to pry open the cabinet's recalcitrant doors.

President Henry David Thoreau Montoya y Florit trembled with something more than the cold. He wondered if Endgame would bite him if he attempted to appropriate a small bit of room under his bed. *I am a sensible man—less stable than before our retreat from Old Washington perhaps, but more stable than most men in similar circumstances would be. There is a rational explanation for the unexcused absence and sudden reappearance of this coathanger. Yes, rational.* He stood in front of the open chifforobe staring at the other coathanger and trembling almost imperceptibly with uneasiness and resentment. *What rational explanation could there be?*

"Please identify yourself," the coathanger said.

The coathanger spoke in English. The coathanger resonated so that its "voice" filled the entire chifforobe and gained a measure of amplification from the cabinet's volume. The coathanger burned like the filament in an Edison-era electric lamp, pulsing with each syllable.

President Montoya, a sane man, did what any sane man would have done in his circumstances. He got down on his hands and knees and looked under the chifforobe. He stood up and wedged his arm behind the cabinet, groping for a tape recorder's telltale cord or a concealed speaker outlet in the bunker's concrete wall. In the morning he would call a meeting and admonish his staff to halt the perpetration of this kind of senseless buffoonery; the country was undergoing a crisis of truly unprecedented proportions; and he, as both titular and acting head of the embattled U.S. of A., needed his sleep. Fuming with anger, Montoya groped and groped. He found nothing. He stood up and poked his head inside the cabinet, as Swearingin had done the previous afternoon. Deliberately, he refused to look at the coathanger from which, as he knew too well, the request to identify himself had come.

"Please," the coathanger said. "We're aware of your presence. No harm will befall you. Speak clearly into the cabinet and express your peculiar selfhood."

"On the contrary," Montoya said. "Express *your* peculiar self-hood!"

The coathanger fell silent for a few moments, as if considering this sternly inflected imperative, and then pulsed again with a vague light, softer than before. "Very well. But first we must ask you to secure yourself inside the artifact wherein this makeshift transponder now hangs. To deny us this request will be not only to forfeit any expectation of an answer but also to terminate this communication altogether. Do you understand?"

"You want me to get inside the cabinet?"

"Please."

"Or you'll stop talking to me—forever. Is that right?"

"You comprehend the conditions for an extended colloquy quite well."

"Good. Now listen to this. I don't want an 'extended colloquy' with you. I particularly do not wish to crawl inside this chifforobe for the pleasure of said colloquy. What I want is, first, my sleep and, second, a degree of responsibility from the asses who've rigged this elaborate ruse. I am the President of the United States, and the people of this country have entrusted me with the trying but joyously undertaken task of saving their—I should say, *our*—collective necks. Whoever went to this trouble to make an ass of *me* is wasting valuable talents, talents that might well contribute to the end toward which we should all be working. If I knew who you were, you'd be shot. Now goodnight!"

And without looking back President Montoya returned to his bed, threw himself upon it, and turned toward the wall. Endgame whimpered but did not emerge from his hiding place. The doors of the chifforobe continued to stand open.

After a long, abashed silence the coathanger trembled with a tentative glow: "At any rate, you have given us a partial identification. Because of this concession and in spite of your intemperate crankiness, we have decided to overlook your initial refusal to enter the artifact. We hereby offer you a second chance to do so. Should you refuse again, all communication with us will immediately cease."

The President did not even look at the 'artifact.'

"Very well," the perfectly modulated voice inside the cabinet said. "If you fulfill our request, we will tell you what became of this wire implement while you thought it inexplicably vanished from the Earth."

His anger mounting, the President rolled over. "My coathanger? What did happen to my coathanger?"

"It vanished from the Earth. To you, inexplicably. Step inside this *chifforobe* (a quaint, dialectical word, we assume), and we will explain its disappearance."

Angrily, President Montoya leapt off his bed, made one long stride across the room, and closed himself up inside the cabinet, banging its doors to with an incredible viciousness. He squatted beneath the clothes bar and stared up at the faintly luminous coathanger. His voice boomed inside the chifforobe, forceful with previously repressed ire: "All right, you've got me. Now send someone down here with cameras and flashbulbs and document it for all time. I've got more important things to worry about than looking foolish before fools. Get it over with, damn you, and let me sleep! Or do you simply wish to keep me awake until New Washington's overrun by Economous's and Podgnornitsyn's troops?"

Again, the coathanger's reply came after a lengthy, taken-aback pause. "Very good. We counted on your innate curiosity to bring you into a more intimate conjunction with our improvised equipment."

"*Ai, Dios*, I'm curious all right. Who's *we*?" The President did not lower his voice. Outside, Endgame made weak moans. "And the word's not *intimate*, it's *cramped*."

"Thank you. We will make a semantical emendation to that effect. However, please do not speak so loudly; we receive you with ample lucidity."

"*Perdóname*. Very sorry, I'm sure."

"We are the Stronolanoneaux of the star system Marl of a necessarily unnamable galaxy in the galactic cluster which your astronomers know as the Hercules group. Currently we reside over three and half billion miles from you on the blissfully hospitable planet of Pluto, ninth from your sun."

"Pluto's a dead chip of ice. If you want this ruse to go any further, you'd better buy a reliable text and pull your heads together." His chin on his upward-jutting knees, the President said contemptuously, " 'Blissfully hospitable'!"

"The heads of the Stronolanoneaux are perpetually together, President of the United States. 'Blissfully hospitable' is terminology which intimates the reformed nature of your ninth planet."

"Reformed?"

"Indeed. Reformed, that is, subsequent to our installation in the planet's sky of a surrogate solar secondary, a satellite of artificially contracted hydrogen which our expedition physicists ignited. They induced in this hydrogen, President of the United States, a self-sustaining meson resonance reaction."

"What?"

"To articulate it concisely, we have given Pluto a little sun, a sun about one-third the size of your own moon."

"Why?"

"No place of interstellar respite need remain desolate when it is so easy to provide the amenities of home. This sun will burn two thousand of your years. We, the Stronolanoneaux, will leave it for you to discover and name as you wish, upon our departure three standard days from now."

"You're going to persist in this masquerade three days?" Disconsolately, the President let his chin slip between his knees. Then he brought his head up and said, "Why would a people capable of creating artificial suns steal a poor imperiled outcast politician's last and only coathanger? *Dígame eso, por favor.*"

"Your last few syllables have no phonemic value to us; we will suppose them an idiosyncratic malediction unworthy of closer scrutiny. However, in the matter of the coathanger, we—"

"That was Spanish, you *hijos de* . . . Well, never mind. But it wasn't a curse, and your feigned omniscience has a few holes in it."

The voice responded after a brief pause: "Very well. Spanish. We have begun to render it intelligible; its syntax, at any rate, is considerably less convolute than this other. *Usted no tiene causa por creernos tocadors de toro.*" The President rolled his eyes upward as far as he was able, but said nothing. "As for your coathanger, we removed it through the process of teledemolecularization from your chifforobe; then, through photon-beam-retraction, we brought it the intervening 3,607,000,000 miles and reconstituted it in its original state as our basis for observation, preliminary hypotheses, and, ultimately, fullscale permutative extrapolation. These procedures completed, we returned the coathanger to you—minus the paper covering from the laundry—and positioned it in such a way as to make instantaneous transmission and reception a likelihood not readily susceptible to contravention. Only the retrieval and the return of the coathanger were accomplished at the irritatingly unexpeditious speed of light; consequently, it was gone not quite ten of your hours, an untoward amount of time and one for which we offer you our profoundest apologies."

President Montoya rubbed his eyes wearily. "Teledemolecularization," he muttered. "Permutative extrapolation . . . instantaneous transmission . . . irritatingly unexpeditious . . ." He let his voice trail off. Then he said, "And why would you settle upon my coathanger of all the coathangers in the world?

"And why would you want it?"

"The Stronolanoneaux do not expend our efforts at contact on indigenous populations of only minimal intelligence. Nor do we believe in plunging physically all the way through the several planets of a solar system optimally constituted to possess higher-level intelligence in order to find it. The result is often waste. Therefore, we establish a base on the outermost planet and focus telemonitored sensor scans on the likeliest planetary body in the system. In your case, President of the United States, we found that a tension field of extreme sensitivity and independence emanated from the artifact wherein this then unfathomed 'coathanger' had its transient domicile. The coathanger was a palpable wrongness in so residually 'intelligent' a container. For over two weeks our probe maintained its exclusive focus on the chifforobe, which was then itself contained by a larger container—then, without preamble, the position of the chifforobe was altered and hardened a negligible degree against our observations."

"You're right," the President said. "Phillips, Swearingin, and Billy took it out of the U-Haul van and moved it into this bunker for me. Everybody in New Washington's aware of that."

"Yes. But to forestall the effects of its undergoing another transferral, perhaps to a place of total inaccessibility, we decided to act at once—therefore, the retraction of the coathanger. The cabinet itself would have been too prodigiously bulky an object to retract, over such a distance, via teledemolecularization. In any case, from the coathanger and from the cumulative evidence of our sensor scan we were able to extrapolate—deduce, you would say—the cabinet's existence. Then, after the more thoroughgoing processes of permutative extrapolation, we returned the coathanger. The Stronolanoneaux, President of the United States, are not unprincipled brigands."

"Wait a minute. Your little game's getting complicated. Let me see if I've been following you correctly. First, you settled upon my chifforobe because it seemed possessed of an after-image, so to speak, of intelligence. Second, you removed the coathanger because it was physically impossible to take the cabinet itself. And third, you deduced from the coathanger the existence of almost our entire civilization, inclusive of the English language but excepting Spanish."

The coathanger chuckled. "Yes. Until we had heard a few words of the latter system, that is." Another chuckle. "On Marl IV our inferior species of humanity, the Frenzilli, have an old proberb: 'From a single fact the great-minded Stronolanoneaux can deduce the entire universe.' Awe provokes them to overstate the case, President of the United States, but through permutative extrapolation we do indeed work small wonders from a finite number of facts.

"From the coathanger we have made well-informed projections about the level of your technology, the morphological development of your species, the weight you give to material as opposed to spiritual cognition (and vice versa), and the psychological derangements attendant upon, as well as the meteorological conditions conducive to, the wearing of clothes. The syntax and the vocabulary of your language we deduced from the slogan on the coathanger's wrapper: 'The Y.T. Blasingame Full Service Laundry and Dry Cleaners of Washington, D.C. We Get You Back on the Street, Looking Neat. Professional Alterations at Inalterably Low Prices.' "

"You didn't return that wrapper, by the way."

"Please forgive us. The wrapper was torn. We thought it of no significant value to the owner of the implement it enwrapped, and we hoped to keep the covering as a small memento of our journey to the, ah, 'Milky Way.' Do you wish its return?"

"It's yours, fellows. Be my guest."

"This graciousness is a meet attitude for the owner of an artifact so wondrously mind-haunted. So wondrously haunted by a *fine* mind, we should specify. You are the owner of the artifact, are you not?"

"Yes, I am."

"And did you not also create and personally effect the concretization of this artifact?"

"Did I design and make it, is that what you mean?"

"Indeed. Pointedly paraphrased."

"No, I didn't. Neither one."

The coathanger, trembling, considered this. "Who, then, among your otherwise limitedly endowed species, conceived the artifact you now possess?"

President Montoya, conscious of a vague tingling sensation in his buttocks, had begun very slowly to believe in the improbable protestations of the coathanger. What other reasonable explanation was there? If nothing else, the 'Stronolanoneaux'—whoever they were—had taken the time to devise a more consistent, albeit more improbable, explanation than anyone else in New Washington was capable of. Without thinking on the ludicrous circumstances in which he now found himself, Montoya forthrightly answered the aliens' question. "Thomas Jefferson," he said. "The third president of the United States."

"Another president. You, then, are Thomas Jefferson's successor?"

"One of them, yes."

"He is dead?"

"Dead and gone."

"At what level of regard do the people of the United States hold the memory of this Thomas Jefferson?"

"He is regarded with the highest esteem."

"By you as well, successor to Thomas Jefferson?"

"Yes. Although there are always revisionists. A few of our historians have found it difficult to grant Jefferson the nebulous qualifier 'great' because like many other men of his time he kept slaves."

"And you?"

"Because of my own background, I see some validity in this line of argument."

Again the coathanger considered. At last it said, "Undoubtedly this Thomas Jefferson, whom you have succeeded, lived during a period of only incipient technological development. Slavery exists almost by universal edict during such periods, for it is technology which ultimately effects the complete supplantation of this barbaric practice— as both the Stronolanoneaux and the Frenzilli well know. Therefore, in spite of the revisionists, we the Stronolanoneaux beneficently grant your Thomas Jefferson the appellative prefix 'great'."

"That's very big of you. I'm sorry I'm not in complete agreement."

"Not?"

"Not completely. An opinion due in part to ethnic considerations. But I'm not a fanatic on the subject. In some ways I respect the man more than the hero worshippers ever could."

"We the Stronolanoneaux consider him great without reservations. It was the residual aura of his presence emanating from the chifforobe that dictated so great an expenditure of our time on the possibilities of your species. Therefore, we ask of you: What have you done to demonstrate your respect for the memory of this man?"

"I saved the chifforobe from imminent destruction by removing it from the historic city of Old Washington during time of peril."

The Stronolanoneaux on the other end of the coathanger said nothing. Then the perfectly modulated voice said, "Such action qualifies you, President of the United States and successor of Thomas Jefferson, as an entity worthy of our commiseration and succor. Your species cannot but benefit."

At this point President Henry David Thoreau Montoya y Florit of the embattled United States of America put aside his last remaining doubts about the identity of his midnight pranksters and talked with them as if their claim of alien origin were legitimate. What did he have to lose? Already he had made a fool of himself. Already he had sacrificed the better part of a precious night's sleep. He talked with these self-confessed 'aliens' for almost four hours. He explained global politics—how the entire world had come to be aligned against his nation for 'crimes' both real and imaginary; how, under Montoya's muddleheaded or self-righteous predecessors, the United States had abdicated not so much its pre-eminent position in world affairs as its own justifiable pride in its people's accomplishments; and how he, president for only eight months, felt a spiritually debilitating disgust for the retreat he had had no choice but to order. He tried to stir the sympathies of his listeners, but he did not lie. H.D.T. Montoya had not risen to the highest office in the land through lying, and even in adversity he refused to succumb to this final recourse of the incompetent.

At last, at the very end of their discussion, he extracted from the Stronolanoneaux a promise which he did not truly believe they had the power to fulfill.

At 0820 hours the coathanger had ceased to glow and Endgame had set up a persistent and reverberating din that rattled even the rafters of the gara— that is, the east wing of the New White House—overhead. In response to Endgame's barking and armed with a tire iron, Colonel "Feisty" Phillips led a party of five men, including Chief Advisor Swearingin and Billy Gilby, through the President's bolted trapdoor and into his private bunker. They battered their way in. And there the six members of the impromptu rescue squad discovered the chief executive of the United States scrunched up in Thomas Jefferson's beautiful chifforobe—sound asleep in spite of Endgame's bewildered barking.

"Well, I'll be damned," said Colonel "Feisty" Phillips reverently.

By the same time the following morning the crisis had passed. It was another week before the last foot soldier of the two foreign alliances disembarked for home—but only thirty-six hours after the President's conference with the Stronolanoneaux, the actualization of this foot soldier's departure was so certain that everyone in New Washington, U.S.A., with the sober but unjudging exception of Montoya himself, wore a beery glow as incandescent as the coathanger's had been. Mrs. Gilby even went so far as to permit Billy a sip of his father's imported California cider. And at the general celebration held that evening in the middle of Highway 61, President Montoya announced that the capital of the nation would remain in what had formerly been Forgan, Oklahoma. The crowd—all thirty-four constituent individuals of it—cheered enthusiastically.

The salvation of the nation befell in this wise:

At 2100 hours of the day following the President's conference with the Stronolanoneaux, a startled but quick-to-compose-himself Gamil Yosef Economous of the A.M.I. Powers materialized to the left of President Montoya inside the antique chifforobe.

The swarthy, mustachioed Economous wore a beige Continental suit and a pair of wire-rimmed, violet-tinged sunglasses, which, of necessity, he at once removed. The Stronolanoneaux had teledemolecularized him while he was engaged in a strategy session on the island of Corfu, one of the subsidiary headquarters of the A.M.I. Alliance, and Economous's first thought was that he had been abducted by a group of fanatically pacificistic Swiss terrorists. In Greek, Hebrew, and Arabic, he told President Montoya that none of his captors' demands would be met; that he, Economous, would die first; and that no evil so pernicious as self-righteous terrorism existed in all the known universe.

It took only twenty minutes for the Stronolanoneaux to apprise him, in perfect Greek, of the real nature of the circumstances and for Economous to accept this apprisal as the truth—or an apprisal as near to the truth as he could anticipate hearing. Then, for two or three physically disconcerting minutes, he and Montoya, scrunched shoulder to shoulder, smiled nervously at each other and waited for the arrival of Maharaja-Premier Podgornitsyn.

At approximately 2124 hours the Maharaja-Premier arrived.

Podgornitsyn was perhaps more surprised than Economous had been, for the Stronolanoneaux had teledemolecularized him out of a sound sleep in his secluded mountain villa in the Caucasus. Podgornitsyn habitually slept without benefit of pyjamas; and his first thought was not that he had been abducted by terrorists (the security precautions at his villa would have delighted Lavrenty Beria of infamous days past), but that he had died and gone straight to the icy hell the guardians of his childhood had told him did not exist. Like Economous, he owed certain aspects of his psychological make-up to the vestigial influence of the Greek Orthodox Church. In President Montoya's chifforobe, without benefit of pyjamas, he shivered and, in shivering, set the chifforobe quaking on its quivering Queen Anne legs—for Valerie Podgornitsyn was a man well over six feet tall who weighed as much as Montoya would have if Billy Gilby had ridden Montoya piggy-back onto the scales.

The Maharaja-Premier recognized President Montoya and demanded, in English, an explanation. How was it that an *Americanski* had gained entrance to his own private hell?

At this point the Stronolanoneaux intervened, indicated to Podgornitsyn the presence of Gamil Yosef Economous, and explained that they had brought the three human beings together in the clothes cabinet of Thomas Jefferson for the purpose of 'substantive negotiations.' "It is abundantly evident to us," the coathanger told the two foreign dignitaries, "that you have not extended the new President of the United States sufficient opportunity to expound the nature of his own programs." To which Podgornitsyn replied, "I do not talk in this condition!" And President Montoya, grateful for the chance to squeeze out from between the hairy flank of the Maharaja-Premier and the bony elbow of Gamil Economous, left the chifforobe briefly, gathered up the yellow dressing-gown from his bed, and returned with it to Podgornitsyn. The big man snorted, but stepped out of the cabinet and put on Montoya's skimpy garment. Then both he and the President, begging Economous's pardon, reassumed their positions in the quaking chifforobe and closed the doors behind them.

The substantive negotiations lasted five hours.

Then the Stronolanoneaux returned the visiting dignitaries to their homelands, and H.D.T. Montoya, President of the United States, was able to catch up on a little of his lost sleep.

At 1220 hours of the day following the President's prolonged cabinet meeting, Chief Advisor Marvin C. Swearingin came through the broken trapdoor and made his way in the semi-darkness to his employer's bedside. He sat down on the edge of the bed.

"Hank?"

The President groaned, but opened his eyes.

"Hank, is it really true that Podgnornitsyn and Economous are going to withdraw their troops?"

"That's right, Marv." President Montoya sat up in his bed, resting his arms over the sheet that covered his knees. He yawned.

"Why would they do that? They had us on the run."

"The Stronolanoneaux threatened to teledemolecularize both of them again and photon-beam-retract them all the way out to Pluto."

Endgame came out from under the bed and allowed Chief Advisor Swearingin to stroke his sleek neck. But the Chief Advisor did so absently, his eyes focused on one of the upper corners of the bunker. "Doesn't it make you a little ashamed, sir, that we didn't get out of this mess on our own? I mean, back at Harvard I took a course in the classical theatre, and whenever one of those fellows like Euripides or Aeschylus had their characters in a bad situation and needed a happy ending, they always had a god come down in a chariot and save everybody. Doesn't it make you a little ashamed that that's what happened to us, sir?"

"Marvin, I take help from whatever quarter it comes. And there's no assurance that the current status quo will hold sway more than a year or two. The Stronolanoneaux are leaving shortly. They're famous among their galactic neighbors, they told me, for interfering in other worlds' affairs, and they simply wanted to give us a chance to restore the balance of power here on Earth or else alter our methods of coexistence away from power politics. And those things, Marvin, we'll have to do ourselves."

"But still—"

"No, wait. There's another thing. The Stronolanoneaux responded to something noble in this nation's heritage, which itself is a part of the heritage of all mankind. It was not a deceitful *deus ex machina* that saved us, Marvin, but our own collective spirit as men."

"Oh," said Chief Advisor Swearingin, brightening.

"And if that doesn't satisfy your longing for a self-reliant resolution of the crisis, I'll tell you something else."

"What, Hank?"

"It won't happen again. The Stronolanoneaux are never coming back."

"Never?"

"No, the universe very seldom grants anyone three wishes. We were lucky to get one."

"I'd say. I thought we'd just about bought the farm."

"And do you know what the Stronolanoneaux told me just before they shut down our coathanger forever?"

"No, sir. What was that?"

"That they've *always* taken an abiding interest in the universe's underdogs."

Endgame had the last move. He licked the President's hand. Then, just as in the clincher of an old cowboy movie or Our Gang comedy, Endgame stalked across the room, squeezed under Thomas Jefferson's chifforobe, and put his paws over his long, mahogany-red snout.

A Flying Saucer With Minnesota Plates

by Lawrence Watt-Evans

Harry nodded. "Yeah, I'll take these," he said.

The customer smiled in relief. "Thanks," he said. "And thanks for the burger." He started for the door.

"Any time," Harry said, waving.

He glanced out the window, trying to decide whether the eastern sky might be starting to lighten a little.

What the hell, he couldn't tell with the lights on, and he wasn't about to turn them off, even if he didn't have any customers in the place just then.

He probably wasn't going to *get* any customers for at least an hour, either; the late-night oddballs who were his best customers, who had provided most of his income for years, wouldn't be coming any more at this time of night, and it was still too early for the truckers catching an early breakfast. The day shift wouldn't be in until eight.

Harry wondered if any of the people who worked the other shifts for him had any idea what kept Harry's All-Night Hamburgers in business. They probably didn't.

He'd been in business for years before he figured out himself just what the story was on the late-night customers. He hadn't done anything to attract them, other than running a decent diner, serving good burgers, and never hassling anyone—but maybe that was enough, because they kept coming.

Harry's late-night customers were not your usual weirdos. Some of them, he was pretty sure, weren't even human.

As long as they paid for their meals, though, he didn't much care what they were.

The kid he'd had helping him on the night shift for awhile had explained it, but Harry had already doped most of it out for himself. The weirdos were from other dimensions. "Parallel worlds," some of them said; "alternate realities," according to others.

"Other dimensions" suited Harry. They were from places that were still Earth, but were *different*, in various ways. They had some way of traveling between worlds, and they came to Harry's because Harry never hassled anyone, because he'd take all sorts of weird trinkets in trade, and because there was a place like Harry's somewhere in this part of the West Virginia hills in millions upon millions of universes, so that they knew where to find him.

And they didn't want to be seen; that gave Harry's another advantage, being out in the woods in the middle of nowhere. Even isolated as the place was, they still only dared show up between midnight and dawn, and usually allowed an hour or so margin on either side.

That last guy had hung around later than most of them ever dared, but even so, Harry had an hour to kill.

Well, that hour would give him a chance to sweep up, maybe clean the grill; the grease was getting a bit thick.

He was out of practice looking after everything himself; he'd gotten spoiled having that kid working the graveyard shift with him for so long, and now that the kid had lit out for wherever the hell he was—he'd sent postcards from Pittsburgh and New York, so far—it was taking awhile to get back into the swing of it.

Maybe, he thought, he should see about hiring another kid—but there was always the question of how a kid would handle the late-

night crowd, and just because the last one had done okay, that didn't
mean the next one would.

The bell over the door jingled as he was pushing the broom along
behind the counter, and Harry looked up, startled.

It was his last customer, back and looking worried.

"Something wrong?" Harry asked.

He hoped it wasn't about the payment; those little coins he'd
accepted looked like the platinum the guy had said they were, and
that meant they were worth several times what the burger should
have cost. He didn't particularly want to give any of them back,
though; after all, he'd have to take them up to Pittsburgh to sell
them, and he deserved something extra to cover the overhead.

"Yes," the man said. "It's my . . . my vehicle. You know anything
about . . . um . . . motors?"

"Well, that depends," Harry said. "What sort of motor are we
talking about here?"

The traveler opened his mouth, then closed it again.

"Um . . ." he said, "Maybe you had better come take a look."

Harry looked him over.

He looked ordinary enough, really. He was definitely human, and
he was wearing pants and a shirt and shoes and a jacket, nothing
particularly weird.

Of course, the shoes were cerise and appeared to be plastic, and
the shirt couldn't seem to decide if it was white or silver, but the
pants were ordinary black denim and the jacket was ordinary black
vinyl—cut a little funny, maybe, but it could pass for European if
you didn't know any better. The little display screen on the collar
could pass for jewelry if you didn't look close.

The guy's head was shaved, but he didn't look like a punk,
especially not with that worried look on his face.

Harry had seen a whole lot worse, in his late-night trade.

"Okay," Harry said, "I'll take a look."

He slipped off his apron and draped it across the counter, and the
two men stepped outside into the cool of a late summer night.

Harry blinked as his eyes adjusted, and the customer pointed and
said, "There."

He hadn't needed to point or say anything. His vehicle was the only one in the lot. Harry stared.

Harry sighed.

The vehicle was silvery, with a finish like brushed aluminum that reflected the light from Harry's signs in broad stripes of soft color. It was round, perhaps twenty feet in diameter, six feet high at the center, but curving gradually down to a sharp edge. A section of one side had lifted up to reveal a dark interior where various colored lights glowed dimly. There were no windows, portholes, or other visible openings, but a band of something milky ran around the lower disk and seemed to be glowing faintly.

It was, in short, a classic flying saucer.

"Oh, Lord," Harry said, "What's wrong with it?"

"I don't know," the customer said, worried.

Harry sighed again. "Well, let's have a look at it."

The customer led the way into the dim interior of the thing, and showed Harry where the access plate for the main drive was.

Harry went back inside, collected his tool box from the furnace room in back, and went to work.

He had never seen anything like the "motor" in this particular vehicle; about half the components looked familiar, but they went together in ways that made no sense at all.

And the other half—Harry didn't even like to look at the other half.

After about fifteen minutes he emerged from the engine compartment and shrugged.

"I'm sorry, buddy, but I can't fix it. I think that . . . that thing on the right might be bad—everything looks okay, no loose wires or hoses, but that thing's got this black gunk on it that doesn't look like it should be there."

The customer stared. "What will I *do*?" he wailed. He turned and looked desperately at Harry. "Is there anyone in your world who knows such machines?"

Harry considered that long and hard, and finally replied, "No."

"No? I am *stranded* here?"

Harry shrugged. "Maybe somebody'll come in who can fix it. We get all kinds here."

"But you said . . ."

"Yeah, well, I meant that *lives* here, there's nobody can fix it. But my place, here, I specialize in you guys, I figure you know that or you wouldn't be here. Tonight, tomorrow, sooner or later we'll get somebody in who can fix your gadget."

"Someone from another time-line, you mean?"

Harry shrugged again. "Whatever. I don't know who you guys are that come here; I just let you come and don't hassle anybody. It's none of my business if you're from time-lines, whatever they are, or from Schenectady, but I do get a lot of you weirdos late at night."

The customer frowned and looked over the controls.

"You are not very reassuring," he said.

"Not my job to be reassuring," Harry said. "My job is selling burgers. Now, would you mind getting this thing out of sight, before the sun comes up?"

The customer turned and blinked at him.

"How am I to do that?" he asked. "Without the primary driver, the vehicle cannot move at all."

Harry's eyebrows lowered.

"You serious? I thought you couldn't do whatever it is you guys do, but you mean it won't go *anywhere*?"

"It will not go anywhere," the other affirmed.

Harry looked out the door of the craft; the sky was definitely getting lighter. Early truckers might happen along almost any time now.

What would they do if they saw a flying saucer in his parking lot? This could be very bad for his daytime business. The late-night trade was important, but the daylight business didn't hurt any, either.

"Maybe we can shove it back into the woods?" he suggested, not very enthusiastically.

The customer shook his head. "I doubt it very much. The craft has a registered weight of seventeen hundred kilos."

"What's that in pounds?" Harry asked.

"Ah . . . about, perhaps, four thousand pounds?"

Harry sat down on a convenient jump-seat. "You're right," he said, "We can't shove it anywhere, unless it's got wheels. I didn't see any."

"There are none."

"Figures."

The two men sat, thinking.

"Can we not leave it here, until someone comes who can repair it?" the customer asked.

Harry glowered. "How the hell am I supposed to explain a goddamn *flying saucer* in my parking lot?"

The customer shrugged.

"I don't know," he said.

Outside, an engine growled. The first of Harry's daylight customers was arriving.

An idea struck him.

"Look," he said, "I gotta go, but here's what you do . . ."

The saucer sat in the lot through the morning and the afternoon, while Harry finished his shift and went home to bed, leaving the day shift in charge. It was still there at about 6:00 P.M. when the county sheriff pulled in and saw it.

He got out of his car and looked the saucer over from every side. The door was closed, and the exterior was virtually seamless. He had no way of knowing that its driver was asleep inside.

Painted on one side, in big red letters, was the legend, "Harry's hamburgers—they're out of this world!"

He smiled and went inside.

Twenty minutes later Harry came out of the back room, yawning, and poured himself a cup of coffee. The evening crew, consisting of Bill the cook and Sherry the waitress, paid no attention to him; they knew, from long experience, that he wouldn't be fit company until he had had his coffee.

The sheriff knew it, too, but between bites of hamburger he said, "Cute gimmick, Harry, that saucer out front."

"Thanks, Sheriff," Harry said, looking up from his cup.

"Is it permanent?"

"Nah, I don't think so," Harry said sleepily. "Takes up a lot of space. Thought I'd try it, though, see if it pulled in any customers."

The sheriff nodded, and took another bite.

"Uh . . . why d'you ask?" Harry inquired uneasily.

The sheriff shrugged and finished chewing.

"Well," he said, "I figured it wasn't there for good when I saw the Minnesota plates. If you keep it there more than a couple of months, you'll want to take those off."

"Oh, yeah," Harry said weakly.

He hadn't noticed the license plates.

Three days later, just after dawn, a trucker pushed open the door.

"Hey, Harry," he called, "What happened to your flying saucer?"

"Got rid of it," Harry said, pulling a breakfast menu out from under the counter. "Wasn't doing any good."

"No? I thought it was a cute idea," the trucker said, settling onto a stool.

Harry just shrugged.

"So, Harry," the trucker asked, "Where'd it go?"

Harry remembered the weird shimmer as the saucer had vanished, several hours before. He remembered all the snatches of conversation he'd overheard, all those years, about parallel realities and alternate worlds, places where history was different, where *everything* was different. He remembered all the strange coins and bizarre gadgets he had accepted in payment, thousands of them by now. He thought of all the stories he could tell this man about what he had seen, in this very place, late at night.

"Minnesota," he said, as he handed over the menu.

Garbage

by Ron Goulart

As to why Marathon Murphy isn't immediately coming back from the Sahara and why I may go to bed with the opposition again.

Let me see if I can explain it to you, sir, in such a way as to avoid causing you to bellow and thump on your chest with your paws.

Okay, you remember you summoned me to your office in DC-2 on Monday last, which was April 5, 2020. It was a pleasant day and even though the force dome over your outdoor office area was malfunctioning in such a way as to suck in those sparrowish sort of birds, you appeared to be in a relatively good mood.

"You're looking remarkably fit, sir," I said, settling into a floating plazchair. "Have you done something to your hair?"

"Growrr," you replied. "Spare me the digs, Tockson."

"No, I meant to compliment you. I think you look very attractive as a blond, sir. Usually one doesn't see too many blond gorillas, but I—"

"Bip off, Tockson!" You pounded on your floating plazdesk with one furry fist. "When are you going to learn to be discreet? You oughtn't to remind a man of his handi—"

"Listen, sir, I don't consider it a handicap at all," I assured you, smiling. "Product Investigation Enterprises doesn't either. Promoting you to investigator-in-chief of the whole—"

"What do those bipheads know? Hell, there's a chimpanzee acting as secretary of state."

"Yeah, but that's the executive branch, sir," I reminded. "For a man who's had his brain transferred into a gorilla's body to rise so high in government is a real feather in—"

"Dan!" you shouted, using my first name finally. "Cease babbling; attend to me. I have an assignment for you. You'd better not dawdle the way you did last time."

"It's no sin to have your brain in a gorilla's body," I continued. "You couldn't help it anyway. Anyone might have hopped onto that faulty teleport pad the way you did on that fateful day back in 2016 and—"

"We won't dwell on it further, Dan!" you snarled.

"Think of how the gorilla must have felt, getting scrambled up with you. You both arrive in White Africa and he finds his brain in your body. He must—"

"There was nothing very wrong with my body!" You scowled, stroking your muzzle. "Perhaps I wasn't lean and young and attractive to peabrained bimbos the way you are, still I—"

"You were dumpy, sir. Pity the poor gorilla having to go home to his native jungle with a dumpy body like—"

"Dan, I have a job for you."

"So I gathered, sir." I gave you an attentive look. "Another faulty and potentially dangerous machine to investigate?"

"No. I'm taking you off things mechanical for a while."

"You're angry because I stayed in fifteenth-century Italy so long?"

"I'm not especially mad, no," you answered, growling. "But the Time Travel Overseeing Committee wasn't much pleased. You shouldn't have dropped in on Leonardo da Vinci with those tips on aerodynamics."

"After I tested out those faulty Japanese-made GE time machines I had some leisure."

You did that little angry chest-beating business you often do. A gorilla holdover, as I've often told you. "I'm sending you to Iveyville."

"Where is it?"

"In Sunnyland-2, in the Florida Sector," you said, shifting your bulky carcass in your floating tinchair. "I suspect, to say the least, we've got a food violation in the making down there."

"Speaking of food, did you get to that vegetarian place I told you about in DC-1? They're very good with roots and tubers. Just the kind of chow a healthy gorilla probably—"

"Mrs. Banks and I don't dine out much."

I nodded. "Your wife, if you don't mind my frankness, doesn't appreciate you. Better a handsome gorilla than a dumpy—"

"Did you ever walk into a clothing outlet, Daniel, and try to get fitted for a nightsuit when you had a gorilla body? Do you know what my neck size is now?"

"I'd guess about—"

"Never mind. Let's get on with this bipping assignment."

Splop!

A stray bird landed on your desk at that point, angering you. After you'd swatted it away and calmed some, I asked, "What do we have to go on? What sort of danger to the consumer does PIE have to face?"

"That is what you're going to Sunnyland to find out," you told me in your throaty gorilla voice. "Some very strange food-induced behavior may be underway there. We have a tip from Marathon Murphy. As you know, he's a dedicated amateur consumer advocate, provided us quite a few other useful tips in the past. This time around, the problem centers in his own hometown in Iveyville." With your left paw you lifted up a faxmemo.

"I notice you're still wearing your Sigma Chi ring. Do they make them that big or did you—"

"This is the bipping code message Marathon sent in last night." You waved the memo pretty wildly. Several circling sparrows went fluttering up through the sunlight. "He's, by the way, using Consumer Code #26, in case you want to send him any notes whilst you're down there."

"Code messages are a waste of time. I prefer a direct contact," I said, slouching slightly in my chair. "What route is Marathon covering these days? I'll catch him on the run."

You let out a husky gorilla sigh. "What a great quantity of puckywits we have in this world of ours, Daniel," you observed, folding your paws over your broad chest. "Here's Marathon, an otherwise rational man of forty-odd years, who devotes all his time to jogging around the streets of the Florida Sector."

"It's a very aerobic way to live. You'd benefit from—"

"And all because he's got to hold on to his bipping World's Record for Continuous Running."

"I bet his respiratory system is in terrific shape," I commented, standing up to my full height of six feet two inches and a fraction. "What did Marathon give us in the way of specifics?"

You brought the faxmemo up close to your ridged brow. " 'A food scandal of major proportions brewing here. Bizarre transformationssuspected. Could spread. Send down a crack investigator pronto. In haste, Marathon Murphy.' There you have the message."

"Could be another bread thing," I said. "Although I doubt Ford-ITT would fool around with imitation sawdust again so soon." I rubbed my hands together. "Okay, I'm on my way to Sunnyland-2. Since this sounds urgent, I'll teleport."

Your little eyes narrowed. "Unk!"

"Really, sir, teleporting is perfectly safe nowadays," I said. "Thanks in good part to dedicated men such as yourself and PIE agents all across the nation. There hasn't been a scramble accident since 2018." I started across the grass of your office area toward the exit spot in the force screen.

"Dan!" you growled.

"Sir?"

"Don't dawdle. PIE is in a budget-cutting phase. They're very much annoyed by dawdlers."

"You needn't worry. The PIE budget computer is a friend of mine." Giving one of my friendly mock salutes, I departed.

I thought about my assuring you how safe teleportation was when I stepped onto the Southbound platform in the depot nearest my condo. There was nothing unsettling about the wide pad itself; the continual low sizzling doesn't bother me the way it does some. The other passengers on the platform, however, each on his individual destination square, seemed a decidedly sinister crowd. Matter of fact, they weren't all exactly on individual squares. That was because some of my fellow travelers, five to be exact, were Siamese Quints. Five rather shifty-eyed gentlemen joined at the hips. They all smiled at me, bowing, cameras jingling. I didn't quite trust them. In addition to these mutants who were, probably, a side effect of those Japanese power-plant riots back around the end of the twentieth century, there were six cowboys on the teleport pad. That, too, was unusual. You don't often get that many cowboys in my part of New Virginia.

"Howdy, pard," hailed one of them. A gaunt, grizzled man in a stained one-piece westsuit. "Don't be afeared to ask for our respective autographs now."

"Why would I want your autographs?" I inquired, keeping a pleasant tone to my voice.

"Cause we is celebs," said another of the cowboys. A toothless fellow with his sooty plazsombrero worn low over his low forehead. "We is the Sons of the Tonto Rim."

"Interesting," I said, though I'd never heard of them.

"Why, may the good Lord bless the pack of you," remarked a slim paranun who was standing at the far end of the teleport pad. "Many's the beam of joy you've brought to the Little Wee Church of Our Lady of Cleveland Mercy Hospital where I work part-time."

Even though she was muffled in the traditional cloaklike habit of her order, I could sense this nun was an attractive young woman. In fact, I had a feeling she was someone I knew. Someone I knew and ought to avoid.

"Teleport passengers, please select your desired destinations," ordered the voice of the dispersal computer. "Jump-off time in 30 seconds."

Bowing easily from the waist, I punched up Iveyville on the tiny panel at my feet.

Still bent, I had an insight. Although I'd only tangled with the the girl twice in my year and a half as an agent for PIE, yet I was now relatively certain the slim paranun was—

Pap!

The usual stomach churning and fuzziness. The slight ringing in the ears. Well, no need to detail it, sir. You know what teleporting feels like.

The surprising thing was, I didn't arrive in Iveyville. Instead I was on a platform situated on a bright yellow beach. I suspected I had arrived on some Caribbean Island.

"Raise them hands, pard." The Sons of the Tonto Rim had come along with me, and the whole half-dozen of them were pointing Old-West-style blaster pistols at various important parts of me.

The paranun had teleported along, too. She eased back her cowl, smiled at me. "Like to talk to you, Dan."

"This isn't ethical, Kassy," I told her. "You can't divert an independent teleport passenger from his—"

"Come on over to my villa," invited Kassy Gulliver, nodding over one slim shoulder.

"Better," advised one of the singing cowboys, "else we mot shoot you up something awful."

I shrugged. You may write it off as dawdling, sir, but to me, fraternizing with the opposition now and then is a great way to learn an awful lot.

Kassy Gulliver is, when not decked out in one of her unflattering disguises, a very pretty young woman. Slim, sleek, well-proportioned, with silky auburn hair. Even though I'm usually able to outwit her, Kassy is one of the Counter Consumer Agency's crack operatives.

The specifics of what went on at her fairly palatial villa on the island of Marafona I won't burden you with. Suffice it to say that as the full moon appeared in the clear tropical sky, Kassy and I were sharing an enormous, circular, floating featherbed.

"Nix?" she inquired, sitting up and reaching for a picnic hamper which rested on a floating cobbler's bench beside the bed.

Waching her tan, supple back, I said, "Afraid so, Kassy."

"We can go as high as $20,000."

"I can earn that much in a month on my present—"

"But, Dan, you don't have to do *anything* for this money," she explained as she extracted several plazpax of junk food out of her hamper. "That's the best thing about bribes."

"It's an idealogical thing really. I'm dedicated to consumer rights, you work for the business community."

"Twenty-five thousand dollars and a lifetime pass to any HoJo Flyin Restaurant in the world."

"Kas, I don't eat any of that garbage. So what's the good of—"

"Okay, $30,000 *and* . . . we'll spend a whole week right here." She unseamed a sandwich, plopped it into her palm and let the package drop to the quilt.

Dumpy! was printed in bold, glowing letters on the packet. *The San With Ever'thing!*

"Dumpy? What the heck is a Dumpy?"

She flushed slightly, bare breasts first, then began to chomp on the thin sandwich. "Oh, only a new product somebody's testing."

I pretended only casual interest. "Kassy, you really ought to pay attention to me. Eventually that garbage you eat is going to take years off—"

"It is garbage, you're right about that much," she said, gracefully wiping a splat of something yellowish off her pretty chin. "An innovative new process allows the Lovin' Sam chain of flyins to produce a totally nutritious sandwich *entirely* from recycled garbage. Not just

food garbage, mind you, Dan, but *all* kinds of garbage. Old magazines, discarded mattresses, plysues, autumn leaves, wrecked—"

"And you're *eating* it?"

"Don't you realize that with technology we can make anything
palatable? Not merely palatable, but darn good for you. Take this
Dumpy!, which you scorn." She snatched up the discarded packet,
breasts tapping gently together, and poked at its ingredient list.
"We'll skip the part where it says: 'DEADLY PERIL! The U.S.
Foodtaster General Warns This Product Is A Probable Cause of . . .'
and then the whole stupid list of spooky diseases which nobody in
his right mind would *blame* a little harmless sandwich for causing.
Here's the interesting part. 'Contains the Minimum Daily Require-
ment of all known vitamins and minerals, plus a dose of Ginseng
sufficient to stimulate a Manchurian ox, plus a perfectly safe tran-
quillizer, plus delayed-release respiratory disease medicine, plus a
brainstim powder, plus a harmless sleep-inducer, plus a cure for
measles, rickets, acne, and Ferman's Syndrome.' Now, admit it, you
don't get that kind of a lift from your so-called organic lettuce."

"Nobody needs all that stuff." I was keeping my face and body
calm, but I'd noticed there was something else printed on the
sandwich wrapper. In tiny letters it said, TEST MARKETED/APRIL
2020/LOVIN' SAM'S IN IVEYVILLE. I began to suspect the reason Kassy
and the Counter Consumer Agency didn't want me to go to Iveyville
had something to do with Lovin' Sam's branch in that town, with
some new products they were testing there. "What eating is all
about, Kassy, is—"

"If you don't take the bribe, I'm going to have to keep you locked
up here." She dug into the hamper again for a packet of explodrink.
"I'll also have the Sons of the Tonto Rim beat the pucky out of you."

"You wouldn't think much of me if I accepted a bribe."

"Sure I would." She paused in the act of unzipping the drink
pouch to pat me on the cheek fondly. "My feeling for you, Dan, is
essentially a physical thing. There's little or no philosophical or
moral basis. I'd sleep with you like this just as joyfully if you took the
dough."

Nodding at the pouch, I advised, "You shouldn't drink that garbage."

"What a cleancut, uneventful life you must lead. I bet if I didn't seduce you every few months there'd be no excitement at all." Tugging the sipper out of the pouch, she inserted it between her lovely lips.

"Too many people nowadays don't realize, Kas, how enjoyable simple solitude is." I watched her as she sipped the explodrink.

"I love the way this stuff starts bubbling once it gets into my mouth," she said, giggling appreciatively. "And what's even . . . ump!" She fell over backwards suddenly, squirting purplish liquid all over her pretty breasts.

This agent work does something to you after a time, sir. A few years ago I would never have reached out of bed, while making love to an extremely attractive young woman, and shot a dose of fast-acting knockout juice into all her soft drinks. Yet that is exactly what I did in this instance.

Swinging off the huge bed, after wiping the sticky explodrink off the unconscious Kassy, I hurried into my clothes. Kassy had a skycar parked on the roof pad of the villa; all six of the Sons of the Tonto Rim were rehearsing down on the lower level. Facts I took into consideration in working out my particular escape plan.

The keyplate for the skycar was in the picnic hamper. I noted, as I swiped it, several of the other imitation foods in there were from that same Lovin' Sam's outlet in Iveyville. Pausing only to make a quick plaz replica of Kassy's forefinger to use on the airships' printlock, I climbed out the bedchamber window and up onto the moonlit roof.

Well, actually, I also stopped to kiss Kassy once on her smooth tan forehead. I try to spare you, sir, most of the sentimental touches.

I couldn't find Marathon Murphy.

I circled his usual route and he wasn't at any of the spots he was supposed to be at. Disposing of the skycar, I even jogged his established course on foot seeking a trace of him. There was nearly a frumus with a feisty band of Venusian joggers who crossed my path, calling out the usual "Green is keen!" slogans and giving me the tentacle. I ignored them, as well as outran them.

Deciding Marathon was obviously not following his accustomed path, I decided to trot over to his starting point on the outskirts of Iveyville. The decorative palm trees and the moderately breathable early morning air made for a pleasant run.

Britzz! Chug!

Brit! Cunk!

I kept running at an even pace, although I felt uneasy.

There were seven of them. At first they pretended to ignore me, went roaring on by me on the nearly empty streetway. Wheelies, the bunch of them. Seven very large louts with jetpropelled skates in place of their voluntarily amputated feet. Each clad in a one-piece black fightsuit. Each suit bearing the name of their Wheelie group emblazoned on its back in glowbeads. *The Skullface Death-Killers.* Not a name to cheer me up on my solitary run through this strange town.

Britzz! Bruk!

Chunka! Cung!

They began circling me, braided hair flapping, augmented teeth gleaming.

"Whiz brzz whirzz," said the guy nearest me.

He'd turned on his motorized teeth and they were grinding away at a tremendous rate. Made it difficult to understand what he was saying.

"Whizz brkk motherfumper whirtzz!"

I caught part of that. "Morning." I grinned in my most ingratiating manner. "Nothing like a good run to start the day off, is there?"

"Grzz schmuck outlander fritzz."

Two more of them were quite close to me, teeth whirring and eyes glistening.

"I'm not actually an outlander. Indeed, this is my old hometown. I grew up right down the street, at the intersection of Grumpy and Dopey Streets. I'm back home again after too long a time away to—"

Pong!

I must admit I never heard the ones who wheeled up behind me. Could be they'd cut the motors in their feet and teeth. At least two of them clouted me over the skull with heavy metallic objects.

I fell down.

There was a very strong animal smell, which I wasn't able to identify immediately, all around. Groaning as unobtrusively as possible, I pushed myself up off the neowood flooring.

Stumbling as I regained my feet, I bumped into several shadowy figures.

"Four score and seven years ago . . . you weigh 164 pounds. . . ."

"Let me make one thing perfectly clear . . . shine 'em up!"

I backed away, realizing I'd collided with a cluster of dusty, cobwebby androids.

"That's going to start them howling for sure," said a portly figure near the warehouse's thick metallic door.

"Can't place you, sorry. Which president are you?"

"I ain't no dingdang andy, I'm Senior Police Chief Tippett."

"Is there a junior chief, too?" I asked as I moved toward him.

"Not in the way you mean, buckeroo. See, we got us two police forces here in Iveyville. One for young folks and one for senior citizens. That there's a custom all over the Florida Sector, I reckon."

"Ask not what your country can do for you . . . three shots for two bits!"

"Oops!" I'd bumped against another android, still somewhat groggy from being coldcocked by the band of Wheelies.

Yowl! Howl!

"What'd I tell you," said the plump Chief Tippett. "It's howling and baying and snarling hereabouts all the live-long day. And I got to tell you, dang it, nothing smells worse than wolf crap."

Halting a few feet from him, I inquired, "There are wolves here?"

"Dozen at least, locked up in the next dangblast warehouse to us," he replied, wiping the back of his hand across his mouth. "Ain't exactly wolves, more what you call lycanthropes."

"Werewolves?"

"You got it, young fella. A dozen, or might be a baker's dozen, of what you call wolfpersons."

"People, you mean, who turn into wolves?"

"What the dickens is a werewolf, if it ain't that?"

Snap!

I snapped my fingers. "This is commencing to make sense," I said, grinning. "Iveyville's been bothered by werewolves for the past few days, hasn't it?"

"We got us one hell of an outbreak," the chief admitted. "Folks getting themselves gnawed on and chased and snapped at. Then yesterday it done stopped. First off I thought the plague was over, but nope. They'd simply rounded up the dang things."

"I admire your vocabulary," I remarked. "Don't often encounter one such in this day and age, except in singing groups."

"Wellsir, I took me a mailorder course in sheriffing once," Senior Police Chief Tippet said.

"Any idea who rounded up these wolf people?"

"Not a one," he said. "I opined it was some jaspers playing vigilante. Now, however, I got me the idee these jiggers want to keep these critters hid for some reason."

"Exactly," I agreed. "They don't want this side effect known until they modify the product. If this got out the publicity would ruin them."

One of his eyes narrowed as he asked me, "You know who started this here hootenanny? Who bopped me on the cabeza when I started investigating the missing wolfpersons? Who dumped me in here with a bunch of semi-defunct patriotic museum andies?"

"Sure, I know all that and more," I assured him. "What we have to do now, though, Chief Tippett, is get out of here."

"I been trying at that for hour on hour, buckaroo. Only time they opened this door was when some walleyed galloot brung me a silly little snack in a plazbag."

"I've got a gadget for getting through that door."

"You maybe had it, young fella." He gave me an amused snort. " 'Cept these jaspers searched us good and proper fore dumping us here."

"Sure, but they're so steeped in the junk-food mystique they tend to overlook certain things." Slipping my hand into my tunic, I tugged out a packet of frylikes with the Frenchies! name bright upon it. Unseaming this packet I'd had the foresight to bring along, I shook out one particular golden-brown fry. "This one isn't exactly what it seems. It is, in point of fact, a highly powerful laser gun made to resemble a french fry."

"Hot diggety, that'll get us clean out of here for sure." Chief Tippett stomped a foot happily. "Oh, but once we gets outside they's a tough galloot with a stunrod out there."

"Don't worry," I said. "I've got another french fry for that."

I hadn't expected to encounter Lovin' Sam himself.

Suitably disguised, I called on the local Lovin' Sam flyin restaurant in the early afternoon. As you know, sir, all of the places in this chain are done up to resemble late nineteenth century bordellos.

An ample woman in a feather-trimmed silky robe admitted me. "Hi, honey. This is Serbo-Croatian-style food week at Lovin' Sam's," she announced by way of greeting. "I'd suggest you try the fried *koljeno* with—"

"Actually, mam, I'm with the Sunnyland-2 Rat Quota Office," I explained, giving her a very brief flash of a recently applied ID tattoo on my chest. "We've heard rumors, unsettling rumors, that the number of rats prowling your kitchen exceeds government-set limits."

"Oh, sure, honey," she said, dimpling. "You want to see the manager, right along this way."

I trailed her broad form through the restaurant, dodging tables and lingerie-clad waitresses. One platinum-haired girl who was serving a heaping plate of neogetti in a dimlit corner seemed vaguely familiar, but I couldn't place her.

"I heard a lot about your new Dumpy! sandwich," I said to my hostess by way of conversation. "Maybe I can sample one while—"

"The what?"

"Lovin' Sam's newest, the Dumpy!"

"Oh, yeah, it is a very popular number, honey. So popular indeed, that we're all out of them today."

"A pity."

We made our way, my hefty guide breathing unevenly, along a dark-paneled corridor. She, keeping her robe shut with one chunky hand, reached out and opened a heavy door. "Right in there, sweetie."

I crossed the threshold onto a thick, flowered carpet and found myself facing Lovin' Sam. The door was quietly shut behind me.

"That's a very unconvincing mother of a moustache," he said from his rolltop desk.

I touched at it. "Oh, so? I had to improvise it out of wolf fur," I said, seating myself in a swivel facing him. "You look exactly as you do in your vidcommercials."

"Why the bejesus shouldn't I?" he said. "I am Lovin' Sam, so naturally I look like him."

"Sometimes there's a media distortion. For instance, when we arrested Granny Malley for excessive adulteration of her applelike pies, she turned out to be considerably frailer than—"

"You are a talkative mother, aren't you?" Lovin' Sam leaned toward me, the zircon in his front tooth flashing. "Just as I heard, talkative Dan Tockson of PIE."

"I see I really am unmasked," I said, glancing around his office. I was pleased to note several large cartons labeled Dumpy! stacked against one wall beneath a dangling imitation-Tiffany lamp. Exactly the sort of evidence I could teleport back to you and our labs, sir. "It doesn't matter, since the jig's up, Lovin' Sam. Senior Chief of Police Tippett has rounded up all those poor unfortunate werewolves the minute I came to. By the way, bopping an accredited agent of the United States gov—"

"You dumb mother, my laboratories are just about into a cure for those people. If you'd left them stashed away another few days, we'd bave got them all fixed up good," said Lovin' Sam, rubbing a black, bejeweled hand across his perspiring face. "Then we'd have let you and that doddering sodkicker go, with nobody the wiser."

"Nope, those wolves were smelly. I knew I was in the vicinity of werewolves the minute I came to. By the way, bopping an accredited agent of the United States gov—"

"You can't prove I had nothing to do with those Wheelie mothers."

"I will be able, however, once I send samples of your new Dumpy! sandwich to DC-2, to prove beyond a doubt you've been using illegal and untested ingredients in your food. There are several known dubious ingredients which have a lycanthropic side-effect on some people, so once—"

"There's absolutely nothing wrong with them sandwiches," insisted Lovin' Sam. "The only reason I'm recalling this test batch is they're not lip-smacking good enough. No other reason."

"Your goons out at the warehouse talked, Lovin' Sam. I know for certain that some of your unfortunate patrons started turning into raving beasts mere seconds after they ventured to sample this newest bit of garbage you—"

"I eat these mothering things myself and I'm okay." He hopped from his chair, rushed to the pile of boxes and ripped a lid open. With both hands he grabbed out a handful of Dumpy! sandwiches. Swiftly he opened three of the things, gobbled them down and then returned to his chair. "You PIE mothers are always trying to frame me for whatever silly . . . woof!"

"Beg pardon?"

"I was saying, mother, that there are any number of reasons why woofy woof yowl!" He finished the sentence on the floor, in an all-fours position.

"What further proof do we need?"

He was covered all over now with bristly hair, and his ears had taken on a definite lupine cast. When he snarled, all his sharp, wolfish teeth showed. The zircon was still there, gleaming.

"You don't want to risk eating a government man," I warned him.

"Growrr! Roff!" He leaped straight for me.

I had a stungun strapped under my tunic, but before I could unholster it the wolfman was upon me.

He growled, snapped at my flesh and tried to take chunks out of my arms and head.

Bringing both knees up, I connected with his snapping jaws and caused them to clamp shut momentarilly.

I rolled away clear, jerking at my stungun.

He got me again, teeth shutting around my wrist.

The office door opened and someone came running in.

Zimmm!

After a few seconds I realized the beam of someone else's stungun had hit Lovin' Sam and caused him to freeze.

Gingerly I worked my wrist free of his now immobile jaws. Rising, brushing myself off, I held out my hand. "Thanks, Kassy."

"Don't try shaking hands, idiot, you're all bloody."

"Excuse it." I accepted the swatch of lingerie she tore from her waitress disguise, and bound up my wound. "I appreciate your—"

"Bad publicity if you were chewed up by one of our clients, Dan," the pretty CCA agent said. "We'll have trouble enough squelching the stories Chief Tippett's been giving out to the media."

"Squelch?" I grinned. "How are you going to squelch this, Kassy? As soon as I ship a few of these deadly sandwiches to headquarters the—"

"You won't be doing that."

"You can't risk killing me."

"We try never to kill anyone." She looked at me with a certain amount of fondness. "Teleportation is much easier. I took you to my island and that nosy Marathon Murphy we zipped over to the Sahara Desert. Turns out, in case you're interested, he *likes* it over there and is going to stay long enough to try out for the Cross

Country Barefooted on Sand World's Record to add to his laurels. As for you—"

Zimm!

At the moment, sir, I'm in the Caribbean once again. Kassy has the notion she'll keep me here until the current batch of faulty Dumpy! sandwiches are safely destroyed and all the fuss dies down and is forgotten. From the news she leaks in, though, I think we can consider the Dumpy! over and done with for good.

Rather than make another daredevil escape, I intend to stay here in her villa. I'm dictating this report into my typevox and you'll receive the usual three copies as soon as I'm back in DC-2.

Meanwhile, there's no telling what valuable intelligence I can pick up by keeping close to her.

Iriadeska's Martians

by Frederik Pohl

Charlie Sanford expected all along that he would be in strange places, doing strange things, because that was what the world was like, even back home in New York. (Who would have thought live Martians would be parading down Broadway one day soon?) It was also what public relations was like because you found yourself doing things like erecting a thirty-foot helium-filled Mr. Pickle balloon in the plaza in front of the United Nations to celebrate International Pickle & Relish Week. Nevertheless, he hadn't expected this. He hadn't expected to find himself in a narrow-bottomed boat with an outboard motor three sizes too big for it, roaring along a sludgy, squdgy river in Southeast Asia, "inspecting" a plantation belonging to the Iriadeskan Army outside the capital city of Pnik. It was very hot. The fact that the Iriadeskans said it was twenty-five degrees did not alter the fact that it felt like pushing ninety in good old Fahrenheit, and soggy damp besides.

"Soon now!" yelled Major Doolathata in his ear, grinning encouragingly.

Sanford nodded, holding onto the windscreen as the driver swerved to cut through a floating green mat of water hyacinth. There was a Mindy Mars doll hanging from the windscreen, its

143

plush fur as soaked with spray as Sanford himself. He had been surprised to see it there. The line had been introduced at the Toy Fair just a few months before. It wasn't even in the stores yet. So how had it reached this God-forsaken part of the world so soon? And why did jolly Major Doolathata wink and glance meaningfully at it every time Sanford caught his eye?

"What I don't understand," Sanford shouted over the roar of the motor, "is why we're poking around out here when I'm supposed to get back to Pnik for my meeting?" He had arrived at the Pnik airport only at five that morning, thoroughly spaced out from the long plane ride through Hawaii, Manila, and Singapore. Jet lag was not easy for Sanford, who hadn't really had much experience of long-distance travel. The flight had not only been interminable, twenty-seven hours of interminable, it had crossed ten time zones and the International Date Line. Sanford could not keep straight in his mind what day it was.

Major Doolathata thumped the boatman, who instantly cut the motor to a purr; Major Doolathata didn't like to have to raise his voice. "General Phenoboomgarat wishes you to do this," he explained. As he had before; and that was all the explanation, it seemed, that Sanford was going to get.

Sanford closed his eyes as the boat picked up speed again. It was better if he didn't look, anyway, because the boatman's driving made him very nervous. It would have been better still if, when this whole idea came up, he had simply said to the Old Man, "Sorry, Chief, but I don't know a thing about Iriadeska, and besides I'm right in the middle of the Fall promotion for the Pickle and Relish Packers Association"—that is, it would have been better in some respects, though it would very likely have meant that he would now be out of a job. And there weren't that many forty-thousand-dollar-a-year jobs for young public-relations executives just three years out of NYU.

"Charles," the Old Man had said benignly, "this is one of those once-in-a-lifetime chances. Grab it, boy! It's a big one for the agency, because it's our first real opportunity to go global. And it's a big one for you, because one of these days we're going to have an

International Division, and who's going to be in front of you in line to head it if you lick this one?"

That was big talk from the head of a seven-person agency, whose biggest previous accounts had been a fading screen star, a toy manufacturer, and the Pickle and Relish Packers Association. But it could happen! Midgets had overnight become titans in the PR field before, and the flunkies they employed had been suddenly carried to dizzying heights.

So Sanford had packed his bag and hopped his plane, and even gone along, bright-eyed and alert after no more than a few winks of sleep, to take this "orientation tour" of the manifold aspects of the institution he was, presumably, supposed to make lovable, namely the Iriadeskan Army.

It had been quite a surprise to discover what the Iriadeskan Army was like. It wasn't just an army. It was practically a conglomerate. Like any immense corporation, it had diversified. It wasn't just a fighting force—in fact, there was no good reason to believe it was any kind of a fighting force at all because Iriadeska had never been in a war. It did possess tanks and cannons. But it was also the proprietor of a whole Fortune 500 string of business enterprises, plantations like the one he was sailing through, newspapers, radio and television broadcasting stations—even its own First, Second, and Third Military Bank and Trust Companies, all of them getting rich on American off-shore deposits that would positively never be reported to any enforcement agency of the United States or anyone else with an urge to tax. The banks and the media companies had particularly interested the Old Man. "Let them know, Charles," he instructed, "that we control the advertising budgets for many of our clients, besides we give them financial advice on investments. Say, for instance, the pickle people ever decide to expand into Southeast Asia. There's no doubt they'd be spending a big buck on radio and TV and space—and why not on the Iriadeskan Army media?"

Of course, the Old Man's agency didn't really "control" much of anything. The shop lived on crumbs the big boys didn't bother to pick up. But no one in Iriadeska, as the Old Man didn't have to point out, was likely to know that. Especially not that particular

Iriadeskan who had walked in the door with this account, the military attaché of the Iriadeskan mission to the United Nations. Sanford was quite certain that if the man had had that much smarts he would hardly have picked the Old Man's agency in the first place.

Sanford hadn't had much of a chance to spread the Old Man's gospel. He hadn't yet met anybody important enough to lie to. Major Doolathata had come to claim him at the airport, grinning and welcoming as he stood under the hanging model of the Algonquin the spacecraft that was on its way back to Earth, and from then on Sanford had been on the move. He had offered a polite conversational gambit, looking around at the airport's exhibit of Mars photographs and ornate red and gold banners with messages he could not read, since they were in the Iriadeskan language—it was surprising that there was more interest in Mars here in Iriadeska than back home—but the major had only grinned and said, "Yes, it's wonderful, now we must hurry because your boat is waiting." And ever since then Sanford had been exploring the rubber, sugar, and cocoa plantation the Iriadeskan Army called Camp Thungoratakma. He had watched a hundred tiny, wiry Iriadeskans in loincloths and rubber sandals slashing away at acre after acre of sugar cane, and hundreds more making their swift, spiral cuts in the multiple wounded trunks of the rubber trees, to catch the milky ooze that would ultimately be converted into automobile tires, hot-water bottles, and condoms for the world. He had putt-putted along miles of those smelly creeks, wincing as the boatman sliced through the tangles of weed, and swatting at the swarms of insects, feeling the spot at the top of his head where the hair was just a tiny bit thin get hotter and redder every minute. He had—

"What?" he asked, startled. The boatman had cut the motor and Major Doolathata was speaking to him.

"I said," giggled the major, "there is one of our Martians."

Ahead of them, in the middle of a mat of water hyacinths, a broad, stupid head was gazing placidly at them. "What the hell is *that*?" Sanford demanded.

"It is what we call a chupri," the major announced. "It is called elsewhere manatee or dugong. It is said that the chupri is the original of the mermaid myth, although I do not personally think they closely resemble beautiful women, do you?"

He giggled again as Sanford shook his head, and added slyly, "Perhaps what they most closely resemble is something you are quite familiar with, Mr. Sanford."

"And what would that be?" Sanford asked absently, staring at the creature. The head, wide as a cow's, whiskered like a cat's, turned away from them and resumed munching the weeds. It certainly did not look like a mermaid. It was even uglier than a sea elephant, and less graceful. It was a lump of water-borne blubber the size of a compact car.

The major was carefully unlocking his shiny pigskin attaché case to pull out a limp, worn copy of *Advertising Age*. "You of course remember this, Mr. Sanford," he said pleasantly.

Mr. Sanford of course did. It wasn't something he would forget. It was the very first time in his life that his picture had made the front page of anything. To be sure, the little snapshot wasn't just him; his was a single face in a group photo of the agency's entire staff, posed at the Toy Fair where they had introduced Mindy Mars and the rest of the line. The caption said, "Executives launch Mars spinoffs," and it was true enough—even the word "executives," because every employee of the agency was an executive, or at least had the title of Director of Something-or-Other or Project Manager for This-or-That—all but Christie, the receptionist, and she was just too pretty to be left out of the picture.

"Yes, that was the Toy Fair," Sanford said, remembering. They had all worked feverishly to get the Martian doll line ready for it; if you didn't exhibit at the Toy Fair you didn't get anything in the stores for Christmas. So they had all been co-opted, even Sanford, though it hadn't been his account. He was the one who stood over the artists while they airbrushed the immense blowup of a NASA photograph of a Martian that was the backdrop for the booth, with the rack of Mindy Mars and Max Mars dolls before it.

The major gave him another unfathomable wink and carefully put the paper away again. "We will say nothing more of this now," he warned. "Now we must hurry back to your appointment in Pnik."

At once the boatman jazzed up the outboard motor and though Sanford immediately asked what the sudden hurry was, the major only shrugged and winked again. Sanford craned his neck to stare after the chupri as the boat circled around and began its return dash. Something was stirring in his mind. What had it been, the major's incomprehensibly irrelevant remark about—

It clicked. He leaned over to the major and yelled, "It *does* look like a Martian!" And the major beamed, and then frowned warningly, shaking his head.

Baffled, Sanford watched the creature out of sight. Yes. Add the stiltlike legs that had been so much trouble to work into Mindy and Max (not too stiff! Children could poke their eyes out. But stiff enough to hold the damn thing—) . . . add a few changes in the facial features, especially the eyes . . . yes, it did look like the Martians, a little bit. At least Sanford thought it did, maybe. It was hard to be sure, since no one on Earth had yet seen a live Martian. The expedition that had discovered them was on its way back to Earth with half a dozen of the creatures, and of course there had been pictures on the TV—endless pictures; in fact, they had become something of a bore.

All right; this chupri thing looked something like a Martian; but what possible difference did that make to anybody?

When they reached the dock he sprang ashore, looking around. There was nothing to see; no one was there to meet them. Major Doolathata erupted into a storm of furious, high-pitched Iriadeskan that sent the boatman off on an agitated run to the parking lot behind the palm trees. "The car will be here in a moment," he apologized. "These people! One simply can't depend on them."

"Yeah," Sanford said absently. He had a new puzzle. At the larger freight-loading pier a few yards downstream a boatload of farm workers was disembarking. As they stepped ashore in their loincloths each one marched past a long table heaped with articles of apparel. *Uniform* apparel. Each little man picked up in turn blouse, shorts, steel helmet and boots, putting them on as they progressed, so that the farm workers at the river end of the table had metamorphosized by the time they reached its far end into active-duty soldiers of the Iriadeskan Army. They filed away through the trees toward dimly visible buses; and, although Sanford could not see clearly, it appeared that as each one boarded a bus he was issued an ugly little rapid-fire carbine.

The major was watching Sanford watch the men. "You see it," said Major Doolathata proudly. "Very tough troops, these men. It is an honor to command them."

Sanford offered, "I thought they were farm workers."

The major giggled. "Farm workers of course, surely. Also combat troops, for who would be better than soldiers to work in the fields of the Iriadeskan Army?"

Sanford smiled. It took some work, but he was making the effort, however irritating Major Doolathata was, to keep on good terms with the man. "And now, I suppose, they're going somewhere to practice close-order drill or something like that?"

"Something like that," Major Doolathata agreed. "Ah, here is your car. In just a short time now we will have you in Pnik for your meeting with General Phenoboomgarat."

It did not, however, work out that way.

When they reached the Fourth Armored Army's headquarters a female officer with colonel's insignia came out and engaged in a long, feverish conversation in Iriadeskan with the major. Then the major, looking angry, strode away, and the colonel turned to Sanford. "General Phenoboomgarat has been called away on urgent business," she explained in perfect, idiomatic American English. "I will take you to your hotel, where you can rest and enjoy an excellent lunch until you are called for."

One had to get used to Iriadeskan ways, Sanford thought with resignation. Anyway, a rest sounded good. Lunch sounded even better, because Sanford hadn't had time for breakfast and his befuddled metabolism was assuring him that, whatever number of clock hours or days had or had not elapsed, it was well past time to eat again. "What's your name?" he asked as the car turned toward the riverfront.

"I don't think you could pronounce my name, Mr. Sanford," said the girl, "but you can call me Emily. Tell me. How are things in America? What's the new music? Are there any good new films?"

Neither of those were subjects Sanford had expected to come up in Iriadeska, but the colonel's face under the uniform cap was pretty and putting on a military tunic had not kept her from adding, Sanford's nose informed him, a charming hint of Chanel. Inside the car she seemed far less an alien military officer and far more an attractive young woman. Sanford did his best to tell her about the Madison Square Garden concert he had attended the month before, and what the reviewers said about the latest batch from Hollywood; and they were at the hotel before he was ready for it.

At the registration desk she was all officer again, firm with the clerk, peremptory with the head waiter of the hotel restaurant—all of it in Iriadeskan, of course. Then she said to Sanford, "I will leave you here to enjoy your meal. All of your expenses will, of course, be met by the Iriadeskan Army, so do not allow them to ask you for any money. Not even tips! Especially not tips, because Americans always tip too much and then these people get sullen when they must serve an Iriadeskan."

"I would enjoy my meal more if you could keep me company," Sanford suggested; and when she smiled and shook her head, pressed a little harder: "I have so many questions about my responsibilities here—"

"Such as?"

"Well, there's this business about the Martians. I wondered—"

But she was suddenly stern. "Please be careful of your conversation here in the hotel! Everything will be explained, Mr. Sanford. Now I must return to my duties."

Sanford sighed and watched her leave, then allowed the head waiter to seat him.

The hotel dining room was vast, marbled, draped, and nearly empty. Sanford puzzled despairingly over the mimeographed menu for several minutes, trying to assess what might be edible among dishes like "twice-cooked fiathia with seven-moons rice" and "cinnamon perch, crayfish sauce." Then an altercation among the idling knot of waiters at the far end of the room at last produced a handsome menu the size of a newspaper page, in English and French.

It didn't end there, though. The waiter shook his head over Sanford's request for the breast of duck with Madagascar pepper sauce; no duck today, he indicated. Also no lamb cutlets with honeyflavored lamb gravy, also no poached filet of Iriadeskan mountain trout. When Sanford finally put his finger on the club sandwich à la Americain the waiter beamed in congratulation; the foreigner had at last struck on a winning choice.

Sanford had the good sense to order tea instead of coffee to go with the meal. The tea arrived in a pewter mug with the Lipton's tag hanging over the side; that, at least, was a known quantity. The club sandwich was less encouraging. One layer seemed to be a sort of egg salad, with unidentified red and brown things chopped into it. The other was meat on a bed of lettuce, but what the meat had been when alive Sanford could not determine.

Still, it was chewable, and not obviously decayed. Sanford's hunger overcame diffidence. He even began to relax. It was the first time in very many hours that that had been possible. What the future held was undecidable but at least, Sanford told himself, he was on an important job in a highly exotic place. He tried to remember if any of his jet-setting acquaintances had ever mentioned dropping in on Iriadeska and came up empty. If only he had brought a camera! It would have been worth doing to be able to say to a date, "Oh, listen, I've got these slides—temples, Buddhas, elephants . . ." And he had actually seen all those things, even though briefly out of the window of a moving car. Maybe if he got this job well started there would be time for sightseeing. Time to get a better look at those funny idols with Abe Lincoln stovepipe hats—if idols was what they were, and not just ornamentation—and get out into the countryside again to see some of those elephants at work . . .

He perceived he had company.

Two saffron-robed monks had entered the dining room, a skinny young one and an immensely fat older one, both holding their begging bowls before them. Six waiters materialized at once to bow to the monks, take their bowls, convoy them to Sanford's table, and race around to bring glasses, pitchers of ice water, even a vase of orchids. The monks seated themselves without invitation. The fat, old one beamed at Sanford, and the skinny young one said, in excellent English, "This is Am Sattaroothata. He bids you good morning."

"Good morning to you too," said Sanford uncertainly. Was he supposed to give them money? Would that be a terrible, unforgivable social blunder? Was this one of the categories Colonel Emily had meant to include under "tipping"?

The young monk went on, bringing the balls of his fingertips together as he spoke the name, "Am Sattaroothata is a very wise and holy man with many, many devoted followers. He is also the brother, on both sides, of General Phenoboomgarat. Furthermore, Am Sattaroothata—" fingers pressed together—"wishes me to inform you that he is really not prejudiced against Americans at all."

Sanford was saved from having to respond to this piece of information by a pleased grunt from Am Sattaroothata. The waiters had come back, bringing the filled begging bowls. Actually, "filled" applied only to the fat monk's bowl. The younger one's contained only a few lentils, a dab of rice, and what might have been a single, thin strip of some kind of dried fish. Am Sattaroothata's, on the other hand, was a symphony. There were crisp stalks of sliced celery, carrot, and other crudites, all tastefully arranged around canapes delicately constructed of pates and bright pink tiny shrimp, topped with rosettes of cheese or scarlet pimientoes or what certainly looked a great deal like caviar. Am Sattaroothata grunted to the young monk to proceed while he waded in.

"It was Am Sattaroothata," said the young monk, resolutely not looking at his superior's bowl, "who choose your firm to assist in our public-relations situation here in Pnik, Mr. Sanford. He was greatly disappointed in the failure of your predecessors to come to terms with the urgency of the matter."

"Now, wait a minute," cried Sanford, suddenly concerned. "What urgency? For that matter, what predecessors? No one said anything to me about having some other PR people here."

The young monk looked alarmed. He turned beseechingly toward Am Sattaroothata, fingers pressed so tightly together that Sanford could see the dark skin whitening around the fingernails. He whispered urgently in Iriadeskan at some length. Am Sattaroothata heard him out, then shrugged. As the younger monk returned to Sanford, Am Sattaroothata glanced casually over his shoulders at the cluster of hovering waiters. That was all it took. They whisked away his now empty bowl and returned it in seconds, wiped spotless, now with a wine bottle in it. Sanford had barely time to read the words "Mouton Rothschild" on the label before one waiter whisked it out of the bowl to uncork, while another set a long-stemmed crystal goblet before the monk, and the remainder bore the empty bowl away.

While the wine waiter was pouring out a drop for Am Sattaroothata to taste, the other monk began to explain. "Six months ago, Mr. Sanford," he said, "even before this matter of the Martians came up—"

Explosion of wine in an angry bellow from Am Sattaroothata, and the younger monk looked up in agony. "It is not important about the Martians yet, Mr. Sanford," he said, cringing. "Allow me to say this in proper order. At that time it was decided that our valiant Iriadeskan Army, while ever unchallenged in battle, had failed to win the hearts and minds of the Iriadeskan people to the degree properly earned by their valor, constancy, diligence, and unflagging loyalty to the state." He glanced at his superior, who seemed to have settled down, and then, longingly, at the sparse and still untouched contents of his bowl. "So therefore, Mr. Sanford, an American public-relations firm was employed to help bring this message to our people, at a cost of many tens of thousands of rupiyit."

Am Sattaroothata, absently sipping his wine, gave a peremptory grunt. The young monk flinched and spoke faster. "To make a long story short, Mr. Sanford, two weeks ago, just when they were most needed, these other Americans resigned the account and left without notice, thus greatly inconveniencing our plans at a critical juncture—"

"Now, hold it right there," Sanford snapped, putting down the remains of his tasteless sandwich. "I want to know more about this other outfit, Mr.—say, what's your name, anyway?"

The young monk turned miserably to the other for instructions, got a negligent nod.

"I am Am Bhopru, Mr. Sanford," he said, "but my name is of no importance. May I proceed? Am Sattaroothata wishes me to explain to you at once your mission and the significant state purposes it will serve."

"Hell," said Sanford, but only in a mutter. The situation was not new. He had felt just this way, back in his freshman year in college, when he had for the first time tried using a computer to whip up a synoptic report on a marketing development in his first business-management course. The thing would give him all the information he wanted. But it would do it at its own pace and after its own style, and if he tried to short-cut its processes he simply fried the program. "Go ahead," he said sulkily, his attention diverted by the waiters hurrying back with Am Sattaroothata's bowl. It now contained what Sanford was quite sure was the breast of duck with Madagascar pepper sauce, flanked by perfectly steamed broccoli and zucchini, with two orchids tastefully laid across the rim. Sanford glared at the remains of his miserable sandwich in disgust, hardly hearing Am Bhopru's long-winded explanations.

The young monk was, after a fashion, answering his question. The previous PR team, it turned out, had come from one of Mad-Ave's highest-powered public-relations firms. They had operated on the grand scale, starting with an all-out public-opinion polling survey. "That was completed within one week of commencement of operations," said Am Bhopru, "and you will be supplied, of course, with complete transcripts of their findings."

"Who did the polling?" asked Sanford.

"Oh, that was quite easy. Am Sattaroothata instructed fifty of his followers to seek enlightenment in this way."

Sanford shrugged; it was seldom a good idea to have interested parties do your polling, but he saw no point in bringing it up yet. And evidently there had been at least a sizeable effort. The monks had covered most of the neighborhoods of Pnik and even out into the fishing villages and farm communities and hill towns. "So the pulse of the Iriadeskan people has been taken," said Am Bhopru, and added proudly, "Of course, all of the data have been stored in our computer, and the printouts are here."

He pulled a thick sheaf of tractor-feed paper out of the recesses of his robe and passed it over the table. "Perhaps you will be good enough to look it over now," he said, and then, with an apologetic fingertip-touch to Am Sattaroothata, began greedily shoveling in the lentils and rice from his bowl.

Sandord struggled with the folded sheets. They were filled with tables and graphs and, although each page was neatly numbered, there was no sort of index to guide him in searching for some sort of summary or overview. In any case, he ran out of time. He had barely begun to read *Major Policy Issues, First Survey*, when Am Sattaroothata, picking duck out of his teeth, signaled the waiters. Immediately they flocked to take his bowl. It reappeared in a moment, scoured clean and filled with petit fours and fresh pineapple chunks, but the fat monk shook his head.

Am Bhopru gamely tried speaking while at the same time scooping the last of his rice into his mouth, and managed, "Is time, Mr. Sanford." (Chew, swallow.) "Is time for us to go to headquarters of General Phenoboomgarat. A car is waiting." And he managed to swallow the last mouthful and give his bowl a brisk wipe with his napkin just as four waiters, two on each side, surrounded Am Sattaroothata and helped him, grunting, to his feet.

The car was a custom-stretched Cadillac, easily fourteen feet long. The seating in it was according to rank. Am Sattaroothata got the huge rear seat to sprawl in all by himself. A jump seat was pulled down for Am Bhopru, while Sanford, with his ten yards of printout, went up front, next to the uniformed driver.

Like every Asiatic city, Pnik's streets were densely packed with human beings using every form of transport possible. There were huge tour buses, mostly empty, and garishly painted city buses, almost as big. There were the converted flat-bed trucks with wooden benches installed that they called mini-buses; there were taxicabs of the standard worldwide sort, and those of the other, three-wheeled variety called tuk-tuks, with their open seats and motorcycle engines. There were real motorbikes and scooters; there were people on bicycles, usually two on each, one impassively riding the handlebars; and, in and around all the vehicles; there were pedestrians. Millions of pedestrians. They dawdled at the open-fronted shops and ambled across the streets and haggled at the hawker-food stands along the curbs; they were everywhere. Almost everywhere. Though the streets were narrow and the traffic nearly solid, somehow the huge limousine purred through. Channels of clear space opened around it, as if it were a water-taxi slashing through the mats of water-hyacinth on the Choomli River. Sanford could not tell exactly how that happened. The pedestrians did not seem conscious of the car. They didn't even seem to look at it, and the soldier-chauffeur never blew his horn. But wherever he chose to turn, aisles of space appeared.

Sanford spent little time looking at the scenery. His big interest was in his bale of tractor-feed, and he flipped it clumsily back and forth as he rode, searching for answers, or at least clues. It was a gift of God that it should have been there for him . . . but there was so much of it! And not just text. There were pie-charts and graphs and histograms, most of them in brilliant color; there were long tables of numerical data, and parenthetical summaries of the statistical tests, chi-squared and more sophisticated ones still, that had been carried out in support of the conclusions.

And there were conclusions.

When Sanford found them he sighed in relief. The relief didn't last. The conclusions were clear enough; his predecessors had measured Iriadeskan public opinion on many questions. It was the questions that were surprising.

The main issues polled were ten:

1. High taxes.
2. Increase in national debt.
3. Corruption in government.
4. Worsening balance of payments.
5. Urban crime and river/canal piracy.
6. Lack of appropriate employment for college graduates.

7. Iriadeskan government attitude toward Martians.

8. Failure to build additional temples.

9. Improper observance of major religious holidays.

10. Lack of sufficient funds to properly train and equip valorous soldiers of Glorious Iriadeskan Army.

Sanford gazed out the window, frowning. Peculiar! Not the first five questions, of course—they were the sort of thing the citizens of almost any country in the world, including his own, might be concerned about. But in the responses to the polls, all five of those were well down on the list of Iriadeskan worries! Even stranger, when the respondents were asked to rank their major concerns in order, the top of the charts, by a large margin, was concern that the army wasn't getting enough money—followed closely by disapproval of the government's attitudes toward the Martians!

It was positively astonishing how often the Martians seemed to come up in this place—and positively annoying how little anyone seemed to want to talk about it.

Sanford swiveled around in his seat, waving the sheaf of papers. "Hey!" he cried. "What's all this Martian—"

He couldn't finish because Am Bhopru leaned quickly forward and pressed a palm over Sanford's mouth; it smelled of fish and cloves and cigarette smoke, and it effectively cut Sanford off in the middle of a sentence. "Please!" the monk whispered urgently. "You must not speak now. Am Sattaroothata is meditating."

It didn't look like meditating to Sanford. The fat monk seemed sound asleep, and in fact Sanford could hear gentle snores coming from the shaved, lowered head. Fuming, Sanford turned back to the printouts.

Riffling through the sheets he found—if not exactly answers—at least supplementary data. There had not been a single poll. There had been, it seemed, one every ten days, and the ranking of matters of concern had changed markedly over the time involved.

There was, for instance, a graph showing the increase in concern over the Martian question that showed almost negligible interest a few months ago, gaining steadily at every sampling until it approached the Number One money-for-the-army question in importance. While the army budget question had started strong, in third place after the two religious questions, and finished stronger, in fact all by itself at the top.

You could understand that, in a way, thought Sanford, frowning to himself. The way the army question was put was highly slanted; it forced an answer, which was bad polling practice. He was surprised that a reputable public-relations agency had phrased it that way, in violation of all established procedures . . . though, no doubt, they had been subject to a certain amount of pressure, since it was the Glorious Iriadeskan Army who had been their, as well as his own, employers. Certainly it meant that there was a substantial chance of error in the numbers generated . . .

But not enough of a chance to alter the fact that Iriadeskans seemed very much to want more money given to their army.

And that did not in any way explain the Martian vote.

Sanford folded the sheets and gazed unseeingly out at the hordes around him. Something drastic had been going on in Iriadeska. But what?

He tried to calculate. The earliest polls had been taken four months earlier. That took him back to June. Had something special happened with the Iriadeskan Army in June?

If so, he realized, no amount of cudgeling his brains would tell him what it had been, since he had barely heard of Iriadeska in June. Maybe someone would tell him if he asked the right questions, but that would have to wait until he was allowed to open his mouth.

All right, then, what about the Martians. Had something special happened with the Martians in June?

He couldn't think of anything. They had taken off in January. One of them had died a month later. The expedition was due to land fairly soon—within the next week or two, if he remembered correctly. But how could any of that account for a sudden surge of interest four months back, while they were doing nothing more interesting than dawdling through space on their interminable return flight?

There was one thing that could account for sudden interest in any subject. He knew what that was because it was what he did for a living. It was called "publicity."

Had the Iriadeskan Army, for reasons not known, hired the PR firm to whip up Iriadeskan interest in the Martians as well as in itself? And, if so, for God's sake, *why*?

"Mr. Sanford?"

He turned, blinking. It was Am Bhopru, leaning forward to whisper urgently in his ear. "We are almost there," he said, contriving to watch worriedly the sleeping older monk while whispering to Sanford. "When we pass the sentries at the entrance to the compound, please be sure not to make any sudden movements."

Sudden movements?

Sanford had another of those nasty, shrinking feelings. What kind of place was he going to, where something might go wrong if he moved the wrong way? He blinked out the window. They were still moving through narrow streets, but most of the traffic was gone. No more buses of any kind, a handful of pedal-bicyclists scattering away out of sight as fast as they could go, pedestrians vanishing into buildings. The big Cadillac limousine had the streets almost to itself, except for an occasional hurrying tuk-tuk.

And, funnily, all the tuk-tuks seemed to have several things in common. They were all going in the same direction—toward the Army compound, along with Sanford's own vehicle. And every one of the tuk-tuk drivers had an identical expression of worry on his face and identically carried a single passenger—an Iriadeskan Army soldier—and each one had one of those nasty carbines across his knees.

The young woman with the colonel's insignia on her uniform conducted Sanford wordlessly into the headquarters building. She did not respond to his greeting. She didn't even smile. She simply led the way to a door and threw it open. Pressing her fingertips together, she said, "General Tupalakuli and General Phenoboomgarat, this is Mr. Charles Sanford."

Sanford wondered if he should bow—or kneel, or crawl on his belly like a worm; he compromised by nodding his head briefly, looking at his employers. General Tupalakuli was short and skinny, General Phenoboomgarat was short and fat. They wore identical gold-braided officers' uniforms of the Iriadeskan Army and sat at identical teak desks the size of billiard tables. Each desk was angled slightly, so that they converged on the spot where Sanford was standing, in the center of the room. On a staff between them was the Iriadeskan flag, three broad bars of green, white, and violet, with twenty-seven stars that represented the twenty-seven islands of the Iriadeskan archipelago.

The colonel—had she said her name was Emily?—pressed her fingertips respectfully together before her breast and said, "This is Mr. Charles Sanford." Then, to Sanford, "General Phenoboomgarat and General Tupalakuli welcome you to the cause of the Glorious Iriadeskan Army. General Tupalakuli and General Phenoboomgarat wish you to know that you will be given every possible assistance in the accomplishment of your mission. General Phenoboomgarat and General Tupalakuli ask how long it will take you to draft your first proclamation, expressing the need of the Glorious Iriadeskan Army for a fifty-five percent increase in its annual budget, with escalator clauses for inflation?"

Sanford swallowed and glanced around. What he had not at first noticed was that there was another door to the room. It was half open, and through it he could see the two monks, the fat one reclining on a love seat, the skinny one hovering nervously behind him. Am Sattaroothata beamed encouragingly at Sanford. Am Bhopru merely looked frightened at being present at this meeting taking place at the highest of all levels.

Sanford returned to Colonel Emily. He licked his lips and did his best with the question she had asked. "Well," he said, "if I had a typewriter and some paper, and someone to fill me in on the issues—maybe a couple of hours, I guess."

The colonel looked scandalized. She glanced at the two generals and lowered her voice, though neither of them showed any signs of comprehension, much less concern. "You do not have hours, Mr. Sanford! There are many, many proclamations and that is only the first. Can't you type fast? Remember, what you write I then have to translate into Iriadeskan and submit it to General Phe—General Tupalakuli and General Phenoboomgarat," she corrected herself, tardily remembering where she had been in the rotation to give each one equal eminence. "No, hours are out of the—"

She stopped before the word "question" because, evidently, there was even less time than she had thought. The phones on the desks of the two generals rang simultaneously. Each general picked up his phone and listened silently for a moment, then they gazed at each other. "Yom?" General Phenoboomgarat asked. "Yom," General Tupalakuli confirmed. They both said, "Yom!" into their telephones and slammed them down in unison.

"It is starting," the colonel whispered.

Outside, in the courtyard of the Army compound, there was a sudden racket of engines starting: deep thudding diesels, yapping little put-puts. In the room still a third door opened, and a lieutenant entered bearing a folded cloth. With an apologetic salute to each of the two generals, the lieutenant began to take down the Iriadeskan flag from its staff.

Sanford said desperately, "What's going on?"

The colonel glanced at the two generals, and then said, "Why, the Iriadeskan people are about to take back power from the corrupt bureaucrats under the wise leadership of General, uh, Phenoboomgarat and General Tupalakuli, of course. See for yourself." And she indicated the window looking out on the courtyard.

Dazedly, Sanford stared out at the scene. The throbbing basso-profundo motors belonged to tanks—big ones, at least twenty of them, with wicked-looking cannon snaking back and forth from their turrets as they began to grumble forward. The higher-pitched noises were tuk-tuks. There seemed to be hundreds of the little three-wheeled vehicles. Each one was driven by a soldier, with three more soldiers crammed into the passenger seat behind him, and all of them armed with the rapid-fire weapons.

"Oh my God," Sanford whispered.

The colonel said crossly, "Now you see why things must be done at once. Please stand at attention!"

Sanford blinked at her. She was standing militarily erect. So were the two generals at their desks. Through the open door he could see Am Bhopru helping his fat superior to struggle to his feet, and all of them raising their right hands in salute.

The lieutenant had taken down the old flag and a new one hung in its place.

At first Sanford thought there had been no change; the broad bars were the same, and the design in the ensign was hidden in the folds of the cloth.

Then the lieutenant reverently pulled it taut, holding his salute.

The twenty-seven stars were gone. In their place, woven in threads of silver, was the image of—a manatee? A Mindy Mars doll?

No. It was the image of a seal-like creature with spindly legs like those of a newborn racehorse, just like the ones that were slowly coasting toward their landing on Earth in the returning spacecraft of the Seerseller expedition.

It was a Martian.

The typewriter was not a typewriter. It was a word processor, and the room it was in was not an office. It was a television studio. The TV station was located in the heart of the military compound, red lights flashing from the tops of its antennae. It was in the tallest building of the lot, surrounded by squat barracks and armories and headquarters buildings; it was a good seven stories tall, not counting the skeletal antenna structure that added another hundred feet.

Crossing the parade grounds to the television studio, Sanford and the colonel had had to dodge for their lives between the columns of ponderous tanks, sorting themselves into a line of march toward the main gate, with the supporting motorized infantry in their tuk-tuks racing their motors to take position behind the armor. Every vehicle bore a brand-new Iriadeskan flag, proudly displayed. And every flag bore the Martian design.

Sanford was full of questions. The colonel forbade him to ask them. "Later," she snapped. "First the proclamations! The march will begin at any moment, and we must have the broadcast ready!"

It wasn't easy. The word processor was a brand unfamiliar to Sanford. The colonel had to set it up for him and stand over him while he typed, grabbing at his hand when he seemed to be reaching for the key that would erase all he had done, or cause the program to suspend operations while it stored a backup record, or perhaps switch to some other mode entirely. But once he had the hang of it, he typed fast.

This sort of thing was in the best traditions of his craft. Many were the times when the Old Man, or some other Old Man, had come beaming and gently deprecating into the copywriters' room at the close of a business day, to announce there was a fire to be put out and they could all phone their wives to say that dinner would be late. Many was the stick of copy Sanford had hammered out, under the gun of a newsbreak, or to counter a competitor's sudden thrust. It had never been quite like this, though. Never before had Sanford had to create powerful prose—powerful *translation-proof* prose, since he knew nothing of the Iriadeskan language his words were to be translated into, and could not risk word-play or jokes—on a subject of which he knew nothing, for an audience he had never encountered, on a machine he had never used before. When he had managed to hit a *Cancel* key a moment before the colonel's hand could stop him, and wiped out three lines, she gritted her teeth and pushed him away from the chair. "Just dictate," she ordered. "I will type. What you must say is that the New People's Reform Government, responding to the righteous needs and wishes of the Iriadeskan masses, has taken over the functions of the corruption-ridden and entrenched old power elite, for the purpose of inaugurating a new era of peace, prosperity and reform for the proud Iriadeskan nation, under the wise leadership of the Glorious Iriadeskan Army."

"Hey," said Sanford, "that's fine the way it is. What do you need me for?"

"Just dictate," she ordered, and after a few false starts they had produced Communiqué No. 1:

People of Iriadeska!
This is the dawn of a new day for Iriadeska! The New People's
Reform Movement, wisely responding to the just needs and
aspirations of the Iriadeskan people, has kicked from office the

petty bureaucrats and corrupt officials of the scandal-ridden and incompetent usurpers of power. This is the first day of the triumphant rebirth of the Iriadeskan nation, moving promptly and surely to a time of peace, prosperity, freedom, and reform for all Iriadeskans. Long live the Glorious Iriadeskan Nation and its beloved allies from afar!

"What's that about allies from afar?" Sanford asked, peering over the colonel's shoulder.

"Later, later," she said absently, beginning to translate it into Iriadeskan. He backed away to leaver her to it, not dissatisfied. It wasn't sparkling prose. It wasn't even *his* prose, or most of it wasn't, because the colonel had edited as she typed. But it was, after all, a pretty fair first try for a man whose major recent work had been devoted principally to the task of persuading American consumers that no table was properly set for a meal without the presence of a jar of pickles and at least one kind of preserved condiment.

The colonel gnawed a knuckle as the printer zipped the words onto paper. Then, without speaking, she rushed out of the room with the copy.

Only minutes later, Sanford had the satisfaction of seeing Am Sattaroothata himself on the desk TV, reading the proclamation aloud in Iriadeskan. He listened attentively to the unfamiliar words that had come, at least partly, out of his own brain. It sounded, he decided, very Iriadeskan. When the old monk stopped reading he gazed benignly into the camera for a few minutes, while music played—no doubt the Iriadeskan national anthem.

Then the screen went to black.

Tardily, Sanford wondered how the revolution was going. In the soundproofed TV studio there was no hint of what went on outside.

But there was a hall just outside the door, and a window at the end of the hall.

There was also a pair of Iriadeskan soldiers standing there with guns at the ready, Sanford discovered when he opened the door. They only glanced at him, though, and turned back to the stairwell, perhaps ready to repel any scandal-ridden and incompetent corrupt bureaucrats who might attack. Sanford walked cautiously to the window and glanced out at the courtyard.

He had supposed that the tank column had already left to fulfill its mission. It hadn't. All the tanks and tuk-tuks were still right there, just as before, except that now they were all motionless and their engines seemed to have been turned off.

The guards stiffened to present arms. Sanford turned apprehensively, just in time to see Colonel Emily appear on the stairs. "Oh, there you are," she said breathlessly. "I just came to tell you that there is a policy matter that must be decided. Study the former proclamations. I will return shortly." And she turned and hurried back out again.

"Shortly" turned out, in fact, to be rather longly. Sanford spent twenty minutes or so puzzling over the last batch of communiques, issued by some previous "New People's Revolutionary Something-or-other Government," trying to find out just what he was expected to do. Many of them had to do with the questions his predecessors had polled—more money for the army, jobs for the unemployed college graduates, temples, subsidies for young men when they put in their customary year of monkhood. But some were quite odd, notably one that said:

> *Humble and reverential Iriadeskans! The Elephant is our Mother and our Beloved! All revere the Elephant for its wisdom, gentleness, and grace! In the symbol of the Elephant lies our strength and our glory. Let no one dare defame the precious Creature, for just as the Elephant is the loving preserver of Man, so will the Holy National Reform Enlightenment Movement be the loving servant, teacher, and ever-righteous guide to the reverential and obedient masses of the Iriadeskan people.*

Perhaps, he decided, it sounded better in Iriadeskan, but it didn't seem to move him very much. And the colonel still had not returned.

Sanford risked another look out the hall window. Nothing had changed. Nothing looked as though it ever would change. The tanks seemed fixed to the parade ground as firmly as war memorials. The soldiers were squatting in groups about the courtyard, smoking fat yellow cigarettes and chatting desultorily among themselves.

And Sanford's physical exhaustion was beginning to catch up with him.

He glanced at his wristwatch, still on U.S.A. Eastern time. He despaired of trying to convert it to whatever they used in Iriadeska, but the watch told him unequivocally enough that it had been either twenty-nine or forty-one hours since he had boarded his first plane at Kennedy, his head full of the Old Man's last-minute instructions. "The first thing you do," he had ordered, "is send me a full situation report. Don't leave out a thing, and don't let them put you on anything that will keep you from doing that *first.*" Well, that certainly hadn't happened the way it was supposed to. Would there be trouble over that when he got back? Could he have done any different? The Old Man had gone on: "This could be The Big One, Charlie, so make sure I know what's what. I want to know everything there is to know about the situation in Irano—Iderian—"

"Iriadeska," Sanford had supplied. "Right, Chief!"

But yessing the Old Man and carrying out the Old Man's orders were two different things, and no one had said anything about Martians, elephants, or an armed revolution. What possible situation report could Sanford now file, assuming he would be allowed to file any, that would convey to the Old Man, sitting in the Old Man's big, bare office overlooking the noisy traffic of Fifty-seventh Street, just what sort of can of worms Sanford was being required to untangle on the steamy opposite side of the world? He wouldn't believe it! Sanford managed a wry grin, thinking of the Old Man's expression if he got such a report—If a truthful report could be filed without once and for always breaching the mutual cozy agency-client relationship the Old Man prized—If any report at all could be filed, anyway, without some potentially very unpleasant consequences to Sanford himself—

He stiffened, staring down at the parade ground.

There in the floodlights, picking his way daintily among the troops and vehicles, was a short, skinny man in a general's uniform.

Behind him were two Iriadeskan soldiers. Their carbines were at the ready, and as they followed they watched the general's every move.

If the man in the general's uniform was under arrest, as it certainly seemed he was, it did not appear to disturb his disdainful poise.

But it certainly disturbed Sanford's poise. Quite a lot. Because, even at that distance, and with the lighting as chancy as it was, he was quite sure that the man being taken away under guard was the co-leader of this coup, or revolution, or spontaneous people's uprising against the corrupt bureaucrats, or whatever it was he had stumbled into. Specifically, it was General Tupalakuli.

Although there was no casting couch in the studio, the armchairs were not hopelessly uncomfortable. Certainly they were a lot better than the airplane seats Sanford had spent so much of his recent past in. When Colonel Emily at last returned he was fast asleep.

"Wake up, wake up," she said crossly, and Sanford did. She helped the process a little by providing coffee—what she called coffee, anyway. She had cups, and a jar of some Asiatic brand of instant, and a huge thermos of nearly boiling water.

By the time he had forced half of the first scalding cup down, Sanford was awake enough to ask questions. The answers he got, though, were not very illuminating. Yes, Emily admitted, the man under guard was in fact General Tupalakuli. Why was he arrested? Why, she parroted, he had revealed himself an enemy of the Iriadeskan masses; therefore the New People's Reform Government had been forced to remove him from his position of trust. But that would not prevent the successful accomplishment of the coup, she explained. General Phenoboomgarat and his brother, the monk Am Sattaroothata, were even now engaged in high-level policy discussions which would in fact have the effect of strengthening still further the invincible New People's Reform Government—

And then she stopped and took a sip of coffee, watching Sanford over the rim of the cup, and finally grinned. "Well," she said, "that's more or less true. Actually it was mostly a question of leadership posts."

"Meaning what?" demanded Sanford.

"General Tupalakuli wanted his wife's uncle to be appointed Iriadeskan Ambassador to the United Nations because it's in New York and he has always been fond of Broadway musicals. General Phenoboomgarat, however, had already promised it to his second son's mother-in-law's brother."

"Are you serious?" asked Sanford, startled. The colonel shrugged, and at last he laughed out loud. "When in Rome," he said, and thought for a minute. He frowned. "General Tupalakuli's wife's uncle sounds like a closer relative," he pointed out.

"Oh, surely. But there are other considerations. Mainly, General Phenoboomgarat's second son's mother-in-law's brother has three estates in California and part of a condo development in Connecticut. He wants to keep an eye on them. It's always useful to have something like that," she explained. "If a coup goes sour and somebody has to go into exile, it's nice to have somewhere to go to."

Sanford opened his mouth to speak, and then closed it again. He looked at her wonderingly, and caught her glancing at her watch. "These high-level discussions," he said. "How long are they likely to take?"

"At least a couple of hours yet," she told him. "Air Chief Marshal Pittikudaru has to helicopter in from his base at the Choomli River delta, but he won't leave until he is assured that the general of either the Fourth or the Seventh Paratroop Brigade is supporting the coup. And they're waiting to see if His Majesty is going to take a position."

"Will he?"

"His Majesty? Oh," she said thoughtfully, "probably not. He's got about as many relatives on one side as he has on the other. But no one is sure because he's on a state visit to America and he hasn't yet said anything. If he turned out to be for us, or neutral, then everything can go ahead as planned—not counting General Tupalakuli, although then he might come back in. But if the king is against, then that's all different. It might mean almost anything. Probably at least somebody from the royal family may have to be included because, you see, General Tupalakuli's father-in-law used to be His Majesty's father's first prime minister, and so he was close to the court. On the other hand, His Majesty *does* have strong feelings now and then."

"So he might intervene for one side or the other?" Sanford offered, trying to keep up.

"No, no! Not for a *side*. His Majesty doesn't get into *politics*. He is—oh, I don't know how to explain this to you—the king is like supreme in matters of *tradition*, and *religion*, and, well, good taste, do you see?"

"I don't see," Sanford said despairingly. "Start from the beginning, won't you?"

Fortunately, Colonel Emily didn't take him at his word. Iriadeskan history went back seventeen hundred years, and all of them were full of plots, conspiracies and coups-d'etat. She went back only as far as World War II, when the then king had been an unusually popular—which was to say, fairly popular—and relatively secure monarch who had made one little mistake. He thought that when the Japanese took over from the French and British, who had divided Iriadeska between them for a couple of hundred years, the Japanese would stay. The 1945 surrender was a crushing blow. He didn't think the returning Europeans would like keeping him on the throne, and he was right. They didn't. So the collaborator king abdicated and spent the rest of his life, happily enough, in Antibes. A nephew was crowned. The boy had been in Oxford when the war broke out. He spent the entire war there, in the uniform of the R.A.F., safely assigned to ground duties. He had developed into a loyal subject of the British crown.

Unfortunately for the dynasty, that didn't work out either. Independence came. The young king didn't get deposed. He was simply required to turn the governance of Iriadeska over to a Council of Ministers. There it had remained ever since, with continual ebb and flow of members in and out as factions jockeyed for power. Or at least for plunder.

Iriadeska was not handicapped by many confusing notions of democracy. They did quite frequently have elections, but the candidates were always from the small list of the elite. No one not at least marginally a member of the Royal Family ever served as police chief or diplomat or military commander in Iriadeska, much less as a member of the Council of Ministers. However, that still left a large pool of available talent for every imaginable government office because over seventeen hundred years the Iriadeskan royal family had come to include many thousands of its citizens.

Still, it was an arithmetical fact that there were, altogether, something like twenty-odd million Iriadeskan nationals. Most of the millions were not related to royalty in any detectable way. They were the ones who chopped the cane, slashed the rubber trees, clerked in the banks for offshore trading, worked in a few factories and staffed the tourist hotels, as well as doing everything else in Iriadeska that produced wealth. Some of them produced quite a lot of it. This was especially true among the Chinese community, where there were many privately owned wholesale establishments, brokerages, and shipping companies. None of these people, even the rich ones, could ever hold any really responsible role in the Iriadeskan government, but that did not make them unimportant. Indeed, the Iriadeskan government always had a very important part for these citizens to play, regardless of who made up the Iriadeskan government of that moment.

They could be taxed.

Sanford, listening to all this, shook his head, uncertain whether to laugh or lose his temper. He said, "So after forty years some people want a redistribution of the loot?"

Emily looked at him in puzzlement. "Forty years? What do you mean, forty years? It has been, let me see, yes, twenty-two months since the last coup attempt, not forty years. That was when two wing commanders of the Royal Iriadeskan Air Force and the Admiral of the Iriadeskan Navy combined to take over the government. They failed because they couldn't get any ground troops to occupy the Palace. In the last forty years there have been, let me see, oh, I think about thirty-three or thirty-four attempts."

"My God," said Sanford. "It sounds like a regular annual event, like the Rose Bowl Parade."

"I think," Emily said stiffly, "that our national struggles are quite a bit more important than that. Anyway, I'll bet more people are probably hurt in your parade."

"Really? Bloodless coups? How many of them are successful?"

"Ah, but don't you see? That's why you're here. None of them are, usually. So this time Am Sattaroothata persuaded General Phenoboomgarat that we could establish a stable regime with good public-relations management, so they hired you."

Briskly she rose, dumped the remnants of his coffee and refilled it from the jar of instant and the thermos of still very hot water. "Can we now get back to work?" she asked. "Many of the communiqués can be used whichever way the discussions go, so let us write them."

"The one about the fifty-five per cent raise in Army allocations?"

"Oh, yes," she agreed. "That and many others. Balancing the budget. Cutting the trade deficit. Limiting the police powers of arbitrary arrest and imprisonment to no more than six months without filing charges. And by all means something about finding work for college graduates; you have no idea how many of our people go off to Europe or America to study and have nothing to do when they come home. Why, I myself—"

She stopped, looking embarrassed. "Yes?" Sanford encouraged. "Were you one of those—or are you part American, with a name like Emily?"

She looked surprised. "My parents named me Arragingamauluthiata, Mr. Sanford. But yes, I was one of those. When I was an English major at Bennington we put on a play. It was *Our Town*, by Thornton Wilder. I played the part of Emily, the young wife who dies and is buried in the graveyard, and as most of my college friends had difficulty in pronouncing Arragingamauluthiata, they generally called me Emily. My years in Vermont made me quite fond of Americans, Mr. Sanford, and I have kept the name ever since."

"And when you came back to Iriadeska you couldn't get a job?" Sanford persisted.

"Not one for an English major specializing in the Lake poets, no. In fact, nothing at all, at first." She looked around the Army television studio without enjoyment. "Then the opportunity came for a commission in the Army, and this sort of work. Which, actually, we had better get busy and do."

"Oh, right," said Sanford agreeably, not quite meaning it; it was distinctly more pleasurable to sit and talk with this rather pretty young woman, who mellowed considerably as you got to know her. "Explain one thing to me, though."

"Certainly, Mr. Sanford."

"Charlie, please?" She smiled and inclined her head. "It's about this elephant release. Communique Number Seven."

She took it from him and he watched with pleasure as she bent her head over it. Actually, he was feeling fairly good, everything considered. The revolution did not seem to be turning violent. His short nap had revived him—or perhaps the coffee had; Emily had been making it progressively stronger, so that now it seemed she was barely dampening the crystals.

She looked up. "Yes," she said, "that was Air Chief Marshal Pittikudaru's idea, two coups ago. What about it?"

"I don't see what elephants have to do with revolutions," Sanford said apologetically.

"Because you aren't Iriadeskan. You do understand that this is an old proclamation? It has nothing to do with what's going on now."

"Well, yes, but still, elephants—"

"Elephants are very important in Iriadeska! That coup attempt adopted the symbol of the elephant because the elephant was the servant of man, just as the new government proposed to be the servant of the Iriadeskan people. They bought it, as a matter of fact, even though Marshal Pittikudaru himself pulled out of the attempt when the others wouldn't agree to make him an admiral as well. Only," she sighed, "some of the hill people thought elephants were holy. They didn't want them used in politics."

Sanford was surprised. "I didn't realize what people thought was that important to an, uh, excuse me, a more or less self-appointed government."

"Not what they *thought*," she explained. "What they *did*. The hill tribes made up most of the Eighth and Tenth Armored Divisions, and they all just ran off, tanks and all, until it was over. So it failed, and Admiral Pilatkatha and General Muntilasia are still in Switzerland over that one." She sighed and stretched. She added sorrowfully, "Anyway, his majesty agreed with the hill people. And in matters of religion or good taste, what His Majesty says is, how would you say it? Conclusive. That's why we chose the Martians this time. No one thinks they're holy."

Sanford said doubtfully, "I still don't see the reasoning there. I mean for putting the Martians on the flag."

"Because they so closely resemble our chupri, of course. The chupri, or manatee, is strong, peaceful, kind, and gentle. It helps keep our canals and waterways clear of weed by grazing on water hyacinth. It is a friend to the Iriadeskans, just as our New People's Reform Movement will be, not to mention it is very newsworthy just now."

"I guess I didn't realize that Iriadeskans were so interested in space," Sanford apologized.

"In space? Oh, hardly at all. But that is what His Majesty is doing, you see. He is in America for that purpose."

"You said he was on a state tour!"

"Yes, exactly. He will address the United Nations tomorrow. Then he will visit Atlantic City, where he has investments in several casinos. Then he has been promised a day in Disney World, and then he goes to Cape Canaveral as a guest of your President to welcome the Seerseller expedition back to Earth. I mean," Emily said sharply, "if the *king* can travel thousands of miles to see the Martians come in, that makes them important, doesn't it?"

"I suppose. I don't know much about Martians," he apologized, and blinked when he saw the effect that had on her.

"You *what*?"

"I said I don't know much about Martians," he repeated deprecatingly.

"But you—Your picture was on page one of the newspaper! Your agency chief claimed you were very familiar with the campaign—"

"Oh, you mean Max Mars and Mindy Mars. Yes, I did help out on that, but only for a week or two. And I don't know anything about Martians. That was just dolls, not the real thing."

"Holy shit," whispered the former Bennington student. Sanford blinked. "Oh, Charlie," she said sorrowfully, "do you have any idea what you're *saying*?"

He said defensively, "Well, I certainly never said anything to give anyone the idea that I was claiming to be an expert on Martians."

"What you claimed? What does *that* matter? Am Sattaroothata told General Phenoboomgarat to hire you because we needed a Martian expert. Do you know, do you have any idea at all, what it would mean to say that Am Sattaroothata was *wrong*?"

Sanford said apologetically, "Well, gosh, Emily, I'm sure it would be pretty embarrassing—"

"Embarrassing? *Embarrassing?* Oh, no, Charlie, it wouldn't be embarrassing. I'll tell you what it would be. It would be—it would be—"

Colonel Emily faltered in mid-tirade. She was listening. So, suddenly, was Sanford, because at long last, and even through the soundproofing of the television studio, there was something to listen to. The building itself was shaking with the steady seismic throb of the tanks.

They were on their way. For better or worse, the coup was launched at last.

From the top of the television tower the whole city of Pnik was spread out before them in the steamy Iriadeskan morning. Off to the west there was the River Choomli with its fringe of high-rise tourist hotels and the bright green mats of water hyacinth swirling upstream as the canal dams were opened for the morning traffic, flushing the weed out into the river. To the north the tall government buildings, all new, all shiny in the glass-sided style of every city in the world. To the east the old city with its temples and towers; glints of gold struck the eye as the sunlight bounced off gilded Buddhas and mortuary columns. To the south the airport, its jumbo jets and private planes all motionless. And in all directions, wherever you looked, it looked empty. When the assault column moved out of the compound it seemed to suck all the life of Pnik after it. There was no one in any street Sanford could see.

Nor was there any sound, either, neither from the streets nor from the airport with its interdicted planes. Least of all was there any sound of cannonfire, or tank engines, or screaming casualties or any of the things twenty years of war movies had trained Sanford to expect. "Shouldn't they be fighting?" he asked Colonel Emily and she looked at him in some surprise.

"The attack is under way," she assured him, "probably. Anyway, Air Chief Marshal Pittikudaru has practically promised to overfly the Supreme Court building as soon as the Seventh Paratroop Brigade takes position around it. So we ought to see the airplanes from here, anyway."

"I don't."

"Well, I don't either!" she stormed at him. "We just have to be patient until we find out what's going on. And don't start again about radio contact; we don't keep in radio contact because then everybody would listen in, since we're all on the same command frequencies."

"I was only trying to say—"

"Don't say it!" Then she peered over the parapet of the building. "That's funny," she said, mostly to herself.

Sanford gripped the hot tile edging of the parapet and leaned forward to see what she was looking at. There was something going on. Down on the parade ground a military figure, erect and sober in its braided uniform and cap, stood waiting. It was General Tupalakuli, and he was surrounded by a smart-looking squad of shoulders with carbines at the ready. From the opposite side of the quad another general stepped out, marching smartly toward him.

It was General Phenoboomgarat. The whole comic-opera scenario suddenly turned ugly for Sanford because it looked very much as though he were about to witness his first execution by firing squad. "He shouldn't kill him," he snapped at Emily. "He's his prisoner! He's entitled to the conventions of war, isn't he?"

She turned to look at him with uncomprehending eyes. "What in the world are you talking about?"

"That's a firing squad for General Tupalakuli, can't you see? Listen, this is carrying things too far! I want to—"

He did not finish saying what he wanted. On the quadrangle below a little drama was being acted out. General Tupalakuli saluted General Phenoboomgarat ceremoniously. General Phenoboomgarat returned the salute. The squad of armed men detached themselves from General Tupalakuli and reformed in a hollow square around General Phenoboomgarat. They marched away with him . . . directly to the door of the military prison Tupalakuli just left.

"Oh, *hell*," moaned Colonel Emily; and behind them on the roof a door opened. The same lieutenant who had changed flags in the room of the two generals, when the two generals seemed temporarily both to be on the same side, appeared again. He saluted Emily perfunctorily and went to the flagpole.

Down came the Martian-bearing flag of the New People's Reform Government. Up went the old twenty-seven-starred banner of the corrupt blood-suckers and tyrants.

Sanford turned a horrified glance on Emily. "Does this mean what I think it means?" he demanded.

"What do you think it means?" she sobbed. "It means we lost."

The limousine was as big as ever, but now it was a lot more crowded. Am Sattaroothata and General Phenoboomgarat shared the back seat, Am Bhopru was in front, Emily and Sanford in the jump seats.

All around them, the city of Pnik was returning to its normal status. The metal shutters were raised again and the cubbyhole stores were doing their nickel-and-dime business in inches of fabric and ounces of meat or poultry. The tuk-tuks had civilian passengers again. Even a great gaudy tour bus rumbled ahead of them, its exhaust choking them, until it turned off to the Temple of the Ten Thousand Golden Buddhas.

General Phenoboomgarat was talking to Am Sattaroothata as

though discussing the results of a recent tennis match. Sanford understood not a word, but Emily gave him a running translation. "The government promised to surrender as soon as the Air Force flew over the Supreme Court building," she said, "but Air Chief Marshal Pittikudaru was waiting for the Seventh Paratroop Brigade to surround the building, and the general didn't go because he'd heard a report that His Majesty had said it was insulting to the proud traditions of Iriadeska to put a child's toy on the flag."

"And did the king really say that?" Sanford asked.

"Oh, who knows that? It's the kind of thing he might have said, and just *thinking* he could have said that was enough to make everybody think a second thought, because in matters of taste and religion—"

"I know," Sanford nodded. "His Majesty's word is, what did you say? Definitive."

"Exactly," she said gloomily. "So General Phenoboomgarat released General Tupalakuli and turned the command of the troops over to him . . . and here we are."

"On the way to the airport and exile," Sanford finished. Emily nodded, pleased with his quick understanding. "Hoping we can sneak out of the country before anyone notices," he added, and she looked indignant.

"Sneak? Who is sneaking anywhere? The airport officials never require exit visas until twelve hours after a coup attempt. Otherwise," she explained, "how would the leaders get away?"

"Get away to where?"

She shrugged. "Wherever they're going. Am Sattaroothata, of course, will only have to stay away for a few months, until things quiet down—he said he wanted to visit Singapore anyway. General Phenoboomgarat has a part interest in the Atlantic City casinos, along with His Majesty. That's probably where he'll go."

"And you?"

"Oh, I'll go to Atlantic City, too. No doubt they'll need some sort of personnel manager . . . and maybe I can go back to school and get my master's degree. What about yourself? Back to the agency?"

"If I still have a job," Sanford grumbled. "I haven't exactly covered myself with glory on this one."

Emily looked sympathetic. Sanford drank it up; sympathy wasn't either a success or a job, but it was the best he'd had that day.

Then Emily looked thoughtful. "Chuck," she said absently. "Does your agency have any casino accounts?"

"You mean gambling? Oh, no. I don't know anything about that, and I don't think the Old Man does, either, and besides he has some funny moral attitudes—"

He stopped because she wasn't listening any more. Her fingertips pressed together, she was whispering deferentially to Am Sattaroothata and the general. They listened absently. Then the monk shrugged and the general said, as though the subject bored him, "Yom."

Emily bowed and turned back to Sanford. "Three hundred million dollars a year," she said, smiling.

"What?"

"That's the handle of our casinos. So there's money for promotion, wouldn't you say? Enough money so that your employer might be interested in the account—with you handling it?"

Sanford said at once, "I think I could learn about casinos very rapidly."

"I think you could, too," Emily said. "I even think I might be able to help teach you."

Hapgood's Hoax

by Allen Steele

LAWRENCE R. BOLGER; Professor of English, Minnesota State University, and science fiction historian.

Harry Hapgood. (*Sighs.*) It would figure that someone would want to interview me about Harry Hapgood, especially since the new collection of his work just came out. The field may not be able to get rid of him until someone digs up his coffin and hammers a stake in his heart. . . .

Okay, since you've come all this way, I'll tell you about H. L. Hapgood, Jr. But, to tell the truth, I'd just as soon leave the bastard in his literary grave.

There were pulp writers from the '30s who managed to survive the times and outlast the pulps, to make the transition from pulp fiction to whatever passes as literature in this genre. Jack Williamson, Clifford Simak, Ray Bradbury . . . those are some of the ones whose work eventually broke out of the pulp mold. They're regarded as the great writers of the field and we still read their stories. They still find their audience. Their publishers keep their classics, like *City* and *The Humanoids* and *The Martian Chronicles*, in print.

Those are the success stories. Yet for every Bradbury or Williamson, there're a hundred other writers—some of them big names back then, you need to remember—who didn't make it out of the pulp era. For one reason or another, their careers faded when the pulps died at the end of the '40s. H. Bedford-Jones, Arthur K. Barnes, S. P. Meek . . . all obscure authors' now. Just like H. L. Hapgood, Jr.

Not that they were necessarily bad writers, either. I mean, some of their stories are no more crap than a lot of the stuff that gets into print today. But when the field started to grow up, when John Campbell began to demand that his *Astounding* contributors deliver realistic SF or else . . . well, Harry was one of those writers who fell into the "or else" category.

But before that, he had been extraordinarily successful, especially when you consider the times. The Depression nearly killed a lot of writers, but those years were kind to him. He had a nonstop imagination and fast fingers, and, for a penny a word, Harry Hapgood cranked out stories by the bushel. I was reading all the SF pulps at the time—I was in high school in Ohio then—so I can tell you with personal authority that there was rarely a month that went by without H.L. Hapgood's byline appearing somewhere. If not in *Amazing* or *Thrilling Wonder*, then in the pre-Campbell era *Astounding* or *Captain Future* or someplace else. "The Sky Pirates of Centaurus," "Attack of the Giant Robots," "Mars or Bust!"— those were some of his more memorable stories. Rock-jawed space captains fighting Venusian tiger-men while mad scientists with Z-ray machines menaced ladies in bondage. Greasy kid stuff, sure, but a hell of a lot of fun when you were fourteen years old. Harry was the master of the space opera. Not even Ed Hamilton or Doc Smith could tell 'em like he could.

You can still find some of his older work in huckster rooms at SF conventions, if you look through the raggy old pulps some people have on the tables. That's about the only place you can find Harry Hapgood's pulp stories anymore. I think his last published story, at least in his lifetime, was in *Amazing* in '45 or '46. The last time any of

his early work was reprinted was when somebody put together a
pulp anthology about ten years ago. When he died in '66, his career
in science fiction had been long since over.

That's the main reason why he's been obscure all these years. But
there was also the New Hampshire hoax. He died a rich man
because of that stunt, but he also blackened his name in the field. I
don't think anyone wanted to remember Hapgood because of that.
At least, not until recently . . .

> *Startled and dazzled by the sudden burst of light, I looked up
> and saw a monstrous disk-shaped vehicle descending toward
> me. Rocket-fighters raced from the sky to combat the weird
> machine, but as they got close, scarlet rays flashed from
> portals along the side of the spaceship. The rockets ex-
> ploded!*
>
> *"Dirk, oh Dirk!" Catherine screamed from the bunker next
> to me, fearful of the apparition. "What can it be?"*
>
> *Before I could answer, Captain Black of the United Earth
> Space Force spoke up. "The Quongg death machine, Miss
> Jones," he said, his chin thrust out belligerently.*
>
> *I reached for my blaster. "Oh, yeah?" I snarled. "Well, they'll
> never take us alive!"*
>
> *Captain Black stared at me. "They'll take us alive, all right!"
> he snarled. "They want us as specimens!"*
>
> —"Kidnappers From The Stars,"
> by H. L. Hapgood Jr.
> *Space Tales*; December, 1938

JOE MACKEY; retired electrical engineer.

If I remember correctly, I first met Harry Hapgood back in 1934 or
1935, when we both lived in the same three-decker in Somerville,
Massachusetts, just outside of Boston. I was about nineteen at the

time and was working a day-job in a deli on Newbury Street to put myself through M.I.T. night school. So, y'know, when I wasn't making grinders or riding the trolley over to classes in Cambridge, I was at home hitting the books. I got maybe four hours of sleep in those days. The Depression was a bitch like that.

I met Harry because he lived right upstairs. His apartment was directly above mine and he used to bang on his typewriter late at night, usually when I was studying or trying to sleep. Every time he hit the carriage return, it sounded like something was being dropped on the floor. I had no idea what he was doing up there . . . practicing somersaults or something.

Anyway, one night I finally got fed up with the racket, so I marched upstairs and hammered on his door, planning on telling him to cut it out 'cause I was trying to catch a few winks. Well, he opened his door—very timidly—and I started to chew him out. Then I looked past him and saw all these science fiction magazines scattered all over the place. Piled on the coffee table, the couch, the kitchen table, the bed . . . *Amazing, Astonishing, Thrilling Wonder, Planet Stories, Startling Stories*. Heaps of them. My jaw just dropped open because, though I read all those magazines when I could afford to buy 'em, I thought I was the only person in Boston who read science fiction.

So I said something like, "Holy smoke! You've got the new issue of *Astounding!*" I remember that it was lying open on the coffee table. Brand new issue. I was too broke to pick it up myself.

Harry just smiled, then he walked over and picked it up and brought it to me. "Here, you can borrow it if you want," he said. Then he added, very slyly, "Read the story by H. L. Hapgood. You might like it."

I nodded and said, "Yeah, I really like his stories." He just blushed and coughed into his fist and shuffled his feet and then he told me who he was.

Well, I didn't say anything about his typing after that, but once he found out I was taking night classes at M.I.T., he stopped typing late at night so I could get some sleep. He figured it out for himself. Harry was a good guy like that.

MARGO CROFT; literary agent; former assistant editor, *Rocket Adventures*.

I was the first-reader at *Rocket* back then, so I read Harry's stories when they came in through the mail, which was once every week or two. Seriously. In his prime, he was more prolific than Bob Silverberg or Isaac Asimov ever were. But the difference was, Silverberg and Asimov were good writers, even in their pulp days.

No, no, scratch that. At a certain level, Harry *was* good. He knew how to keep a story going. He was a master of pacing, for one thing. But it was all formula fiction, even if he didn't recognize the formula himself. Anyone who compares him to E.E. Smith or Edmond Hamilton is fooling you. His characters were one-dimensional, his dialogue was vintage movie serial. "Ah-ha, Dr. Zoko, I've got you now!"—that sort of thing. His understanding of real science was non-existent. In fact, he usually ignored science. When it was convenient, say, for a pocket of air to exist in a crater on the Moon, there it was.

But his stories were no worse than the other stuff we published, and he got his share of fan mail, so we sent him lots of checks. For a long time, he was in our stable of regular writers. Whenever we needed a six thousand-word story to fill a gap in the next issue, there was always an H.L. Hapgood yarn in the inventory. He was a fiction factory.

I finally met him at the first World Science Fiction Convention, in New York back in '39. I think it was Donald Wollheim who introduced us. I was twenty years old then, flat-chested and single, ready to throw myself at the first writer who came along, so I developed a crush on Harry at once. He might have been a hack, but he was a good-looking hack (*Laughs*).

He had fans all around him, though, because he was such a well-known writer. I spent the better part of Saturday following him around Caravan Hall, trying to get his attention. It was hard. Harry was shy when it came to one-on-one conversation, but he soaked up the glory when a mob was around.

Anyway, I finally managed to get him into a group that was going out to dinner that night. We found an Italian restaurant a few blocks away and took over a long table in the back room. There were a whole bunch of us—I think Ray Bradbury was in the group, though nobody knew who he was then—and I managed to get myself positioned across the table from Harry. Like I said, he was very shy when it came to one-on-one conversation, so I gave up on talking to him like a pretty girl and tried speaking to him like an editor. He began to notice me then.

His lack of—well, for lack of better term, literary sophistication— was mind-boggling. He had barely heard of Ernest Hemingway, and he only recognized Steinbeck as the name of his neighborhood grocer. The only classics he had read were by H. G. Wells and Jules Verne. In fact, the only thing Harry seemed to have ever read was science fiction or *Popular Mechanics*, and that was all he wanted to talk about. I mean, there I was trying to show off my legs—maybe I had no chest back then, but my legs were Marlene Dietrich's—and Harry only wanted to discuss the collected work of Neil R. Jones.

So I lost a little interest in him during that talk, and after a while I started paying attention to other people at the table. I *do* distinctly remember two things Harry said that night. One was that his ambition was to get rich and famous. He was convinced that he would write for the pulps forever. "Science fiction will never change," he proclaimed.

The other was a comment which sounds routine today. Every other SF writer has said it at least once, but I recall Harry saying it first, at least as far as I can remember. It probably sticks in my mind because of what happened years later.

"If aliens ever came to Earth to capture people," he said offhandedly at one point, "they wouldn't have to hunt for me. I'd volunteer for the trip."

JOE MACKEY:

Harry Hapgood was a hell of a good person back then. You can quote me on that. He put me up to a lot of meals when I was starving, and he always had a buck to spare even when his own rent was due. But the day I saw him begin to hurt was the day John Campbell rejected one of his stories.

I had dropped by his place after work. It was in the middle of winter . . . 1940, I think . . . and the M.I.T. semester hadn't yet started, so I had some time to kill. The mail had just come, and when I came into Harry's apartment he was sitting at his kitchen table, bent over a manuscript which had just come back in the mail. It was a rejection from *Astounding*.

This almost never happened to him. Harry thought he was rejection-proof. After all, his stories usually sold on the first shot. That, and the fact that *Astounding* had always been one of his most reliable markets. But Harry's old editor, F. Orlin Tremaine, had left a couple of years earlier, and the new guy, John W. Campbell, was reshaping the magazine . . . and that meant getting rid of the zap-gun school of science fiction.

So here was Harry, looking at this story which had been bounced back, "Enslaved On Venus." Just staring at it, that's all. "What's going on?" I asked, and he told me that Campbell had just rejected this story. "Did he tell you why?" I said. Harry told me he had received a letter, but he wouldn't show it to me. I think it was in the trash. "Well, just send it out again to some other magazine," I said, because this is what he had always told me should be done when a story gets rejected.

But he just shook his head. "No," he said. "I don't think so."

Something John Campbell had written in that letter had really gotten to Harry. Whatever Campbell had written in that letter, it had cut right to the bone. I don't think Campbell ever consciously tried to hurt writers whose work he rejected, but he was known to be tough . . . and now he had gotten tough on Harry.

Anyway, Harry told me that he wanted to be alone for a while, so I left his place. I wasn't really worried. I had confidence that "Enslaved On Venus" would be published somewhere else. But I never saw that story make it into print, and Harry never mentioned it to me again. I think he trashed it along with Campbell's letter. It wasn't even found in his files.

Lawrence Bolger:

Harry Hapgood became a dinosaur. His literary career died because he couldn't adapt. The World War II paper shortage killed the pulps, so there went most of his regular markets, and the changes in the genre swept in by John Campbell, H.L. Gold, Frederik Pohl, and other editors made his kind of SF writing unpopular. Raymond Palmer continued to buy his stories for *Amazing* until Palmer, too, left the field in the late '40s. By then, science fiction had grown up.

But Hapgood didn't grow with the genre. His stories were pure romanticism. He paid no attention to scientific accuracy or character development. He persisted in trying to write Buck Rogers stuff. Other writers learned the new rules, changed their styles to fit the times, but Harry Hapgood wouldn't—probably couldn't—change chords. So while Robert Heinlein was creating his "Future History" series and Ted Sturgeon was writing classics like "Baby Is Three," Harry was still trying to get away with space heroes and bug-eyed monsters. The more sophisticated SF mags wouldn't touch that stuff.

It was sad. He still went to science fiction conventions on the East Coast, but he was no longer surrounded by fans. They just didn't want to talk to him anymore.

The magazine editors tried to tell him where he was going wrong, why they weren't buying his stories any more. I remember, at one Science Fiction convention in Philadelphia, overhearing John Campbell patiently trying to explain to Harry that, as long as he persisted in writing stories which claimed that rockets could travel to another solar system in two days or that Jupiter had a surface, he simply could not accept any of Harry's work.

Harry never listened. He stubbornly wanted to play by his own rules. Gregory Benford once criticized science fiction that "plays with the net down," SF stories which ignore basic scientific principles like the theory of Relativity. In Harry Hapgood's case, he was playing on a different court altogether. All he could write were stories in which lizard-men kidnapped beautiful women and the Space Navy always saved the day. But he was playing ping-pong among Wimbledon champs, and he wouldn't realize that he was in a new game.

MARGO CROFT:

After *Rocket Adventures* folded, I went down the street to work as an associate editor at Doubleday, helping to edit their mystery line. That was in '48. I had all but completely withdrawn from the science fiction scene by then, but I still had a few contacts in the field, people with whom I'd touch bases now and then.

Anyway . . . one of Doubleday's whodunnit writers lived in Boston and I occasionally took the train up there to meet with her. On one of those trips I had some time to kill before catching the train back to New York. I had my address book in my purse and Harry's number was written in it, so I called him up and told him I'd buy him lunch downtown. It was mainly for old time's sake, but also I wondered if he had recovered from the collapse of the pulp market. By then, I hadn't seen him in a few years.

Harry wasn't looking good. He had lost weight and he had started chain-smoking. He wore a suit which looked as if it had been new in 1939, and I knew it had to be his best suit. The last time he had made an SF magazine sale had been the year before. He wouldn't admit it, but I knew that he had been trying to pay the bills by writing articles for some furniture trade magazine. It was ironic. Harry, who had practically thrived during the Depression, was on the skids during the postwar boom. Ironic, but not funny.

It was a painful lunch. He didn't want to talk much. He knew I was paying, so he ordered the biggest item on the menu. It was probably the best meal he had eaten in months. I told him that I had married— my first husband, Phillip—and though he tried to take it well, I could see that he was disappointed. I suppose he had noticed that girlish crush I'd had on him ten years before, and was sorry now that he hadn't done anything about it then. (*Shakes her head.*) Poor man.

His personal life was a wreck, so I tried to talk to him about his writing. I told him that Doubleday was starting to publish science fiction and that they were looking for established authors; he should take a crack at it. He didn't say much, and I got the impression that he had lost interest in SF. Somehow that didn't make sense. Harry was a science fiction writer top to bottom. He should have jumped at the chance.

He had stopped at a newsstand before meeting me at the restaurant, and he had picked up a handful of magazines. It was his usual reading matter—all the SF magazines—but in the stack was also the first issue of a new magazine which I had heard about through the grapevine. That was *Fate*, the UFO digest that Ray Palmer started publishing after he left *Amazing* to take advantage of the flying saucer craze.

Sure, it was the type of thing which Harry Hapgood would read. Nothing sinister about that. But I remember, over dessert, watching him absently pick it up and thumb through the pages. Then he casually asked me what it would take for him to write a bestseller.

"I'm talking about a science fiction novel," he said. "I mean, something that would sell like crazy."

Coming from Harry Hapgood, that would have been hysterical if it hadn't been so sad. I didn't really think he was capable of writing an SF novel that was even publishable—and it would be years before science fiction scratched the bestseller lists. But I told him that he had answered his own question.

"Write something that a lot of people will want to read," I said. The obvious answer, of course. Harry just nodded his head and kept flipping through *Fate*.

JOE MACKEY:

I remember Harry's disappearance very well.

By then I was working as a draftsman for a refrigerator company in Boston, but I still lived downstairs from Harry, in that three-decker in Somerville. I had gotten home from work and was settling down on the couch to read. Harry knocked on my door, stuck his head in, and said that he was going out for ice cream. Did I want to come along? I told him, no, thanks anyway, and so he left. I heard the front door downstairs open and close . . . and that was it. That was the last time I heard from him for five days.

Next morning I went up to his place for coffee before going to work—something I did every morning—and found his door unlocked. His lights were still on, but he was missing. I was a little worried, but I figured, what the hell. I turned off the lights and went to my job. But when I got home that evening and found that he still hadn't returned, I called the police.

Nothing was missing. His suitcase was still in the closet, his toothbrush was still next to the sink in the bathroom, there was even a half-finished furniture article in his typewriter. He had just walked out to get ice cream and . . . *phhtt!* Vanished. The cops searched the neighborhood, thinking he had been mugged, maybe killed and left in an alley somewhere, but there was no trace of him. He hadn't checked into any hospitals and the cab drivers didn't report picking him up anywhere. The newspapers reported his disappearance the next day, as a minor item buried in the back pages. Nobody seemed to be really concerned, though. Except me. I was worried sick about the whole thing. Y'know, maybe Harry was going to be found floating in the Charles River or something.

Then . . . well, you know what happened next. He turned up in the boonies of New Hampshire, saying that he had been kidnapped by a flying saucer.

A lone pedestrian, found on Route 202 in Hillsboro, was brought to Hillsboro Police station Tuesday night, after he wandered out of the woods and flagged down a driver. The man, identified as a Somerville, Massachusetts, writer, has been sought by Massachusetts police as a missing person since last week.

Harold LaPierre Hapgood, Jr., 38, of 19 Waterhouse St., Somerville, was found on the roadside near the Antrim town line by the Rev. Lucius Colby, minister of the First Episcopal

Church in Henniker. According to Hillsboro Police Chief Cyril G. Slater, Mr. Hapgood stumbled out into the highway in front of the Rev. Colby's automobile, waving his arms and forcing the driver to halt. The Rev. Colby then drove Mr. Hapgood to the Hillsboro police station.

Chief Slater says that Mr. Hapgood, a magazine writer, has been sought by the Somerville, Boston, and Massachusetts state police departments since Friday, May 7, when he apparently vanished after leaving his residence in Somerville. Chief Slater says that although Mr. Hapgood appears to be in good health, he was delirious when brought to his office. Mr. Hapgood claims that he was kidnapped by a space-ship piloted by creatures from another planet . . .

> —*Hillsboro News-Register*,
> Hillsboro, N.H.
> Thursday, May 13, 1948

LAWRENCE BOLGER:

Did Harry Hapgood really get kidnapped by a UFO? Not a chance. If he got kidnapped by anything, it was the Trailways bus he caught at the station in Boston.

When a reporter from one of the Boston papers retraced Hapgood's trail, he found that the driver remembered someone who looked like Harry getting on in Boston and getting off in Keene, New Hampshire. He used false names when he bought the ticket and when he checked into a hotel in Keene for four days, but his description was matched by the bus driver, the hotel clerk and chambermaids, even the waitress at the diner where he ate breakfast and dinner. The only thing which wasn't established was how he got from Keene to Hillsboro, so one can only assume that he hitched a ride . . . and it sure as hell wasn't in a flying saucer.

It wasn't an iron-clad story at all. Hell, it was a blatant fraud. He didn't have a shred of evidence to support his claim that he had been teleported off the street in Somerville, taken into space in a UFO, and examined by strange little men for four days.

On the other hand, he didn't need any proof. The country was in the midst of its first big flying-saucer flap, started by Kenneth Arnold's sighting of UFOs over Mt. Rainier the year before. There were a lot of true believers like the Fortean Society, and whenever newspapers or the Air Force debunked a sighting or a kidnap story, these people would claim that it was part of a government conspiracy to cover-up the UFO "invasion" or whatever.

Harry Hapgood knew what he was doing. First, he sold a first-hand account of his experience to Ray Palmer at *Fate*. After that story was printed and enough newspapers had written about his "ordeal," he wrote his book and sold it to a minor hardback publisher, changing his byline to H. LaPierre Hapgood so that he wouldn't get confused with H.L. Hapgood, Jr., the pulp writer.

(*Laughs*). No one noticed the name change, because no one paid any attention to science fiction in those days. The only people who really knew that H. LaPierre Hapgood had started his career as a science fiction hack were SF fans. Since they were considered to be even further out on the fringe than the UFO cultists, no one paid any attention to them.

And what do you know? It became a runaway bestseller . . .

MARGO CROFT:

The odd thing about Harry's first book is, if you take it as science fiction, it's a pretty good yarn. His narrative skills, developed from all those years of grinding out stories for the pulps, really lent themselves to this sort of thing. It has an almost-convincing sense of realism. I mean, if you checked your skepticism at the door, you could have ended up believing him. And a lot of people did.

If Harry had applied himself to writing science fiction, he could have re-emerged in the field as one of the major writers of the '50s. (*Shrugs.*) But maybe he was fed up with science fiction. I dunno. I guess he was more interested in making money, at that point.

One of the funnier stories about the hoax was that, after *Abducted to Space* was published and made it to the bestseller lists, he got invited to be the commencement speaker at graduation ceremonies at some small liberal-arts college in Illinois. As academic tradition sometimes has it, for his services he was presented an honorary doctorate in astronomy from the school. It didn't mean a damn thing, but Harry and his publisher milked it for all it was worth. So Harry overnight became Dr. H. LaPierre Hapgood, the professional astronomer. (*Laughs.*) He didn't even graduate from high school!

When I awoke, I found myself lying in a circular chamber. The walls rose around me as a hemispherical dome, white and featureless except for a pulsing red orb suspended from the apex of the ceiling.

The room seemed to hum, just above the range of audibility. I was lying on a raised platform which seemed to be made out of metal, except that it was soft where I lay. I attempted to move my arms, then my legs, but discovered to my alarm that I was completely paralyzed. Yet there were no visible restraints on my arms or legs.

Then, directly in front of me, a section of the wall faded and became a screen. I saw the black expanse of outer space. In the center of the screen hung Earth, and I realized that I was thousands of miles out in space. I was terrified. How did I get here? What would be done to me? Most importantly, would I ever be released?

A few moments later, a low section of the wall to my right slid upward, and the first of the Aliens slowly walked into the chamber . . .

—H. LaPierre Hapgood;
Abducted To Space

JOE MACKEY:

Harry moved out of the place in Somerville as soon as he got the advance money for *Abducted to Space*, but by then he and I weren't on speaking terms. I was pretty upset with him by that time. I thought we were friends, but he had used me to establish credibility for that cock-and-bull story of his. Hell, when the reporters starting showing up to interview him about his experience, he would send them downstairs to interview me as a "reliable source." Of course, they never printed my opinion that he was making the whole thing up. Just the part about how I found his place empty one morning.

So I didn't really mind when he moved out to one of the ritzier parts of Chestnut Hill, but I did keep up with him, from a distance. I'm sure you know a lot of this already, right? After he and his publisher made a mint from *Abducted to Space*, he did *UFO!*, which was just a rehash of the first book, except that he embellished the story a little. Seems he "remembered" a lot of details in his dreams, which he claimed were buried in his subconscious by the aliens. That's a lot of horseshit—excuse my French—because I could see he was just recycling stuff from his old pulp stories. Probably had his copies of *Thrilling Wonder* and *Amazing* right there on his desk when he was writing the thing.

It was after he put out *Odd Visitors*, the third book, that he really went for the nugget. He started that UFO cult of his—whachacallit, the International Center For Extraterrestrial Studies—and soon had every dingbat in the country sending him donations. Ten dollars got you a mimeographed newsletter every couple of months, and a hundred bucks put you on a list of "honorary contactees."

The money was supposedly going for the construction of a "UFO spaceport" on some land he had purchased out in the western part of the state. The line was that, when the spacearks arrived, they would land at the spaceport and take aboard human passengers for a voyage to another planet, which Harry called Nirvanos. Complete crap—but, y'know, there's a lot of mixed-up people out there who'll buy into just that sort of thing.

My wife and I drove out there one Sunday to check it out. Found a three-acre plot in Leicester, off a dirt road in the middle of nowhere. Just a big cleared cow pasture, surrounded by a barb-wire fence with an empty shack in the middle and a big billboard at the end. It had some weird symbols painted on it and was strung with Christmas lights. Some local kid was hired to switch them on each night. And that was his spaceport.

I bet Harry spent no more than five hundred dollars on the thing . . . and he probably took a million to the bank, in donations from a lot of sick, gullible folks.

I can't tell you how much I despised the son of a bitch.

MARGO CROFT:

Harry dropped out of sight for about a dozen years, and while he did the UFO craze of the '50s ran its course. By the time Alan Shepard went up in space, flying saucers were a joke. The company which put out Harry's three UFO books went under—I think the publisher went to jail for tax fraud—and no respectable house would touch the ravings of Dr. H. LaPierre Hapgood. He kept his UFO cult going for a little while longer, after he moved it to Mexico to escape the IRS, but eventually it ran out of steam. On occasion I heard scuttlebutt about some millionaire American expatriate who had made his money writing UFO books, now living in a mansion-compound just outside of Mexico City, and never seen by outsiders. I knew who he was, and I didn't give a damn.

Then it was 1965, and I had left Doubleday and was starting my own literary agency. I wanted to take on some science fiction writers as clients, so I started hitting the major SF conventions, trying to find the next Robert Heinlein or Isaac Asimov. I found myself at an SF convention in the Chicago area, in a private party filled with the hot young writers of the day—Roger Zelazny, Harlan Ellison, Larry Niven, some others I can't recall. The hotel room was crowded and smoke-filled, so I went in search of a quiet corner of the room. And when I got there, I found Harry Hapgood.

He was old, old before his time. I was only a few years younger than him, but he seemed (*long pause*) so wasted. Used up, like something had been sucking blood out of him for fifteen years. If he was a millionaire, it didn't show. His clothes looked like they had been bought off the rack at Woolworth's, and he was so thin, so pale . . . I might not have recognized him if it hadn't been for his nametag.

"H. L. Hapgood, Jr." it read. He had gone back to his old byline, but if anyone had recognized his name, they didn't want to meet him. "Hapgood" was a foul name to conjure in SF circles. Science fiction writers and fans had long been misassociated by the general public with the UFO crazies, just as they're now lumped in with the New Age crystalfreaks. H. L. Hapgood was the name of one of their own, a writer who had turned Quisling and sold out to the lunatic fringe. In a crowded party, he was all alone. I couldn't believe that he had dared to show his face at an SF convention.

He recognized me at once. He might have even been waiting for me. I wanted to turn and walk away. But then he said my name, and I stayed. I sat down on the windowsill next to his chair, and listened to a dying old man.

He said . . .

(*Sighs*). I'm sorry. I can't go on. Will you turn off the recorder now, please?

"I've been asked, 'Why did you try, when you knew 99 percent of the people wouldn't believe you?' My reply, when it wasn't self-incriminating to answer the question, was simple. 'You're missing the point,' I said. "It doesn't matter if 99 percent of the people won't believe you. It only takes the remaining 1 percent to make you a rich man.'

"I have done many terrible things to become rich, and I won't apologize for all of them. The New Hampshire hoax was only the first of many. I have deceived and manipulated countless

people. I have no regrets about bilking total strangers for their money. If they were silly enough to send me money for the privilege of hearing more of my lies, then they deserved what they received. You get what you pay for.

"Yet, for those whose friendship I betrayed, I feel a vast, unspeakable shame. The wealth I reaped is a poor substitute for the friends I have lost. The debt I owe them can never be repaid, even by the division of my estate.

"The greater part of my estate, though, I bequeath to Minnesota State University, for the continuance of its English department's science fiction research program. My actions have tarnished the genre. Perhaps this will help to make amends. However, there is no reason why the program should be blackened by the name of a liar, which is why this donation will be made anonymously.

"As for my three UFO books, I commend them to death. I have appointed Margo Croft to be my literary executor, and she has been instructed to make sure that they are never again reprinted. They will follow me into the grave, never again to rot anyone's mind.

"As for my remaining works . . . Margo, you may do with them as you please."

—Harold L. Hapgood, Jr.
Last will and testament
(Recorded July 28, 1966)

LAWRENCE BOLGER:

Shortly after Harry Hapgood's funeral, the University sent a couple of graduate researchers from the SF program down to Mexico, to visit Hapgood's mansion. They went along with Margo Croft, who had yet to set foot in Harry's house, even though the two of them had reached sort of a reconciliation just before he died. Both our students and Margo were interested in the same thing, the vague reference to "remaining work" Hapgood had alluded to in his will.

Outside the high walls of the compound, a few of Harry's remaining followers were still holding vigil—wild-haired old ladies clutching frayed copies of *Abducted to Space*, intense young men with madness lurking behind their eyes, a smiling married couple wearing aluminum-foil spacesuits, waiting for Harry's spaceark to arrive and carry them to the promised land in the sky. Within the mansion, men were packing in crates his furniture and belongings—jade and porcelain vases, Spanish iron sculptures, Elizabethan tapestries—in preparation for Sotheby's auction of the estate. As Hapgood had directed, the house itself and its grounds would be donated to Mexico for a mental institute. Perhaps this was a final, wry joke on his part.

Margo and the researchers found Harry's office virtually untouched. Only the lawyers had been in there, to retrieve the file cabinets containing Harry's financial records. There was another file cabinet in the office, though, and a desk; in the drawers, they found the last literary work of H.L. Hapgood, Jr.

They counted sixty four short stories and three novels: meticulously typed, almost all completed, and none previously published. All had been written since the early 1950s, most in the last few years of his life when Harry had been fighting his cancer. All science fiction . . . not a UFO book in the whole bunch. Enough writing to fill a career.

Yet there were no rejection slips in the files, nor were there copies of cover letters. No indication that Harry had ever submitted any of these stories to magazine or book publishers. It was as if he would write a story, then simply stash it away and start another one. Hapgood had lived alone; there had been no one to read his work.

Why? (*Shrugs.*) Who knows? Maybe he couldn't face rejection . . . he didn't want to see any of those stories come back in the mail. But they were good stories, nonetheless. Hapgood had obviously learned something about writing in the intervening years.

You know the rest, of course. Margo brought the manuscripts back to New York, and one of her clients culled the best short stories from the stack, edited them into a posthumous collection, and managed to get it published. The damn thing's been selling like crazy ever since. (*Laughs.*) Perhaps Harry's legion of UFO cultists is still out there, loyally buying multiple copies from the bookstores. That's the only explanation I have for the new book getting on the New York *Times* bestseller list last week. And now the same publisher is going to issue his novels in a uniform edition. They'll probably become bestsellers, too. So go figure . . .

So who got the last laugh? Maybe this is Harry's final revenge. His place in the genre's history has been revised, and hardly anyone out there remembers the New Hampshire hoax. That's the conventional wisdom. But, y'know, he didn't survive to see his new acceptance in the field. Literary success doesn't do you much good if you're dead, right?

Look at it this way. Harry always said that the UFOs were coming back to get him. And he was right. The flying saucers got him in the end.

The Abduction of Bunny Steiner, or a Shameless Lie

by Thomas M. Disch

When Rudy Steiner's agent, Mal Bitzberg, called up with the idea that Rudy should produce a UFO book after the manner of Whitley Strieber's *Communion, a True Story*, Rudy thought Bitzberg was putting him on. It was April 1, but Rudy's situation was too desperate for April Fool's Day jokes. Bitzberg knew how desperate Rudy was at the present moment, the latest, lowest nadir of a career rich in nadirs. He was: (a) in debt well over his head; (b) apartmentless; (c) obese; (d) an apostate member of A.A.; (e) in his third month of writer's block; and, the crown jewel among Rudy's woes, (f) all the royalties for his best-selling fantasy series, *The Elfin Horde*, et al., were being held in perpetual escrow pending the settlement of a lawsuit that had been brought against him and his subsequently bankrupted publisher, Djinn Books. The lawsuit had been initiated by a Baltimore attorney and professional litigant, Rafe Boone, who specialized in charging best-selling authors with plagiarism and settling with them out of court. Rudy had balked at shelling out $100,000.00 to Boone, a jury had decided in Boone's favor, and then an appeals court had reversed the verdict. While Boone was contesting that appeal, he had been shot dead on the steps of the courthouse by another of his victims. Shortly afterward, the legal remains of Djinn Books had been swallowed up by a German publishing consortium. Boone having died intestate, his estate was now being contested by five separate claimants, and the bulk of that estate consisted of their potential seizure of Rudy's royalties. It was the opinion of Rudy's attorney, Merrill Yates, that Rudy had as much chance of finding the pot of gold at the end of the rainbow as of seeing any further proceeds from *The Elfin Horde* and its six sequels. Worse, he'd been enjoined from writing new books in the series and even from using the pseudonym of Priscilla Wisdom. The experience had been embittering.

"A UFO story?" Rudy had marveled. "You've got to be kidding. Besides the Streiber book, Random House is bringing out one just like it by that other jerk."

But Bitzberg was not a kidder. "So? That means it's a trend. All you need is a slightly different angle. Strieber's angle is he's the first name writer who's been inside a UFO. Hopkins has got this whole club of UFO witnesses, which anyone can join: that's his angle, democracy. The whole thing could become a religion. Anyhow that's what Janet Cruse thinks. It was her idea. And she thinks you're the person to write the next book."

"Janet Cruse? You've got to be kidding!"

Bitzberg shook his head and smiled a snaggletoothed smile that had been known to frighten small children. "She's with Knopf now, and she wants *you* to write a UFO book."

"Janet Cruse is with Knopf? I can't believe it."

Years ago, when Janet, a Canadian living in London, had been handling Rudy's English rights, she had sold several of his Priscilla Wisdom titles in foreign markets without telling him. By the time he'd discovered what she'd done, Janet had absconded to Toronto. She'd sold three books in Belgium, two in Portugal, four in Israel, and those were just the sales Rudy had found out about. He'd never seen a cent of the money.

"She realizes you've got reason to be angry with her. But she hoped this might make it up to you."

"If she wants to make it up to me, she could just pay me the money she stole."

"She doesn't have it. Believe me, I've seen where she's living. She's no better off than you."

"And she's at *Knopf*? And Knopf wants a UFO book?"

"Knopf brought her in, because she's considered an expert on occult writers. UFOs are as respectable as astrology these days. Random House, Atlantic Monthly Press—those are not your typical exploitation publishers. Anyhow, do you want to have lunch with her or not?"

"What kind of money are we talking about?"

"Fifty thousand. Half with the portion and outline, half on publication."

"Fifty thousand? Strieber got a *million*."

"So? Maybe he's got a better agent. Or maybe he's got a bigger name. Or maybe it was because he was there first."

Rudy sighed. He had no choice, and Bitzberg knew it. "Set up a lunch."

Bitzberg exposed his terrible teeth. "It's already set up. Tomorrow, one o'clock, Moratuwa Wok."

"And *morituri te salutamus* to you too, old buddy."

Bitzberg lit a cigarette. His fingers trembled, making the flame of the match quaver. His fingers had trembled as long as Rudy had known him. It was some kind of nervous affliction. "I do what I can, Rudy, I do what I can."

"So this is my idea," Janet Cruse explained the next day, sipping lukewarm tea from a dainty cracked teacup. "Strieber's book shows that the audience is there, and Hopkins's book shows that anyone can tell essentially the same story that Strieber did and the similarity only goes to *prove* that something strange has to be happening, or how is it that *everyone* is telling the same story?"

"How indeed," Rudy agreed.

"Now the one thing you *have* to promise, Rudy, is that you never joke about this. Flying saucers are like religion. You've got to be solemn. Have you read Strieber's book?"

He nodded.

"Then you know the basic line to take. You're upset, you're confused, you're skeptical, you can hardly believe what's happened to you. And you're terribly grateful to Strieber and Hopkins for having had the courage to tell their stories, because now at last you can tell the world about you—and Bunny."

"Bunny?"

Janet dabbed at the crisp, crimson corners of her lips with a paper napkin. "Bunny is your daughter." She tilted her head coquettishly and waited for him to express some suitable astonishment.

He maintained a poker face, however, and their waitress chose just that moment to arrive with their bowls of millet, steamed vegetables, and a condiment made of onion and raisins. Moratuwa Wok was a Sri Lankan vegetarian restaurant, and it did not have a liquor license. There were gaudy posters of Hindu gods on the wall, and scented candles burning on each of the six tables. Janet and Rudy were the only people having lunch.

"How old is my daughter Bunny?" he asked, after the waitress had gone away.

"Oh, I'd say five or six. Four would be ideal, it's when kids are cutest, but you've got to consider that a lot of the text will be Bunny's account while she's under hypnosis."

"Mm-hm."

He considered Janet's proposition while she nibbled a stalk of asparagus still so crisp it barely drooped as she lifted it to her lips. Sri Lankans did not overcook their vegetables.

"You see how inevitable it is, don't you?" Janet said, halfway down the stalk. "Strieber *played* with the possibility. His little boy was allowed to hear the reindeer on the roof, so to speak, and who knows but that in his next book he'll go all the way and have the dear boy abducted. And *missing* for a few days. Imagine the anguish a parent must suffer. Especially a *father.* How long was Cosby's *Fatherhood* at the top of the list? And how many copies did it sell? It set a record, I think, and it's still going strong. And what could be a greater torment for a loving father than to have his daughter abducted by aliens, who perform unspeakable acts on her? Which is what mainly goes on, as I understood it, in all those unidentified flying objects. So there you've got another hot issue for a cherry on the sundae: child abuse. Can you imagine any paperback house turning down a package like that?"

"It sounds like a very marketable commodity, Janet, I agree. There's only one problem."

"What's that? Tell me, I'll solve it." She snapped decisively at a carrot stick. "You don't have a daughter, is that it? *That* is why you are the ideal dad for little Bunny. Because *obviously* we can't rely on a kid that young to go on talk show circuits and be cross-examined. So what *you* say is that Bunny has been so traumatized by her abduction that she can't possibly be exposed to the brutalizing attentions of the press. She has to be protected from all that, which is why there are no photographs in the book. And as for the fact that Bunny doesn't exist, that's what makes it perfect. That way even Woodward and Bernstein themselves couldn't find her."

Rudy shook his head. "No one will buy it."

"Believe me, they'll buy a million copies."

"Anyone who knows me knows I don't have a daughter."

"But who knows you, Rudy? No one, a dozen people. You don't have a job to go to every day. You've been in and out of A.A. You're broke. Obviously you haven't been the best father in the world to Bunny, but that's part of your anguish. She's being raised by her mother, somewhere upstate, and you visit them whenever you can."

"And what's her name, Bunny's mother?"

"Kimberly, Jennifer, Melissa, take your pick. You can spend a couple chapters filling in the background on the guilt you feel for having let her bear all the responsibility for Bunny's upbringing. You've offered to marry her, because she's a beautiful, talented woman, but she's refused to consider it until you've proved you can stay sober one full year. And of course you can't, but you still visit them whenever you can. They live in this *chalet* in the Catskills.

Melissa handles real estate. Or does she paint? No, real estate, that's a daydream anyone can handle. So that's Bunny's background. The story proper can begin in June."

"This coming June?"

"Mm-hm, when you've agreed to go and look after Bunny, while Melissa takes a well-deserved vacation. You can guess what happens then."

"She's abducted by the aliens."

"Right. For *five days* she's missing, and you are frantic, but even so an obscure impulse keeps you from notifying the police. You search the woods. You see the clearing where the UFO must have landed. You find Bunny's doll there in the matted-down grass. No, better than that: her dog, her faithful dog who followed her everywhere."

"Wouldn't it be better if the dog were abducted with her?"

"Of course! What am I telling you all this for, anyhow? *You're* the writer."

"Do you really think I've sunk so low that I'd write the book you're talking about?"

"Oh, I think you'd always have *written* it, Rudy. The only difference now is that you'll sign your name to it."

"You think I'm shameless."

She nodded.

She was right.

Five weeks later he'd finished a first draft of 340 pages. *The Visitation* was shorter than either Strieber's book or Hopkins's, but it was intense. If Knopf insisted, he could pad out the middle chapters with more paternal anguish and add any number of pages to the transcript of Bunny's testimony under hypnosis. After the nature descriptions—an idyllic walk with Bunny through blossoming mountain laurels and the thunderstorm on the night she disappears—that transcript was the best thing in the book. The Xlom themselves (such was the name he'd given the aliens that both Strieber and Hopkins had left nameless) were no more incredible than darling four-year-old bright-as-a-button Bunny. "Honey Bunny" he called her in moments of supreme paternal doting, or "Funny Bunny" when she was being mischievous, and sometimes (but never in the book, only when he'd finished his day's quota of ten pages), with a fond, bourbon-scented smile, "Money Bunny." Margaret O'Brien had never been more endearing, and Shirley Temple was crass by comparison. Bunny was sugar and spice and everything nice.

And the Xlom were unspeakable. Strieber and Hopkins had both been very equivocal about their aliens. Strieber even allowed as how they might not come from Outer Space but maybe from some Other Dimension or else perhaps they were gods. *Quien sabe?* Half Strieber's book was devoted to such bootless speculations. Hopkins was less accommodating. His aliens seemed to be conducting genetic experiments on their captive humans, impregnating the women with genetically altered sperm stolen from the men and then, when the unwilling brides were a couple months pregnant, abducting them again and stealing their fetuses. Hopkins supplied no explanation as to why his aliens did this, but it certainly was not an activity that inspired trust.

Rudy himself went easy on the enforced pregnancy fantasy (Bunny, after all, was only four), but he bore down hard on the details of the little darling's physical examinations and on the mysterious scar tissue that came to be discovered all over her body. Hopkins had also done a lot with scars, including some blurry photos of what looked like knees with squeezed pimples. Sometimes Rudy felt a tad uneasy about the transparency of *The Visitation*'s S & M sub-text, but Janet had told him not to worry on that score. The target audience for UFO books could read the entire works of the Marquis de Sade, she insisted, and if the Sadean cruelties were ascribed to aliens, they would remain completely innocent as to what it was they were getting off on. Such had been the wisdom of Priscilla Wisdom in her time, as well, so Rudy didn't have any problem letting it all hang out. He wrote at a pace he hadn't managed for the past five years and enjoyed doing it. It might not be art, but it was definitely a professional job.

Two weeks after he'd turned in the manuscript to Bitzberg and had been duly patted on the back for his speedy performance, Rudy still had not heard from Janet, nor (which was more worrisome) had he got back the executed contracts from Knopf. Feeling antsy, he called the Knopf office and asked to speak to Ms. Cruse.

"Who?" the receptionist asked.

"Janet Cruse," he insisted. "She's my editor there."

The receptionist insisted that there was no editor with Knopf called Janet Cruse, nor any record of there ever having been one.

He realized right away that he'd been conned. The walk back to the Knopf office after the lunch at Moratuwa Wok, the good-bye at the elevators, the freebie copy of the Updike book (*Trust Me*, indeed!), the boilerplate contracts with the Knopf logo (something that any agent would have had many opportunities to acquire, alter, and duplicate), and then the constant barrage of phone calls "just to kibbitz," but really to keep him from ever needing to call her at the Knopf office.

But what about Bitzberg: hadn't *he* ever tried to call her at Knopf? Or talked to someone else there about *The Visitation*? On the other hand, if Bitzberg knew Janet wasn't at Knopf, if he'd been in collusion with her from the start, why would he have advanced Rudy $10,000 from his own pocket to tide him over until the nonexistent Knopf advance came in?

"I didn't," Bitzberg explained, "know that, at first. And when I came to suspect it, I admit that I didn't at once tell you. At that point the book was half done, and I'd received money. Not from Knopf, admittedly, but the check didn't bounce for all that. If you want to bow out now, I expect we could take the money and run. On the other hand, there is a bonafide contract for *sixty* thou, and they're not asking for any revisions. They love the book, as is."

"They?"

"The People."

"Who are the people?"

"A cult, I gather. I asked Janet, and she was not particularly forthcoming. But they have their own imprint, Orange Bangle Press." Bitzberg raised a cigarette in his trembling fingers: "I know what you're going to say. You're going to be sarcastic about the name of the press. *But* they have had a major best-seller, *I Wish I May.*"

"I've never heard of it."

"Well, maybe 'major' is an exaggeration. It sold almost forty thousand copies in a trade paperback over the last two years. And they expect to do a lot more with your book."

"You've got a contract?"

Bitzberg smiled, he nodded, he cringed. "I'll show you," he said.

Rudy read the contract.

He signed it.

Only then did he go to the library and find out what there was to be known about The People.

The People had begun, humbly enough, in 1975 as a support group in San Diego for smokers trying to kick the habit by means of meditation and herbal medicine. This original narrow focus gradually came to include other areas of concern, from the therapeutic use of precious stones in the cure of breast cancer and diabetes to the need for a stronger defense posture. One of the group's founding members and the author most often published by Orange Bangle Press was Ms. Lillian Devore, the sole heir of Robert P. Devore of the munitions firm Devore International, contractors for the Navy's Atreus missile. Most of the information in the library about The People focused on the recent legal proceedings concerning the mental competence of Ms. Devore, and her subsequent demise only two months ago just after a court had found that she was not provably insane, notwithstanding certain passages in her published works and the opinions of psychiatrists hired by her niece and nephew, who had brought the case against her.

Needless to say, that niece and nephew had inherited nothing from Ms. Devore's estate, all of which was bequeathed to The People with the sole proviso that the organization continue to advance the study of herbal medicine and to investigate UFO phenomena. UFOs had become a matter of concern only late in Ms. Devore's life, after she had entertained the hypothesis at her trial that her niece and nephew might conceivably have been the issue of secret genetic experiments being conducted by aliens on the women of Earth (and on her half-sister Sue-Beth Smith in particular). This was essentially the same hypothesis being advanced by

Budd Hopkins in *Intruders*, and Ms. Devore's defense attorney was able to introduce as evidence both Hopkins's book and an open letter by the head of Random House, Howard Kaminsky, stating that the publisher and his associates were persuaded of the book's veracity, intellectual integrity, and great importance. It followed from this, Ms. Devore's attorney had argued, that his client must be considered at least as sane as Howard Kaminsky, and the jury had agreed. Two weeks later, at the ripe old age of ninety-four, this monument to the efficacy of herbal medicine died in her sleep, and the last to be heard of The People in the news concerned the unsuccessful efforts of one of The People to have Ms. Devore's estate divided equally among the 150 members of the sect. That effort was quickly quashed, and the direction of the organization and the control of its funds was to remain under the direction of Ms. Devore's former financial adviser and dear friend, B. Franklin Grace, the man who had figured so prominently during the competency hearings for his role in protecting Ms. Devore from the attention of the press. It was Grace, as the head of Orange Bangle Press, who had signed the contract for *The Visitation*.

Books In Print listed four titles by Lillian Devore, including her reputed best-seller *I Wish I May*, but none were available either from the library or at any bookstore where Rudy asked for them. So that was the end of his research efforts. Anyhow, it seemed pretty clear what had happened. Janet had contacted B. Franklin Grace and pitched her idea for the *Communion* rip-off to him, got a go-ahead, and then scouted for someone desperate enough to write it. Why she'd felt she had to diddle Rudy into thinking he was doing the book for Knopf was still a puzzle. Either she thought he needed the extra bait of Knopf's respectability before he took the hook, or else she might have figured he would have been greedier if he'd known he was dipping his royalties from The Fund for The People, Inc. He also wasn't sure whether Janet had come up with the whole scheme by herself or if she and Bitzberg had acted in collusion. But since the final result was a valid contract and money in the bank, Rudy was willing to put his legitimate anger on hold, take the money, and sit tight. On the whole, he felt he'd be happier being published by Orange Bangle instead of by Knopf, since on the basis of Orange Bangle's previous track record, no one might ever find out that *The Visitation* existed. His poor dear imaginary daughter might have endured all her indignities in vain, like the fabled tree that falls, unheard, in the middle of the forest. With luck, he might not even be reviewed in *Publishers' Weekly* (Orange Bangle verged on being a vanity press), and his authorship would remain a secret shame, the easiest kind to bear.

He celebrated his windfall by renting a tape of *Close Encounters* and watching it, soused, with the sound off and Mahler's 8th on the stereo. He fell asleep as Richard Dreyfuss was heading for Wyoming to rendezvous with the aliens' mothership. He woke at 4 A.M. feeling just the way he'd felt in *The Visitation* the first time he'd been returned to his summer cabin after having been abducted and experimented on by the Xlom: his head ached, he was ravenously hungry, and he had an obscure sense that something terrible had just happened to him but he didn't know what.

The Visitation appeared in October and disappeared at once into the vast limbo of unreviewed books, at least as far as New York was concerned. Janet assured him that the real market for UFO books was in the sticks and that there the book was selling reasonably well. The lack of reviews was par for the course with crackpot books, since anyone credulous enough to take such revelations seriously was probably too dumb to write coherent prose. What was a source of concern was the lack of media attention due to what Janet diplomatically referred to as Rudy's image problem, meaning his weight. TV talk shows did not like to feature fat people unless they were famously fat. Similar consideration had prompted Orange Bangle not to put Rudy's picture on the book jacket.

Then, early in November, little Bunny Steiner made her TV debut on a late night talk show in St. Paul. The next day Rudy's phone didn't stop ringing. He claimed, quite truthfully, to know nothing about Bunny's appearance and said that until he saw a tape of the show he could not be certain it had actually been *his* Bunny who'd given such a vivid account of her abduction by the Xlom. When he tried to reach Janet, she was unreachable, and B. Franklin Grace (whom Rudy had not, previously, tried to talk to) was likewise not taking calls.

He let it ride.

The phone calls continued: from Milwaukee, from Detroit, from somewhere in West Virginia, from Buffalo, New York. Bunny got around, and everywhere she got to she seemed to make a considerable impression. Some of the phone calls were accusing in tone, with the unspoken suggestion behind them that Rudy had been personally responsible for his daughter's ordeal, a suggestion he indignantly resisted. "What kind of monster do you think I am?" he would demand of his unseen interrogators.

"Maybe a Xlom?" one of them had replied, and then hung up without awaiting his answer.

Finally, by agreeing to go to Philadelphia for his own late-night inquisition (albeit on radio), Rudy was able to obtain, as his quid pro quo, a VHS tape of Bunny's appearance on *The Brotherly Breakfast Hour.* He slipped the tape into his player, and there she was on his own TV, in the living color of her flesh, his imaginary four-year-old daughter, pretty much the way he'd described her: a blonde, curly-haired, dimple-cheeked, lisping mini-maniac, who rolled her eyes and wrang her hands and commanded the willing suspension of any conceivable disbelief as she re-told the story of her abduction. While her delivery was not verbatim, Bunny rarely strayed beyond the boundaries of the text that Rudy had written, and she never was betrayed into a significant contradiction. Her few embroideries were all in the area of the ineffable and the unspoken, quavers and semi-quavers and moments of stricken silence when she found herself unable to say just where the funny bald people with their big eyes had touched her or what they'd asked her to do. When asked such intimate questions, she would look away—into the camera— and cry real tears. This child had clearly been through experiences that words could not express. Little wonder that the media was picking up on Bunny's performance. She was a miniature Sarah Bernhardt.

Bunny's star reached its zenith just before Xmas, when *The Nation* (which you'd think would have had more dignity than to interest itself in UFOs) published a long article examining the books of Rudy, Strieber, Hopkins, and the Atlantic Monthly Press's contender, Gary Kinder, whose *Light Years* (released in June) featured color photos of UFOs taken by a one-armed Swiss farmer, Eduard Meier. The Kinder book had been expected to enjoy an even larger success than *Communion*, being buttressed not only with its snapshots but with quotes from bonafide scientists, including Stevie Wonder's sound engineer. However, before *Light Years'* release it was discovered that Wendelle Stevens, one of the investigators who'd acted as matchmaker between Meier and the author (and therefore shared in the book's royalties) was serving time in an Arizona prison on a charge of child molestation. There had been no child involved in the Meier UFO sightings, so Stevens's crime should have had no bearing on the book's credibility, as Kinder was at pains to point out in a last-minute Appendix. Nevertheless, the critic in *The Nation* made every effort to tar all four UFO books with the same brush, concentrating his most sinister innuendos on the possibility that Bunny may have been subjected to a false abduction in which Rudy had been an accomplice.

"Young children believe in Santa Claus," the man had argued, "because they *see* him, in his red suit and his white beard, filling their stockings with presents. Who could he be *but* Santa? They have no reason to suspect deceit, no suspicion that for many grown-ups bamboozling the young is its own reward. Might Bunny Steiner not have been put in the same position vis-a-vis the Xlom? Perhaps the reason her testimony has such a distressing fascination, even for UFO skeptics like myself, is that she is not lying. Perhaps the terrible events reported in *The Visitation* really did take place. Only Mr. Steiner can say with any certainty whether his daughter is one of the hoaxers—or one of the hoaxed."

Rudy's problem, of course, was that he couldn't say anything with any certainty. Janet, when he finally did get through to her, would only burble on about what a brilliant marketing strategy Bunny's TV appearances represented. She brushed aside all of Rudy's questions about who Bunny was and where she came from and how the book was selling.

"But her *scars*," he insisted nervously. "They don't look fake. How did she . . ."

Janet laughed. "Surely you don't think only aliens can perform surgery. Kids are always falling down and getting stitched back together. You shouldn't let yourself be upset by one article in one magazine."

"But what if the *police* become interested? What if they say they want to talk with Bunny?"

"*What* police, Rudy? Be reasonable. No one knows what state Bunny lives in, for heaven's sake, much less what city. And *you* are not legally responsible for her, are you? Only her mother is, only Melissa, and she's been very careful to keep both herself and Bunny out of the limelight *except* for her carefully scripted minutes before the cameras. The minute they leave that studio, Bunny's little blonde wig comes off, and she's another girl."

"But is it all an act, or . . . ?"

"No, of course not, it's all true, and she really is your daughter, conceived on board a flying saucer with the semen the Xlom stole from you one night when, according to the false memory they've implanted in your brain, you thought you were watching a rerun of the *The Sound of Music*. And *I'm* the reincarnation of Marie Antoinette."

"You know what I mean," Rudy protested, uncajoled.

"I have never met Bunny, or Melissa X. or B. Franklin Grace for that matter. And I don't see what difference it makes, whether Bunny believes what she's saying or not. She's still a consummate little actress, and her performances are earning us all a pot of money. So why look a gift horse in the mouth?"

"For the Trojans those were famous last words."

"You want reassurance? I'll reassure you. I wasn't going to tell you about this till the deal was firmed up, but at this point we're just haggling over sub-rights percentages, so what the hell. Harper-Collins is taking over distribution for Orange Bangle, *on condition* that you write a final chapter bringing the story up to date. Which means you've got a real shot at the list."

"And what's in the last chapter—a searing account of my trial for child molestation?"

"No, an account of your disbelief, amazement, horror, and shock when you go to visit Bunny and her mother on Christmas Eve and you find that they've *both* been abducted. This time, since it's winter, you'll be able to take photos of where the UFO landed in the snow. Then after the first thaw you report them missing."

Rudy's jaw dropped. "To the *police?*"

"Do you know how many people are reported missing every week? Thousands. You're not saying abducted, not to the police. You just say that two people are missing who *are* missing. Who knows why? Maybe all the publicity was too much for Melissa and she decided to take Bunny and the money and disappear. Or *maybe* the Xlom decided that Bunny had to be taken somewhere where scientists couldn't examine her. In either case, your fatherly heart is broken, and all you can hope for is that some day, somewhere you'll see your little Bunny again."

"HarperCollins *wants* this? You laid this out for them in advance?"

"Well, I couldn't come right out and say what the Xlom may be intending to do. I just promised them that the last chapter would contain sensational new material. I think they got my drift. Of course, you'll have to split your royalties fifty-fifty for the new edition. On the other hand, it's not a sequel, it's just a final chapter that you can write in a weekend."

"Fifty-fifty with whom?"

"With your original publisher, Orange Bangle. I expect a good part of their cut will go to pay off Bunny and her mom. They can't be doing all this for nothing."

"Do you know what the penalty is for reporting a spurious abduction? A $10,000 fine and five years in prison."

"It won't be spurious. Bunny and her mom will have genuinely disappeared. If you *speculate* in your book that the Xlom have taken them from the face of the planet, that's just your theory. And if, later on, they should turn up somewhere else *on* the planet, all that can be inferred from that is that they're trying to avoid public attention, including yours, which they're entitled to do. But I think it highly unlikely they'll be found. The FBI isn't going to make it a top priority, and where are they going to start looking? It's a big country."

"You've discussed this with Grace?"

"Mm-hm. And he's even thrown out hints that Bunny and her mom will be returning to their original happy home, complete with a daddy and sibs. So anyone trying to track down a single woman and her blonde daughter will be following a false scent."

"And when the police ask me for information about them?"

"Grace has created a paper trail that is fairly close to the 'facts' presented in *The Visitation*. Remember all those little changes that appeared in the book after you returned the galleys? That's why they're there. That's why we made Melissa such a mystery woman. Maybe *she* was an alien! Have you ever considered that? Or maybe she's one of the first generation of genetically altered human beings that the aliens have been training to vamp humanity! But that's too good an idea to waste on this book. Keep that one in reserve, and in the ripeness of time we can approach HarperCollins with a sequel: *I Married a Xlom.*"

"But I *didn't* marry her."

"Rudy, you are such a *pedant*. Anyhow, when can I see that last chapter?"

There didn't seem to be any point in further argument. He'd written Bunny into existence. Now he would write her out of existence. "When do you need it?"

"Yesterday."

"You've got it."

The disappearance of Bunny and Melissa, when that event was finally staged, was like a long-postponed visit to the dentist. The worst of it was in the anxiety beforehand, especially in the week from Christmas through New Year's Day that he had to spend alone in the newly vacated chalet. Most of the neighboring vacation houses were standing empty at that time of year, so he was spared having to make a spectacle of himself going about and asking after his missing significant others. Of those people he did approach, only the crippled woman who tended the nearest convenience store claimed to recognize Bunny and Melissa from the photo he showed them, and all she could remember of them was that the little girl had been particularly fond of Pepperidge Farm cookies, which seemed a precocious and expensive taste in such a very young girl. "Mostly at that age their mommies buy them Ding-Dongs or Twinkies, but not that little lady. *She* got Brussels cookies, or Milanos, or Lidos. Did they skip out on their bills, is that why you're asking?" Rudy had assured her it was nothing like that.

With the police he had to be more forthcoming. He could not withhold the fact that the missing girl had figured in *The Visitation* for an earlier disappearance, which the book had ascribed to UFOs. To his relief, though the policemen obviously suspected that Bunny's latest disappearance was a repeat performance of her first, they did not seem annoyed to have been called in. Indeed, both men had their own UFO stories to relate to Rudy concerning mysterious lights that had appeared in the area around the Ashokan reservoir, moving at higher speeds and lower altitudes than could have been the case if they'd been ordinary airplanes. Rudy ended up taking more notes about their UFO sightings than they did concerning the missing girl and her mother. As the friendlier of the two policemen suggested, with a conspiratorial wink, maybe Melissa was just trying to avoid him. Maybe her arranging to spend the holiday with him had been a kind of practical joke. In any case, while it might be mysterious, it was not the sort of mystery the police ought to take an interest in.

When they left the chalet, Rudy called up Janet to jubilate and to ask her to hold up the final production of the new revised edition until he could add something about the testimony of the two policemen.

Saleswise the new edition was something of a letdown. Disappearances are in their nature hard to ballyhoo, since the person who might do the job best isn't around. An effort was made to have Rudy, despite his obesity, appear on the talk shows where Bunny had been such a hit, but most of them declined the opportunity. The few times he did appear, the shows' hosts were openly derisive. Most of their questions had to do with his earnings from *The Visitation* and his relationship with B. Franklin Grace and The People, who were in the news once again for allegedly having tried to poison Ms. Devore's litigious niece and nephew in the period before her competency hearings. Rudy was not enough of a showman to make emotional headway against such currents, and he came off looking sheepish and creepy. He retired from the talk show circuit with a strong conviction that his fifteen minutes on the parking meter of fame had expired, a conviction that was strengthened when Janet Cruse's phone number began to connect with an answering service instead of with Janet. For a little while the answering service went through the motions of taking Rudy's ever-more-urgent messages, and then he was given the address, in Vancouver, where Janet could be contacted. So that, he thought, was the end of the Bunny Steiner story and of his own career as a father. He was wrong on both counts.

Bunny arrived in New York at the end of May, unannounced except by the driver of the taxi who had taken her from the Port Authority bus terminal to Rudy's new sublet in a brownstone on Barrow Street in the nicest part of the Village. "Your daughter's down here," the man had shouted into the intercom, and then, before Rudy could deny he had a daughter, he added: "And the charge on the meter is $4.70."

"Hello, Daddy," Bunny said, clutching her little knapsack to her chest and smiling at him as sweetly as if he were a camera.

"Bunny!"

"Mommy said I've grown so much you probably wouldn't recognize me."

"This is none of my business, Mister," the taxi driver said, with a sideways commiserating glance in Bunny's direction, "but don't you think she's a little young to be traveling around New York on her own? I mean, this isn't . . ." He raised his voice and asked of Bunny: "Where'd you say you came here from, sweetheart?"

"Pocatello," she said demurely. "That's in Idaho."

"You came all the way to New York from Idaho *on a bus*?" the taxi driver marveled.

She nodded. "That's how my dress got so wrinkled."

Rudy paid the driver six dollars, took Bunny's knapsack, and held the door open for her.

"Thank you," she said, stepping inside and heading straight for the stairs. Her hand reached up to grasp the banister. Rudy realized he'd never seen a child on the wide wonky staircase in all the time he'd been subletting his apartment. She seemed so small. Of course, children were supposed to be small, but Bunny seemed smaller than small, a miniature child.

"What is the number of your apartment?" she asked from the head of the stairs.

"Twelve. It's two more flights up."

By the time Rudy had reached the fourth floor, huffing and puffing, Bunny had already gone into the apartment and was leaning out the window that accessed to the fire escape. "You really live high up."

"Not by New York standards."

"I hope you're not mad at me," she said in a placatory tone, turning away from the window and wedging herself into the corner of the sofa. "I know I should have phoned first, but I thought if I did, you might call the police before we had a chance to talk together. I didn't know *what* I'd do if you weren't here. Do they have shopping-bag kids in New York? That's what I'd have become, I guess."

"Am I to understand that you're running away from home?"

She nodded.

"From Pocatello?" he asked with a teasing smile.

She laughed. "No, silly. That's where *Judy Garland* was from, in *A Star Is Born*. Which is one of my favorite movies of all time. We made a tape of it, and I must have seen it twenty times."

"Who is 'we'? And for that matter, who are you?"

"It's all right if you call me Bunny. I like it better than my real name, which is—" She wrinkled her nose to indicate disgust: "Margaret."

"Just Margaret? No last name?"

"On my birth certificate it says Margaret Dacey. But The People don't use last names with each other."

"Ah ha! I *wondered* if you weren't one of The People. They never told me anything about you, you know. I thought I was just making it all up, everything in the book. Even you."

"I know. They always used to make jokes about that. How surprised you were going to be when I appeared on TV. Anyhow, I'm not one of the People. My mother is, but that doesn't mean I have to be. Before The People, she was in something like the Hari Krishnas, only they didn't march around in orange clothes. I *really* hated that. Finally the Baba, who was the old man who ran the place and pretended he was an Indian (but he wasn't, he came from Utah), finally he got busted for cocaine. That was two years ago, in Portland."

"It sounds like you've had an exciting life. How old are you?"

"Guess."

"You must be older than you look. Maybe six?" ·

She shook her head.

"Seven?"

"No—eight and a half. I'm like Gary Coleman, everyone thinks I'm *pre*-school. When the inspectors came round to the commune to see if they were sending their kids to school like they were supposed to, they always made me go with the little kids. I've never been to a real school. But I can read almost anything. I read *your* book a couple times. And I read *The Elfin Horde*, too. And the other ones that came after. When we were living up in the cabin there wasn't much else you could do but read, you couldn't get TV. Mom was going crazy."

"So? What did you think?"

"Of *The Elfin Horde*? Oh, I loved the whole series. Only I hated it when Twa-Loora died. Sometimes at night when I'm going to sleep I'll think about her riding up to the edge of that cliff and looking back and seeing the Black Riders. And then *leaping* to certain death.

And I'll start crying all over again. In fact—" She furrowed her forehead and frowned down at her hands, primly folded together in her lap. "In fact, that's why I decided to come here. Because if I went anywhere else, they would just send me right back to the commune. But I thought *you'd* understand. Because you understood Twa-Loora."

"What about your father? Couldn't you go to him?"

"I'm like the Bunny in your book. I don't have a dad. Unless *you'd* be my dad."

"Hey, wait a minute!"

But Bunny was not to be checked now. She insisted on sharing her fantasy in its full extent. And it was not (Rudy gradually, grudgingly came to see) so entirely bizarre as to be unfeasible. As Bunny herself pointed out, millions of TV viewers had already come to accept as a fact that she was his daughter, and her mother had been deeply involved in that deception. Admittedly, Bunny's birth certificate (she produced a Xerox of it from her knapsack) could not confirm Rudy's paternity, but neither did it contradict it: the space for Father's Name had been left blank. Assuming that her mother and Mr. Grace agreed to letting Rudy assume the responsibility for bringing up Bunny, it would probably not be difficult to arrange the legal details. And with the material in the knapsack it was hard to imagine them withholding their cooperation.

"You realize, don't you, that what we're discussing is blackmail?"

"But if I just took all this to the *police*, it wouldn't make things better for anyone. They'd probably put Mr. Grace in jail, and I'd be sent back to my mother, and she'd be furious with me, and we wouldn't have anywhere to live. Anyhow, she doesn't like me any more than I like her. When we're in the commune we hardly ever even talk to each other. I do have *friends* there, or I used to, but Billy's in jail now. We used to play backgammon, and he really didn't mind if I won sometimes. Mother would get furious. I'll bet she'd be tickled pink to let you have custody. She'd have been glad if the Xlom were real and they did take me away in a flying saucer. She said so lots of times, and pretended it was a joke but it wasn't, not really. It's Mr. Grace who's the problem. Every time reporters would come to the commune, he'd always have someone take me down to the basement laundry room, and I wouldn't come out until the reporters went away. It made me feel like a prisoner."

The more Bunny told about her life in The People's commune, the more Rudy realized that the girl was an As-Told-To diamond mine. What's more, she knew it too, for when he suggested that he turn on his tape deck in order to have a permanent record of the rest of the story, she agreed that that would be a good idea and she even was so thoughtful, when they started taping, to return to the point in the story when Mr. Grace first discovered Bunny and her mother busking in downtown San Diego. Bunny, in addition to her other talents, was a proficient tapdancer, and one of her objects in adopting Rudy as her father was to be able to study dance—tap, jazz, and classic ballet—in New York City, the dance capital of the universe.

"But also," she confided, "I just *like* you. I could tell that from reading *The Visitation*."

"Yes, but that's all made up," Rudy pointed out. "That book is just one lie after another. *You* know that."

"But you tell *nice* lies," Bunny insisted. "If you had a *real* little girl, I'll bet you'd be just the kind of daddy you say you are in the book. Is it the money you're worried about? Mother was always saying how expensive it is to have a kid."

"I hadn't even considered that side of it."

"Because when I was in Mr. Grace's office and took those other things, the dirty pictures and the rest, I also took this."

Out of her wonderful knapsack Bunny produced a file of papers showing sales figures for *The Visitation* that were, even at a glance, distinctly at variance from the figures Orange Bangle Press had provided to him. Bunny's competence as a fairy godchild was coming to seem uncanny. "How did you know . . . ?"

"They always talked to each other as though I weren't there. Maybe they thought I was that dumb. Or maybe they just forgot about me."

"And where do they think you are now? Did you leave a note, or tell anyone?"

"I left a note saying I was going to visit one of Baba's people and I told them not to go to the police. I don't think they would have anyhow. I didn't steal much more money than I needed for the bus trip. I knew if I took a lot, Mr. Grace *would* go to the police. Do you have something to eat?"

"Sure. What do you want? Is a sandwich okay?"

"Just some cookies and milk would be nice. I didn't have any breakfast when the bus stopped in New Jersey."

Rudy went into the kitchen and poured out a Daffy Duck glass-full of milk. Then he arranged three kinds of cookies on a plate. He took it as an omen that Bunny should have arrived at the moment when his cupboard was so well supplied with her favorite brand of cookie.

"There's clover for bunnies," he called out from the kitchen, quoting from his book.

And Bunny, from the living room, quoted the book back to him, making it theirs: "And here's a Bunny for the clover!"

PART TWO

Life on Other Worlds

Caduceus

by C. R. Faddis

The mummy was in an excellent state of preservation. Even the soft neural tissue beneath the arachnoid's anterior exoskeleton was intact. Eighteen centuries had taken a toll of most of the corpses in the catacombs, despite the permafrost of Alcestis's upper strata.

Doctor Calvin was ecstatic. A preliminary scan showed that the mummy was not shot through with the usual tumors of plague; perhaps the creature had survived the plague. Maybe it had died of natural causes, later. It was a lead. After five years of scattergun research and hunch-driven theorizing, it was the first *real* lead. Calvin wasted no time suiting up in the anticontamination gear and entering the sealed dissection cubicle. This cadaver demanded his direct attention, no manipulation by remotes.

An hour vanished as he charted the major organs, making verbal and visual notes for the overhead recorders. The arachnoid was almost certainly an ancestor of the nomadic Keeris—another datum to back Calvin's hypothesis. Humming happily, the doctor prepared cultures of every tissue and began a comp-analysis on the traces of frozen circulatory fluid. It wasn't until he plunged a specimen of cardiac tissue into the cryovat that he noticed—violently—that one of his gloves had a puncture.

"Damnation!" He dropped the specimen and stormed to the decontamination booth, sealing the door behind him. Stripping, he stuffed his garments into the disintegrator and, with another curse, kicked it shut. The booth's cleansing beams came on and scrubbed and bombarded him with antiseptics. For safety, he ran through the process a second time. Then, yanking on a sterile lab coat, he stepped through the outside seal into the control room once more.

The recording system shut down at a snap of the switch. Calvin glanced at the monitors gloomily. He programmed the remotes to return the mummy to the airtight preservation pod in which he'd brought it to the lab. The mummy itself was still of archaeological value, but the flaw in his glove had done double damage: when the evidence had contaminated him, he had also contaminated it. The cadaver, the cultures, all the medical data were compromised by the zoo of bacteria and viruses that are the barnacles of human existence.

The mummy was safely sealed away. Running his hands through his thinning hair, Calvin shut down the monitors. Then, releasing the safety cover, he pulled the lever on the sterilization unit. Inside the dissection chamber, unseen by human eyes, a terrible blaze of white light vaporized every organic particle—specimens, culture medium, microorganisms. The throat of an erupting volcano could not have been more sterile.

In need of a cup of coffee, Calvin left for the canteen that was the heart of Clifftown Station. The alien infection he'd absorbed was already on its way through his bloodstream.

Thin snow dusted the upland deserts of the planet Alcestis, splashed into the north-facing crevices by the persistent winds. Doctor Darwin MacNeil leaned forward in the copilot's seat and peered through the tranship's windows, drinking in the view below. It suggested a skin-cracking dryness; the patches of snow were incongruous.

Andre Iyevka, the tranship's pilot, pointed eastward. "There it is," he said. "Clifftown Station."

Bright vermillion surveyors' domes perched on the rim of a distant mesa, their color an intrusion in the pervasive pastels. Iyevka banked the craft for an approach.

"Clifftown Station to supply tranship," the radio crackled. "We have you on visual."

"This is the *Casper* acknowledging," Iyevka said. "ETA in four minutes. Stand by with those anchors, it's breezy around here."

"Standing by, *Casper.*"

"Brrrr." MacNeil swiveled in the seat as his assistant, Caroline Sommerville, entered the cockpit, her arms wrapped around herself. "If we have to go out in that, I'm breaking out the thermals," she said.

"*Da,* you'd better," the pilot grinned. "Siberia is a resort compared to this."

"Cheer up, kid." MacNeil rose and clapped the pilot on the back. "After four months, those surveyors will be so happy to see new faces that you'll never get a chance to notice the weather."

"Happy to see *me,*" Iyevka called after him. "Don't be too sure about yourself."

Shrugging, MacNeil waved Caroline ahead of him to the storage stow aft and helped her locate the thermals among the jam of medical supplies.

"Is all of this for Clifftown Station?" she said.

MacNeil picked up the inventory slate, ran his eyes down it. "Whoever this J.D.C. is, he or she's been putting in orders like this all year. This latest one is extra heavy on antibiotics." He didn't like the implications. "Either Clifftown Station is peopled by the most accident-prone drillers in the galaxy, or someone's black-marketing the stuff."

"Or they have a legitimate medical problem." Caroline paused in shaking out the thermals and her handsome face tilted up to meet MacNeil's. "Surveyors have a way of 'forgetting' their immunity boosters."

"Don't remind me." MacNeil scanned the slate again. "Well, I don't see anything out of the ordinary in the reports. Whatever is going on, our little surprise visit should shake it out into the open. Two will get you ten, it's nothing worse than a nice embarrassing round of Anthasian clap."

"Doctor, really!"

Grinning, MacNeil thrust a leg into a thermal jumpsuit.

Iyevka set the *Casper* down near the waiting ground crew and killed the power as the craft was anchored to bedrock. Even so, it shuddered in the wind.

Suited up, they stepped into a bitter squall. The forty meters to the nearest prefab dome were ice-stinging, hang-onto-the-guide-ropes-for-dear-life minutes that left everybody shivering, lips numbed and eyes and noses streaming. MacNeil let himself be led to a bench, seeing the inside of the hut through tear-blurred eyes. The howl of the wind died as doors whined shut, and a blast of heated air drove out the cold.

Someone began helping MacNeil out of his thermals, and he dragged a freed arm across his eyes. What he saw chilled him more than the squall had. His helper, a tarnished-brown young man, was marred with dry white blisters. The other surveyors in the hut were similarly marked, yet their movements were vigorous and their color under the blisters was good.

Climbing out of his suit's leggings, MacNeil unpacked his medical remote and passed it over the nearest man, frowning at the ambiguous readings.

"We weren't expecting anyone but a pilot," the man smiled, "but we're always glad to have visitors." He offered a hand. "I'm Telerio Takanna, drilling engineer."

MacNeil drew back from the proffered hand. "Caroline, Andre—don't touch anyone. Andre, the anticontamination suits are in the blue pack. Break out three of them and get into one."

"What for?" Iyevka said.

"Do it *now.*" MacNeil peered at Takanna's face, examining the lesions more closely without touching them. "I'm Doctor MacNeil from Company Central. How long have you had these blemishes?"

"Oh, this?" Shrugging, Takanna folded MacNeil's thermals. "It's just a rash, everyone's got it. Just some little bug."

"We'll see about that. Where's your team medic?"

"I'll take you below to the infirmary and let Doc Calvin fill you in," Takanna said.

"Calvin?" Something snagged at MacNeil's memory, but then Iyevka handed him an anticontamination suit.

Takanna tore his eyes from watching Caroline Sommerville pull the clear, skin-like suit on over her exquisite legs. "Ah, did you say something, Doc?"

The light, anticontamination hood settled over MacNeil's shoulders, and he closed the seals and started the rebreather. "Let's go below," he said. "Someone has a lot of explaining to do."

A steeply sloped tunnel cut neatly into the heart of the mesa. The soft intermittent lighting revealed rich textures on the surfaces, sculpted reliefs crazed like porcelain by the stress of fluctuating temperatures. The abstract carvings spiraled down the passage, linked together as though narrating a myth or prayer of some bygone hero or deity.

"Watch your step," Takanna warned. "I trip over myself every time I come through here."

"Is this a kind of writing?" Iyevka asked.

"Nothing anyone can deciper. It's pretty, isn't it? Makes you sorry the race died out."

The tunnel became damp as they penetrated the permafrost layer. A form of fungus or algae grew over the carvings, tinting the beige stone with bright patches of orange and pink wherever the surveyors had mounted lights that warmed the stone.

"Why are you living down here instead of in the prefabs?" MacNeil asked the Freyan chemist beside him.

Yed-Paolor's heteroplastic head, offset on the alien's shoulder and grafted to the left clavicle, turned to converse while her natural head watched the passage ahead. "We have determined that it is—how do you humans say?—more 'comfortable' in the grottoes, and more spacious. You may have noticed as your tranship approached that there are no surface remains of the civilization that flourished here. The beings did not disturb the surface environment; they built beneath it."

"I've heard about that," Iyevka said. "Is that why Alcestis is nicknamed 'Catacombs'?"

"It's probably some explorer's morbid idea of a joke," MacNeil snapped.

"Not so," the Freyan replied. "It is a most appropriate epithet."

Leading the group into a brighter side passage, Takanna added, "Most of this part of Alcestis is one big graveyard, and this particular mesa seems to have been the main 'chapel'." He waved at the walls. "There's tombs behind most of the passages."

"*Tombs?*" Iyevka gulped. The young pilot shook his head and walked closer—much closer—to the others. But then the tunnel ended in a fitted doorway scavenged from one of the huts.

Beyond it, the living quarters were a series of dry chambers strung together by passages, an elaborate macrame executed in stone. The spaces were pleasing even to human senses, but Mac-Neil gave them scant attention. He scrutinized every person they passed, mentally ticking off any visible signs of illness. Discounting the few nonhumans, he noted a variety on different people. But the one consistent symptom was the white blistering that marred faces, hands, and arms. He was still grinding through mental texts when Takanna knocked at a door marked **TEMP INFIRM** in yellow engineer's chalk.

Inside, a clutch of cots held several patients in the immense, echoing room. Off to one side, an iron-haired man in a rumpled lab coat sat with his back to the door, examining one of the patients.

Takanna harrumphed, then spoke up. "Hey, Doc? We have visitors."

The man turned slowly, blinked, then zeroed on MacNeil. "Darwin. I should have known. I'd heard you joined the Company. You always were a prize snoop."

MacNeil's mouth dropped open. Then his wit came to his rescue. "Hello, J.D. You haven't mellowed a microgram, have you?" he heard himself drawl. Moving to Calvin's patient, he inspected the dressings on the woman's arms. "Your practical skills haven't improved much, either."

"Pill-pushing and sprain-splinting are your racket, not mine."

Waving Calvin out of the chair, MacNeil sat down to redo the bandages. Out of the corner of his eyes, he watched as the older man made awkward apologies to Sommerville and Iyevka. Jefferson Davis Calvin! The once-famous researcher had not aged gracefully. He looked a good bit older than the sixty or so years MacNeil knew he carried. The leftover babyfat Calvin had had while head of Exomedicine at MacNeil's alma mater had melted away to stooped gauntness, and the yellow-grey hair was overdue for a trim. How far the man's fortunes had fallen, to reduce him to a surveyors' medic— a post usually filled by doctors right out of an undistinguished internship. MacNeil's frown deepened, but he wiped it carefully from his face before turning to the others.

"I hate to break up the party, but I want to know what these people have contracted." He eyed Calvin, decided not to press immediately for why Calvin hadn't reported the situation. "Caroline, get a list of patients and personal statistics, and begin matching up symptoms for the data bank. Andre, as soon as the wind outside lets up, bring down the diagnostic computer and the other supplies. Calvin, we'll start by taking a look at your logbook."

Iyevka took care of transferring the medical equipment to the infirmary, then left the doctors to their work and made a tour of the station with Takanna. The mesa was a maze of tunnels, many of which were barren of decoration. Iyevka stepped up to one of the passage walls and inspected the stone. It was as smooth and glazed as if it had been melted out by a laserdrill.

"Not our work, Andre," Takanna said. "Doc Calvin knows a lot about archaeology, and he figures this place is over three thousand standard years old."

"The extinct native culture did this?"

"Who else?"

"Have—have you ever followed the tunnels to their end?"

"We've never found an 'end,' so to speak. Most of the tunnels take a sharp dip, too steep to walk, and they just keep going down."

Iyevka's sense of adventure was aroused. "Has anyone ever climbed down very far?"

"Mikki Fo tried, a few months ago, when the winds got too high to go out to the drilling sites. She hit a cross-passage about a thousand meters down, but when she explored it, there were only more tunnels. One of these days, if I ever get the time, I want to rig a power-lift so we can take a look in some of the really deep wells."

Iyevka laughed, shaking his blond bangs out of his eyes under the close-fitting anticontamination hood. "We could set up the pulleys, you and I, when we both have a few free hours. Tomorrow, maybe?"

Ruefully, Takanna held up his hands. They were freshly bandaged. "I can't climb. But I'll run the motor for your line, if you're game to go down alone."

The grin widened on Iyevka's face as he punched Takanna on the arm. "Now tell me, who could turn down a challenge like that?"

The footsteps behind MacNeil clomped back and forth, pacing interminably. Every once in a while, Calvin would pause long enough to peer over MacNeil's shoulder at the computer readouts, then he'd resume his pacing.

"Sit down, will you?" MacNeil growled. "I can't concentrate with you jogging in place behind me."

Calvin ignored him.

Sighing, MacNeil pushed back from the console. "Except for these blasted lesions, it's one confounding symptom after another. I haven't the slightest idea of what we're dealing with."

"There's the sinus problem. Most of us had that the first day after the blisters appeared."

"Well, the computer's never heard of a combination like that, and neither have I. For all I can tell, we could have at least four completely unrelated infections going here at once."

Calvin finally picked a spot and stood still. "At least I've lived to hear the summa cum laude *wunderkind* admit he doesn't have all the answers."

A sarcastic comeback formed on MacNeil's lips, but he bit it back. There was no point in provoking Calvin. The old man was proud as Lucifer, and he'd already been caught with his pants down once this week. MacNeil looked up. "Look, J.D., it's been twenty years. Can't we shelve the war? The damage is done. There's work to do."

Calvin just stared at the reflections in a polished metal cabinet and scratched absently at the blisters on his hands. His mouth was a thin, sealed line.

Snapping off the computer, MacNeil turned his mind back to the problem at hand. "This isn't getting us anywhere; we may not get anything from the tissue cultures for weeks." He spun in the chair to face Calvin. "Maybe we can backtrack the infection. Tell me, who turned up with the first lesions?"

Calvin shifted uneasily. "I did."

"You? Do you have any idea how you got them?"

Tearing himself from his contemplation of his reflection, Calvin gave a new set of instructions to the computer. The readout promptly displayed a holotape of an autopsy—an autopsy of a mummified alien, the species of which MacNeil recognized immediately.

"A Keeris—space gypsies?"

"No, not a modern Keeris," Calvin corrected. "An inhabitant of Alcestis, dead eighteen hundred and nine years, though I do think the gypsies' species originated here."

"What does this have to do with the infection?"

Calvin grimaced. "A flaw developed in one of my gloves while I was dissecting this cadaver. The lesions appeared the next day; but by then, I'd spread it by touch to some of the surveyors; and soon everyone had it. I didn't think it would affect humans seriously, and that antibiotics would knock it out, but—" He swallowed, gestured at the readout. "It's probably the same plague that destroyed the Keeris here."

"Plague? Wait a minute. What were you doing poking into the tombs here? I thought this planet—this whole system—is under archaeological interdict."

Folding his arms, Calvin locked eyes with him. "Archaeological interdict by my own recommendation, Darwin. There were three surveys here before. I was with two of them. Archaeopathology is my specialty, or have you forgotten everything I taught you?" In a more reasonable tone, he added, "There are archaeological and—I think—medical treasures here that must be protected from the insensitive. Do you know what the surveyors are finding here? Do you know why Company keeps sending them back to take another look around? They've found traces of high grade *oil*. Natural petroleum. Maybe by the carrier loads."

"Natural oil's pretty rare stuff, Calvin; what makes you think there's enough here to make profiteering worthwhile?"

"It isn't rare on certain classes of planets. Earth itself used to be swimming in it—used to burn it for *fuel* half a millennium ago. But the base molecules of Alcestin crude are the makings of jewelers' plastics, and worth—oh, it would take a financier to estimate the wealth."

"And what does oil have to do with opening tombs?" MacNeil insisted.

Calvin looked at him as though he were brain-damaged. "Why, the planet would be overrun. Miners, heavy equipment, large-scale operations—then looters and grave robbers—it would be horrible. There'd be no valid evidence of Keeris culture inside of a year."

"If you knew about all this, you should have notified the Company. And if you suspected a viable plague here, you should never have opened a single tomb!"

"I don't have to apologize for my decisions to you."

"Damn you, I think you do!" MacNeil yanked open the seal on the sleeve of his anticontamination suit and stuck his bare arm under

Calvin's nose. Tiny white pustules were beginning to raise on his skin.

Calvin stared, horror slowly displacing his rage. Then he turned on his heel and was gone out the door.

The chamber set aside for the mess hall, called "the canteen," was also the station's social center; and aside from having to wear the slightly confining anticontamination suit, Caroline Sommerville felt as comfortable there as she felt at the Company's home base on Comstock II. She'd been teaching the more healthy of the surveyors basic nursing skills so there would be more help with the bedridden patients; and she and the Freyan woman, Yed-Paolor, became friends.

Playing cards with the Freyan was a startling experience, though. Paolor, the heteroplastic personality, would presumably be playing her hand when Yed would look over and make a suggestion about strategy. Watching two parts of a single being debate each other over a card game was disconcerting. On top of that, Yed felt no compunctions about discussing Paolor's hand in detail, so that Caroline could hardly help knowing every card her opponent held. It was a hopeless situation. Freyans simply did not understand the concept of secrecy, even on so limited a scale. Yed-Paolor left after several hands, with a deprecating but humorous opinion of human entertainments.

Caroline was due back at the infirmary in ten minutes. She was just leaving when Dr. Calvin came in, trailing a cloud of ill temper. She nodded to him as she passed him.

"Oh, Ms. Sommerville?"

She stopped. "Yes, Doctor, is there something I can do for you?" Polite. Noncommittal. The man was a mystery to her.

"I realize I was somewhat . . . curt . . . when we met yesterday. I've been meaning to apologize properly. If you're not in a hurry—if you have time—would you join me for a chat?"

She met his eyes, and his anger was gone, replaced by shy

hopefulness. "I do have a few minutes," she said; and putting her first impression firmly aside, she joined him at a table.

"I'm afraid my—" he began.

"Is it true—" she said at the same instant.

They chuckled nervously, and Calvin waved her first.

"I asked Dr. MacNeil where he'd known you before. I hope you don't mind, but it was obvious, and I'm a curious person. He told me you were a Korbel Prize winner in medicine where he went to medical school," she said. "I'm interested because my husband was Paul Sommerville, another Korbel winner—maybe you've heard of him? I was hoping you might have known him."

"Sommerville? I thought the name sounded familiar. The Sommerville of eugenic revitalization. Yes, I know his work quite well, it was vital to some of my own, years ago. I heard he was killed in an accident. I didn't know he had a wife."

"We'd only been married five months," Caroline said softly. She studied a pattern on the opposite wall.

Calvin changed the topic. "Yes; well, then. What do you think of our 'digs,' if you'll excuse a poor pun?" He gestured at the vault of carvings that capped the room.

Caroline snatched at the overture of levity. "I think," she said animatedly, "that I would never have dreamed of living underground until I came here. When I was ten, my parents took me to New Islam on my first offworld vacation, and we saw dozens of mosques with carved lattice domes. They were wonderful, but they couldn't hold a candle to this."

Calvin's smile was a pleasant change in his seamed face. "Interesting that you should compare this to a place of worship. I have reason to believe that these grottoes once housed a religious order."

"It's a kind of monastery?"

"Very much like that. I call it 'the Order of the Caduceus'."

"The caduceus is the Terran symbol for medicine."

"That's correct, but the name's associations fit here, in their way. The cult here was a mingling of religion and medicine." He leaned toward her as though to convey a confidence. "If I'm right, the members studied to attain the capability of curative empathy."

Caroline blinked, not sure she followed what he was trying to say. "I thought the only curing empaths are born that way, and they usually die before puberty. What makes you think someone could *attain* empathy?"

"Have you ever heard of space gypsies?"

"Keeris? What about them?"

"They are the descendents of the race that lived here," Calvin said. "And none of them are empaths. Espers, yes, but not empaths. Yet empaths existed here two thousand years ago, before a plague came."

"What makes you think that?"

He lowered his voice. "You're skeptical, of course. But you seem to be a very perceptive woman. I have data from preserved remains of Keeris who died around the time of the plague, yet show signs of having been cured of the plague itself, to die of other causes. I believe an empath cured them. Also, I can read some of the hieroglyphs."

Caroline stared at him. He was completely serious. This world was supposed to be an archaeological enigma, and Dr. Calvin seemed to be keeping his incredible discoveries almost to himself. It didn't make sense. "If empathy is a learnable technique," she said, "that knowledge would be a breakthrough in medicine comparable to—to Pasteur's discovery of microörganisms. Why haven't you contacted Authority to get professional archaeologists here?"

"Oh, I have," he said. "They don't believe me. They said my findings are ambiguous. They warned me to keep out of the tombs."

"Then what you've been doing is illegal." She said it playfully, but he missed her humor.

"That's not important. It's absolutely vital that I find out how the ancient Keeris artificially stimulated empathic healing. I *must* discover it! Think of what it would mean in ending suffering. No price would be too high to find it."

Sitting back in her chair, Caroline looked at Calvin as though she were seeing him for the first time. He reminded her acutely of Paul:

the social awkwardness, the singleminded view he took of his work's importance, the incredible drive for knowledge. Calvin wasn't much older than Paul would be, now. She decided she liked the creases around his eyes. She knew they came of too much squinting at computer readouts, but she began to think of them as smile lines. She couldn't imagine what Darwin MacNeil found in Calvin that he disliked so vehemently. Then she noticed the time.

"Oh no, I'm late. I've got to get back." She rose.

Calvin caught at her arm. "Please, Ms. Sommerville, I hope I didn't bore you," he said. "And I am sorry about the poor greeting I gave you yesterday. I hope you'll have time for another chat after your shift?"

She smiled her warmest smile. "That sounds very nice," she said, and headed for the infirmary. She decided she definitely liked Dr. Calvin. He stirred feelings in her that she had thought long dead . . . and buried.

"I think we're ready," Telerio Takanna said. He hauled the dummy weight out of the well and unfastened it from the lifeline.

"How many meters of line are there?" Iyevka asked, snapping the lifeline onto the harness at his chest.

"Twenty-five hundred. This well bounced bottom at twenty-one, so you'll have plenty of line if you want to wander around down there."

Iyevka peered into the inky vertical hole into which he was about to drop. He could see down about ten meters, where the illumination of Takanna's mining lamp ended. A stiff, icy breeze came up from the depths.

"Having second thoughts, Andre?"

Iyevka straightened and met Takanna's toothy grin. It was a friendly face, a trustworthy face. "Not on your life," Iyevka said; and, gathering the short loops of slack line, he scrambled over the ledge.

"Okay, Andre?"

"Lower away."

The motorized pulley hummed to life and fed out cable in a smooth descent. Relaxing in the harness, Iyevka looked up, watching the circle of light shrink at the rim of the well. Within a minute, it had diminished to a pinpoint. Complete blackness closed around him, and the peculiar environment of the well pressed on his senses. The updraft stripped away his body heat even through his sealed jumpsuit. The wind penetrated the suit's filters with an odor he hadn't noticed before: dank, like moist earth, with a tinge of sulfur.

Alarmed, Iyevka flashed his lamp into the pit coming up at him. Empty. He switched the lamp off again, feeling foolish, and wondered how long it would take to reach bottom.

As on cue, the speaker at his belt crackled to life. "Half-way mark, Andre. Everything all right?"

"Just fine. I always wanted to freeze to death," he complained, but he was grateful to hear Takanna's voice. He dropped the rest of the way in silence.

Sans warning, solid ground leapt up to meet him and he found himself on his knees before he could orient himself. The cable kept coming down on top of him. "Ho! Telerio! I'm here!"

The cable stopped feeding.

"One small step for a man, . . ." he muttered.

"What was that, Andre?"

"I said, there's a nudist colony down here."

"What?"

"I said I'm here!"

"Oh. What's down there?"

Iyevka stood up and freed himself from the excess cable, reaching for his lamp. Then he realized that he could *see* the walls around him. They were dimly defined by a delicate glow that seemed to emanate from the stone itself. He shut his eyes and opened them again to check whether what he was seeing was retinal "noise." It wasn't. There was light, and he seemed to be adapting to it very quickly; already he could make out one of the mysterious carvings that appeared at every tunnel intersection. "I think I found another street sign," he told Takanna.

"A what?"

"A street sign. I think that's what the intersection carvings are."

"Speak up, Andre, I can't hear you."

"Turn up the damn receiver!"

"It's all the way up," Takanna said.

"Oh." Iyevka could make out the carving clearly now. It seemed that a natural phosphorescence in the rock, possibly reacting to his body heat, was the source of the glow. It wasn't enough light to move around in, though, so he snapped on his lamp. The sudden glare stabbed his eyes, and he shut it off immediately. When he opened his eyes again, the tunnel had brightened enough to see without the lamp. He saw that he was in yet another featureless tunnel.

"Feed me some slack, nice and slow," he radioed, remembering to raise his voice. "I'm going for a walk."

"It's about time."

Iyevka's footsteps crunched on scattered debris, and he listened to the echoes kick around the passage. There was a turn in the tunnel ahead. Then he heard it: the plink-plink of dripping water. Enduring the blaze of his lamp, he negotiated the downward-spiraling rotation of passage and found himself in a luminous chamber.

There was no altar, no idol, no seating matrix, yet Iyevka knew he was in a place set aside for ritual or meditation. It had that universal quality that transcended architecture or decor, sect or species—a sense of *presence*, perhaps a lingering impression on the place itself of the aspirations and prayers of its users. A wide pool of green-glowing water dominated the chamber. Water dripped into it from a place high in the stalactitic ceiling. Then something moved behind one of the stalactites, and Iyevka swung his lamp to spotlight it.

Beady multiple eyes stared down at him from a profusion of thin, hairy limbs. One of the limbs moved to shield the red eyes from the glare of the lamp. Another limb felt around on the ceiling for a firmer foothold.

Iyevka wheeled, scrambling for the vertical well, nearly garroting himself on the tangled line underfoot. "Telerio! Pull me out!"

"Hey Andre?"

"Up, man!" He heard spidery legs scrabbling behind him. "*Get me out of here!*"

He reached the well, the slack line snaking up beside him. The scrabbling sound was closer, and then reflective red eyes came around the turn in the tunnel. Abruptly, Iyevka was yanked off his feet and hauled upward. Spinning, he cracked his head on the vertical wall. The red eyes below him winked out along with everything else.

No one believed him.

Doctor Calvin listened to him attentively, but made no comment, only grabbing some tapedecks and cornering Dr. MacNeil at the other end of the room. Caroline Sommerville nodded patiently as Iyevka repeated his story for her, but she was much more interested in getting the adhesive patch to stick to the shaved spot on his skull. Finally, Dr. MacNeil checked him over and sent him off to rest. Even Telerio Takanna seemed to think it was all an hallucination.

Slumped in a chair in the canteen, Iyevka held his throbbing head.

"Look," Takanna told him, "whatever you saw, it wasn't real. It's true that beings like the Keeris used to live here. But no one's lived on Alcestis in a couple thousand years. No one could. What would they live on; nothing'll grow but mushrooms."

Iyevka shook his head, wincing.

"Maybe you saw a statue, then."

"I saw a living being. It followed me back to the well," the pilot said. "If I hadn't panicked—"

"If you hadn't panicked, you wouldn't have hit your head; and that's all," Takanna said, not quite suppressing a smile.

"I want to go back down and find it."

The smile fell off Takanna's face. "No one's going back down. Haley Druen is sick, and now Yed-Paolor. That leaves me in charge, and there are fourteen rigs to shut down. Soon we'll all be too ill to work. There's no more time for adventure, Andre. Besides—" He reached across the table and pulled Iyevka's now-bare hand from his coffee cup. "—look at those blisters. And Doc MacNeil said you're running a temperature."

"So's the doctor, and you haven't accused him of hallucinating."

Takanna frowned, looking suddenly older, more tired. "Look, even if there are Keeris in the wells, they never come up here, so what does it matter?"

"It matters to me! Don't you see? I saw it and ran like a kid seeing his first real dragon. All my training—everything I believe in—told me I should have tried to communicate with it. But all I could think of was that I had to get out of there." An aura of self-disgust projected from him as he slouched back in the chair.

Takanna inspected the bandages on his own hands for a moment, then leaned forward. "Listen, Andre, your case of whatever-we-have isn't as advanced as ours. We need you right here. Maybe after the crisis is over, you and me can go down the well together and hunt your spider. What do you say?"

Squinting skeptically at the engineer, Iyevka managed a look of resignation. "Whatever you say. You're in charge."

Mirrors were Caroline Sommerville's enemies. They chronicled more than the passage of years; for her, they were an inexorable conscience that mocked her with every frown line. She could camouflage the wisps of grey in her ash brown hair; but at forty, she had a face full of sighs. Staring now at her reflection, she waited to see the first blisters encrust her cheeks as they had the backs of her hands. She was the last of the newcomers to develop the infection, which they'd apparently contracted when the ground crew had helped them out of their thermals the first day they'd arrived on Alcestis.

She'd retreated into the washroom to escape the constant bickering between MacNeil and Calvin. She didn't care for this embittered side of the previously genial MacNeil. And, she was finding herself increasingly drawn to Calvin, spending more and more of her time with him. She didn't know why the two men detested each other. She wasn't sure she wanted to know. She just wished they'd call off the battle; people were short-tempered as it was.

After a few minutes, she slapped water onto her face, dried it, reset her features to prim neutrality, and went back into the lab.

MacNeil and Calvin were still at each other, pitted in a verbal duel that roared around the stone chamber. The computers chattered away quietly, sorting data that no one was scanning.

"Your suppositions are based on pure fantasy," MacNeil barked. "We don't have time to chase after Iyevka's hallucinations—or yours. There are half a dozen people dying in the next room!"

Florid with indignation, Calvin practically sputtered. "Then stop speaking to me as if I were some irresponsible, raving lunatic. I'm a scientist! I have proof!"

"Some scientist. You'd gamble lives and precious time on a myth."

Calvin picked up a box of tapedecks and slammed it on the table in front of MacNeil. "If you'd look at the evidence, you'd know I'm right. If we've got the Keeris' plague, then finding the secret of the Caduceus is our only chance."

MacNeil caught Caroline's withering look. He bowed his head, took a deep breath, and spoke more calmly. "I did look at your 'evidence.' But you're so goddamned wrapped up in your treasure hunt that you're oblivious to everything else. Even if there were a Caduceus once, it couldn't save its own race from the very plague we're fighting now. They *died*, J.D. The Keeris here are all *dead*."

"The gypsies are Keeris, and they're alive," Calvin said. He pounced on MacNeil's attempt at reason. "And your pilot saw a living Keeris in the pits. Some of them survived, so there has to be a cure. There has to be."

MacNeil hammered the computer console. "Yes, there's a cure! It's right in this data, or we're all dead."

"The computer will tell us nothing. Not in time."

"Then I hope you've made out your will." MacNeil turned back to the console and punched the reset button. Over his shoulder, he said, "Are you going to help with this morning's test results, or are you going back to the infirmary?" His voice carried a tone of dismissal; and Calvin complied, vanishing into the next room in silent fury. MacNeil turned his gaze on Caroline—as cold a stare as she'd ever seen. "And what are you going to do, stand there all day?"

Stung, she followed Calvin.

In the infirmary, she went directly to the ward monitor and checked to see which of the fifteen patients were due for medication. MacNeil was prescribing a pan-spectrum antibiotic, which seemed to slow the disease in some of the patients. She loaded an inject-gun with the drug and made the rounds.

As she approached, Andre Iyevka looked up from the patient he was tending.

"How do you like your new career as a nurse?" she asked, forcing a smile.

He shook his head, eyes grim. "I don't know how you can do it, day after day."

"You get used to it," she said. Setting the injector, she uncovered Iyevka's patient to give him the shot. Takanna was unconscious. Iyevka looked miserable. "Don't worry, he's holding his own—"

Conversation was aborted by a piercing alarm. Dropping the injector, Caroline scrambled to get the emergency kit and hurried after Calvin to the bed of the endangered patient.

Yed-Paolor's skin had gone the frightful orange of Freyan asphyxiation. Calvin jerked the pillows out from under the woman's heads and demanded the respirators. Caroline slapped one into his hand and pressed the other over the Freyan's heteroplastic face. The lungs inflated, deflated, but neither brain initiated another inhalation. Calvin filled the lungs again mechanically. No response. Again. Nothing. Grabbing an injector, he shot stimulants into each neck artery in the hope of jolting at least one brain into automatic function, but it was useless: the Freyan had decided to die. Her skin was flushed to near-scarlet.

"All right!" Calvin stood back helplessly and watched the encephalon readings plummet. "All right." His voice wavered. "Die if you want to."

After a long minute, he reached over, removed the respirators, and switched off the monitors. The corpse relaxed. The lidless faceted eyes filmed over, and the Freyan's faces set in tranquil expressions. Caroline Sommerville, who had seen many friends die, sobbed in the privacy of her mind.

Behind her, unnoticed until now, MacNeil spoke softly. "The first one. It's started."

The seventh day at Clifftown Station was particularly quiet. Most of the survivors were in the infirmary. Those still on their feet divided their time between caring for the bedridden and aiding the desperate research effort. The station itself was shut down.

MacNeil pondered the autopsy he'd performed on Yed-Paolor. The cause of the disease was still unknown, but its effects were before him in graphic detail: the Freyan's body was a ghastly clump of intertwined tumors, tissue gone mad. The abnormality had affected every gastrointestinal and lymphatic organ until the torso was strangled with bulk and the vital systems collapsed.

There were the beginnings of the tumors in all of them, now. MacNeil had tried everything he knew: antibiotics, cultured serums, and other chemotherapy; transfusions of circulatory and lymphatic fluids; radiation therapies; electropuncture and electrolytic alignment; treating the symptoms where he could not find the cause. All, so far, had been ineffective.

And then Caroline, tired to the bone, mixed up the culture plates. And there it was. MacNeil pounced on the computer scope and sent Caroline scurrying for Calvin.

"That's the culprit," MacNeil said. The scope displayed three slides, each a specimen from a different organ, each clustered with colorless, featureless spheroids that had not been there before.

"What about the other microbes you were tracking?" Calvin asked.

"I ruled them out. They're concurrent infections that our immunological injections would normally have countered. But these are from two-day-old plates. Apparently, it doesn't show up on fresh slides. It was an accident that we even looked at these."

Calvin nodded, peering at the glassy spheroids. He reprogrammed the moleculanalyzer, and the computer constructed a holo of the atomic structure. The spheroids were featureless to the eye, but their molecular composition was bizarre. Several of the valences were anomalous.

"An insidious thing," MacNeil said. "It wrecks our immunology, opens the gates to other infections, and meanwhile fills us with tumors like some amok supercarcinoma. And I have no idea what it is. It isn't a spore, or a bacterium, or even quite a virus."

"But an ugly killer," Caroline breathed.

Eyes narrowing, Calvin turned to MacNeil. "Darwin, now more than ever, we have to find out how the Keeris' descendents survived the plague. If the secret of acquired empathy is still known—"

"Not that again!"

"Admit it, Darwin." He jabbed a finger at the monitors. "We can't fight that thing. Iyevka saw a Keeris, here, and if a Keeris survived, there must either be an immunity or a cure. And a cure is what we need!"

"Andre didn't see anything. He's hardly more than a kid." Mac-Neil eased back in a chair. He was beginning to ache inside.

"We have nothing to lose by hunting the Keeris."

"We'd lose time," MacNeil growled, "which we have very little of. There are several treatments we haven't tried yet."

"No, you haven't tried standing on your head, or signing a treaty, or farting on the slides!"

MacNeil did a slow burn. "Ms. Sommerville," he said neutrally, "one of us should be on call in the infirmary. Would you take that post, please?"

Caroline threw him an inscrutable look and left.

When the door had shut, he glared at Calvin. "You jackass! You ignorant, glory-seeking son of a bitch!" When Calvin made no reply, he added, "I never wanted to see your goddamned face again, but here we are and we're stuck with each other. At least have the decency not to undermine morale by attacking me in front of my staff. And while I'm on the subject, I don't like what you've been up to behind my back. Keep your slimy hands off my assistant!"

Face flushing, Calvin jerked up straight, but his voice was deadly quiet. "Unless you have a personal claim on Ms. Sommerville, I suggest that you mind your own business."

"Caroline is my associate and my friend, and I won't have some emotional jackal preying on her sensitivity. She deserves better than you. Just leave her alone."

"You have no right—"

"I have every right," MacNeil said with baiting relish. "What you did to my marriage gives me that right. You're the lowest kind of lecher there is!"

Calvin's temper cracked; but instead of the expected tirade, he launched himself at MacNeil, tipping the chair over backwards and crashing them both to the floor. Papers and slide mounts flew as Calvin pummeled at MacNeil. Fending off the clumsy blows, MacNeil twisted away and captured thin arms. Gaining his knees, MacNeil pinned the arms behind the older man's back.

"You bastard! You stupid bastard!"

"Calvin, calm down," MacNeil said, shaken. "Calm down and I'll let you go."

"No, do what you will, you've got me where you want me," he blurted. "You want your revenge, take it!"

MacNeil shoved Calvin from him, but the bottled-up bitterness poured out. "Twenty years ago I'd have beaten your face in. You damn near killed me when you seduced Ella away from me. Now, you just make me sick." He swayed to his feet, wanting to be away from this man, this room, this planet.

"Is that what you think?" Calvin rolled over and sat against a cabinet. "That I stole her from you?"

MacNeil's malice dissipated, leaving only exhaustion. He flopped down on the lab stool. "What should I think? You were the most prestigious name at the university, the Korbel Prize winner, attractive, single, wealthy. . . ." Despair crept into his voice. "I was a nobody, an intern on a shoestring budget, living in a two-room student apartment with a wife and child. You offered Ella everything she ever wanted. How could I hope to hold on to her?"

Calvin winced. "No . . . Darwin, it wasn't that simple. Ella went after *me*."

"Bullshit."

"We were friends once, Darwin, I'm not lying to you. In the beginning, I tried to discourage her, but I'd never had a beautiful woman pay much attention to me before. I wasn't for socializing, you know that. The great Solitary Academician." He closed his eyes, swallowed. "She seduced me. She—so young, so exquisite—*loved* me, she said. And she made a fool of me. Just as she did of you."

"I don't believe any of it."

Calvin only stared at the overturned chair.

"She was the mother of our child!" MacNeil persisted. But his words mocked him. Ella had never wanted the baby, not really. He'd hoped to bind her to him with doting, worshipful attention, and then, with their daughter. But she'd used him. She'd always used him, and he'd let her. And now he knew he'd hidden his wounded ego behind a lie, let it rule his life, forbid him commitment to any other love. In a way, he'd always known the truth of it. *I wonder,* he thought, *who she's using now?*

Calvin seemed to have wrestled out of his own miasma. "You haven't kept track of her?" he said. It wasn't a question as much as an appreciation.

"No. No, I didn't want to know anything. Our daughter got letters from her for a while. Then they stopped coming."

"She left me for Quentin Hsu," Calvin said. "After him, there was Moultren, the concert synthesist. And after him. . . .Lord, what does it matter?"

MacNeil nodded. He sorted through the wreckage of his illusions. Curiously, he felt more relieved than grieved. "Calvin—" he began, then amended, ". . . J.D." His voice shook. "I didn't know any of it." Suddenly, he pushed himself up, crossed the space between them, offering a hand to the older man still on the floor. Their eyes locked in mutual sympathy. Then Calvin accepted the proffered help.

"I suppose," he said, "we'd better get to work on the next tests."

* * *

Calvin was too ill to think. He stared vacantly into the mouth of Iyevka's well and contemplated it. It was there. He was there. There was nothing else.

His hands were useless now, gone spongy in a mass of lesions. A day ago he'd become unable to reason with enough clarity to back up MacNeil's research, and now he couldn't even tend the bedridden. But he'd refused to take to a bed himself, though Caroline had coaxed and nagged him. No, he'd had to come here. To the pit. He felt as though he still had unfinished business here.

But when he could think, between the long temporal blackouts, he thought mostly of his guilt. People were dying—some were dead—because of him. He'd wanted only good things, to recover lost knowledge, to find a way to end pain. He'd gone about it the best way he knew how. He didn't know why he had failed, or what had gone wrong.

Footsteps approached behind him, and he turned lethargically.

"Jeff?" Caroline's lantern flashed toward him, picking him out of the gloom. She crouched next to him at the rim of the well. A part of Calvin's mind noticed how worn she looked. The blisters blemished her lovely features.

"I've been worried about you," she said. She seemed to mean it. "I think you ought to come back with me to the infirmary."

Calvin blinked in the light, and he came awake slowly, looking around as though this were the first time he realized where he was. He couldn't remember coming here. Then Caroline tugged at his arm, pulling him up. He managed to collect his mind. "Any progress?" he asked.

Supporting him with her arm around his waist, Caroline led him very slowly up the tunnel. "Not yet," she said.

It seemed that she was about to say more, but when she didn't, he didn't press her. Obviously, their luck was running out. His knees grew suddenly weak. "Caroline, I—please, let me sit down."

They hadn't gone ten meters. She eased him down, setting his back against the wall, and slumped down next to him, pointing the lantern at the opposite wall.

"I'm terminal," he said. It wasn't a protest, just the truth. "I won't last another day. We're all going to die here."

"Yes," she said simply.

He tried to see her eyes in the reflected light, but it was too dim. Feeble, he touched at her cheek with one bandaged hand, turned her face to him. Flustered, she met his gaze. He tried to smile. "Darwin said . . . you're still in love with Paul Sommerville. After twelve years."

She closed her eyes, made no answer.

Calvin nodded. Wistfully, he said, "I envy him."

She shuddered to the depths of her soul. "Don't," she said, and put her free hand over his. "Please. Don't."

He saw that she was crying, and swallowed painfully. "I . . . I could love you. Caroline?"

"I know." Her head bowed. "We're dying, Jeff. Darwin went up to the radio hut to inform Company Central."

There seemed nothing left to say, and they embraced with soft sadness. They didn't hear the quiet scratching at the well's edge, the scuttering behind it. Spidery limbs the length of a man skittered over the rim, and clusters of red reflective eyes glittered in the gloom.

It was the third shift at Company Central's communications complex on Comstock II when MacNeil called. Rashi Sriram was at the monitors. MacNeil was relieved that it wasn't the first watch's troubleshooter, Jeanne Decoteau. It would have been harder to say goodbye to her.

For it was goodbye. There was no longer hope of finding a cure in time. Eight of the surveyors were dead, the rest were dying; and neither himself or Caroline had the strength of mental acuity to continue the research. Sriram offered to send medical volunteers to continue the research, but MacNeil reluctantly forbade it; the volunteers couldn't possibly find an answer in time to save those already infected, and they might only contract the disease themselves. No, Authority had to be notified. The planet had to be quarantined indefinitely, and he and the other carriers of the plague left to their fates.

Across the communications hut, Andre Iyevka shut down the transmitter. The few clicks were as loud as clods of soil falling on a coffin. Wrapping his arms around himself, Iyevka glanced out at the cold. "Doctor, how long do you think we have?"

Honesty was the only available response. "The three of us should have a few more days. The others won't last that long."

"I watched Telerio die."

"I'm sorry. You shouldn't have stayed. Caroline was with him."

"We were friends."

From his own haze of pain, MacNeil's heart went out to the pilot—so damned young, and rightfully afraid. "He didn't suffer, Andre. None of us will suffer. I'll see to it."

A shout interrupted. Caroline burst abruptly from the tunnel. "Doctor MacNeil!" Her arms flailed wildly. "Doctor!"

MacNeil caught her wrists. "Caroline! What's wrong? You shouldn't exert yourself like this."

"We saw them," she gasped. She couldn't catch her breath. "—saw them—Jeff and I—three of them—we saw—"

"Jeff? Caroline, pull yourself together and make sense."

But she shrugged out of his grasp and clutched at Iyevka. "You were right! The Keeris—we saw them too!"

"I wasn't crazy?" he said.

"Three of them," she said more rationally. She swung back to MacNeil. "Jeff and I saw them. They were exactly like Jeff's autopsies, and they were Keeris. They came up out of the shaft Andre went down, and they scared the daylights out of us, let me tell you!"

"What did they do?" MacNeil said, bewildered that he'd ever be asking that question.

"They came right up to our lantern, only they walked upside-down on the ceiling. They had red eyes, and they looked just like the gypsies, with hairy legs and markings on their bodies that glowed. They just looked at us, Jeff and me, and I was so frightened that I screamed, and they turned around and went back down the shaft. And Jeff sent me to get you."

"I'm not crazy!" Iyevka laughed.

MacNeil stared up at the sky through the dome's transparent roof. He'd been wrong about Calvin again—and never so glad to admit it. He dragged in a deep breath. "Mister Iyevka, do you think you're still up to a climb?"

"You bet I am."

"Caroline?"

"I'll take care of things in the infirmary."

"Where's Calvin?"

"I'll find someone to help me get him into a bed."

"Telerio and I left all the equipment we used in a storeroom," Iyevka said. "We can set up the pulleys as soon as you're ready, Doctor."

MacNeil still gazed up at the sky. Stars spattered the zenith. Comstock II orbited one of those twinkling lights, and Jeanne Decoteau was there. "I'll never be readier," he said.

Tired and aching through and through, MacNeil eased down onto a broken stalagmite and closed his eyes, listening to the roar in his ears as it gradually quieted. Iyevka sat beside him and unsealed the collar of his miner's jumpsuit. The breeze was cold, but the hours of trudging had left both of them sweating.

Descending the shaft that Iyevka had gone down earlier, they'd explored the chamber with the pool of glowing water, but it had been deserted. Beyond that room, the catacombs had begun. MacNeil and Iyevka had followed endless galleries, passing numberless tombs. There had been other chambers like the first, each with its greenish pool, none with attendants. Always, the natural walls glowed with an unnatural light, transmuting the invisible heat of their bodies into dim but visible illumination.

MacNeil dragged his gloves off and fumbled in his medical bag for the inject-gun. Setting it for a strong stimulant, he slid next to Iyevka and pressed the dosage home against the pilot's bared chest. Then he administered a dose to himself.

"How long have we been at this?" he asked.

Iyevka held his chronometer up to the light. "Almost six hours."

"Seems like six weeks."

"*Da.*"

"How're you holding up?"

"I'm fine," Iyevka lied.

"For a wet-behind-the-ears youngster," MacNeil smiled, "you have your share of pluck."

"You're not doing badly either, Doctor—for an antique."

"Antique, eh? Hmph. Ready for more spelunking, sonny?"

Iyevka's grin was game. "Ready when you are."

Sudden agony scorched through MacNeil's insides and he doubled over. He must have made some pain-sound, because the pilot had hold of his arms and called him urgently. When the inner searing eased, MacNeil straightened.

"Doctor?"

"It's passed," he breathed. "I'm all right now."

Iyevka pulled him up. "Are you sure you can walk?"

Nodding, MacNeil took a deep breath, reached for his gloves— and froze. A cluster of red eyes stared down at him from a few steps away. Scalp prickling, he glanced at Iyevka, who likewise had gone still.

The Keeris had them bracketed. Several hung with acrobatic ease from the ceiling overhead, but at least a dozen blocked retreat on the ground. They made no immediate move, either, and MacNeil took a good look at them. Having seen space-Keeris, he was not repulsed. He'd found them an exotically attractive species, with their glossy, filament-covered appendages, green-marbled abdomens, and startling multiple eyes. But the gypsies were a likable, nonviolent bunch. These two-meter cousins were an unknown.

"Don't move," he whispered, but Iyevka was already reaching toward his pack. Instantly, sticky loops of thread sailed across the intervening space, catching and tangling the pilot's arms. In seconds, both he and MacNeil were immobilized by the extruded silk.

"We're friends!" MacNeil said. "We have no weapons!"

One of the Keeris skittered down from the ceiling to settle itself in front of MacNeil. It seemed to study him, as though looking for an appendage he didn't own. Then it reached with one of its forelimbs and touched tentatively at his scalp. MacNeil tried not to flinch. He'd seen the gypsies do this. Esper-talk. He concentrated on thinking friendly thoughts, calming thoughts. *We are friends. . .*

Alien perceptions explored in his skull, but they formed in sensations that approximated language: *Soft-limbed worms speak? Your thoughts touch us!*

We are peaceful beings, MacNeil assured. *We come in peace.*

Truth. Why have you come?

Relieved, he realized the Keeris read only his surface thoughts. *We have an illness. We hope you can help us.*

What can be done?

If you take us to your healers, they may cure us.

The concept of healer precipitated a flurry of confused images. Then, *Explain. Allusion unclear.*

MacNeil reviewed what he knew of Calvin's research, and his hypothesis about acquired empathy. He was careful to emphasize Calvin's scientific interest and the surveyors' ignorance of the existence of sentient beings in the mesa. The Keeris absorbed it, and broke the esper contact.

"What is it doing?" Iyevka whispered.

"Shhhhh."

The Keeris touched, very briefly, the arachnid next to it, which touched the being next to it, and so around to complete a circle.

A council of war? MacNeil wondered, but a cold, hairy pedipalp reached for him again. The impact of combined alien minds nearly jolted him to insensibility. But they probed him, supporting his weight as he sagged.

There seemed to be a madman's argument going on in the back of his head, like hearing a debate from the rear of an empty, reverberating auditorium. He felt as though his brain were swelling, about to boil, but the pressure dissipated as quickly as it had built, leaving only himself and the one Keeris mind.

We shall take you to the Aged One. It cannot help you, but we shall take you to it, as you wish.

The Aged One—is the healer?

Yes. And no. It dissolved the link.

MacNeil's legs wouldn't hold him and he began to slide to the ground, but more appendages caught and lifted him. He squeezed his eyes shut as he was portaged up the cavern wall, comfortably supported in the arachnids' powerful grips.

The Keeris were agile beyond belief. Despite his dead weight, they skimmed along the uneven ceiling, and in a few minutes entered a brightly lit part of the caverns. The rock faces were finished and sculpted like the chambers the surveyors occupied. Myriad cul-de-sacs trickled with the glowing water, and in them grew clumps of fungi. Some of the plant-forms, obviously culti-vated, were as iridescent as mother-of-pearl. One grotto held mushroom-like shoots that blazed with their own inner light, a saturated magenta, and they perfumed the corridors with a fra-grance like cloves.

The group's passage took them by other Keeris, each of which ceased its activities and joined the silent, ceiling-skimming proces-sion. They came to a halt in a vast, vaulted room.

Their bonds released, MacNeil and Iyevka climbed to unsteady feet and looked around. The place was permeated with a compelling aura of sanctity. Ponds of radiant water made an emerald diadem around the periphery, but the center of the room drew the eye: from the highest vault dropped a massive, cylindrical canopy, like a curtain around a Holy of Holies. Woven of the Keeris's own silk, it fell to the surface of the great central pool, reflecting the green glow its full length.

The chamber was filling with Keeris, which scuttled across the floor or took to the ceiling. The one that had posted itself next to MacNeil approached and extended its pedipalp toward his head again, as though asking permission. MacNeil lowered his eyes, trying to relax or accept the communication.

The Aged One is within, the Keeris imparted.

Inside the veil?
Always.
May I enter to communicate with it?
Useless. It cannot.
It is the healer?
Yes. Also, no.
No? Then why were we brought here?
It is what you named Caduceus. It is what you desire.
I don't understand. Why is it the healer, but not the healer?
It is the healer; it no longer heals.
It once healed?
Yes.
But no longer?
Yes.
Why?

A barrage of histories, myths, theories, and private doubts poured from the Keeris, information coming so fast that MacNeil couldn't endure the influx. Sensing that, the Keeris disengaged the contact and eased the doctor to the intaglio floor.

His mind cleared slowly. It took him a minute to realize that the arm supporting him belonged to Iyevka.

"Doctor? Doctor, what did it do to you?"

MacNeil hugged his knees. "We're sunk," he said. "Calvin was wrong. There's no technique to acquire empathy. Only a mutant empath who survived the plague but couldn't stop it. And it's senile or demented, now. It hasn't healed anyone since its civilization fell."

"It told you all that?"

"That's the gist of it."

"But there must be a thousand of them here, Doctor." Iyevka waved at the Keeris surrounding them. "Some of them did survive."

MacNeil's head was beginning to throb, whether from the esper links or the disease, he didn't know. But there was something to what Iyevka said. "Let me see what else I can find out," he said. Putting his fingers to his temples, he motioned to the Keeris. Obligingly, the pedipalp descended, and the alien minds touched.

How is it, MacNeil asked, *that the plague destroyed the others, but you still live?*

The Aged One was able to cure some. Eight-tens and two lived to lay eggs. Few hatched live, but we are the children's children's children. The illness comes to hatchlings yet. Some grow; most die.

Natural mutational immunity, MacNeil reasoned. *But the Caduceus cured eighty-two.*

Means? the Keeris questioned.

Means I am confused. The Aged One was the healer of the eighty-two?

So it comes by touch from the forebears.

Oral tradition by touch-telepathy, MacNeil translated. *How is it that you live briefly, then, but the Aged One lives yet from the time of the plague?*

It is the curse of the Stone.

Stone?

The Keeris registered amusement that the Soft One was so ignorant, but it explained patiently. *The Stone gives the curse of life. The Aged One does not die.*

Immortality is a curse?

If life is agony, is not death to be desired?

It was starting to make some sense. *Does the Stone also give the gift of healing?*

Yes. And no.

Ambiguities again. *How 'yes'?*

The Aged One was born on the Stone.

MacNeil felt hopeful, pressed on. *Then, how 'no'?*

One who only touches the Stone cannot heal. But if one is born there, it becomes the One.

That had the feel of a myth-confused correlation. *How is one born on the Stone?* MacNeil persisted.

You must become the New One.

Can it be done?

Who would wish to take the curse upon itself?

That was certainly straightforward enough. MacNeil thought

furiously, trying to piece everything together. The Keeris mind withdrew gently, leaving him alone to think his own thoughts.

The Stone—that was the source of—what? Immortality of a sort, and an incomplete empathy: the healer cured by absorbing the injuries or illnesses of others . . . but *it couldn't heal itself.* When the empathic ability eventually burned out, the empath persisted, sustained by some power within the Stone. All the accumulated suffering was bound up in it, and it had no escape, no relief. The curse of the Stone that came from . . . God knew where.

MacNeil's mind cowered. He knew he was at the threshold of a decision. That "born on the Stone" business—it implied a way to transfer the empathic ability. But, as the Keeris had pointed out, who could face such a fate? None of the Keeris had done so since the time of the plague, though with the high hatchling mortality, even a limited empath would be an enormous boon to the race.

A blitzkrieg of pain ripped through MacNeil again. He gasped, twisting his hands in Iyevka's sleeves, trying to master it, trying to weigh the choices. If he became the One, he would have this pain, and the others', and there'd not even be the mercy of death. He'd go mad, no doubt of it. He'd be a raving, screaming lunatic far into the future, generations after those he might save now would be dust. If he chose the other alternative, he'd still suffer this, but in a few days at most, it would be finished. He'd be dead along with the others.

The seizure was long in passing, this time. As soon as he could control his limbs again, he let go of Iyevka and groped for the Keeris. There was more he needed to know. And time was growing short.

The Keeris mind centered in his again.

Can the Aged One never die at all? MacNeil asked.

It caught the drift of his thoughts; and while there was not disapproval, there was honest warning. *It is said that if you are born on the Stone, the Aged One will find rest; but there would be none for you.*

Am I permitted to view the Aged One, MacNeil asked, *before I decide?*

It is not forbidden. Only do not touch it while it is on the Stone unless you have made that choice. And it left his mind.

The broad lake was before him, the milky shroud brushing its surface. Within the translucent curtain, MacNeil could make out a dark shape atop a lighter, much larger mass. What would it be like—look like—after all the centuries, all the suffering? Terrified, but compelled, he struggled up, Iyevka helping him.

"Where are you going?" the pilot begged. "For God's sake, Doctor MacNeil, what's happening here?"

The water glowed, pea-green, like Earth's new leaves filtering sunlight. It rippled gently, inviting him, its surface serene. "Wait here," he told the pilot, and stepped into the pool, sinking up to his thighs. It was agreeably warm. He began to wade out to the veil.

All was silence but for the little lapping sounds of the water as he walked, and the muffled roar of distant echoes. His mind lolled into a tranquil, vapid unconcern. The soothing, tepid water girdled his waist as he neared the curtain, and with a soporific lethargy, he lifted it and stooped inside the sanctuary.

For six heartbeats, he stared. Then he came back to life, reeling away into the veil as every cell of his being revolted. He wanted out, had to get *out,* but his legs refused him. He scrabbled in the filmy water and choked and clung to the curtain to keep from going under again.

It was too grisly to contemplate, that seat of all ugliness, that living tangle of disease-infested loathsomeness. Its exoskeleton bulged with deformity, and inner tissue extruded from each abscessed joint, oozing with a cloudy syrup that seeped over the pearly Stone and scummed the veil-ringed inner pond. How the creature still lived was beyond his comprehension. To look at it again was beyond his strength. Stupefied, he could only think, *Not that for me. Not that!*

After an eon of paralysis, MacNeil regained his feet, though the curtain still took most of his weight. The shock receded, and he tried to stifle his asthmatic gasps, calm his tide of hysteria. Forcing his eyes open, he gazed out through the gauzy veil—*away* from the Stone—with a frantic compulsion.

They were out there: a sea of red eyes, watching. He watched back numbly, gathering what tendrils of sanity he could still find. The Keeris watched, and they waited, hanging from the great ceiling like so many scarlet-sparkled chandeliers, or standing on the vast carved floors like many-legged candlelabra. Iyevka, a solitary taper, glowed silver in his miner's jumpsuit. MacNeil tried to read the human's face, but it was too far away. No matter. He knew what they all wanted: a nimbus of breath-held hopefulness filled the room. They were waiting, and they hoped. Their need converged on him like an electrical field, running cold chills over his wet skin. He hugged the veil and shivered.

Decide, they seemed to plead.

I can't! he wailed. *Not that!*

His thoughts wove a flight that touched at home and dreamt of stars, of love; of Jeanne and Caroline and his grown child; of Calvin and the surveyors; of death and songs and shadows; and he chose.

He turned around.

It was a dreary tune that Caroline hummed, not realizing she hummed at all. Had she known, she would have recognized it: *Dies Irae;* and had she had the strength, she would have been annoyed. But it took all her strength simply to stay at her post—the lab chair she'd set by the infirmary's central monitor. Nine of the monitor lights still registered. She watched them for any change, her only aid an inject-gun loaded with sedatives.

The smell of suffering was heavy in the room. She'd kept the deathwatch too many hours. The oppressive odor, the oppressive gloom, the oppressive and constant pain had dulled her other senses and narcotized her thoughts. She barely noticed when the door swung in.

Arachnid forms pushed through the opening and clambered up the walls, and she gawked at them, jamming her gloved fingers into her mouth. But she didn't scream, because two silver-suited humans appeared behind the Keeris, one supporting the other. Stumbling to them, Caroline fixed her gaze on Iyevka, and it had to be a wish-fulfilling illusion, because the pilot was untainted—as healthy as when they'd left Comstock II.

"You found the empath, you found—"

Her eyes fell on MacNeil. Or a parody of MacNeil. His features were lost under the lesions, and he had no neck for the tumorous glands in it. For every symptom Iyevka had shed, the doctor seemed doubly inflicted. Only the pilot's grip kept MacNeil from crumpling. But that ghastly face looked up at her, and the leprous lips moved.

"How . . . many?" he rasped. Even his voice was shattered.

She couldn't bear to look at him. "Ten of us," she managed. She made an effort to stand straighter, and didn't realize she'd been falling until Iyevka draped her in her vacant chair. He returned in a moment with MacNeil and arranged him on the floor, kneeling before her. She bit her lip, not knowing what to expect.

The doctor raised his hands, swathed in a silky fabric, and clasped her face tenderly between his palms. "Caroline," he breathed, and his eyes seemed to roll up into his head. Then his grasp tightened, pinching her flesh against her cheekbones; and he went rigid as though electrocuted.

A stab of impossible pain penetrated Caroline and she fell against MacNeil. But it was wonderful pain, the cries of healing tissues, and it cascaded through here, peaking, then ebbing to nothing so quickly that she slipped from the chair and sprawled with MacNeil on the floor.

"Ms. Sommerville? It's all right, it's over now. Let me help you up." Iyevka untangled her from MacNeil and deposited her back on the chair, then bent to aid the doctor.

Never in her life had Caroline felt as exhausted. At the same time, she felt . . . completely well. Holding her breath, she looked down at her arms. The blisters were gone. Hesitantly, she drew off a glove. Her hand was unmarked. Eyes widening, she looked back at MacNeil. If anything, he was more loathsome than before. But behind the sunken eyes was a remarkable preternatural vitality.

"Oh my God. *You*. You're the empath," she breathed. "Can you do the same thing for the others?"

The vitality flickered, then steadied. "Help . . . me . . . up."

Between them, Caroline and Iyevka walked him to the nearest cot. Caroline saw the changes this time. MacNeil's flesh literally crawled. A scream erupted from the patient, then; and MacNeil rolled away from her—was pushed away by hysterical flailing. Caroline held the woman's shoulders until her screams declined into sobs. But the medical monitor showed nearly normal readings.

The empath was a depleted heap in the chair where Iyevka had put him. Leaving the other patient, Caroline ran the monitor remote over MacNeil and tried to decipher the readings. The bp and pulse were impossibly high, the pain level incredible. The metabolic rate was nowhere near that of a human being. Yet there were no signs of imminent breakdown, no dangerous dysfunction. It was as though he'd been infused with an upshifted vitality, like a nuke-powered ship overhauled with an ion engine.

Pushing aside her revulsion, Caroline helped MacNeil to sit up straight. "Darwin. Darwin, there are eight more to go. Can you keep it up?"

The monstrosity almost seemed to laugh. "Forever."

No nightmare would ever match the reality to which Calvin awakened. He'd closed his eyes expecting to die, and reopened them to a form of death he'd never imagined. Death by disfigurement.

Appalled, he witnessed the subsequent healings: the physical contact, the sudden rictus, the transfer of the patient's symptoms to the empath. Each successive contact diminished MacNeil's kinship to humanity. The personality dubbed Darwin MacNeil was guttering out. What little would survive would be caged forever in a stinking clump of pain-swamped tissue. Unthinkable.

The last of the surveyors was healed to throat-torn screams, and MacNeil collapsed. Caroline pumped an injector of sedatives into the whimpering form, but the pain reading on the monitor stayed off the top of the scale.

"What can we do for him?" Caroline asked.

"I don't know," Calvin said. "Probably nothing."

Abruptly, the Keeris skittered down from the walls. Two of them faced off and began to spit silk at each other, constructing between them what looked like a cat's cradle. As more silk was added, it became a litter.

"They brought him up that way," Iyevka said. "I think they want to take him back to the Stone, and use whatever powers he has left for their hatchlings."

"We can't let them take him!" Caroline said. "Good God, he'll never see humans again."

"It's no use," Calvin said. His insight shook him. "He's finished for us, Caroline. Look at him. He isn't even human any more."

The Keeris arranged their net around MacNeil, suturing him into it with more loops. The strands joined and covered him like a cocoon, hiding the deformities that had split his silver miner's suit.

"They'll take care of him," Calvin breathed. "He'll be cared for. Forever."

"Or until the next Caduceus releases him," Iyevka said.

Finished, the Keeris lifted the limp form and bore it slowly from the room. Calvin stared after them, his soul in turmoil. He didn't hear the agitated surveyors, didn't notice when Caroline bowed her head into her hands and finally wept. Eighteen people had died in this place—because he, Calvin, had let his obsession get the best of caution. It had all gone wrong! This wasn't the "gift" he'd pursued. It was an abomination, a gruesome anomaly of empathy. It was a perverted form of suicide. Or murder.

A hand on his arm startled him back to the present.

"Jeff?" It was Haley Druen, the chief surveyor. "Jeff, listen, what do we do now? Can we get out of here, or are we still carrying this disease?"

Calvin pulled his thoughts together. "The monitors say we're clean of it. But there's no guarantee that we won't come down with it again, or pick up something else in our depleted conditions. We must leave and not come back."

"What about the station?" someone piped up. "What about the oil?"

"Damn the oil," Druen said. "We're calling Comstock for transports and getting the hell out of this hole while we can."

Iyevka roused himself. "They'll put us in quarantine, won't they?"

"They damned well better had," Calvin said. He rose and made his way to the doorway. The Keeris disappeared around a bend in the passage as he watched. To Druen, he added, "Take our medical records to be copied, but incinerate the originals. And make sure Central informs Authority that Alcestis is to be declared a plague world. No one is ever to set foot here again."

"Understood, Doctor. Will you come with me to the communications hut to make the call?"

"I have another matter to attend to," Calvin said. Turning back to the corridor, he saw Caroline watching him. The fear in her eyes held him. She'd read him, seen his decision.

"Jeff," she mouthed from across the room. "Don't do it."

He caressed her with his eyes. How could he explain all the debts he had to pay? He said, "If I'm not back by the time the transports arrive, go without me."

"Jeff!"

He rushed down the echoing passage.

The last four of the survivors were suiting up to make the chilling walk to the transport when the Keeris appeared out of the tunnelway. They bore a slack human form: Darwin MacNeil. He was not the loathsome remnant they'd taken from the infirmary, but the man in his original human state, whole and unblemished. The Keeris eased him into the humans' arms and vanished back into the bowels of their world as Caroline and the others huddled over MacNeil.

"He's alive," Caroline said. "But he's totally prostrated. We'd better get him back to the clinic on Comstock right away. He needs care."

They hurried to stuff his lax limbs into a thermal, but Caroline left that to the others and turned to stare down the passageway into the mesa. It was vacant, plunged in gloom and silence.

The radio came to life. "What's the delay, Iyevka?" the transport's medic demanded.

"The Keeris just brought back Doctor MacNeil," Iyevka reported. "He's alive!"

"MacNeil?" There was a pause. "What about Dr. Calvin?"

Iyevka's gaze flew to Caroline, and they locked eyes. He passed the comm to her.

"Ms. Sommerville here," she said dully. "Doctor Calvin is dead." In a sense, it was the truth.

"Then come on, let's get out of here before you catch something else," the medic said.

Caroline stepped next to MacNeil and took his arm. He was stirring, not quite conscious; but at least he wouldn't have to be carried to the transport. Pulling him closer, Caroline took one last look through the dome at the frozen little planet clad in twilight. Then she stepped out into the gale, glad to be going home to the stars.

Seasoning

by Hal Clement

The onshore wind had slackened, but was still strong enough to make the sturdiest bushes lean inland. The little sloop should be able to beat out against it, but Faivonen couldn't help watching. The *Fahamu* was his only link with the rest of Medea's humanity—a small population, but the only one that could mean anything to him now. Earth's billions were no longer part of his life.

Sullivan had promised to be back by midsummer, thirty Medean days from now. Faivonen trusted him, of course, since unreliable people had been pretty well combed out of the colony's leadership, but any commitment on the new world carried the unspoken qualification, "If I'm still alive." In spite of the numerous children, there were very few more human beings on the satellite than had landed two decades before. Learning as much as possible as soon as possible about the new world was admitted to be a necessity for the colony, but had been hard on individual members.

Faivonen, though his enjoyment of society had died with Riita, had not become a misanthrope, and he could not bring himself to turn his back on his vanishing friends just yet. There would be plenty of loneliness, not mere solitude, for the next couple of thousand hours, even with Beedee along.

The vessel was getting hard to see, but he could make out that she was going onto the starboard tack, after a long reach which had carried the individual figures of her crew well out of sight. The light was dim, probably dim enough to have made him give up the watch thirty years before; but the human eye is adaptable, and the human memory constantly edits the standards of what can be expected. Even though the principal suns were not up yet, their location below the horizon revealed only by flecks of hydrogen crimson from their vast halo of prominences, Castor A and B were nearly overhead. Together they provided less light than Earth's full moon had done, but it was enough to satisfy him.

"They'll clear the bay on the next tack." The voice was only slightly filtered by the speaker in the man's left ear; it would have sounded perfectly human to anyone not acquainted with the being who had spoken, who could hardly have been less so. Faivonen, without even glancing down at his arm, nodded.

"That was my guess. Are you making a linear extrapolation, or allowing for wind changes?"

"The wind will grow weaker for hours yet. Of course I allowed for that." There might have been indignation in the voice. "I have no reliable information on the currents, of course, but with no river flowing into this bay they should be simple. Are you going to watch the ship out of sight? That will waste valuable hours."

"I'll watch for a while. There's no use getting started until the real suns are up, and there's nothing to check before we go. You wouldn't have let me forget anything important, and even if you had there'd be nothing that could be done about it now."

The voice made no answer; its owner knew it had taken the man's thoughts away, to some extent, from his vanishing companions. Faivonen, however, had little else to think of for the moment. The job ahead was already planned in as much detail as possible; it was to stay alive and to learn what he could about as much of the area as he could cover—preferably, but not quite necessarily, in that order. If he didn't actually manage to stay alive, the things he learned could still be useful as long as his body and Beedee were found. It was this fact that had gripped his thoughts for the moment—the fact, and the memory it always evoked. He himself had found Beedee on Riita's skeleton; he had been searching for her, against the best advice. Success had made him for a time almost useless to himself, to their children, and to the colony. This time, he had extracted a firm promise from Sullivan: if Faivonen himself should fail to reappear to meet the ship, and it was decided that someone must go after Beedee and the information, it was not to be any of his and Riita's children. It was all right if they turned out to be explorers when they got old enough—as they nearly were, he suddenly reminded himself—but that sort of picture was too much to inflict on anyone of closer status than casual friend. The kids couldn't—

"Watch the ship, if you must, but get your mind off that line," Beedee's voice cut into his thoughts. "If you have nothing more constructive, or less destructive, to do than brood, I insist on getting started. The suns are practically up."

This time Faivonen did glance down at the object strapped to his left wrist. He knew that Beedee could not actually read minds. He—or she, or it; the man had vacillated about the correct pronoun for most of the twenty-four years since he first met Riita and her strange possession—could do a very good job of reading the expression of anyone it knew, however. During the twenty years of their marriage, and the year since he had found and inherited the black diamond, it had plenty of opportunity to get to know him.

"You're in no position to insist on anything," he pointed out, as usual when one of their conversations reached this point. Beedee made the usual counter.

"Very true, but you know I'm right. We can see well enough for research. Get the rest of your equipment on, and let's start."

"I'm hungry."

"Well, you won't eat anything but cheese until you get moving.

You managed to kill one meal here at the shore an hour after we landed, but nothing else has—"

"All right. Hiking is easier than arguing." Faivonen attached knife, shovel, canteen, cheese incubator, shoulder pack, bow, and quiver to various parts of his person. Then he took a last look at the *Fahamu* silhouetted against the dull red patch on the horizon where Argo had set a few hours before, turned his back on the bay, and set off up the valley.

From the sea, this had looked like a product of glaciation. No one had been surprised, since it led toward the cold hemisphere. However, there had been no sign of any stream or river flowing into the bay, in spite of the heavy vegetation which could be seen from shipboard. The plant life itself was a little startling for the latitude— eighty-six degrees north of the equator—where Castor C gave very little assistance to Argo in heating the world. When a careful check failed to show even a cove where a seasonal stream might have emptied, it was agreed that information was needed. Elisha Kent Kane Faivonen drew the job of getting it.

A few facts had been ascertained before the ship had hoisted sail. There were animals which could serve as food, and plenty of the plants whose sap would serve as culture medium for the "cheese." This was the mixture of gene-tailored bacteria which produced the half-dozen amino acids needed by human beings and lacking in Medean life forms—one of the very few products of advanced Earth technology which the colonists had retained. They had not wanted to be dependent on anything which had to be replaced from Earth, but had little choice in this matter. Terrestrial plants were still struggling to become adjusted to the satellite, and until real crops of these could be grown, people lived on native food and cheese.

Faivonen kept well to the left wall—his own left—of the valley as he travelled away from the bay. This would get the better light when the suns were a little higher, and they did have to see. Everything had to be examined; plants, animals, soil, rocks, wind, weather. The wind had been blowing on shore and up the valley for days before the *Fahamu* had reached the bay; a surface wind blowing toward the cold side of Medea was another peculiarity to be explained, though the explanation might be as trivial as the explanation of local weather so often was. Beedee had claimed a special interest, however, and was constantly asking the man to hold it as high as possible so that its delicate pressure senses could record air currents with a minimum of ground disturbance.

Faivonen didn't object, usually. The black diamond weighed only about three quarters of a kilogram, a negligible fraction of the equipment he was carrying. Whether the thing should be called equipment or personnel was still an open question, of course; he knew it was of artificial origin, but could not bring himself to regard it as merely a computer. It said too many things which smacked of personality. Somewhere in the lattice of carbon atoms which formed the thing's basic structure was a tendency—programmed, grown, or learned—to imitate human speech mannerisms and even voices. When he had found it with Riita's body it had spoken to him with her voice. . . .

They had reached an understanding on that, right away; Beedee had promised not to repeat the offense. Courtesy? Sympathy? Faivonen couldn't know, but also couldn't help thinking of the device or creature as a person, as his wife always had.

Of course, a person is alive, and living things don't operate from such simple energy sources as the flow of heat from a man's forearm to a near-freezing environment, or the potential difference between two metal bracelets with human sweat as an electrolyte. Living things, when their energy sources vanish and they stop operating, don't start up again after indefinitely long periods of time.

Beedee had been "dead" for over two years between Riita's death and Faivonen's discovery of her body. He(?) had been "dead" for over two billion years between the time he(?) had sunk with a surface vessel on the Earthlike world of his(?) makers, and the time he(?) had been discovered by Riita's grandmother on an airless planet, blistering under a red giant sun, in a pile of calcium oxide which had once been a deposit of marine limestone.

Only machines can be turned off and on, so Beedee must be *it*, not *he* or *she*. So Faivonen's experience insisted—most of it.

"Elisha! There is a fairly large animal beyond the bush—thirty meters at two o'clock. You're hungry; get ready!"

They were two kilometers from the bay, and the man was even hungrier than when they had started; his bow was bent and an arrow nocked before the diamond had finished speaking. Silently, avoiding the ankle-high puffballs whose bursting would give audible warning of his approach, Faivonen stalked toward the bush. He was still a dozen meters away when a calf-sized creature with six legs leaped into view on the far side, clearly bent on departure. He put his arrow high in the trunk, between the first and second pairs of legs. If it were like the animals he knew closer to the equator, it had no centralized heart; but a major aorta ran along its body just below the backbone. Severing the blood vessel or the major nerve cord should be equally effective. It was; the creature dropped on the next bound.

Faivonen performed a combined butchering and anatomical dissection, with Beedee recording the data. Then he collected fuel, lighted a fire with pyrite and steel, and cooked a meal. He didn't enjoy eating it much; neither the Medean flesh nor the cheese was particularly tasty, but hunger was even less pleasant.

He cut a couple of kilograms of the meat into thin strips for his next few meals, extracted the few remaining lumps of ripe cheese from the incubator's tank and put them in the storage chamber, refilled the tank with sap from the Cheddar plants he had already identified, and resumed his hike, after asking Beedee if his(?) own battery needed charging.

"Oh, no—I'm running on—oh, you're being funny. Excuse me."

It had happened before. The diamond's calculating processes, or reasoning if that was really what it could be called, operated at electronic speed; it had known he was joking long before its first word had been uttered. Nevertheless, it had imitated a human double-take; it had been playing up to his humor. Whether it had felt anything corresponding to the strange relay-chatter with which the human nervous system responds to incongruity was something

Faivonen couldn't guess. Whether it *felt* at all was an equally open question.

By the time the Castor C twins were halfway around to their midday position a few degrees above the southern horizon, Faivonen was tired; even with frequent pauses to examine biological or geological data, they were more than thirty kilometers from the sea. He rested and ate again, and then settled into his sleeping bag. He knew that his own biological clock would never reset itself to Medea's seventy-five hour rotation, but sleep was as necessary as food; he slipped the blinders over his eyes and relaxed. Beedee would guard; it was unlikely that anything could approach without registering on its supersensitive pressure sense. Guarding might be necessary; Medean predators could get no more adequate nourishment from human tissue than the other way around, but none of them seemed to know it.

This time the man was lucky, not waking up until Beedee's voice began hammering "Eight hours, loafer," into his ear. He sat up, slipped the pads from his eyes, and looked around. The suns were almost in the south, now, just above the spot where Argo had long ago disappeared. Two balloons floated a hundred meters overhead; Beedee might not have heard them, since they always seemed to ride with the wind, but it didn't matter. No one knew much about the organisms—Faivonen wasn't even sure whether they were actually inedible, or merely had too little tissue to be worth hunting— but they were certainly harmless. At the moment they didn't seem to be moving at all, which was interesting.

"Sullivan thought the wind was getting a little weaker each cycle," Faivonen remarked. "It looks as though he was right."

"He was," agreed the diamond. "There was a pretty good chance of it when he was speaking, but there were too many unknown variables for real computation. You know, I am beginning to suspect that some of the variables lie in the shape of this valley. We'll have to get a long way inland to make sure."

"Too far inland and Argo won't be rising at all. I want no part of Coldside," Faivonen pointed out. "You wouldn't like it either. There may be a lot to learn, but with your power off you wouldn't be learning it."

"You could rig me a battery. I can think of ways you could set it up to operate even at dry-ice temperatures."

"It gets colder than that—and you don't like being turned off any better than I'd like dying, even if you can switch on again."

"I know. I hate to miss arriving information. Still, I believe right now that I'd like to take the chance; and I've heard you, and Sullivan, and many other people say that danger gives spice to existence."

"I think we said life, not existence. And I know we said danger, not suicide. Forget it, Beedee; you stay with me, and I stop a long way short of dry ice even if this valley goes that far. You figure out what you can from the rocks and the weather and the life; that should be enough."

"There is never enough. I can calculate, but then I have to see whether I was right. You should allow for that; your wife always did."

Faivonen's silence was pointed. A human being would have been embarrassed at the *faux pas*, but Beedee didn't make such mistakes. He must have had—*it* must have had a reason, and it must have been a good one.

The man knew that he probably wouldn't be able to guess it. The score of black diamonds which had been brought back by the Tammuz expedition had made no secret of their composition, though the knowledge had done human engineers no good—the techniques needed to make one of the things were far beyond current human ability.

They were just what they were called—diamonds, structures of carbon with replacement atoms and crystal defects built deliberately into their lattices in ways which resembled mankind's operations on silicon chips for the last century or two—resembled them in much the same way that the circuit chips resembled a flint knife. About twelve hundred unit cells of the diamond lattice composed a single basic structural unit of the devices; a much less reliable estimate, usually guessed at about five thousand, of these units had about the recording and decision-making capacity of a single human brain cell.

The things themselves—Beedee was typical, though no two were identical—looked as though someone had made a cylinder of black glass a little over six centimeters in radius and not quite ten in length, fitted the ends with hemispheres of the same material, and split them lengthwise to make two units. With that volume—a little over two hundred milliliters—they had theoretical capacity for the equivalent of not quite 200,000,000 four-billion-cell human brains. Some people were afraid of them, and there had been loud demands—to destroy them or get them off Earth—by some of that planet's more paranoid inhabitants. It had not been entirely the high regard for private property rights characteristic of the culture of that time which had allowed Beedee to come to Castor.

Faivonen himself was no more afraid of the thing than his wife had been, but he took for granted that it could think many times faster and with far more precise consideration of myriads of variables than any human being could. It had been one of Beedee's fellow machines, or beings, who (which?) had proved that chess was as trivial a game as tick-tack-toe.

Some people had not forgiven them for that.

Faivonen didn't go back over all that, consciously. He merely wondered why Beedee had mentioned Riita when it knew the man would be pained, assumed he would not be able to guess the answer, and turned to the day's work. He cooked and consumed another meal, loaded up his equipment, and not until they were under way did he speak to his computer-recorder again. Even then he changed the subject to one of more immediate importance.

"There's still no river in this valley—"

"There could hardly be one at all, if none reached the sea," Beedee pointed out.

"There have also been no pools or puddles, though there is plenty of vegetation. I'm halfway through this two-liter canteen. Have you any practical suggestions?"

"There was snow visible at the top of the cliffs from the sea. The temperature here is distinctly above freezing. Some water should flow over the edge, if only occasionally. Let's examine the base of the cliff more closely; the geological information will be useful in any case."

Faivonen refrained from comment, and started toward the nearer side of the valley. They had already learned that the valley had been cut in sedimentary rock—a fine sandstone—whose present elevation above sea level implied much about the tectonic forces available on Medea. There was rubble, inevitably, at the foot of the cliffs. Near the bay, this had been deposited so as to give a U-shaped contour to the valley, leading the explorers to assume former glaciation; closer examination had revealed only very fine material which appeared to have been wind-borne. This far from the bay the roundness persisted and was even exaggerated; the cliff, on this side at least, seemed slightly undercut.

Away from the walls, the soil was a fine-grained loess. Closer in, it contained rocks whose size increased with decreasing distance from the cliff. Exposed portions of the rocks were well rounded by some form of erosion.

The soil itself was very dry, in spite of the abundant vegetation. The man had dug up several of the smaller plants, and found that their root systems did not go particularly deep; Beedee had agreed with his conclusion that there must be a fairly frequent supply of surface or near-surface water, since the plants themselves showed nothing unusual in the way of liquid storage capacity.

The diamond, as usual, was right; the soil was detectably moister near the cliff, and part way up the slope they found occasional shallow puddles where the rocks had made dams to hold them. With a good deal of relief, Faivonen took the first long drink he had allowed himself since landing, and refilled his canteen.

He was in a better humor now, willing to go on farther toward the cold. His garment was another bit of Earth technology which had been kept for special uses, a coverall of thin polymer whose thermal conductivity was extremely low, though it was quite transparent to near infra-red radiation—he could appreciate the heat of a fire or of the Castor C twins without having to take off anything to let the light in. With a headpiece like an ancient skiing mask, he would be able to face air temperatures well below the freezing point of water, even with fairly high winds. Dry ice temperatures would be something else, but it should take many days of foot travel to bring him anywhere near that sort of environment.

He chatted good-naturedly with Beedee as they resumed their way up the valley, slanting back toward its level floor where walking was easier. The discussion was almost entirely about the facts they were observing—the diamond was seldom willing to play human to the extent of indulging in gossip or idle chatter—but it included much speculation. What had elevated this entire region of sedimentary rock practically as a unit for more than five hundred meters? Beedee had made several dip measurements where the exposure permitted, and nowhere found more than two degrees. What had cut this canyon, if not a river or glacier? and if it had been a river or glacier, why was there no trace of it now? Valleys without central streams are most unusual except the ones in deserts—and even those usually have empty stream beds where water once flowed.

The two balloons had drifted *down* the valley—the wind had finally reversed, instead of merely slowing down. Could this be a tidal phenomenon, as Sullivan had guessed as they were approaching the region in the *Fahamu*? Beedee agreed that it could be, but declined to risk a prediction.

"If this is really a tidal current in the atmosphere, and is being funnelled into this valley from both ends, the width of the valley itself, the height of the walls, and the size of the feed areas are all relevant. At the sea end the supply reservoir is effectively infinite, but we have no observations about the other factors. Guessing that the canyon keeps its present width and height for its whole length is pointless as long as I don't know the length or the other variables. I can treat it mathematically as an organ pipe of rather unusual cross section with a forced input of one Medean day's period, but—"

"Forget it." Faivonen was a perfectly good mathematician as

human beings went, but knew the futility of trying to follow Bee-dee's brute-digital-force "estimates." "You keep your ideas inside, and we'll check their accuracy as we get farther up the organ pipe. Isn't that a new plant?"

"Not really. It's quite common on some of the islands near the equator. It is the first time I have seen it so far north. Of course latitude means much less than longitude here as far as climate is concerned." The last sentence came after a slight pause, as though it were an afterthought.

"Yes, *I* keep forgetting. It was very tactful of you to talk as though you forget too, but I don't really need that kind of coddling. I know what your brain is like."

"Does it offend you? I have noticed that most human beings seem more at ease when I use such conversational artifacts."

"Well—no, not really. Just don't ever let it waste time if we're in trouble."

"Of course not."

Whatever Faivonen may have thought consciously of Beedee, his feeling toward the thing was essentially ordinary friendship. It was a personality. It was even a person. Their running conversation might almost have been taped at a dining table during a scientific convention; and for the first two Medean days it was little more exciting than dining-table talk. The only complications arose from the endless phase problems between Faivonen's twenty-four-hour cycle and the satellite's seventy-five-plus-hour rotation. He had to waste waking hours at "night." The white suns and the continuous aurora gave enough light to permit travel when the orange suns were below the horizon, but the man and the machine were both reluctant to do this. Seeing was poor enough to give a high risk of missing important data, a possibility which bothered Beedee even more than it did the man. Gathering and storing information was the diamond's prime motivation—its equivalent of hunger, thirst, and libido combined.

On the third day, Faivonen was awakened early from his morning sleep by Beedee's voice in his ear.

"Elisha! Something is trying to creep up on us very silently! Have weapons ready."

The man snaked out of his sleeping bag as quickly and quietly as possible. "How far away?" he asked, wondering whether bow, axe, or knife would be most appropriate.

"I cannot tell the linear distance, since I don't know how much sound energy it is producing. If it maintains its recent average rate of approach, it will arrive in about one hundred seconds."

Faivonen was on his feet by now; he nodded, seized the bow, and nocked an arrow. "Direction?" he asked.

"Four o'clock from where you're facing now." The man whirled to his right. Nothing was yet visible, but there were many shrubs up to three meters in height which blocked the line of sight. He could not hear anything yet; the hard-packed soil was almost completely covered with the bladder-covered, mosslike growths which filled the ecological niche of grass over much of Medea's surface, and even a very heavy animal would have made little noise.

Argo was just rising, and its dull red disc, rimmed on the upper left by the brighter crescent where the twins lit its farther hemisphere, provided a blood-tinted background against which the newcomer should be silhouetted any moment. Faivonen wondered whether the creature were following his trail, or had simply winded him—the air tide, if it were actually that, had gone much more negative during the last couple of cycles and blown a stiff breeze down the valley toward the sea. This had fallen in the last few hours as the fire-planet rose, but could still be carrying the human scent to anything down-valley equipped to detect it.

"It's stopped. It's only breathing now," Beedee said suddenly. Faivonen lifted his bow, and drew the arrow part way back. Some of the Medean predators could leap many meters—

This one didn't. It suddenly came into sight to one side of a large bush, running toward him at high speed. It was moving too fast, and the back-lighting was too poor, to let him count legs or spot other details; but research didn't occur to him until later, anyway. He drew the shaft back the rest of its length, aimed as best he could in the second or two available, and loosed. The creature swerved slightly, knocking him off his feet as it brushed by him. It must have had twice his own mass. He struggled back to his feet as rapidly as his muscles would permit, dropping his bow and drawing his machete.

"Relax. It's still running. Your arrow is about half-shaft deep in a front left shoulder; you hurt it badly, perhaps killed it."

"Any other details?"

"It was a species of lancer, the largest I've seen. It had a radula—the toothy-tongue arrangement they all do, and was running with tongue extended. If you had missed with that arrow, the tongue would have hit your throat and left very little of your neck. I thought of telling you to dodge, but it was obvious that your reaction would have been very much too slow."

"And it's still heading away from us?"

"Yes. I see no likelihood of recovering your arrow."

"That wasn't quite what I was thinking about."

At least, the incident killed boredom for a time. The diamond claimed not to understand this, pointing out that if Faivonen had been killed he would have attained ultimate boredom. Faivonen failed to see any humor in this, but couldn't help wondering whether Beedee were actually trying to display some such human emotion. He put a leading question.

"Do you really want all your predictions fulfilled and your calculations correct? I've heard you say that your fun consists of checking your figures against observation. Isn't it sort of—well—deadening if you're right all the time? Life needs some kind of spice."

"I assume you speak figuratively, if the word you just used actually refers to the taste-only foods you left on Earth. I am aware that no research can be done without a little risk, but fail to see how adding to the danger improves the taste, if that matches your figure of speech, of learning or discovery."

"You're just trying to make yourself sound more like a machine," retorted Faivonen.

"Gambling should obviously be saved for the time the odds are with you. My knowledge of human gamblers is limited, but manipulating the odds in their favor has always appeared to be one of their standard procedures."

"Those weren't gamblers. Look—you've just won a bet, since your existence is tied in with mine. If you don't get a kick thinking about that, you're just not alive."

"I have never claimed to be alive," was the diamond's rather overwhelming answer. "Thank you for forgetting."

Faivonen could think of nothing to say.

There was no more night, even the brilliant night of aurora and the white Castor suns. The trip had started at the equinox; four Medean days later, sunrise and sunset points had met ahead of the travellers. The Castor C twins were in the sky for the rest of the journey; they would not set for thirty of Medea's revolutions around Argo. This at least resolved the question of whether or not to travel at night.

No more attacks were experienced in the next few days, and boredom again began to threaten the morale of the human member of the exploring team. On the seventh day he felt the need to do something about it.

Beedee, with its precise visual sense, had measured the distance they had travelled, mapping the valley as exactly as the human race was ever likely to find necessary. They were now just over five hundred and fifty kilometers from the bay as the balloons travelled—as many of them did. The winds were increasing in speed both ways, and more and more of the organisms were apparently getting swept into the valley. The down-valley winds, back toward the bay, were less intense and shorter in duration than those blowing from behind the travellers, but a change in both qualities was becoming evident as the days went on.

"Beedee," Faivonen remarked as he finished a breakfast during the seventh day, "I'm getting a little tired of waiting for something to happen. I was inclined a couple of days ago to liven things up— season this meal of knowledge you find so tasty—by making a bet or two with you. Then I couldn't think of anything either of us could use to pay off with; but I just have. The only trouble is that I'm not sure any bet could be really fair, since you can calculate things so much better than I can. Still, it's worth trying, if you'll tell me the truth."

"Trying what? Why should I tell you anything but the truth?"

"To the latter, I don't suppose you would; it would demand human characteristics you claim to lack. What I want to try, as I said, is a bet. For example, I've been wondering about those balloons— they're being carried farther toward the cold side than back this way by the winds, so far. If they get there, it's hard to see how they could do anything but freeze. We could bet on how much frozen balloon there is in the glaciers we both believe are a few hundred kilos along, with the uncertainties being things like natural methods of escape which I haven't been able to think of.

"Or we could bet about the winds, which we both think are affected both by the season and the tides. How intense will they get by, say, the third noon from now? I can only extrapolate roughly, and you say your calculations wouldn't mean anything without data on the shape and length of the valley and the area beyond which feeds wind to it."

"True. My set of possible solutions so far is so broad that any one of them would qualify as merely a guess. Yes, we could bet on that; but what possible currency could we use?"

"If I lose, we go fifty kilometers farther than the point where my judgement says we ought to start back. You will collect that much more knowledge."

"A very tempting offer. Will you state in advance the criteria on which you would base that judgement?"

"Don't you trust me? I can give you several, actually, but can't guess which might happen first or demand highest weight. For example, if we went twenty hours or so without finding a food animal, I'd certainly think about return. If wind-chill got too close to the lower limit at which this suit could keep me alive . . ."

"But if we went beyond those points, you might die. Those are the same sort of factors which would make *me* recommend turning back."

"Well, that would be just another bet. If I didn't survive, you'd still be found sometime, so you'd be the winner again."

"I don't want to be turned off, even temporarily. I wouldn't regard it as a win."

"And you won't bet?"

"No. What are you trying to arrange? You haven't suggested what I should pay you if you win. I have never heard of a gambler who didn't give that factor his prime concern."

"I told you—you've never met a real gambler. I'd be content with being right in a dispute with you. Didn't Riita ever challenge you to anything like that—both make predictions, and see who was right?"

"I thought you didn't want to discuss her with me. It seemed to cause you grave emotional distress."

"This is not a discussion. I simply asked a question."

"Yes, she sometimes tried to outguess me about what was to happen, but she never made a formal challenge of it."

"Well, I want to."

"I get the impression that you are trying to confuse me. The set of possible explanations—or rather, the set of explanations I can think of—for your action is larger than the set of possible solutions to the problem of the valley wind."

"I have thought of something you could pay me. Just stop with those artifacts. The correction in your choice of words was intentional; you had planned that sentence long before the first sound wave came out of the speaker."

"You said that this did not bother or annoy you."

"It's beginning to. It reminds me, each time you do it, how much faster your brain works than mine does."

"Then I will stop. No bet is needed."

"Thanks—I guess. Well, I'm making a prediction anyway. I say that the wind coming down this valley at noon on the third day from now will have a speed greater than seventy-five kilometers an hour. Do you agree?"

"This is very close to the median of my set of possibilities."

"What's the median?"

"Seventy-seven point one four."

"All right, I say it will be higher than that—or do you want to take the high side?"

"I see no basis for a choice. Let it be as you say. I will not, however, hold you to the pledge of extra distance if you turn out to be wrong."

"You can't stop me from paying off if my conscience demands it," pointed out the man.

"You mean you are doing all this to remind both of us that you control all our actions? It seems silly."

"I hadn't thought of that. Thanks."

"I wonder if that is really true."

Faivonen made no answer, though the diamond's remark startled him considerably. He fell silent, and gathered up equipment in readiness for the "day's" next hike. The suns circled the horizon, hiding first behind one set of cliffs and then the other.

Some ninety hours later the trip became interesting again without the aid of bets. Over a space of about two kilometers the hard soil of the valley became first slightly damp, then quite wet, and finally coated with frost. The man's first thought was radiation cooling, even though there had been no real night. Then he noticed that the frost extended about equally far on both sides of the valley, and part way up its walls, as though something had come down to this point to chill everything, and then retreated. The fact that frost crystals grew as deeply on the underside of branches and overhung rocks implied the same: things had cooled by some other process than radiating to the sky.

"This is a good one," Faivonen remarked aloud. "Any ideas?"

"Of course," replied Beedee. "This fact has narrowed my set of possible solutions by more than ninety-five percent."

"Where does it leave my bet?"

"You are well ahead. You are also in about fifty times as much personal danger as I had estimated."

"How bad is that? You mean we should turn back now?"

"I should be able to give you warning. Actually, the estimate remains grossly unreliable in view of the unknowns in the physiography ahead of us. If you are willing to face the risk of learning more of the pertinent facts, I most certainly am."

"But what caused this frost? And why is it taking so long to melt, even with the suns shining on it?"

"Before I answer that question, I must ask you one—one which involves your wife. Do you object?"

Faivonen hesitated, then said, "Go ahead."

"It was her very clearly expressed wish that I not solve a problem for her which I believed she might reasonably solve by herself. She may never have told you in so many words, but she did not wish to become dependent on me; she felt some guilt about bringing me to Medea at all. She fully supported the policy that you colonists should not be or become dependent on anything they could not produce here. If you share her policy views, I cannot answer your question. I know you have enough data, and I think you have enough reasoning power, to solve it yourself."

Faivonen thought silently for several seconds. He was willing to take on the problem himself—it would help fight the boredom of pure fact collecting. However, he was less sure of the general policy suggested. Beedee, in spite of the need for independence, was highly important to the colony; it carried most of the data so far accumulated about Medea in its memory. Some of the group had objected to letting the device go out on exploring trips, yielding the point only because so much better quantitative information could be obtained through its senses. Several of the *Fahuma's* crew had been clearly more concerned about the machine than about Faivonen when they left the ship.

If, as Beedee had just said, the danger were now greater, perhaps it would be better to turn back now and get the information so far gathered back to the colony.

On the other hand, as he was quite sure the diamond would claim, what they had learned already would be greatly multiplied in value if more were known about this area; the local meteorology, especially, would provide clues to the cold-side conditions which might take years to gather any other way or from any other place. It was not just a matter of Beedee's burning thirst for information; Medea's weather, and still more its climate, could be very literally matters of life and death for Medean humanity. There was no way of getting knowledge without risk, and knowledge itself was life.

"All right," he finally said. "I'll figure it out myself. Let's go on." Beedee approved briefly.

The suns were slowly melting the frost from the branches and leaves of the bushes, but were making much less progress with the coating on soil and rocks. The presumption was that the latter had been chilled to a considerable depth, which in turn suggested conductive rather than radiative loss of heat; beyond this, for the moment, Faivonen could not get. The only change made by ten kilometers of travel was a thicker frost, with some evidence of snow as well—piles of feathery crystals which had apparently blown into sheltered areas by wind coming down the valley, and then, strangely, had had frost crystals grow on top of them. The distinction between the material which had blown from elsewhere and that which had grown in place was quite definite, according to Beedee, and Faivonen himself could see it.

He could not see the physical situation which would produce such a phenomenon. There had been no clouds even a few kilometers down the valley; it was hard to see how snow could fall without them. On the other hand, it was hard to see how radiation cooling sufficient for frost could occur if clouds were present. A brief snow shower, possibly, followed by a quick clearing, would explain things after a fashion. However, it did not explain why he and Beedee had seen nothing of the shower. Such a phenomenon should have been part of a travelling system—a weather front; and why such a thing should have stopped and retreated, or died out after coming within a few kilometers of the last camp, was hard to see. There had not been a cloud; all that either of them had seen in the sky since the suns had stopped setting had been the balloons.

These had been floating in ever-increasing numbers, sometimes back toward the bay, sometimes passing the explorers on the way toward the cold side. The tides, if the valley winds really were tidal phenomena, still seemed to favor motion away from Argo.

The creatures seemed to be drifting lower each day. A hundred hours ago some had been only a few tens of meters up; now many were practically skimming the frost. It occurred to Faivonen that he might actually catch one of the things by its trailing roots, or tentacles, or whatever they were. Then it occurred to him that the converse was also true. However, he refused to worry, as usual.

"I suggest," Beedee cut into this line of thought, "that we examine some of the clefts or chimneys in the cliff. We might get more evidence about the nature of this strange heat sink."

"All right," agreed the man. "While I'm climbing, you might look out over the valley for animal life. We're short of meat, and I can't live indefinitely on cheese. I can't help wondering whether this freeze may not have driven the local animals away, or into underground hibernation, or something like that."

"A good thought," agreed the diamond. "It would be a pity to have to turn back just as data are starting to cut down the possibilities to a really manageable set. I predict that the valley will at least double its width in the next ten kilometers."

"I'll go that far without any food, if you're that near a solution. But let's check this chimney first."

The feature in question was a fairly typical crack, ranging from one to two meters wide, in the cliff wall. It appeared to start at the point where the rock itself became nearly vertical; probably it went lower, but was hidden by the rubble which formed the rounded base of the wall. A climb of nearly a hundred meters was necessary to make the study they wanted.

This took only a few minutes. The numerous projecting rocks which served as steps were worn very smooth, presumably by blowing dust or sand, but were so firmly buried in loess as to be completely safe. With frost crystals crunching under his feet, Faivonen took a zigzag path to the bare rock; from that point he was able to follow a shelf where coarser and evidently softer sandstone had been eroded away, straight to the chimney itself.

The examination was brief; the crack was almost solidly choked with frost.

"Not radiation cooling," Faivonen remarked categorically.

"I agree," replied Beedee.

"You know what did it." The man's words were a declaration, not a question.

"I believe I have a unique solution for this aspect of the problem."

"And I should be able to find the same one."

"You should. All pertinent data are available to you."

Faivonen thought deeply as he picked his way back down to the valley floor and headed up the valley once more, but failed to come up with any solutions, unique or even believable. Increasing hunger finally diverted his attention from the problem.

"Did you see any animals while we were up there?" he asked the diamond.

"None, nothing moving in any part of the valley I could examine. I did not mention it because you said you would go at least ten kilometers farther anyway."

"Thanks. What do you think the chances are of finding them in this frozen area?"

"I have not enough information for a reliable estimate."

"Could these animals survive the conditions which you believe caused the frost?"

"Not by any special physiological machinery we have found in them. Such techniques as hibernation would involve biochemical factors not obvious to gross examination, of course."

"Could I survive those conditions?"

"No."

"But you can warn me in time to escape them."

"I believe so. There are variables—"

"I know there are variables, blast you. Are you walking me into something I'd have to catch a couple of dozen balloons to lift me out of?"

"That number would be insufficient, and you might have trouble securing their cooperation—"

"Cut it out! You know perfectly well when I'm being figurative!"

"I am never certain about it. Your wife was much easier to judge in such—"

"Shut up!"

Faivonen strode on in silence for two or three kilometers. After the first five minutes or so, he realized that Beedee had done a competent job of changing the subject on him, and he still didn't know how much risk he was taking; but he didn't see any use going back to the matter, and he felt reasonably sure that the diamond would not take really serious chances with its own transportation. Gradually, he cooled down to the point where he could pay attention to his business once more.

The frost was slowly vanishing from the near side of the valley, under the rather unimpressive glow of the twin suns—a glow currently reduced by the fact that one of them was eclipsing the other. Argo, the real heat source for its satellite, was too low to help even if a slight turn in the canyon, some scores of kilometers back, had not blocked its radiation from the valley floor anyway.

When he finally spoke to Beedee again, it was not about personal risks.

"How much useful information do you really think we can get by going, say, a hundred kilometers farther, if that is possible?" he asked. "We have a good idea of the local geology—at least, as good as we can get without drilling—and an even better one of the biology and ecology. Of course, any additional information is always good—I go along with you on that, even if I don't have your burn for detailed knowledge—but aren't we maybe getting to the point where what we've already learned should be brought back and reported?"

"In those fields, perhaps yes," was the answer. "However, the meteorology still baffles me seriously. We really must learn more about the atmospheric tides which I believe are controlling so much of what goes on in this valley. If I can work them out in detail, I believe we can infer more about the physiography of the cold side of Medea than could be learned by many hundreds of man-days of surface mapping even if men could venture there. I consider it vital that we go on for a while yet."

"Regardless of risk." It was not a question.

"Not entirely, of course. I will do my best to keep you well enough informed to get us back safely, though like you I accept the fact that research entails risk. After all, while I was quite certain that you would come looking for your wife and therefore would find me, I am not nearly so sure that anyone would—or could or should, in this part of the world—come looking for you."

"They'd surely come for you."

"I doubt it. Sullivan would be the most strongly tempted, but would certainly not leave his ship. I would not be willing to bet my consciousness on the chance of anyone else on the *Fahuma* coming, even if Sullivan were willing to work such a trip into the ship's schedule. I am as strongly concerned about your safety as I was about—" The machine's voice broke off.

Faivonen knew what the missing word would have been, just as well as he knew that the interrupted sentence had not actually been a mistake; it was another deliberate action by the diamond. He decided not to play up, this time.

"All right. We'll go on for at least twelve hours, unless you warn me back. Keep your senses tuned up for animals, please. The food situation is getting a little tense."

Beedee acknowledged the request, and another score of kilometers were traversed with little worth noting except the melting of most of the frost and the fulfilling of Beedee's valley-width prophecy. They finally stopped for rest. There was nothing to eat but cheese, since they had seen no animal life, but he lit a fire anyway; and, with some trouble, dug a shallow sleeping pit in the not-quite-frozen ground. The wind was starting to strain the performance of coverall and sleeping bag; balloons were now sweeping by them from behind at running speed, at times bouncing against bushes.

"Do you suppose it's the low temperature that brings them down this far?" the man wondered aloud.

"Not for simple physical reasons. A given mass of hydrogen or other light gas would have the same lift in a given atmosphere at any temperature. The balloons do not seem to have shrunk, and a temperature drop for a given *volume*, if shared by the surrounding atmosphere, would increase the lift. Of course, if the creatures can alter internal pressure by muscular contraction of their sacks, or do something to raise internal temperature, the set of possible responses is greatly enlarged. A detailed examination of one of them would be interesting and useful."

"Hasn't anyone done it already?"

"It has not been reported to me. The creatures seem to have been given a very low research priority after being found inedible. I would not have approved, myself, of such an evaluation."

"Naturally not. Well, we'll fit that in if we can. Stay on your toes; I'm going to sleep for a few hours." Faivonen slipped the blinders on.

He woke up five or six hours later, unpleasantly chilled. Keeping as low as possible behind the low pile of soil he had excavated—the wind was not strong, but very noticeable—he placed most of the fuel he had stacked beside his sleeping pit to help break the wind on the remains of the long-dead fire, and lighted it. When it blazed up he rose to sitting position to let its radiation reach more of his body; and as he did so, Beedee's voice—no, it was Riita's voice!—suddenly sounded.

"Elisha! Get to the cliff and start climbing at once! Waste no time!"

Being human, Faivonen did waste a little time. He reached for the equipment he had discarded on lying down, which cost him a second or two; as he ran toward the nearby valley wall, still fastening gear about his person, he looked up the valley and almost lost several more.

Some kilometers away—he could not judge more precisely—an

almost featureless white cloud was bearing down on them. It spread low across the valley from wall to wall. Its upper surface was sharply defined, but he could see for some distance into the lower portion. Its height was somewhat under half that of the canyon walls.

From ground level he could not judge its speed, but had a strong impression that it was approaching rapidly. Beedee's evident opinion that it was dangerous could probably be trusted, anyway, and Faivonen ran his hardest.

It was only a short distance to the point where the wind-rounded rubble began to slow him down. It also, very shortly, brought him to a height where he could judge the distance and speed of the menace for himself. Neither item of information was encouraging. He saw little chance of getting above it before it reached him, but he had no idea of giving up and spending the time before it arrived in thinking up reasons why it was probably harmless.

Details became clearer as the thing drew closer and the man climbed higher. He remembered seeing something like it in a museum on Earth, in a wave demonstration tank where two inmiscible liquids sloshed back and forth. He remembered the crawl of the denser fluid along the tank bottom as the container slowly tilted, and how the lighter material was forced up and out of the way.

He remembered pictures of a similar situation which had seen later, when he was studying meteorology—the cross section of a cold front. . . .

And suddenly he realized what it must be, and redoubled his climbing effort. Cursing his own shortsightedness could come later, when the breath might be available.

"Beedee!" he panted, "I suppose this was your solution. I take it you didn't call the time quite correctly."

"It is. I couldn't. The region beyond our sight must broaden into a bowl in its general arrangements, but I have no data on the bowl's size. Hence, the sloshing of the dense gas under tidal influence has a natural period which I was unable to calculate, though the observed changes in the valley wind eliminated many possibilities. There must be funnelling effects at various places along the valley, and these were quite impossible to calculate. There must be some critical time, as spring advances, when the contents of the bowl not only pour for some distance down the valley but actually start a siphoning effect. I trust this is not the time. When that happens, there will be a high, uninterrupted wind of carbon dioxide all the way to the sea—no doubt the cause of the peculiar erosional features we have observed from the beginning."

"I guessed about the CO_2 when I saw how sharp the upper surface of the gas river was. It's the coldest cold front anyone ever saw—"

"Don't waste your breath in speech. You seem to have analyzed the situation correctly, but you will have to get above that gas surface or drown. You probably see now as well as I do how the thing formed in the first place, but this is not the time to discuss it. Climb!"

"All right. Just don't use Riita's voice again, no matter how urgently you want my attention."

Beedee made no answer to this, and Faivonen continued up the steepening slope, still snatching occasional glances at the approaching river of frigid gas. Its boundary was clearly marked by the water it froze out of the air it met. Tiny snowflakes settled through it, giving the mass a foggy appearance from a distance. The upper surface looked sharp mostly because the man's line of sight was nearly parallel to it.

It was also marked, he saw as it drew nearer, by larger specks which he finally realized were balloons. Their buoyancy, as he and Beedee had seen, was for some reason low enough to let them reach the ground in ordinary air, but they floated on top of the carbon dioxide to emphasize the outline provided by the snow.

Looking back and down, in the brief instants he dared do so, he could see the creatures being scooped up as the front reached them. They looked as helpless as he was beginning to feel. His arms and legs ached, his breath was scratching at his throat, and his heart was pounding. He was tempted to drop some of his equipment, but it was already at a minimum likely to keep him alive if he got through the present jam.

The front at the valley floor level was within a kilometer of his camp—farther back, thank goodness, at his present height—it had a shallow slope; every meter he climbed was giving him more time—that would be a good calculus exercise—no, waste of time, Beedee must have it figured out already except for a few variables involved in the terrain he was trying to climb over—it was funny what a person's mind would do when it wasn't being put to important work.

Now the ground-level leading edge of the front had passed below him. The valley to his right was floored with a foggy whiteness which became sharper and more opaque as the eye followed it toward the horizon. The top of the snowstorm was climbing toward his feet, the site of his camp disappearing through the thickening precipitation. The fire had vanished between two breaths; its only trace was a vague patch of smoke which had been lifted like the balloons and was spreading into invisibility as it rose toward him.

"Elisha! To your right—ten meters—a chimney. Get into it!"

"Why?" Faivonen slanted in the direction mentioned, even though the reason was not yet clear to him. "It will fill with gas as quickly as the rest of the valley, and there's no reason to suppose I can climb any faster there."

"You probably can't, but I sense turbulence at its edges. The gas is mixing with air there, and should remain breathable longer. Try it. As I read the currents where the front has reached it lower down, there must be good air being forced up from below inside the crack."

Faivonen didn't see what he could lose, and where hand- and foot-holds permitted a choice he favored the way toward the opening. He was by now well above the talus and climbing bare but greatly weathered rock. As had been the case farther down the valley, occasional layers of softer sediments had eroded more rapidly to provide shelves and steps; the climbing was not essentially difficult, but hoisting his eighty kilograms of self and equipment even with good footing at the speed which seemed necessary called for a high power consumption.

But climbing inside the chimney would be too slow, though he knew the techniques well enough. Beedee saw this, once they were able to look in, as quickly as the man did.

"Stay as close as you can. There'll be oxygen for longer. Another fifty or sixty meters will get us out of danger anyway."

"I—"

"Don't talk! Keep quiet and climb! I'm talking so you won't. Listen all you want, but if you disagree with me keep it to yourself until later. I just remembered another factor; I wish I could evaluate it numerically. The gas lake feeding this river must not only be sloshing under tidal influence, but be expanding thermally as spring advances. It's getting deeper, and would overflow down this valley, I judge, even without the tides. The diurnal variation in solar heating would have the same frequency as the tide, of course, but probably not the same phase—a really interesting new family of variables—"

Faivonen glanced back and down, which was what Beedee had been hoping to forestall. The snowflakes were very close below.

"Twenty more meters should make us relatively safe. There's a good ledge there—"

Cold suddenly bit through the coverall. The rock seemed almost hot by contrast, and he was tempted to press against it and stop climbing. The air coming into his nose felt like fire, and he pulled his mask completely over the lower half of his face. The chill may have helped save him; he could feel the urge to breathe faster as the gas reached his blood, but the pain drove him to inhale as slowly as possible. Hyperventilation, especially in Medea's oxygen-rich atmosphere, could have cost him his physical coordination.

There must be some mixing; he was holding on to consciousness, so there must be enough oxygen—or nearly enough; there was a curtain of darkness twisting about the edges of his field of vision. Beedee was talking again, giving very precise directions where to put his hand, and then his other hand, and then one foot, and then the other . . .

His vision cleared, and his mind slowly followed. The snow was below him again, and he could breathe without pain. He was not, however, out of trouble.

He was on a ledge, presumably the one Beedee had mentioned, and seemed in no immediate danger of falling from it; but there was no obvious way of getting off it by any other method, either. Below, the way he had come, the cliff was climbable but bathed in the frigid gas. Above, the rock was sheer and, at first glance at least, impossible to negotiate. To his left as he faced outward, the shelf came to an end several meters short of the chimney; in the opposite direction it extended farther, but its end was quite visible.

"Is the gas going to get this high?" he asked.

"Not as long as it flows this way. The gas lake, I judge, is now emptying smoothly."

"Then maybe its level will go down as it empties," the man hoped aloud.

"Maybe. I have no basis for estimating its total volume. It seems obvious that it is fed by glaciers of alternating layers of water ice, flowing under pressure even at farside temperatures, and carbon dioxide ice, deposited in alternate seasons. No numbers are available, I fear."

Faivonen got wearily to his feet; there seemed nothing to do but make really sure about other ways off the ledge. Fifteen minutes later he settled to the same spot with a grunt of greater weariness. No ways up, and the only ones down all led into the gas.

"Well, Beedee, I guess I can only wish you luck. Maybe someone will come by in a few years looking for you. I just hope it isn't one of the kids."

The machine responded only to the first sentences.

"Perhaps you could improvise a cell to power me and keep me conscious until then. You have several metal objects in your possession, and if you strapped two pieces of different composition on my round and flat faces respectively, using a strip of leather from one of the balloons, there should be an adequate potential difference. Natural moisture in the tissue should provide electrolyte, probably to very low temperatures—it would be far from pure water. You should try before the balloons blow off the shelf."

Faivonen had paid no attention to the half dozen of the creatures which had apparently been blown into the relatively calm area of the shelf. Even though they were big—some of them over two meters in diameter—it would have taken dozens of them to support his weight even if he had trimmed off their excess tissues and left only gas bags.

"You do want to do a bit of gambling, then? I told you it was the spice of—let's call it existence, since you don't claim to be alive."

"I don't see it as gambling; I am merely trying to increase my odds of remaining able to observe. You said that wasn't true gambling."

"So it isn't. All right, I'll do my own gambling. There's a bush farther up the cliff, between us and the chimney. I have twenty meters of line, and a climbing grapnel. If I can hook to the bush, I can work across to the chimney with the rope carrying our weight."

"I noticed the bush. It is twenty-seven meters from the nearest point on the shelf."

"Then let's use leather, if you can call it that, from the balloons to lengthen my line."

"I doubt that it could be strong enough; lightness must be its primary quality."

"Right. *That's* what I call gambling."

He rose and approached the nearest of the balloons. It was obviously alive—the rootlike tentacles were moving, apparently aimlessly. It showed no obvious awareness of his approach, and did not react even when he stepped within reach of the tentacles and poked it experimentally with his machete. The gas bag was rather taller than his own height, thin enough to be translucent, delicately tinted pink and orange. The vital organs, if they could be called that—no one was sure if the things were animals, plants, or something entirely new—were clustered in a structure about the size of a human head at the lower end; the roots radiated from just above this, at what Faivonen couldn't help thinking of as the Antarctic circle.

If the thing were really animal in any sense, however, it seemed to be unresponsive—perhaps the cold, the man thought. Deciding it was safe, he squatted down and examined the "head" closely. The roots continued their aimless writhing.

After close examination which told neither of them anything useful, he dissected the central mass rapidly, letting Beedee see everything he did. The organs, their shapes, and their arrangements conveyed no meaning to the man, and the machine cast no illuminating comments although its insatiable thirst for information was presumably being slaked. The balloons, Faivonen judged, must form a kingdom of their own; they showed no clear relation to other life, Medean or Terrestrial.

The tissues of the deflated gas bag were as flimsy as predicted, but Faivonen began cutting strips from them. Rope making would be a long job, and time seemed limited.

"You will have to make the cord as far overstrength as we can estimate," remarked Beedee. "It is unfortunate that we have no way to test it before completion. How long do you think you will need?"

"Longer than we probably have. I'm hungry and thirsty now; there's little cheese; and, by that time, less water."

"We should have started sooner, but it was impossible. I fear our lack of data has cost another human life, though I tried to avoid my earlier mistake."

Faivonen snapped a startled question. "You mean it was a situation like this that caused Riita's death?"

"Not exactly, though her problem involved the use of the balloons. There were human emotions involved which I had not evaluated properly, long as I had known her. She refused to kill any of the creatures, which could have been put to effective use, when I told her they were intelligent. I was more careful this time, fearing that you might react in the same way."

Faivonen fought off an urge to retch. "I certainly would have. How do you know they are intelligent? Are you sure?"

"Of course. The motion patterns of their tentacles and the changing colors of their gas bags are repetitious, and seem to correlate with their actions in rising and sinking. I have been watching relays of messages going up and down the valley from one of the creatures to the next."

"Then they can see? We didn't find anything like eyes in this one."

"A very interesting problem, I agree."

Faivonen fell silent, and thought for several minutes. Then he removed and opened his shoulder pack, groped through its contents, and pulled out several pieces of metal.

"You're giving up on your gamble?" asked the diamond.

"Not exactly." Faivonen said no more. He selected two of the metal fragments, and cut a long strip from the gas bag, five or six centimeters wide. Then he removed the straps which held Beedee to his wrist, placed one piece of metal against its flat surface and the other on the curved one, and wrapped the skin around everything. He left the rounded ends of the machine, where its eyes and pressure senses were located, clear. Then he cut several much narrower strips and used them to tie the "bandage" in place. The package seemed secure.

"Current flowing, Beedee?"

"Adequately, thank you."

"Good. I've noticed that there is a breeze at our level coming from down the valley, while the gas river is still flowing in the opposite direction. Any explanation?"

"Certainly. The gas is siphoning—enough weight has flowed down the valley to maintain the current. The last time it got to the point where we first met the frost, and then was forced back by the tidal wind; this time it's set for the season, I judge. What we feel is the regular wind, riding over the carbon dioxide."

"So the gas river will flow for several weeks."

"It seems likely."

"And I can't get away."

"I don't see how."

"All right." Faivonen picked up the diamond and approached another of the balloons, now shifting a little in the rising wind. With more strips of skin, he bound the package to one of the thicker tendrils, still taking pains to leave the diamond's sense organs unobstructed. Then he stood up and looked down at the glassy half-cylinder for several seconds.

"Nothing personal," he said at last. "You put my wife in a situation which would kill her unless she changed her personality. You've done the same with me. Perhaps you aren't guilty of killing us—those human quirks you've mentioned, which are good for species survival but not for individuals, are probably doing that—but I don't choose to quibble. If my kids ever come looking for me, I don't want them to find you."

"The balloon won't support me." Beedee's voice was fainter, but quite audible.

"It will support you in carbon dioxide. Try calculating which wind will carry you. I'm betting on coldside—you wanted to see it anyway." Faivonen pushed the balloon off the shelf with his foot.

"Thank you, Elisha." The voice was much fainter, but the words could be made out. "I am coming to understand human beings. This was the action I hoped you would take. Depending on glacier speed, I should be back with your people in a few millennia—I, too, am betting on the wind toward the cold side. I seem to be winning. Of course, if these creatures have a way of coming back, I may see men sooner. I regret that you won't be there; you have been almost as interesting a property as your wife. Of course, if I do happen to get back in months instead of centuries, it would be inadvisable to have your report of my admittedly unhuman behavior waiting for me."

The voice stopped. Faivonen watched the balloon for several minutes as it drifted slowly up the valley. Then he walked to the end of the shelf nearest the chimney, took out his rope and grapnel, and made sure the latter was firmly attached.

Then he began climbing down.

"But how will we do without the diamond?" Sullivan was quite frankly horrified.

"Quite well, I should think," replied Faivonen. "We do without simpler calculators, aircraft, radios, and all sorts of other things we decided to eliminate until we could make them ourselves from local materials. This ship of yours shows we *can* do what has to be done. Come on—you know we couldn't afford to be dependent on anything we couldn't produce here. Beedee was left out of the original deal because he, or it, was private property, and anyway no one could decide whether he was alive or not—he might have been a citizen. Some of the younger generation have been claiming there was no use learning to read and write—Beedee would remember everything and tell us everything—that he wanted us to believe. That, friend Sullivan, is very bad indeed, and you know it."

"I know it, but a lot of others don't. They'll want to lynch you for losing all the knowledge of Medea we've picked up in twenty years, and they'll be right; we can't live without it."

"They won't and they'd be wrong," said Faivonen. "In the first place I didn't lose it; most of what has been learned is either common knowledge, or has been written or remembered by someone with special interest. In the second—look, Sully: Beedee knew years ago that the balloons were intelligent, but didn't tell anyone because he foresaw it would interfere with his life style. He knew perfectly well that with the carbon dioxide river flowing one way and the air the other, the gases would be turbulent and mix at the interface—there would be oxygen enough for meters below the so-called surface of the gas river, which he wanted me to think of as the drowning line, to let me breathe and climb over to the chimney and back up again. It hurt, and was hard to keep breathing control, but I could do it and did do it. Did he tell me? No. He didn't really care whether I died there on the shelf, but he wanted to make sure I sent him off to coldside. He wants knowledge the way a baby wants milk or a teen-ager wants sex, and he's as completely selfish about the appetite as a baby or an untrained adolescent; humanity is a convenience to him, but its individual members are expendable conveniences. The key fact is that we can't trust him, and once people realize that, no one's going to want to lynch me."

"You mean he's done this sort of thing to us before? We don't know what to believe, out of what he's recorded for us?"

"Just that. I'd have smashed him for killing Riita, only the fact that he didn't get away or stay conscious makes me believe he made an honest mistake that time. Maybe, if he gets back early and I'm still alive and cooled off enough, I'll be able to ask him for the real details."

"You've been calling Beedee *him* instead of *it*. You really regard— him—as alive, don't you?"

"Yes. As alive as I am, or you are, and potentially just as much a member of society. But what use is a liar to any society?"

Sure Thing

by Isaac Asimov

As is well-known, in this 30th Century of ours, space travel is fearfully dull and time-consuming. In search of diversion many crew-members defy the quarantine restrictions and pick up pets from the various habitable worlds they explore.

Jim Sloane had a Rockette, which he called Teddy. It just sat there looking like a rock, but sometimes it lifted a lower edge and sucked in powdered sugar. That was all it ate. No one ever saw it move, but every once in a while it wasn't quite where people thought it was. There was a theory it moved when no one was looking.

Bob Laverty had a Heli-worm he called Dolly. It was green and carried on photosynthesis. Sometimes it moved to get into better light and when it did so it coiled its worm-like body and inched along very slowly like a turning helix.

One day, Jim Sloane challenged Bob Laverty to a race. "My Teddy," he said, "can beat your Dolly."

"Your Teddy," scoffed Laverty, "doesn't move."

"Bet!" said Sloane.

The whole crew got into the act. Even the Captain risked half a credit. Everyone bet on Dolly. At least it moved.

Jim Sloane covered it all. He had been saving his salary through three trips and he put every millicredit of it on Teddy.

The race started at one end of the Grand Salon. At the other end, a heap of sugar had been placed for Teddy and a spotlight for Dolly. Dolly formed a coil at once and began to spiral its way very slowly toward the light. The watching crew cheered it on.

Teddy just sat there without budging.

"Sugar, Teddy. Sugar," said Sloane, pointing. Teddy did not move. It looked more like a rock than ever, but Sloane did not seem concerned.

Finally, when Dolly had spiralled half-way across the salon, Jim Sloane said casually to the Rockette, "If you don't get out there, Teddy, I'm going to get a hammer and chip you into pebbles."

That was when people first discovered that Rockettes could read minds. That was also when people first discovered that Rockettes could teleport.

Sloane had no sooner made his threat when Teddy just disappeared from its place and re-appeared on top of the sugar.

Sloane won, of course, and he counted his winnings slowly and luxuriously.

Laverty said, bitterly, "You *knew* the damn thing could teleport."

"No, I didn't," said Sloane, "but I knew he would win. It was a sure thing."

"How come?"

"It's an old saying everyone knows. Sloane's Teddy wins the race."

To Bell the Cat

by Joan Vinge

Another squeal of animal pain reached them from the bubble tent twenty meters away. Juah-u Corouda jerked involuntarily as he tossed the carved gaming pieces from the cup, spoiling his throw. "Hell, a triad . . . Damn that noise; it's like fingernails on metal."

"Orr doesn't know the meaning of 'surrender'." Albe Hyacin-Soong caught up the cup. "It must be driving him crazy that he can't figure out how those scaly little rats survive all that radioactivity. How they ever evolved in the first place—"

"He doesn't know the meaning of the word 'mercy'." Xena Soong-Hyacin frowned at her husband, her hands clasping her elbows. "Why doesn't he anesthetize them?"

"Come on, Xena," Corouda said. "They're just animals. They don't feel pain like we do."

"And what are any of us, Juah-u, but animals trying to play God?"

"I just want to play squamish," Albe muttered.

Corouda smiled faintly, looking away from Xena toward the edge of the camp. A few complaints, hers among them, had forced Orr to move his lab tent away from the rest. Corouda was just as glad. The noises annoyed him, but he didn't take them personally. Research was necessary; Xena—any scientist—should be able to accept that.

305

But the bleeding hearts are always with us. No matter how comfortable a society became, no matter how fair, no matter how nearly perfect, there was always someone who wanted flaws to pick at. Some people were never satisfied; he was glad he wasn't one of them. And glad he wasn't married to one of them. But then, Albe always liked a good argument—

"Next you'll be telling me that *he* doesn't feel anything either!" Xena pointed.

"Keep your voice down, Xena. He'll hear you. He's right over there. And don't pull down straw men; he's got nothing to do with this. He's Piper Alvarian Jary; he's supposed to suffer."

"He's been brainwiped. That's like punishing an amnesiac; he's not the same man—"

"I don't want to get into that again," Albe said, unconvincingly.

Corouda shook his head, pushed the blond curls back under his peaked cap and moved further into the shade. They sat cross-legged on the soft, gray-brown earth with the studied primitivism all wardens affected. He turned his head slightly to look at Piper Alvarian Jary, sitting on a rock in the sun; alone as usual, and as usual within summoning range of Hoban Orr, his master. Piper Alvarian Jary, who for six years—six years! Was it only six?—had been serving a sentence at Simeu Biomedical Research Institute, being punished in kind for the greatness of his sin.

Not that he looked like a monster now, as he sat toying endlessly with a pile of stones. He wore a plain, pale coverall sealed shut to the neck in spite of the heat; dark hair fell forward into his eyes above a nondescript sunburned face. He could have been anyone's menial assistant, ill at ease in this group of ecological experts on an unexplored world. He could have been anyone—

Corouda looked away, remembering the scars that the sealed suit probably covered. But he *was* Piper Alvarian Jary, who had supported the dictator Naron—who had bloodied his hands in one of the most brutal regimes in mankind's long history of inhumanity-to-man. It had surprised Corouda that Jary was still young. But a lifetime spent as a Catspaw for Simeu Institute would age a man fast

. . . Maybe that's why he's sitting in the sun; maybe he wants to fry his brains out.

"—that's why I wanted to become a warden, Albe!" Xena's insistent voice pulled his attention back. "So that we wouldn't have to be a part of things like this . . . so that I wouldn't have to sit here beating my head against a stone wall about the injustice and the indifference of this society—"

Albe reached out distractingly and tucked a strand of her bound-up hair behind her ear. "But you've got to admit this is a remarkable discovery we've made here. After all, a natural reactor—a concentration of uranium ore so rich that it's fissioning. The only comparable thing we know of happened on Terra a billion years before anybody was around to care." He waved his hand at the cave mouth 200 meters away. "And right in that soggy cave over there is a live one, and animals survive in it! To find out how they could have adapted to that much radiation . . . Isn't it important for us to find that out?"

"Of course it is." Xena looked pained. "Don't patronize me, Albe. I know that as well as you do. And you know that's not what I'm talking about."

"Yes, I know it isn't . . ." He sighed in surrender. "This whole expedition will be clearing out soon; they've got most of the data they want already. And then the six of us can get down to work and forget we ever saw any of them; we'll have a whole new world all to ourselves."

"Until they start shipping in the damned tourists—"

"Hey, come on," Corouda said, too loudly. "Come on. What're we sitting here for? Roll them bones."

Albe laughed, and shook the cup. He scattered the carved shapes and let them group in the dirt. "Hah. Two-square."

Corouda grunted. "I know you cheat; if I could just figure out how. Xena—"

She turned back from gazing at Piper Alvarian Jary, her face tight.

"Xena, if it makes you feel any better, Jary doesn't feel anything. Only in his hands, maybe his face a little."

She looked at him blankly. "What?"

"Jary told me himself; Orr killed his sense of feeling when he first got him, so that he wouldn't have to suffer needlessly from the experiments.

Her mouth came open.

"Is that right?" Albe pushed the sweatband back on his tanned, balding forehead. "Remember last week, he backed into the camp-fire . . . I didn't know you'd talked to him, Juah-u. What's he like?"

"I don't know. Who knows what somebody like that is really like? A while back he came and offered to check a collection of potentially edible flora for me . . ." And Jary had returned the next day with the samples, looking tired and a little shaky, to tell him exactly what was and wasn't edible, and to what degree. It was only later, after he'd had time to run tests of his own, that he had understood how Jary had managed to get the answers so fast, and so accurately. "He ate them, to see if they poisoned *him*. Don't ask me why he did it; maybe he enjoys being punished."

Xena withered him with a look.

"I didn't know he was going to eat them." Corouda slapped at a bug, annoyed. "Besides, he'd have to drink strychnine by the liter to kill himself. They made Jary into a walking biological lab—his body manufactures an immunity to anything, almost on the spot; they use him to make vaccines. You can cut off anything but his head and it'll grow back . . ."

"Oh, for God's sake." Xena stood up, her brown face flushed. She dropped the cup between them like something unclean, and strode away into the trees.

Corouda watched her go; the wine-red crown of the forest gave her shelter from his insensitivity. In the distance through the trees he could see the stunted vegetation at the mouth of the reactor cave. Radiation had eaten out an entire hillside, and the cave's heart was still a festering radioactive sink hot enough to boil water. Yet some tiny alien creatures had chosen to live in it . . . which meant that this expedition would have to go on stewing in the sun until Orr made a breakthrough, or made up his mind to quit. Corouda sighed, and looked back at Hyacin-Soong. "Sorry, Albe. I even disgusted myself this time."

Albe's expression eased. "She'll cool down in a while . . . Tell her that, when she comes back."

"I will." Corouda rolled his shirtsleeves up another turn, feeling uncomfortably hot. "Well, we need three if we're going to keep playing." He gestured at Piper Alvarian Jary, still sitting in the sun. "You wanted to know what he's like—why don't we ask him?"

"Him?" Incredulity faded to curiosity on Albe's face, "Why not? Go ahead and ask him."

"Hey, Jary!" Corouda watched the sunburned face lift, startled, to look at him. "Want to play some squamish?" He could barely see the expression on Jary's face, barely see it change. He thought it became fear, decided he must be wrong. But then Jary squinted at him, shielding his eyes against the sun; and the dark head bobbed. Jary came toward them, watching the ground, with the unsure, shuffling gait of a man who couldn't find his footing.

He sat down between them awkwardly, an expressionless smile frozen on his mouth, and pulled his feet into position.

Corouda found himself at a loss for words, wondering why in hell he'd done this. He held out the cup, shook it. "Uh—you know how to play squamish?"

Jary took the cup, and shook his head. "I don't g-get much chance to play anything, W-warden." The smile turned rueful, but there was nothing in his voice. "I don't get asked."

Corouda remembered again that Piper Alvarian Jary stuttered, and felt an undesired twinge of sympathy. But hadn't he heard, from somebody, that Jary had always stuttered? Jary had finally loosened the neck of his coveralls; Corouda could see the beginning of a scar between his collarbones, running down his chest. Jary caught him staring; a hand rose instinctively to close the seal.

Corouda cleared his throat. "Nothing to it, it's mostly luck. You throw the pieces, and it depends on the—"

Another mindless squall came from the tent behind them. Jary glanced toward it.

"—the distribution, the way the pieces cluster . . . Does that bother you?" The bald question was out before he realized it, and left him feeling like a rude child.

Jary looked back at him as though it hadn't surprised him at all. "No. They're just animals. B-better them than me."

Corouda felt his anger rise, remembering what Jary was . . . until he remembered that he had said the same thing.

"Piper! Come here, I need you."

Corouda recognized Hoban Orr's voice. Jary recognized it too, climbed to his feet, stumbling with haste. "I'm sorry, the Doctor wants me." He backed away, they watched him turn and shuffle off toward Orr's tent. His voice had not changed; Corouda suddenly tried not to wonder why he was needed . . . *Catspaw: person used by another to do something dangerous or unpleasant.*

Corouda stood up, brushing at his pants. Jary spent his time outside while Orr was dissecting: Piper Alvarian Jary, who had served a man who made Attila the Hun, Hitler, and Kahless look like nice guys. Corouda wondered if it were possible that he really didn't like to watch.

Albe stood with him, and stretched. "What did you think of that? That's the real Piper Alvarian Jary, all right. 'Better them than me . . . just a bunch of animals.' He probably thinks we're all a bunch of animals."

Corouda watched Jary disappear into the tent. "Wouldn't surprise me at all."

Piper Alvarian Jary picked his way cautiously over the rough, slagged surface of the narrow cave ledge, setting down one foot and then the other like a puppeteer. Below him, some five meters down the solid rock surface here, lay the shallow liquid surface of the radioactive mud. He rarely looked down at it, too concerned with lighting a path for his own feet. Their geological tests had shown that a seven-meter layer forty meters down in the boiling mud held a freakish concentration of fissile ores, hot enough once to have eaten out this strange, contorted subterranean world. He risked a glance out into the pitch blackness, his headlamp spotlighting grotesque formations cast from molten rock; silvery metallic stalactites and stalagmites, reborn from vaporized ores. Over millenia the water-saturated mass of mud and uranium had become exothermic and then cooled, sporadically, in one spot and then another. Like some immense witches' caldron, the whole underground had simmered and sputtered for nearly half a million years.

Fumes rising in Jary's line of sight shrouded his vision of the tormented underworld; he wondered vaguely whether the smell would be unpleasant, if he could remove the helmet of his radiation suit. Someone else might have thought of Hell, but that image did not occur to him.

He stumbled, coming up hard against a jagged outcropping. Orr's suited form turned back to look at him, glittered in the dancing light of his own headlamp. "Watch out for that case!"

He felt for the bulky container slung against his hip, reassuring his nerveless body that its contents were still secure. Huddled inside it, creeping over one another aimlessly, were the half dozen sluggish, rat-sized troglodites they had captured on this trip. He turned his light on them but they did not respond, gazing stupidly at him and through him from the observation window. "It's all right, D-doctor."

Orr nodded, starting on. Jary ducked a gleaming stalactite, moved forward quickly before the safety line between them jerked taut. He was grateful for the line, even though he had heard the warden named Hyacin-Soong call it his leash. Hyacin-Soong followed behind him now with the other warden, Corouda, who had asked him to play squamish this morning. He didn't expect them to ask him again; he knew that he had antagonized Hyacin-Soong somehow—maybe just by existing. Corouda still treated him with benign indifference.

Jary glanced again at the trogs, wishing suddenly that Orr would give up on them and take him home. He wanted the safety of the Simeu Institute, the security of the known. He was afraid of his clumsiness in these alien surroundings, afraid of the strangers, afraid of displeasing Orr— He let the air out of his constricted lungs in a long sigh. Of course he was afraid; he had good reason to be. He was Piper Alvarian Jary.

But Orr would never give up on the trogs, until he either broke the secret code of their alien genes or ran out of specimens to work with. Orr wanted above all to discover how they had adapted to the cave in the geologically short span of time the reactor had been stable— everyone in the expedition wanted to know that. But even the trogs' basic biology confounded him: what the functions were of the four variant kinds he had observed; how they reproduced, when they appeared to be sexless, at least by human standards; what ecological niches they filled, with such hopelessly rudimentary brains. And particularly, how their existence was thermodynamically possible. Orr believed that they seined nutrients directly from the radioactive mud, but even he couldn't accept the possibility that their food-chain ended in nuclear fission. The trogs themselves were faintly radioactive; they were carbon-based, could withstand high pressures, and perceived stimuli far into the short end of the EM spectrum. And that was all that Orr was certain of, so far.

Jary clung with his gloved hands to the rough wall above the ledge as it narrowed, and remembered touching the trogs. Once, when he was alone, he had taken off his protective gloves and held one of them in his bare hands. Its scaled, purplish-gray body had not been cold and slippery as he had imagined, but warm, sinuous, and comforting. He had held onto it for as long as he dared, craving the sensual, sensory pleasure of its motion and the alien texture of its skin. He had caressed its small unresponsive body, while it repeated over and over the same groping motions, unperturbed, like an untended machine. And his hands had trembled with the same confusion of shame and desire that he always knew when he handled the experimental animals . . .

There had been a time when he had played innocently with the soft, supple, pink-eyed mice and rabbits, the quick, curious monkeys, and the iridescent fletters. But then Orr had begun training him as an assistant; and observation of the progress of induced diseases, the clearing away of entrails and blood, the disposal of small, ruined bodies in the incinerator chute had taught him their place, and his own. Animals had no rights and no feelings. But when he held the head of a squirming mouse between his fingers and looked down into the red, amorphous eyes, when he caught its tail for the jerk that would snap its spine, his hands trembled . . .

The ground trembled with the strain of pent-up pressures; Jary fell to his knees, not feeling the bruising impact. Behind him he heard the curses of the wardens and saw Orr struggle to keep his own balance up ahead. When his hands told him the tremor had passed, he began to crawl toward Orr, using his hands to feel his way, his palms cold with sweat. He could not compensate for unexpected motion; it was easier to crawl.

"Piper!" Orr jerked on the safety line. "Get up, you're dragging the specimen box."

Jary felt the wardens come up behind him, and heard one of them laugh. The goad of sudden sharp memory got him to his feet; he started on, not looking back at them. He had crawled after the first operation, the one that had killed his sense of touch—using his still-sensitive hands to lead his deadened body. The lab workers had laughed; and he had laughed too, until the fog of his repersonalization treatment began to lift, until he began to realize that they were laughing at him. Then he had taught himself, finally, to walk upright like a human being; at least to look like a human being.

Up ahead he saw Orr stop again, and realized that they must have reached the Split already. "Give me some more light up here."

He moved forward to slacken the line between them and shined his lamp on the almost meter-wide crevice that opened across their path. The wardens joined him; Orr gathered himself in the pool of their light and made the jump easily. Jary moved to the lip of the cleft and threw the light of his headlamp down, down; saw its reflection on the oily, gleaming water surface ten meters below. He swayed.

"Don't stand so close to the edge!"

"Just back up, and make the jump."

"Don't think about it—"

"Come on, Jary; we don't have all day!"

Hyacin-Soong struck at his shoulder just as he started forward. With a choked cry of protest he lost his footing, and fell.

The safety line jerked taut, battering him against the tight walls of the cleft. Stunned and giddy, he dangled inside a kaleidoscope of spinning light and blackness. And then, incredulous, he felt the safety line begin to give . . . Abruptly it let go, somewhere up above him, and he dropped six meters more to the bottom.

"Jary! Jary—?"

"Can you hear us?"

Jary opened his eyes, dimly surprised that he could still see—that his headlamp still functioned, and the speakers in his suit, and his brain . . .

"Are you all right, Piper?"

Orr's voice registered, and then the meaning of the words. A brief, astonished smile stretched Jary's mouth. "Yes, Doctor, f-fine!" His voice was shaking. The absurdity of his answer hit him, and he began to laugh.

"Get a hold of yourself; you're going into shock. What about the specimens?"

Jary breathed deeply, obediently, and looked down. He found himself up to his waist in steaming water. His legs would not respond when he tried to move them; for a moment he wondered if he'd broken his back. But his groping hands found thick mud thirty centimeters below the water's surface, and he realized that he was only trapped, not paralyzed. The specimen case drifted half-submerged, almost out of his reach. He lunged, caught the strap and pulled it back, floundering. The trogs inside had been shaken out of their torpor; their frantic scrabbling startled him.

"Well? What happened?"

Jary noticed that his lunge for the box had driven him deeper into the mud; the water was up to his chest now. "I've g-got it. But I'm st-st-stuck in the mud; I'm sinking." He glanced up at the external radiation meters inside his helmet. "Every dosimeter's in the red; my suit's going to overload f-fast." He leaned back, trying to see Orr's face past the convex curve of the cleft wall. He saw only a triple star, three headlamp beams far above him, shafting down between the vertical walls of the slit.

"Keep your head up so we can see you; we'll throw you down a line." He recognized Corouda's voice, saw the rope come spiralling down into his piece of light. "Tie it around your waist."

The end of the rope hung twisting half a meter above his head. He struggled upward, clinging to the wall, but his muddy gloves could not hold the slick fibers and he dropped back, sinking deeper. "It's too short. I c-can't do it."

"Then tie on the specimen case, at least."

"I can't reach it!" He struck at the rock wall with his fist. "I'm sinking deeper, I'll fry. G-get me out!"

"Don't thrash," Corouda said evenly, "you'll sink faster. You'll be all right for at least fifteen minutes in that suit. Find a handhold on the wall and keep it. We'll be back soon with more equipment. You'll be all right."

"B-but—"

"Don't let go of that case."

"Yes, Doctor . . ." The triple star disappeared from his view, and he lost track of the cleft's rim. He could touch both walls without stretching his arms; he found a low ledge protruding, got the specimen case and one elbow up onto it. Steam clouded his faceplate and he wiped it away, smearing the glass with water and mud instead. The trogs had grown quiet on the ledge, as if they were waiting with him. There was no sound but his own quick breathing; the trap of rock cut him off utterly from even the reassurance of another human voice. he was suddenly glad to have the trogs for company.

The minutes stretched. Huddled in his cup of light, he began to imagine what would happen if another earth tremor closed this tiny fracture of the rock . . . What would happen if his suit failed—Sweat trickled down his face like tears; he shook his head, not knowing whether he was sweating with the heat of the mud of the strain of waiting. His suit could have torn when he fell; the radioactive mud could be seeping in, and he would never know it. He had been exposed to radiation in some of Orr's experiments; it had made him sick to his stomach, and once all his hair had fallen out. But he had never had to see the flesh rot off of his bones, his body disintegrating in front of his eyes . . .

His numb hand slipped from the ledge, and he dropped back into the mud. He hauled himself out again, panting, sobered. He had too much imagination; that was what Orr had always told him. And Orr had taught him ways to control his panic during experimentation, as he had taught him to control his body's biological functions. He should know enough by now not to lose his head. But there were still times when even everything he knew was not enough. And it was then that he came the closest to understanding what Piper Alvarian Jary had done, and why he deserved his punishment.

He relaxed his breathing, concentrating on what was tangible and real: the glaring moon-landscape of the mottled wall before his face, the bright flares of pain as he flexed the hand he had bruised against the stone. He savored the vivid sensory stimulation that was pain, that proved he was alive, with a guilty hunger heightened by fear. The gibbous, mirror-like eyes of the trogs pooled at the view-window of the box, reflecting light, still staring intently through him as if they saw into another world. He remembered that they could, and turned his head slightly, uneasily. He froze, as the small, beslimed face of another trog broke the water beside his chest; then two, and three . . . suddenly half a dozen.

Moving with a sense of purpose that he had never seen them show, they began to leap and struggle up the face of the wall—and his own suit, as though he was nothing more than an extension of the stone. He stayed motionless, not able to do anything but stare as stupidly as his own captives. His captives—A trog dropped from his shoulder onto the ledge; they were all trying to reach the box. Had the captive ones called them here? But how? They were stupid, primitive; creatures with rudimentary brains. How could they work together?

But they *were* working together, clustered now around the box, some probing with long webbed fingers, the larger ones pushing and prying. They searched its surface with their bodies, oblivious to the light of his headlamp, as though the only way they could discover its nature was through their sense of touch. He remembered that they were blind to the segment of the EM spectrum that to him was visible light. He *was* only a part of the rock, in their darkness. And here in the darkness of the cave they were reasoning, intelligent creatures—when outside in the camp they had never shown any kind of intelligence or group activity; never anything at all. Why? Did they leave their brains behind them in the mud when they surfaced . . . ?

Jary wondered suddenly if he had lost his own mind. No, it was really happening. If his mind was ever going to snap, it would have happened long ago. And there was no doubt in his mind that these animals had come here for one reason—to free the captives from their cage. These animals . . .

He watched their tireless, desperate struggle to open the cage, knowing that it was futile, that they could only fail in the end. The captive trogs were doomed, because only a human being—

His hand rose crookedly, dripping mud, and reached out toward the case, the trogs seemed to recoil, as if somehow they sensed him coming. He unsealed the lock, and pulled up the lid. The trogs inside shrank down in confusion as the ones on the outside scrambled over the ledge. "C-come on!" He pulled the box to him angrily and shook it upside down, watched their ungainly bodies spill out into the streaming water.

He set the case back on the ledge and clung there, his mind strangely light and empty. And then he saw the second circle of brightness that lapped his own on the wall, illuminating the empty cage. He looked up, to see Corouda suspended silently from a line above his head, feet braced against the shadowed rock. He could see Corouda's dark eyes clearly, and the odd intentness of his face. "Need some help, Jary?"

He looked back at the empty box, his hand still holding onto the strap. "Yes."

Corouda nodded, and tossed him a rope.

IsTHP: But we must contact these creatures. We have seen at last that they *are* beings, alien, but like ourselves; not some unknown force. They have mobiles with forms which can be known.

(Warm heavy currents billow upward)
(Mobiles rise together)
(Sussuration of thermal neutron clouds)

MNG: They have souls which can be reached. The shining mobile that released our captives, when all we did could not—we must contact that one's sessile, and make our problem known. These aliens must have space flight too, they are not native here. They can help us.
(My tendrils flatten)
(Golden-green carbonaceous webs)
(Bright gamma deepens to red as we rise)

AHM: Our problem is that these aliens wish to destroy us! That being did not truly shine with life—it was a cold creature of darkness, dripping warm mud.
(Silly currents, growing colder as this one rises)
(Soft darkness above, we rise toward darkness)

MNG: But its sessile realized our distress. It released your mobiles. It showed good will. We did not know of the aliens' true nature; perhaps they only begin to grasp our own.
(Silent absence of neutron flux)

AHM: But how do we know they would leave us in peace, even then? We have sent our mobiles into the upper darkness to begin the ritual three times already. And three times they have attacked us viciously. We have only six months left. Our mobiles must complete the ritual in the soft upper reaches, or there will be no new sessiles. We are growing old; it takes time to focus the diffision, the obliqueness of a new young mind. We cannot wait until the next Calling.
(It grows softer, colder)
(The bright world dims around us)
(Grayed, delayed radiation)
(Only whispers from the neutron clouds)

Isthp: That is true. But surely we can make them understand . . .
We must take the risk, in order to gain anything worthwhile.
(Cool sandy cross-currents)

Scwa: And what is there worth risking our wholeness and sanity for
that we do not already have? We set out to colonize a new world—
and we have done so.
(Darkness; dimming, whispering darkness)
(Soft atmospheric spaces, hard basalt)

Isthp: But we have not! We are trapped in this pocket of light, with
barely room to exercise our mobiles, on a dark and hostile world.
Every century our lifespace grows less. The ore concentration is
only a fluke, undependable. This is not the world you wanted,
one like our own that generates perpetual light, There is no
future here.
(Crackling gusts of prompt neutrons)
(Swept upward, swept upward)
(Hold back, Swift One, wait for the rest)

Ahm: What do you propose, then? That we return to *our* world,
where there is no room for us? That we should depend on these
alien monsters to take us there?
(Darkness, blind darkness on all sides)
(Dim warm radiance of mud)

Mng: They are not monsters! They might help us find a better
world!
(****************)

Kle: We are content here. We are colonists, not explorers; we ask
only to be able to breed our mobiles together . . . *such pride, to feel
the quickness of body, or the grace of supple fingers; to know that I
have chosen the best to breed with* . . . and to meditate in peace.
(Mud-pools pulse with dim ruby radiance)
(Smooth basalt . . . and the rarified atmosphere of the upper
reaches)
(I perceive that I shine in all my parts)

MNG: What is the point of breeding the finest mobiles, if they have no purpose? They build nothing for you, they contribute nothing—you are not a whole being; you are a debased breeder of pets. *To breed mobiles that can gaze upon the starry universe; that is truly beautiful.* If it were possible to breed mobiles like ours which ran the ship, which could perhaps see the true nature of the aliens from the upper darkness—that would be worthy. But we have no way to create anything worthy here.

    (Crackling gusts grow dim and gentle)
        (Push this mobile; currents slip)
            (Bright depths below us now . . . they halo the mobiles of my radiant friend *Isthp*, Gamma-shine-through-Molten Feldspar)

AHM: Worthy—breeding artificial mobiles and building artificial machines? Machines that fail, like all ephemeral, material objects.

BLLR, RHM, TFOD: Technician *Mng*!

MNG: After five hundred years, still you have not reconciled an accident. You are well named, *Ahm*, who is Darkness-Absence-of-Radiation.

    (Begin first alignment)
        (How they shine . . . how I shine)
            (Shine against darkness)
                (Shine)

AHM: It was spaceflight that brought true Darkness into our lives. It is the purpose of the body's sessile to remain fixed, to seek the perfection of mind and mobile, not to tumble like a grain of silt through the nothingness between worlds.

    (Cluster)
        (Form first pattern)
            (Gray-ruby gleaming mudpools)

ISTHP: *The 'nothingness' of space is full of light, if one has mobiles to perceive it. Strange radiation, that trembles in my memory still.* Technology frees the sessile as meditation frees the soul. So do sessiles become the mobiles of God.

(All gather, to form the patterns)
   (Heaviness of solid rock density)
     (Beautiful to behold)

AHM: Heresy. Heresy! Blasphemer.
   (All gather, my mobiles)
     (True breeding. Fine breeding.)

MNG: *Ahm*, you make me lose control—!
   (****************)

ISTHP: Peace, my beloved *Mng*, Cloud-Music. I am not offended. As our Nimbles differ from our Swifts, so do our very souls differ, one being's from another's. We were never meant to steep quietly in the depths, you and I.
   (Gently, my Strong One, move with control)
     (Vibration ripples lap the shore; mudpools settle)
       (Pass under, pass through)

MNG: *Ahm*, you must think of the future generations—why do our mobiles answer the Calling now, but to create new sessiles, who will soon be breeding new mobiles of their own? Our space here will shrink as our numbers increase, and soon it will become like the homeworld . . . and then, much worse. We do not have the resources, or the equipment, or the time, to restructure our lifespace here. You are selfish—
   (Stray whisper of the neutron breeze)
     (Pressure shifts the rock)
       (Tendrils brushing)

ZHEK: *You* are selfish! You only wish to return to space, to inflict more danger and discomfort on us all, for the sake of your perverted mechanical-mobile machines.
   (Subtle flow of color on radiant forms)
     (First movement of receptiveness)

SCWA: *I remember dim blackness and killing cold . . . anguish in all my mobiles, as they bore my sessile container over the pathless world-crust.* We have suffered too much already, from the failure of the ship; we few barely reached here alive. I for one am not ready for more trials. *Mind the mobiles! Enter a new phase of the pattern* . . .

    (All circle together)
      (Weave nets of life-shine)
        (The patterns multiply)

RHM, TFOD, ZHEK, KLE: Agreed, agreed.

ISTHP, MEG: We must contact the shining creature!

Jary lay back on the examining table while Orr checked his body for broken bones and scanned him with a radiation counter. Out of the corner of his eye he could see the empty specimen box, still lying on the floor where Orr had dumped it when he entered the tent. Orr had kept him waiting while he talked with Corouda outside—but so far he hadn't said anything more about the loss of the trogs. Jary wondered how much Corouda had really seen—or whether he had seen anything. No one had ever looked at him the way Corouda had, at the bottom of the cleft . . . and so he couldn't be sure what it really meant.

"There's nothing wrong with you that's worth treating." Orr gestured him up. "Hairline fractures on a couple of your ribs."

Jary sat up on the table's edge, mildly relieved, pressing his bruised hand down against the cold metal surface. Orr was angry; he knew the way every line settled on that unexpressive face. But Orr might only be angry because he'd lost the specimens.

"Something else bothering you?"

"Yes—" he answered the graying back of Orr's head, because Orr had already turned away to the storage chests. "You l-let me fall. didn't you?" He had found the muddy safety line intact, and the unfastened latch at the end.

Orr turned around, surprised, and looked at him. "Yes, I did. I had to release the rope or you might have dragged me into the crevice with you."

Jary laughed sharply.

Orr nodded, as though he had found an answer, "Is that why you did it?"

"What?"

"Turned the specimens loose. Because I let you fall—is that it?"

"No." Jary glanced unwillingly at the case on the floor. "I m-mean, it just c-c-came open; I told you. When if f-fell." The stutter was worse when he got nervous.

"Why didn't you tell me that immediately?"

"I didn't know!" His hands tightened on the metal; he slid down from the table.

"Stay there." Orr set a tray of instruments and specimen plates on the table beside him. "Those locks don't just 'come open.' You opened it, Piper, and let them go—out of personal spite."

"No." He shook his head, enduring Orr's pale scrutiny.

"Don't lie to me." Orr's expression changed slightly, as Jary's face stayed stubborn. "Warden Corouda told me he saw you do it."

No—The word died this time before it reached his mouth. His gaze broke. He looked down at his feet, traced a scar with his eyes.

"So." The satisfied nod, again. Orr reached out and caught his wrist. "You know how important those animals are. And you know how much trouble and risk is involved in bringing them back." Orr forced Jary's hand down onto the shining tabletop, with the strength that was always a surprise to him. Orr picked up a scalpel.

Jary's fingers tightened convulsively. "They'll g-g-grow back!"

Orr didn't look at him. "I need some fresh tissue samples; you'll supply them. Open your fist."

"Please. Please don't hurt my h-hands."

Orr used the scalpel. And Jary screamed.

"What are you doing in here, Orr?"

A sharp and angry woman's voice filled the tent space. Jary blinked his vision clear, and saw Warden Soong-Hyacin standing inside the entrance, her eyes hard with indignation. She looked at the scalpel Orr still held, at the blood pooling in Jary's hand. She called to someone outside the tent; Corouda appeared beside her in the opening. "Witness this for me."

Corouda followed her gaze, and he grimaced. "What's going on?"

"Nothing that concerns you, Wardens." Orr frowned, more in annoyance than embarrassment.

"Anything that happens on our world concerns us," Soong-Hyacin said. "And that includes your torture—"

"Xena." Corouda nudged her. "What's he doing to you, Jary?"

Jary gulped, speechless, and shrugged; not looking at Corouda, not wanting to see his face.

"I was taking some tissue samples. As you can see—" Orr picked up a specimen plate, set it down. "My job, and his function. Nothing to do with 'your world', as you put it."

"Why from his hands?"

"He understands the reason, Warden . . . Go outside and wait, Piper. I'll call you when I want you."

Jary moved around the table, pressing his mouth shut against nausea as he looked down at the instrument tray; he slipped past the wardens and escaped, gratefully, into the fresh air.

Corouda watched Jary shuffle away in the evening sunlight, pulled his attention back into the tent.

"If you don't stop interfering with my work, Warden Soong-Hyacin, I'm going to complain to Doctor Etchamendy."

Xena lifted her head. "Fine. That's your privilege. But don't be surprised when she supports us. You know the laws of domain. thank you, Juah-u . . ." She turned to go, looked back at him questioningly.

Corouda nodded. "In a minute." He watched Orr treat the specimen plates and begin to clear away the equipment. "What did you mean when you said 'he understands the reason'?"

Orr pushed the empty carrying case with his foot. "I questioned him about the troglodytes, and he told me that he let them loose, out of spite."

"Spite?" Corouda remembered the expression behind Jary's mud-spattered faceplate, at the bottom of the crevice. And Jary had told Orr that the lock had broken, after they had pulled him up . . . "Is that how you got him to admit it?" He pointed at the table.

"Of course not," irritation. Orr wiped the table clean, and wiped off his hands. "I told him that you'd seen him do it."

"I told you I didn't see anything!"

Orr smiled sourly. "Whether you told me the truth, or not, is of no concern. I simply wanted the truth from him. And I got it."

"You let him think—"

"Does that matter to you?" Orr leaned on the table and studied him with clinical curiosity. "Frankly, I don't see why any of this should matter to you, Warden. After all, you, and Soong-Hyacin, and the other fifteen billion citizens of the Union were the ones who passed judgment on Piper Alvarian Jary. You're the ones who believe his crimes are so heinous that he deserves to be punished without mercy. You sanctioned his becoming my Catspaw—my property, to use as I see fit. Are you telling me now that you think you were wrong?"

Corouda tuned and left the tent, and left the question unanswered.

Piper Alvarian Jary sat alone on his rock, as he always did. The evening light threw his shadow at Corouda like an accusing finger; but he did not look up, even when Corouda stood in front of him. Corouda saw that his eyes were shut.

"Jary?"

Jary opened his eyes, looked up, and then down at his hands. Corouda kept his own gaze on Jary's pinched face. "I told Orr that I didn't see what happened. That's all I said. He lied to you."

Jary jerked slightly, and then sighed.

"Do you believe me?"

"Why would you b-bother to lie about it?" Jary raised his head finally. "But why should you b-bother to tell me the truth . . ." He shrugged. "It doesn't matter."

"It matters to me."

Something that was almost envy crossed Jary's face. He leaned forward absently to pick up a stone from the pile between his feet. Corouda saw it was a piece of obsidian: night-black volcanic glass with the smoothness of silk or water, spotted with ashy, snowflake impurities. Jary cupped it for a moment in his lacerated palms, then dropped it like a hot coal, wincing. It fell back into the pile, into a chain reaction, cascading a rainbow of colors and textures. Two quick drops of red from Jary's hand fell into the colors; he shut his eyes again with his hands palm-up on his knees, meditation. This time Corouda watched, forcing himself, and saw the bleeding stop. He wondered with a kind of morbid fascination how many other strange abilities Jary had.

Jary opened his eyes again; seemed surprised to find Corouda still in front of him. He laughed suddenly, uncomfortably. "You're welcome to play with my rocks, Warden; since you let me play squamish. B-but I won't join you." He pushed a rock forward carefully with his foot.

Corouda leaned over to pick it up: a lavender cobble flecked with clear quartz, worn smooth by eons rolled in the rivers of some other world. He smiled at the even coolness and the solidity of it; the smile stopped when he realized how much more that must mean to Jary.

"Orr lets me have rocks," Jary was saying. "I started collecting when they sent me to the Institute. If I held still and did what I was told, sometimes somebody would let me go out and walk around the grounds . . . I like rocks. They don't d-d-die," his voice cracked unexpectedly. "What did you really see, there in the cave, W-warden?"

"Enough . . .?" Corouda sat down on the ground and tossed the rock back into the pile. "Why did you do it, Jary?"

Jary's eyes moved aimlessly, searching the woods for the cave mouth. "I d-don't know."

"I mean—what you did to the people on Angsith. And on Ikeba. Why? How could anyone—"

Jary's eyes came back to his face, blurred with the desperate pain of a man being forced to stare at the sun. "I don't remember. I don't remember. . ." He might have laughed.

Corouda had a sudden, sickening double vision of the strutting, uniformed Jary who had helped to turn worlds into charnel houses. . . and Jary the Catspaw, who collected stones.

Jary's hands tightened into fists. "But *I* did it. I *am* P-piper

Alvarian Jary! I am guilty—" He stretched his fingers again with a small gasp; his palms oozed bright blood like a revelation. "Fifteen b-billion people can't be wrong . . . And I've been lucky."

"Lucky?" Corouda said, inadequately.

Jary nodded at his feet. "Lucky they gave me to Orr. Some of the others . . . I've heard stories . . . they didn't care who they gave them to." Then, as if he sensed Corouda's unspoken question, "Orr punishes me only when I do something wrong. He's not cruel to me . . . he didn't have to make sure I wouldn't feel p-pain. He doesn't care what I did; I'm just something he uses. At least I'm useful—" His voice rose slightly. "I'm really very grateful that I'm so well off. That I only spend half my time cut up like a f-flatworm, or flat on my back with fever and diarrhea, or vomiting or fed through a tube or cleaning up the guts of d-dead animals—" Jary's hands stopped short of his face. He wiped his face roughly with the sleeve of his coveralls and stood up, scattering rocks.

"Jary— wait a minute." Corouda rose to his knees. "Sit down."

Jary's face was under control again; Corouda couldn't tell whether he turned back gladly or only obediently. He sat down hard, without hands to guide him.

"You know, if you wanted to be useful . . ." Corouda struggled with the half-formed idea. "The thing you did for me, testing those plants; the way you can synthesize antidotes and vaccines. You could be very useful, working on a new world—like this one."

Jary gaped at him. "What do you m-m—" he bit his lips. "— mean?"

"Is there any way Orr would be willing to let you work for some other group?"

Jary sat silently while his disbelief faded through suspicion into nothing. His mouth formed the imitation of a smile that Corouda had seen before. "It cost too much to make be a b-biochemical miracle, Warden. You couldn't afford me. . . Unless Orr disowned me. Then I'd be nobody's—or anybody's."

"You mean, he could just let you go? And you'd be free?"

"Free." Jary's mouth twitched. "If I m-made him mad enough, I guess he would."

"My God, then why haven't you made him mad enough?"

Jary pulled his hands up impassively to his chest. "Some people like to l-look at my scars, Warden. If I didn't belong to a research institute, they could do more than just look. They could do anything they wanted to . . ."

Corouda searched for words, and picked a burr from the dark-brown sleeve of his shirt.

Jary shifted on the rock, shifted again. "Simeu Institute protects me. And Orr n-needs me. I'd have to make him angrier than he ever has been before he'd throw me out—" He met Corouda's eyes again, strangely resentful.

"Piper!"

Jary stood up in sudden reflex at the sound of Orr's voice. Corouda saw that he looked relieved; and realized that relief was the main emotion in his own mind. Hell, even if Orr would sell Jary, or loan him, or disown him—how did he know the other wardens would accept it? Xena might, if she was willing to act on her rhetoric. But Albe wasn't even apologetic about causing Jary to fall—

Jary had gone past him without a word, starting back toward Orr's lab.

"Jary!" Corouda called after him suddenly. "I still think Piper Alvarian Jary deserved to be punished. But I think they're punishing the wrong man."

Jary stopped and turned back to look at him. And Corouda realized that the expression on his face was not gratitude, but something closer to hatred.

"All right, you're safely across. I'll wait here for you."

Jary stood alone in the darkness on the far side of the Split, pinned in the beam of Orr's headlamp. He nodded, breathing hard, unsure of his voice.

"You know your way from here, and what to do. Go and do it." Orr's voice was cutting; Orr was angry again, because Etchamenday had supported Soong-Hyacin's complaint.

Jary reached down for the carrying case at his feet. He shut his eyes as he used his hand, twitched the strap hurriedly up onto his shoulder. He turned his back on Orr without answering, and started on into the cave.

"Don't come back without them!"

Jary bit down on the taste of unaccustomed fury, and kept walking. Orr was sending him into the cave totally alone to bring back more trogs, to complete his penance. As if his stiffened, bandaged hands weren't enough to convince him how much of a fool he'd been. He had lost half his supper on the ground because his hands could barely hold a spoon . . . he would catch hell for his clumsy lab work tomorrow . . . he couldn't even have the comfort of touching his stones. Orr didn't give a damn if he broke both his legs, and had to crawl all the way to the cave's heart and back . . . Orr didn't care if he broke his neck, or drowned in radioactive mud—

Jary stopped suddenly in the blackness. What was wrong with him; why did he feel like this—? He looked back, falling against the wall as the crazy dance of his headlamp made him dizzy. There was no echoing beam of light; Orr was already beyond sight. Deliberately he tightened his hands, startling himself back into reason with a curse. Orr wouldn't have made him do this if he thought it would get him killed; Orr hated waste.

Jary pushed himself away from the wall, looking down at the patches of dried mud that still caked his suit. Most of it had fallen off as he walked; his dosimeters barely registered what was left. He started on, moving more slowly, picking his way across the rubble where the ledge narrowed. After all, he wasn't in any hurry to bring back more trogs; to let Orr prove all over again how futile it had been to turn them loose . . . how futile his own suffering had been; how futile everything was—

And all at once he understood. It was Corouda. "Corouda—!" he threw the word like a challenge into the blackness. That damned Corouda was doing this to him. Corouda, who had done the real act of torture . . . that bastard Corouda, who had pretended interest to draw him out, and then used false pity like a scalpel on his sanity: Telling him that just because he couldn't remember his crimes, he was guiltless; that he was being punished for no reason. Trying to make him believe that he had suffered years of hatred and abuse for nothing . . . No, he was guilty, guilty! And Corouda had one it to him because Corouda was like all the rest. The whole universe hated him; except for Orr. Orr was all he had. And Orr had told him to bring the trogs, or else—He slipped unexpectedly and fell down, going to his elbows to save his hands. Orr was all he had . . .

ISTHP: We must make the shining mobile understand us. How shall we do it, *Mng*? They do not sense our communication.
(Thin darkness)

MNG: But they see us. We must show them an artifact . . . a pressure suit, perhaps; to reveal our level of technology, and our plight, together.
(Mudpools vibrate with escaping gases)
(Patterns of light)

ISTHP: Exactly! I will rouse my second Nimble; it is my smallest, perhaps it can still wear a suit . . . *I summon.* . .
(Find the suit, and bear it upward)
(Weave the circle together)

AHM: We will not allow you to do this. We are the majority; we forbid contact with the alien's mobile. We will stop you if you try it.
(Cold fluid lapping basalt)

ISTHP: But its sessile is a creature of good will; even you must admit that, *Ahm*—it set your mobiles free.
(My patterns are subtle)
(Pulse softly and glow)

AHM: *Great shining fingers reaching toward me . . . fear, hope . . . to set my mobiles free . . .* But the thing we must communicate is that we wish to be left alone! Let us use the shining mobile as a warning, if the aliens return again. It can make the invisible aliens visible, and let us flee in time.
(Draw in the circle)
(Draw in)
(Strange radiance)

MNG: No, we must ask more! Show it that we are an intelligent life form, however alien. We must seek its help to rescue us from this forsaken place!

> (Close the net)
>> (Mobiles draw in)
>>> (A light in the darkness)

AHM, SCWA, TFOD, ZHEK: No. No.

> (Radiance, strange light)

ISTHP: Yes, beloved friend Mng—we will have our freedom, and the start: Look, look with all your mobiles; it shows itself! It shines—

> (Strange radiance)
>> (Light flickering like gamma through galena)
>>> (Hurry! Bear the suit upward)

AHM: The shining one returns! Take care, take care—

> (Patches of radiance flowing closer)

BLLR: Break the pattern, prepare to flee. Make its light our warning.

> (It shines)
>> (Prepare for flight)
>>> (Prepare)

MNG: Make it our hope!

> (Patches of radiance)
>> (It shines)

Echoes of his fall came back to Jary from a sudden distance; he guessed that he must be close to the main chamber already. He climbed to his feet, unable to crawl, and eased past the slick patch of metallic ore. It flashed silver in his light as he looked down, making him squint. The red path-markers fell away beyond it; he fumbled his way down the rough incline, half sliding, feeling the ceiling arch and the walls withdraw around him.

Here in the main chamber a firm, ore-veined surface of basalt flowed to meet the water-surface of the radioactive depths; here they had found the trogs. He passed a slender pillar bristling with spines of rose quartz, touched one with the back of his hand as he passed. In the distance he saw the glimmer of the water's edge, rising tendrils of steam. His stomach tightened, but he was barely aware of it: in the nearer distance the filigree of ore-veins netted light—and a cluster of trogs lay together on the shore. He swept the surface with his headlamp, saw another cluster, and another, and another, their blind, helpless forms moving sedately in a bizarre mimickry of ritual dance.

He had never had the chance to stand and watch them; and so he did, now. And the frightening conviction began to fill his mind that he was seeing something that went beyond instinct; something beyond his comprehension—But they were just animals! Even if they cared about what happened to their fellow creatures; even though they had risked death to perform a rescue . . . it was only instinct.

He began to move toward them, trying to flex his bandaged fingers, trying not to imagine the pain when he tried to keep his hold on a squirming trog body. . . . He stopped again, frowning, as the trogs' rhythmic dance suddenly broke apart. The small clumps of bodies aligned, turning almost as one to face him, as if they could see him. But that was impossible, he knew they couldn't see a human—

A dozen trogs skittered back and disappeared into the pool; the rest milled, uncertain. He stopped, still five meters up the bank. They were staring at him, he was sure of it, except that they seemed to be staring at his knees, as if he were only half there. He risked one step, and then another—and all but two clumps of trogs fled into the pool. He stood still, in the beginnings of desperation, and waited.

His numb body had begun to twitch impatiently before another trog moved. But this time it moved forward. The rest began to creep toward him then, slowly, purposefully. They ringed his feet, staring up at his knees with the moon-eyes reverence of worshippers. He went down carefully onto one knee, and then the other; the trogs slithered back. They came forward again as he made no further motion, their rudder-like hindquarters dripping mud.

They came on until they reached his knees, and began to pluck at his muddy suit-legs. He held himself like a statue, trying to imagine their purpose with a mind that had gone uselessly blank. Long, webbed fingers grasped his suit, and two of the trogs began to climb up him, smearing the suit with fresh mud. He did not use his hands to pull them off, even though his body shuddered with his awareness of their clinging forms. The dials inside his helmet began to flicker and climb.

He shut his eyes, "L-leave me alone!" opened them again, after a long moment.

Almost as if they had heard him, the trogs had let go and dropped away. They all squatted again in front of him, gazing now at his mud-slimed chest. He realized finally that it must be the radioactive mud they saw—that made his suit shine with a light they could see. Were they trying, in some clumsy way, to discover what he was? He laughed softly raggedly, "I'm P-piper Alvarian Jary!"

And it didn't matter. The name meant nothing to them. The trogs went on watching him, unmoved. Jary looked away at last as another trog emerged from the pool. He stared as the mud slid from its skin; its skin was like nothing he had ever seen on a trog, luminous silver reflecting his light. The skin bagged and pulled taut in awkward, afunctional ways ways it moved, and it moved with difficulty. All the trogs were staring at it now; and as he tried to get to his feet and move closer, they slithered ahead of him to surround the silver one themselves. Then abruptly more trogs swarmed at the edge of the pool; he watched in confusion as the mass of them attacked the silver trog, forcing it back into the mudpool, sweeping the few who resisted with it.

Jary stood waiting in the darkness while seconds became minutes, but the trogs did not return. Bubbles of escaping gas formed ripple-rings to shatter along the empty shore, but nothing else moved the water surface. He crouched down, staring at the tracks of wet mud where the trogs had been, staring down at his own muddy suit.

They weren't coming back; he was sure of that now. But why

not? What was the silver trog, and why hadn't he seen one before? Why had the others attacked it? Or had they only been protecting it, from him?

Maybe they had suddenly realized what he was: not Piper Alvarian Jary, but one of the invisible monsters who attacked them without warning.

And he had let them get away. Why, when they had climbed his suit, begging to be plucked off and dropped into his box—? But they had come to him in trust; they had put themselves into his hands, not knowing him for what he was.

Not knowing him . . .

And from that moment he knew that he would never tell Orr about the rescue, or the dance, or the silver trog—or the way the trogs had gathered, gazing up at him. Their secret life would be safe with him . . . all their lives would be safe with him. He touched his muddy suit. Inadvertently they had shown him the way to make sure they could be warned whenever he came again with Orr. Maybe, if he was lucky, Orr would never see another trog—Jary closed his hands, hardening his resolution. Damn Orr! It would serve him right.

But what if Orr found out what he'd done? Orr might even disown him, for that: abandon him here. . . . But somehow the thought did not frighten him, now. Nothing they could do to him really mattered, now—because his decision had nothing to do with his life among men, where he lived only to pay and pay on a debt that he could never repay. No matter how much he suffered, in the universe of men he carried the mark of Cain, and he would never stop being Piper Alvarian Jary.

But here in this alien universe his crime did not exist. He could prove what he could never prove in his own world, that he was as free to make the right choice as the wrong one. Whatever happened to him from now on, it could never take away the knowledge that somewhere he had been a savior, and not a devil: a light in the darkness . . .

Jary got to his feet and started back up the slope, carrying an empty cage.

Strangers

Poul Anderson

Last night as I stood on the clifftop at Hrau, seeking dreams, a ghost sailed by. The moon was well aloft, full, so bright that it flooded most stars out of heaven, for clouds had whitened nearly all its face. The light shimmered over darkful waves as if to make a path to Lost Motherland. Afar on my left, the northern horizon flickered with the campfires of the dead.

Wind lulled and ruffled my fur. It was cool, and full of salt odors to which my tendrils quivered. The surf broke utterly white, so far beneath me that the sound came low and steady, like the murmur of First River on its way to the sea when I was young. Here was a good loneliness in which to hope for dreams that would help me understand what this life has meant that now nears its end. I had not thought myself to be the kind that does—I am no saint or familiar of the Unseen—but the Watermother says I should, because of what happened long ago. Aia, how long ago!

Then as I waited, something glimmered yonder. It might have been a leaf, pale with autumn, which the wind hunted along the foam-crests. Yet it was too large, and fared too steadily, and it came not down the wind but across, from the east. Was this the form of my guide into sleep? A shiver and a shiver passed through me.

Still it neared, until suddenly it swung about. But that time it was so close that I could see what was below, the knife-lean shape cleaving its way, with a wake behind on which the moonlight shattered and swirled. My fin, already lowered, shut itself hard against my back. That was no canoe of ours passing by. That was a boat of the Night Folk.

Why have they come to seek us out, after these many years? What has changed in the Forest or in Lost Motherland, and is it of horror or of hope? Almost, I called out, but fear choked me and I crouched down, not to be seen against the western stars and the Sky Flow.

The ghost boat sailed on in swiftness and silence, following the shoreline but well clear of the breakers. As it moved away, dread left me. Might those be aboard whom I had known? I sprang to my feet, raised my fin to the full that moonlight might gleam off it, shouted and sprang about.

The boat sailed on. I do not know if they saw me. Surely they could have, as great as their powers are; but I do not know. The boat vanished southward. Grief welled up in me. I dropped to all fours, my tail lashed to and fro, I wailed for my loss, if it was indeed a loss.

No dream would come to be before dawn. Presently, though, calm did. I rose again and sang the song of farewell. After that I went home. Today I tell you of this that I have seen.

Most of you are young. You have heard the tales and learned the songs, but you do not know Lost Motherland as we few aged do who were born there and once walked on the downs and offered at the ancestral tombs. And I alone remain of those who ever saw the Night Folk. I alone sought them out in the Forest. We who remember have paid the price and suffered that loss which mortals must who deal with them; but mine was the sacrifice over and above this. Therefore you others do not know what you believe you know. I must try to tell you. Hear me.

It may be that the ghost boat was bound past on its way to some mystery beyond sight. It may be that the Night Folk have many times flitted about these islands unbeknownst to us. Did I only chance to see last night, or did they want me to see? That may have been the sending I sought, to make me ready; and after I am in my dolmen they will come by moonlight and whisper to me. Who can say? If they do seek you out, you will need the awe, the wariness, and also the eerie gladness that were ours, not as words but deep in your dreams. It is for your children and their children, who will not have countless ancestors to watch over them as we did, but merely us. Though you believe you have heard my story before, you have not really. Hear me.

For two days, people at home saw smoke drift up in the distance above Gneissback Fell. Ktiya had been a large thorp; it and its croplands were long in burning and longer still in smoldering after the Charioteers torched them. The sullen sight brooded behind us through our return to Oaua and haunted the following sunrise. At last it grew thin and merciful winds scattered what was left. They could not blow the memories out of us, nor the forebodings. Ktiya was large, I say, and it had gotten the help of such other Wold People as spied the beacon fires that meant Charioteers were on their way to it. Nevertheless Ktiya perished. Oaua was small; and belike it would stand alone when next the destroyers came, for our kindred around the land would be in despair.

"But we drove them off, Ak'hai'i," my oath-comrade Izizi protested when I forced myself to utter this. "We killed several and hurt more—as you know better than anyone else among us—until they wheeled about and lashed their ehins to full speed eastward."

"They were a small party," I answered. "We had thrice the count of them, I think. Even so, they left our dead and wounded wide-strewn. They withdrew in good order, taking their own fallen along, except for those two it happened we surrounded."

"You should sing of that, Ak'hai'i," he said.

I might well have, for it was I who led the charge that split the enemy line. We cut a single chariot off from the rest, and Hgi of Thunder Bay put a spear in the driver but it was I—I—I who sprang up over the rail and killed the warrior himself. My ax smashed his head before his blade gave me more than a shallow slash, and now that blade rested sheathed upon my breast.

But darkness had risen in me with the smoke of Ktiya. "They rallied at once," I said. "They could have cloven us asunder and hunted us down one by one as we fled. They did not, because it was not worth their trouble. They had done what they meant to do, and longed to get back to their horde."

We lay in the Male Lodge, we who had gone forth to battle and lived. Soon we would seek the females and their wisdom, but first we must come to terms with those of us whom we had carried home for burial, and with ourselves. Afterward we would explain as best we could to the females, and take counsel, and all together try to come to terms with the Unseen. Thus did the Wold People do in the old times. It is different today. Everything is different.

Coolness dwelt within the thick clay walls. Sunlight filtered through the matting in the doorway to make dusk for us. The thatch smelled of nightwort and dry forage, a peaceful smell. Our gaze we kept on the lampflame on top of the Block.

"What was it, then, that the Charioteers came to do?" asked Ngi. He and his family lived by themselves, strand-fishing or venturing out into the bay on a raft more than they worked the soil. Therefore he had not heard as much as we did in our thorp, and until this moment, time and breath had been lacking for him to learn.

"To lay waste," I told him. "They have cleared that vale of people and crops. Naught will meet them when they return but the whistlewing above and the wanderbeast on the ground. Naught will be growing but forage for their herds. In this wise, piece by piece they take the world away from the Wold People."

"What drives them to such deeds?" Izizi cried.

I shrugged my fin. "Who knows? Maybe not even themselves. Or maybe the years have worsened still more in the far east than they have here, as the sun slips from her rightful path."

"They fall on us who never harmed them!"

"A flippertail may think the same of me when my net hauls him from the water," said Ngi harshly.

"They have the power, true," breathed from me, "the chariots and the iron." So did we call the terrible material that cut and stabbed, unbreakable, keener than the finest-knapped sharpstone. Nobody knew who first named it. The Watermother said the word might have come from the users. Sometimes they bore off captives, and maybe a very few of these had escaped over the years and made their way back.

"If I did," rumbled Ngi, "I would use it against them just as they do against us."

"But the fate is otherwise," I replied. "Now let us be silent, mingle our spirits with the lampflame, and find peace."

Stillness fell. It did not in me. I lay there with rage on my right side and grief on my left. What to do? At heavy cost, we had slain four or eight of a raiding party and I had brought back a weapon of theirs. What good was that when the horde had blades like stalks in a swale and we knew not how to make a single one?

At last I drew mine. The others were rapt and did not see. I looked at it and felt of it as I had done whenever we stopped to rest while homebound. It was almost as long as my arm, but at the middle no more thick than my outer thumb. A stone blade shaped like that could only be for ceremony, would shatter in use; the iron did not even chip. It sheened darkly, ice-smooth. The edges, which drew blood if I stroked them, had the beautiful curve of a sunseeker leaf. There was a guardian crosspiece at their top. The haft beyond was not merely wrapped, it was a thing to itself, carven hardwood somehow fastened on and wrapped with leather, flaring out to a knob in which was set a crystal. When I lifted the weapon, it was heavy as stone, but so balanced that it came alive in my hand. The crystal gleamed in the dusk, an eye that watched me like the eye of a beast of prey.

For I was the prey. My people were. Surely I was not the first who ever won an iron blade for himself. It must have happened here, and there, as our kind met the invaders. But what was the use? Unskilled, its possessor would fare worse in his next battle than if he bore familiar arms. Better he leave his prize behind in the tomb of his ancestors, to wait for him. Better still, maybe, that he sink it in a pool or thrust it into a hilltop. The Unseen might accept such an offering and grant peace of soul, or the Night Folk might take it and be pleased enough to give his kindred some small help.

The flame on the Block wavered. It called me, and my spirit followed. I came back to my body knowing what I must do.

In those days the Watermother of Oaua was Riao, old, wise, and deep in the mysteries. When I told her of my intent, we two alone in her house, she said more quietly than I had awaited, "This is a wildness in you."

"It is a hope," I answered. "I see none other."

"You are likeliest to find death or worse, you who have wife and children."

"I go because I have them."

"What is your plan?"

"None. How can I make any when I know naught? I will seek until I find the Night Folk, then I will beg of them or try to compel them, whatever seems best. There are tales of ancestors who had to do with them. My own grandmother saw one."

"They flit from the Forest, across the Wold, sometimes—oftener than we know, I think," Riao agreed. "Most people who have a glimpse are afraid to tell of it afterward. If you must venture this, why do you not rove the darkness closer to home?"

"How can I be sure I will meet any, though years pass in waiting? They come and go like the wind. Or they may well spy me and stay clear of me. Also, should I catch one, their anger may fall on the whole thorp; they may blight the crops and put a murrain on the livestock. By myself, off in their own country, I may well draw them, and they should understand that any offense against them is mine alone."

"That is well spoken," she said, "and you have hunted in the fringes of the Forest, at least. Depart, keep silence, and let me dream on this."

I left that dim hut behung with strange things and went to my home. When I entered, Hroai looked hard at me and sent our young outside. "Your fin is nearly white," she whispered. Waves of violet pulsed between the ribs of hers.

"It is in my mind to brave a certain danger," I told her.

"Again?"

"This is not another battle. It would be unlucky for you to hear more. Have I your leave to fare?"

She was a long while mute, though her fin darkened and lightened and darkened, her tail twitched, her fur stood briefly on end. At last she said, "I believe I know what you intend. For the children's sake, I will not speak of it. For good or ill, there is a fate in you. Let us have each other while we still man." And that night she loved me often and fiercely.

In the morning I went back to Riao. "You shall go," she declared, "but first I will teach you and give you that which may help."

And so I abode with her for three days and nights. What she taught me I may not reveal, only that certain signs I could watch for and certain spells I could cast were therein. At the end she took me to First River, where it cascaded into a shadowy coomb otherwise forbidden to males, and purified me. After that she gave me a lasso. "The groundvine whose fiber is in this grew on the tomb of my ancestors," she said. "I twisted it together by night, singing moonbeams in among the strands. It may bind one of those whom you seek. Be on your way."

"Let me return home and make my farewell," I asked.

"You dare not," the Watermother said.

Dawn was breaking above the mist and clangor in the hollow. I prostrated myself before her, rose, and climbed out to begin my journey.

From a hilltop I looked widely across the land. That sight is before me as I tell of it, clearer and more colored than this around us; but I was young then.

Shadows reached long and blue in the morning light. They brought forth the strong curves of the Wold, the downs rolling away and away on every side until I saw a thin gleam in the west that was the sea, the vales between their slopes, the river winding and shining through a web of lesser streams that trickled or tumbled to mingle with it. Autumn-tawny the land was, save where cultivation made small dark patches. A few scattered trees stood northward, stunted and wind-gnarled, forerunners of the Forest. Dolmens and passage graves brooded gray on heights.

Tiny and very dear was Oaua, the round huts clustered close together, hearthfire smoke seeping up out of their thatch. Hurdle-fenced pens encircled it like a lover's arms and legs. I knew the bustle and clatter of awakening, I knew that Hroai was already out in our fleshroot field with her digging stick while little Uo fed the animals and littler Lyang cleaned house and cared for the infant yet nameless, but none of this could I hear or see from where I was. I whispered, "Farewell," and started north.

The weather was chill. Even in the afternoon I needed only half unfold my fin to stay cool. Clouds drove low on blustery airs. It should not have been so. The sallowness of forage and shrubs recalled a wet, cold summer. When my mother was a child, snow seldom fell in winter; now most years saw several nights of black frost.

Late that day, following the river upstream, I came upon the Henge. I did not linger; those standing stones were too grim. The Wold People no longer met there for rites, as my grandparents had told me they once did. It was not that we believed a curse had fallen on the halidom. But when a watcher stood on the Flagstone at solstice, the sun did not rise above either Altar of the Seasons. Sacredness had gone after the heavenly paths turned awry; and weather bleakened and presently the Charioteers began arriving.

Nevertheless this remained a good land, Motherland, and I would keep it for us if my fate had might enough. So did I vow, then.

At eventide I made camp. My plan was to enter the Forest when the moon was full. Belike it would give more power to the Night Folk, but it would give sight to me. Meanwhile, though, I would use the dark for resting. I cut some withes, fashioned a weir, and staked it in the stream hoping my breakfast would be there at sunrise. I kindled no fire, which would have been troublesome to do and might draw a heed I did not yet want. Instead, I found pebbles to serve as a henge around me, within which I unrolled my blanket hide and ate of the dried provisions I carried.

Besides these things, I bore a casting spear and my ax: the weapons in my hands, the skin and pouch on my shoulders. A knife hung on a cord at my throat. Should any of my gear break, I could readily replace it, for sharpstone was plentiful on the Wold. Moreover, across my chest lay the iron blade, with Riao's lasso wrapped about its sheath.

I slept lightly, and my dreams were of home. I did not know what that meant.

Trees became more and taller as I trotted on. By the third day I had truly entered the Forest.

Most that grew around me were stonewood, their ruddy boles soaring aloft till the branches arched in leafage that tented off the sky. Sunlight filled the shadows overhead with flickery turquoise and the shadows beneath with white flecks. Distances reached boundless, for sight soon lost itself yonder. In places I saw bluecap blooming upward, low nightwort, moonfruit aglow, a tangle of groundvine, fangthorn crouched cruel; but mainly it was clear between the trees, except for old leaves that rustled underfoot. Sometimes a whistlewing flew from a bough, a redflit piped, a buzzbuzz blundered past; and when I stood still a while and listened closely I might hear scuttering go through the brush. Such noises hardly broke the stillness. It was warmer here than out on the Wold, and full of earth odors.

I had ventured this far in the past, hunting uk'ho or trihorn. Thus had I once come upon a field of the Night Folk. Others had done likewise. Always we called aloud that we purposed no trespass, and veered off. Today I must do what I earlier denied. I touched the rope that encoiled the blade and hastened onward before courage should bleed out of me.

My course took me from First River and the comfort of open sky above it, for here the land began to climb. The fields had been in damp, shady places. I followed a tributary brook up its own stream. It glided slow, dimly aglimmer. Shadows thickened. Evening was nigh when I found what I sought.

All those clearings were small. I think this was to have trees close around, that they might keep full sun off the witchplants. Much water was needed too; the brook ran through the middle. High and strange and in straight rows grew the plants. When last I saw them they were brilliant green, but that was in a different season. Now they were nearly white, had dried out, and bore long berries encased in husks. Four trees rose in their midst, dwarfish and gnarly. Leaves of a paler green and large red fruits clustered upon them.

I touched naught. Stories told of reckless hunters who had stolen from plots like this. They hoped the trophies would bring luck, but only misfortune came to them. A child of one ate, and although the taste made him spit it straightway out, he was sick for days. And then there are tales of Night Folk who visited wise females, talked with them, sometimes warned that something people were doing was unwise, but refused any food offered, or any drink save water. It alone may pass between the worlds without bearing death.

Casting about, I found what I had not found earlier, when I merely stared and fled. A trail ran along the farther side of the clearing, in easy curves that soon went beyond my sight. It was no game track, but wide and hard-packed, kept clear of growth. Peering close, I made out marks in the dirt, grooves that ran side by side about two tailspans apart. Wheel marks? Who had taught the Charioteers?

I flinched from that question and looked for a blind. A canebrake at an opposite corner of the field seemed best. I settled myself within to wait.

The sun sank until its beams speared through rare breaks in the wall of woods, as long as my thoughts. When would the Night Folk arrive to see to their harvest? Could I abide for that? What should I do? What would they do? The songs and the stories told how ill it was to cross them. Yet tales also went of kindnesses they had done, wonders they had worked, when the mood blew into them. These happenings took place in olden times, when they came out more freely upon the Wold and it was not unheard of for people to encounter them. No living person in Riao's knowledge had done so, aside from glimpses. She knew not what had changed or why. One

story said that a powerful Watermother grew overweeningly proud
and took such a visitor captive by spells and force; she met a frightful
end when others appeared in her doorway, and afterward they
never guested anyone. Many more stories said that to have anything
to do with the Night Folk, even though it was help they gave, cost
heavily; some said the price was half one's soul.

Nonetheless I meant to dare it, for next year the Charioteers
would be back.

The sun went down. The moon rose, but the Forest shut it off.
Darkness weighed on me. Its creatures hooted, chirred, and thrice
from afar howled. I sat on my tail as moveless as I was able. At last I
dozed.

A new sound brought me fully awake. For a moment I was aware
of thirst. Time had worn on until the moon was over the treetops
around the clearing. Fear thrilled everything else out of me. What I
heard coming from the west was the beat of ehin hoofs.

The moon stood huge. Its clouds covered entirely the mottlings
on its face. Light frosted leaves, poured down them to drench the
field and melt into the brook. The edges of things were stark,
the shadows they cast were dappled. Air had gone cool and still. The
water whispered of secrets.

Hoofs thudded. He of the Night rode forth from under the trees.

Rode. His ehin did not draw a chariot but stepped as proudly and
gracefully as if in the wild, with him upon its back. Bewilderment
whirled in me. How could this be? Then I remembered that the
Night Folk have no tails.

Tall he was, tall as I am long from muzzle to tailtip, and slender.
The moonlight revealed him moon-pale, without fur; but hair grew
in a fallow mane on his head and in a bristle on his lower face. That
face was flat, save that the eyes were deep-set (and no tendril fronds
above) and a beak jutted outward. The ears were small and round.
No fin grew from his back. You have heard weird rumors of how the
Night Folk look. This is the truth.

He came to the edge of the field and drew on cords he had
fastened about the ehin's head. The animal halted and he sprang
down to earth. I saw that he had bound a kind of seat to the ehin's

back. . . . Aia, I forgot most of you have never seen such a beast. Like many large four-footed creatures of the mainland, instead of a real fin it has a low ridge of ribs and membranes along neck and back. A pad flattening part of this is harmless; the female does it to the male when she mounts him in breeding season.

My gaze went wholly to the rider. He stood as straight as he sat, needing no tail to balance himself. Through me flitted a wondering: what did he use when he must strike a heavy blow and had no ax? At once I asked myself: what would dare attack him?

I would, if I must.

The rope felt slippery as I unwound it and made a coil to carry in my left hand. My right was empty, ready to snatch out the blade, for my stone weapons were surely of no avail here. Did cold iron have power against Night Folk? Or had they made a pact with the warriors of the east, teaching them about iron and wheels? That thought stiffened my will.

He entered the field, handling the witch-plants like any farmer who wants to see how the crop ripens. Somehow that made it all the eerier. What would his harvest be? I raised my courage and trod forth into the moonlight.

He heard, turned about, stood for an instant as though startled. I lifted my right hand. "Hail to you, strong one," I heard myself call. "Forgive that I trouble you. The need of my people is great."

I stopped. The ehin stamped and whistled. For what seemed a very long time, he of the Night stayed moveless. Finally he walked toward me. You or I could never do that gait. A tailspan away he paused, and we were silent before each other.

"I am Ak'hai'i of Oaua," I said when I became able. "Lately the Charioteers came as near us as Ktiya and laid its territory waste, in spite of the Wold People who live within sight of its beacons sending males to help. Next year or next, they will be upon us. After that, year by year, they will take all for themselves. The last of us will lie untombed and none be left to light the ancestors home on Hallows' Eve. To come to you was my choosing and nobody else's. But I beg you, help us."

His mouth, below the beak, opened. The teeth that gleamed in the moonlight were like none I had ever seen before in person or beast. As he spoke, his mouth writhed around them. His voice was an eldritch singing, full of overtones and sounds we cannon make; and it changed the sounds we can make until I barely knew what they were meant to be. When I was small, my father had a tame redflit that could say a few words. They were less alien than what I now heard.

And these words stumbled. I hear them anew, even as I see that moonwashed space, the light like rimefrost on the crowns of trees and in the murmurous water; even as I feel the cold that went through and through me. "You . . . people . . . never . . . come . . . so."

"Death drove me," I pleaded. "You know us of old. Our ancestors remember you. Help us, lest we die!"

He spread his hands. Each bore an extra finger, and only one of the curiously shaped five was a thumb. Or thus it seemed. "No can help," he said. "You go."

I braced myself foursquare. "You must."

He pointed at me. "Go."

I stood where I was. No lightning blasted me, no curse withered me. He backed off a step. Was he afraid? That could not be, could it? He was immortal.

Yet the tales told of bounds upon what they did when they might well have done much more. And why did they shun daylight?

He moved toward his ehin. Belike he had wand or weapon tied to the animal. If it did not act at once, I could soon be dead— unentombed—or stricken mad or turned to stone.

Before fear froze me, I whipped the charmed lasso upward. It whirled about my head and pounced. I am a hunter. I noosed him by the legs, hauled, and brought him to earth.

He shouted and struggled. I leaped close and tossed coil after coil around him, snugged them taut, made him lie trussed like a taorhi for slaughter. I secured the bonds and had him.

He glared. Moonlight glistened off the white that was in his eyes. "Let me go," he panted. "No can help."

"I think you can but will not," I answered. "Or your folk can. We shall see."

He stiffened and defied me. "What you do?"

Dismay winged through my spirit. How indeed could I compel the Night Folk? What doom had I already brought on myself?

Nevertheless . . . he lay there snared. He spoke poorly, must be ignorant of speech, he, the lord of lore. None of his brethren had come on the wind to save him.

Through the awe that held me glided a thought. "You shall lie where you are till daybreak," I told him.

He gasped. Emboldened, I bent low to look closer at this that I had, incredibly, captured. What I had taken for skin wrinkled and folded with his movements. I forced myself to feel. It was covering, like a cap we put on in the bitterest weather, through this was woven so fine that warp and woof were lost within it, and was fitted to his limbs.

I drew the iron blade. Its living heaviness became my own will. "You shall have no shade from the sun," I threatened. Carefully, I slashed. His true skin shone bone-pallid under the moon. When I tugged at the fabric to get it clear of the rope, it ripped. I peeled him from shoulders to hips and left his belly naked to the sky.

What I then saw struck me with such astonishment that I dropped the blade and sprang back. "But you are female!" I cried. What evil had I been about to wreak?

His mouth twisted upward. A wild barking noise broke from him. "I male," he choked.

I mastered myself again and looked harder. Indeed that which sprouted between his thighs did not much resemble the female organ. Were the Night Folk wholly deformed?

It came to me how unwise he had been. Had he let me believe him female, I might well have released him. The charioteers kill everyone, but the Wold People respect the Life Power.

Or would I have set him free? He was not of my people, and their need was great. I did not know, and it did not matter. He *was* male; and he was not clever, regardless of what he knew. He was mine, unless and until his vengeful rescuers arrived.

He keened words in his own language, if that was what they were, and strained against his bonds. I stood by. Dawn, was still far away.

Patience was my single strength. I must be the rock that outlasts the night wind.

But it was just a short while before he calmed. His uncanny gaze met mine. I compelled myself not to look away. "Sun kill me," he said. "Sun, fire, burn, I dead."

"Unless you help my people, they are dead," I answered.

"Not know how."

"There are those among you who do." I must believe that. "Take me to them."

Silence brimmed the well of moonlight that was the clearing. My spirit was cold. At last he said, "I take you."

The cold became a rushing tide. "Will you swear to that?" I asked. "By the honor of your ancestors, will you bring me unharmed to the home of your folk and will they hear me out?"

He bobbed his head up and down. "I take you, I take you."

That was no oath. Maybe the Night Folk could not swear any. Maybe, immortal, they lacked ancestors. Well, if he intended treachery, my hope was lost anyway. "We will go," I said. Stooping, I undid the knot.

Meanwhile I commanded, "Hold still." He obeyed. I kept my blade lying ready to stab while I drew the lasso off him and used it to tie his hands behind his back. He rose, and for a little while we stared again at each other.

"I . . . Sten," he said. "Sten Granstad,"—as nearly as I can make the sounds.

Did he offer me his name for a hostage, as I had offered mine? My throat shut tight. It was a moment before I could repeat, "Ak'hai'i" and his gesture.

His mouth curved, though he did not bark. "Come, Ak'hai'i," he said quite softly, and turned about.

I did not risk breaking the spell by fetching my gear from the canebrake. If ever I started back home, it would be easy to chip out a hand ax, and that would be enough for the journey.

We walked west down the broad trail. He had me lead the chin by the cords. My other hand held the enchanted rope that leashed him.

As time and distance passed, my grip eased. He had made no trial of escape, nor done anything else to alarm me. He gave no sign of wrath at my binding him and spoiling his garment. Rather, he went by my side almost as a comrade might.

Of course, we were bound for his kindred, and once among them I would become the captive. What I had gained was, at most, the right to speak with them; and my gain could well prove to be no more than death, and helpless homelessness forever afterward.

Only our footfalls and the ehin's hoofbeats spoke while we followed that moonlit path. The shadows shifted, shortened; dew began to glitter on boulders and fallen trees; coolness deepened toward chill; stars trekked across heaven. My thoughts were few and dreamlike. I had gone beyond myself as well as beyond my world.

We passed more stands of witchplants, and once a shelter. It was of wood, timbers shaped to a fineness no sharpstone adze could achieve. The form was square-sided, altogether foreign. And yet that was ordinary naoi wood.

My dream broke apart like dawnmists when suddenly hoofs tramped ahead of us. Sten's ehin whistled. We halted. I stood stiff, awaiting my fate.

It happened the boughs here were thin above us. The moon hovered enormous behind their lattice. Its light poured over the trail. Around a bend, out of the speckled shadows, another mount came into that hueless brilliance, and upon it another of the Night Folk. Behind paced two beasts of unknown kind. Fourfooted, they stood about as high as my hip. Thick hair covered them from long muzzle to short tail. When they sensed me and growled, fangs gleamed.

The rider stopped, stared, reached for something. "Nadia!" Sten called. The rider drew a hollow canc of iron from a sheath and pointed it. Sten spoke fast in a lilting language that no throat among us could ever form, unless partly and brokenly. The rider replied. I stood awaiting my fate.

Sten turned to me. "Nadia Zaleski," he said, and made a gesture with his head. I cannot speak it any better than that, but I knew it was a name. He barked and added, "She female."

In truth? I stared. She too had covered her body, but I could find some differences. Her mane was black, longer than his. Apart from the thin lines of hair the Night Folk have above their eyes in place of tendrils, none grew on her face. Her form was smaller, slighter, rounder, with twin swellings at the chest. Had they not told me, I would have taken her for the male, him for the female. But they did give me this knowledge into my hands, and therewith a brightening of hope.

I stepped behind Sten and loosed his arms. "Is she your Water-mother? I asked unsteadily. "If so, I will beg of her."

Nadia spoke from her seat. Although she could not make words of ours sound right, they flowed much more readily, in a voice more high and sweet, than his. "We have no Watermother," she said. "You have wandered far from your world, Ak'hai'i."

"But surely you have traveled into ours, mighty lady," I had courage to reply.

She moved her head up and down. The mane rippled about her shoulder. "I have that. What is your home, Ak'hai'i?" When I told her, she murmured, "It is long since I was in Oaua. You cannot have been born. But I met with its Watermother—secretly seeking her out, lest fear of me make her people dread her too—and we spoke of many things. She was Kiluo."

I shuddered. "Kiluo is in her tomb. Riao now deals for us with the Unseen." Bracing myself: "But why should this be strange? You never grow old, you Night Folk."

A sound like a breeze through darkness blew from her mouth. Did I hear sorrow? "We do not grow old as fast as you, Ak'hai'i."

At that, somehow, the hope within me turned from fire to ice. I had trapped and tricked Sten. I had made him guide me here, because else I would have made the sun burn him alive. Now Nadia said they also must someday die. "Have you no power to save us?" I howled.

They talked together.

"I will go," I said dully. "Forgive my people that I troubled you. They knew naught of it."

Nadia raised her hand. "Wait," she called. I turned back. The blood knocked in my head. "You have dared what none before you ever did, Ak'hai'i," she said low. "We would help you because of that, if we can. I make no promise. And I fear the price to you must be heavy, whether you win or lose. Are you willing?"

"I am, I am," I sang.

A moment she sat quiet. Her teeth gnawed her mouth. "Can we bring ourselves to this?" she wondered.

"I think we must, whatever it costs us," replied Sten, likewise in my language.

She commanded her ehin to go west. "Follow," she said.

He mounted his. I came behind. The hunting beasts loped at my tail.

Of what happened therafter I can say very little. We lack the words. We lack the eyes and the thoughts. Do you understand? A thing may be so strange that you cannon *see* it. You do not know how to look. It is like a mist where colors go swirling, now bright, now dim, never the same. Sometimes the mist rolls aside somewhere, and for a breath a shape stands forth, but it is like an icicle or a lightning bolt; and what you hear is like voices in a dream that seem to have meaning until you awaken and cannot imagine what the meaning was.

We three had fared a ways when Sten gaped and stretched and mumbled something. Nadia spoke back to him before she explained to me—how kindly they both had become!—"He is weary."

By that time my surprise could only be dull, but she observed it. Her mouth curved as she said with a ghost-wind of breath, "We grow weary and must sleep the same as you. Sten has been traveling on his rounds since sundown."

"Was it a hard journey?" I asked, wondering what dangers he might have encountered.

She barked a tiny bit. "Not until he met you. He was just seeing if all was well with our fields. But it has been a long wakefulness for him." She was quiet a spell. The hoofs of the ehins thudded, the leather of the seats upon them creaked. "In the place where we should be, the days and the nights are but half as long as here."

"Why do you not stop and rest?" I blurted.

"We must be sure to return before dawn."

"Is it true the Night Folk cannot endure daylight?"

Her head moved up and down. "Your sun burns too cruelly bright for us."

Bewilderment silenced me.

I was tired myself when we ended our journey. But what I found there took from me every sense of mortality. I was like the spirit of one unentombed, bodiless awareness in a world no longer mine. This world, though, had never been mine; I had not even a memory of it.

The stronghold of the Night Folk stands on high ground above the sea. Forest is at its back and trees grow around three sides of it. The fourth looks down into a bay that was then a broken path of light under the sinking moon. Mightily rear those wall, stone and timber, beneath a roof that is also of cloven wood. The windows are filled with clear ice that never melts, and dawn-soft yellow light glows through it. Nearby are the worksteads. Of them I can say naught, except that I saw flames flicker and heard iron ring upon iron, with undergroundish noises as of whirring and tramping. I was brought to the house.

Forth they came to meet us, the tall Night Folk, and more from the woods and the worksteads, carrying lights in their hands that I thought at first, seeing them at a distance, were stars descended upon earth. By this and the shining windows I saw how garb upon the Night Folk was colored, fire-red, sunseeker-orange, springleaf-yellow, gem-green and sea-green, heaven-blue and sea-blue, blood violet, the white of snow and the black of oracular pools. Their speech caroled and surged about me. I believed some were angry and would have stricken me dead with the iron things they bore, but maybe I was mistaken. Sure it is that the will of Nadia and Sten prevailed; and who had better right to spare my life than Sten? The first brightening was above the Forest when they led me within.

And there—I cannot say what was there. I am not forbidden, but I am not able. No mortal would be. I may speak of soaring rooms and rainbow hues and music that bore me on its tide, but how shall I conjure this up out of the passage grave that is my memory? That I can never share the miracle has set me apart forever.

They gave me a place to be by myself. They brought me food I could eat, and pure water. They heard me out, questioned, listened, talked one with another, went off and left me alone, came back and questioned further. Sometimes they named names I remembers, Wold People, though all whom I had ever heard of or known as a child were dead. Indeed the Night Folk had gone among us.

"Mostly we sought to learn about you, to understand you," Nadia said once. "Certain things that happened were bad. I suppose that is inescapable, when races are altogether unlike. We cherished hopes—but they came to naught, and now we seldom leave the Forest."

Day broke. The dwellers drew into their great house of many rooms. They closed wooden slabs over the windows. When any of them must venture out, he went muffled and shaded, with pieces of black ice masking his eyes.

"This is not our world, you see," Nadia told me.

"Whence came your forebears?" I whispered.

"It was far away, beneath a gentler sun," she said. "They fell from the sky long ago, long ago . . . as you reckon lifetimes. Since then we have made what we could out of what we have."

In my puzzlement I could not ask further.

The day wore on. About noon, I met with one who seemed almost a Watermother, though male. The hair on his head was white. "Did the Charioteers learn their arts from you?" I made bold to question him; for I had seen ehins drawing wheels.

"They did not," he avowed. "We knew no more about them than that there are herders on the eastern plains. Nor did we know, until you bore us the tidings, that any have moved this far west."

"They ravage and slay," I said. "In the name of whatever friendship ever was between the Night Folk and the Wold People, help us. Else we perish."

"What would you have us do?"

"You can tell better than I. Give us iron weapons and chariots of our own, and school us in their use?"

"The invaders are too many for you, I fear. That is an enormous country which bred them. Also, would you gladly become what they are?"

"Then go against them yourselves," I urged. "Ride to their camps in the dark, strike them with the lightning that the stories say you can wield, drive them back from us."

"Nor can we do that," he said, gentle and merciless. "They have their own right to life. Drought holds the plains, and will not let go for generations to come."

My anguish lashed at him: "How can you know this?"

His straightness sagged a little. "We do know. We always did. Your heavy sun and your huge moon pull so hard upon this world of yours that its spinning changes swiftly . . . as the stars reckon lifetimes."

Thus he said. The words echo in me like words from a Hallows' Eve dream, never to be understood, never to be forgotten. In my later years, I have thought that maybe he meant the skewing of the heavenly pathways.

I crouched down in that dim room full of gleaming things, tail raised as if for battle, and screamed, "But have *we* no right to live?"

He turned and went from me. His garb billowed with his haste. Did he flee? I sought the room that was mine, lay there with eyes shut, and tried to call Hroai and our children to my spirit. They could not come. I had wandered too far, into a land too other.

The sun trudged west.

Sten entered my refuge, which had become my cage. The times we talked had given him a better command of earthly language. His voice wavered. "We may have discovered what we can do for you," he said.

You may think this is the end of my story. The rest you have heard, since first you could listen, until it is woven into flesh and bone. I say to you, it was not the end. Through the rest of my life grew a slow understanding, for whose fullness I strove last night when I stood on the clifftop and the ghost boat sailed by. Today I would give you what understanding I do have, if I am able, for you may have need of it after I have gone home to my Hroai in our dolmen.

You know how I went in another ghost boat, on the tide that followed the sunken sun, with two of the Night Folk. Nadia and Sten, they were. The wind filled the sails and we bounded over long, murmurous waves, across which the moonlight flowed in rivers. Smells of salt and the deeps filled my tendrils. Great creatures broached and wings skimmed low, but we fared unharmed across the waste, and at dawn we raised the easternmost of these islands.

I went about it during the day, while Sten and Nadia sheltered in a tent on the strand. "It is good country," I told them. "The soil is rich and the springs are fresh."

"We are glad," Nadia answered. "We knew simply that it was here."

"But it is lonely," I said.

"That is well," Sten replied. "None will dispute your settlement. None will pursue you."

He spoke truth. I could not bring myself to say it was barely half a truth. Where were the tombs? How could we remain one with our ancestors if we forsook Motherland?

At darkfall we three set homeward. winds were ill-humored and morning found us still at sea. The Night Folk stretched the larger sail across the hull and huddled. For me that might have been an empty day, rocking on an endless gleam of waters. Instead it became a time of magic; for we talked freely together, we three. I came to learn a litte, little about the Night Folk. Sten said they knew how to make a thing that would drive a boat without sails or paddles, but had never found time to build it, they being few in a foreign world—

Well, this is not what I mean by understanding. It is merely words. Water and words may pass between the worlds without carrying death; water, however, quenches, while words raise a thirst that can never be slaked.

We landed early in the dark and found that the Night Folk in their stronghold had the canoe ready. Often have I had to make clear why this was what they made for me, instead of a boat like their own. I will tell you again. To make a ghost boat and to handle it are craft, wizardry, beyond us people. We might have learned how, but it would have taken more time than we had. For us the Night Folk devised the simple dugout with paddles and square mat sail that you know. In the next few days in the house and darks in the open, they taught me will how to make more and how to bring them over the sea to the islands.

And then they sent me back. I returned with my hands empty but my spirit full. I prophesied and I taught—the help of Watermother Riao and the strength of Hroai upbore me—and those months were bitter, for who would willingly leave Motherland? We did at last, we Wold People, thorp by thorp, with our homes aflame behind us; and here we are, and *this* is your home and you are happy in it.

But our ancestors are all alone.

That, and a memory of dawn stealing over the downs, are the price that we, your mothers and fathers, must pay. Will you and your children and your children's children repay us, care for our tombs and call on our dream? Or will there be only the Night Folk whispering to us?

And I, I gave more. Half my soul it was, as the old songs warned. I have been in the house of wonder; it will always haunt me. None else will ever know what I have known, and so I too am forever lonely. Yet I remember the look upon Hroai when I brought hope to her.

And also the Night Folk have paid. I have not understood what it was they must give up to the Unseen because of what they did. But as we said farewell, Nadia caught me in her arms. "When we were beginning to know you!" she cried softly, and laid her mouth upon mine. Water welled from her eyes. It tasted salt.

The God and His Man

by Gene Wolfe

Once long, long ago, when the Universe was old, the mighty and powerful god Isid Iooo IoooE, whose name is given by certain others in other ways, and who is determined in every place and time to do what is good, came to the world of Zed. As every man knows, such gods travel in craft that can never be wrecked—and indeed, how could they be wrecked, when the gods are ever awake and hold the tiller? He came, I say, to the world of Zed, but he landed not and made no port, for it is not fit (as those who made the gods long ago ruled) that a god should set his foot upon any world, however blue, however fair.

Therefore Isid Iooo IoooE remained above the heavens, and his craft, though it travelled faster than the wind, contrived to do so in such a way that it stood suspended—as the many-hued stars themselves do not—above that isle of Zed that is called by the men of Zed (for they are men, or nearly) Land. Then the god looked down upon Zed, and seeing that the men of Zed were men and the women thereof women, he summoned to him a certain man of Urth. The summons of Isid Iooo IoooE cannot be disobeyed.

"Man," said the god, "go down to the world of Zed. For behold, the men of Zed are even as you are, and their women are women."

Then he let Man see through his own eyes, and Man saw the men of Zed, how they herded their cattle and drove their plows and beat the little drums of Zed. And he saw the women of Zed, and how many were fair to look upon, and how they lived in sorrow and idleness, or else in toil and weariness, even like the women of Urth.

He said to the god, "If I am ever to see my own home, and my own women, and my children again, I must do as you say. But if I go as I am, I shall not see any of those things ever again. For the men of Zed are men—you yourself have said it—and therefore crueler than any beast."

"It is that cruelty we must end," said the god. "And in order that you may assist me with your reports, I have certain gifts for you." Then he gave Man the enchanted cloak Tarnung by which none should see him when he did not wish to be seen, and he gave Man the enchanted sword Maser, whose blade is as long as the wielder wishes it (though it weighs nothing) and against which not even stone can stand.

No sooner had Man tied Tarnung about his shoulders and picked up Maser than the god vanished from his sight, and he found he rested in a grove of trees with scarlet flowers.

The time of the gods is not as the time of men and women. Who can say how long Man wandered across Land on Zed? He wandered in the high, hot lands where men have few laws and many slaves.

There he fought many fights until he knew all the manner of fighting of the people of the high, hot lands and grew shamed of killing those men with Maser, and took for himself the crooked sword of those lands, putting Maser by. Then he drew to him a hundred wild men, bandits, and slaves who had slain their masters and fled, and murders of many kinds. And he armed them after the manner of the high, hot lands, and mounted them on the yellow camels of those lands, that of times crush men with their necks, and led them in many wars. His face was like the faces of other men, and his sword like their swords; he stood no taller than they, and his shoulders were no broader; yet because he was very cunning and sometimes vanished from the camp, his followers venerated him.

At last he grew rich, and built a citadel in the fastness of the mountains. It stood upon a cliff and was rimmed with mighty walls. A thousand spears and a thousand spells guarded it. Within were white domes and white towers, a hundred fountains, and gardens that leaped up the mountain in roses and ran down it like children in the laughter of many of many waters. There Man sat at his ease and exchanged tales with his captains of their many wars. There he listened to the feet of his dancers, which were as the pattering of rain, and meditated on their round limbs and smiling faces. And at last he grew tired of these things, and wrapping himself in Tarnung vanished, and was seen in that citadel no more.

Then he wandered in the steaming lands, where the trees grew taller than his towers, and the men are shy and kill from the shadows with little poisoned arrows no longer than their forearms. There for a long while he wore the cloak Tarnung always, for no sword avails against such an arrow in the neck. The weight of the sword he had fetched from the high, hot lands oppressed him there, and the breath of the steaming lands rusted its blade; and so he cast it, one day, into a slow river where the black crocodiles swam and the riverhorses with amber eyes floated like logs or bellowed like thunder. But the magical sword Maser he kept.

And in the steaming lands he learned the ways of the great trees, of which each is an island, with its own dwellers thereon; and he learned the ways of the beasts of Zed, whose cleverness is so much less than the cleverness of men, and whose wisdom is so much more. There he tamed a panther with eyes like three emeralds, so that it followed him like a dog and killed for him like a hawk; and when he came upon a village of the men of the steaming lands, he leaped from a high branch onto the head of their idol and smote the hut of their chief with the sword Maser and vanished from their sight. And when he returned after a year to that village, he saw that the old idol was destroyed, and a new idol set up, with lightning in its hand and a panther at its feet.

Then he entered that village and blessed all the people and made the lap of that idol his throne. He rode an elephant with a blood-red tusk and two trunks; his war canoes walked up and down the river on a hundred legs; the heads of his drums were beaten with the white bones of chiefs; his wives were kept from the sun so their pale beauty would lure him to his hut by night and their fresh skins give him rest even in the steaming lands, and they were gorged with oil and meal until he lay upon them as upon pillows of silk. And so he would have remained had not the god Isid Iooo IoooE come to him in a dream of the night and commanded him to bestir himself, wandering and observing in the cold lands.

There he walked down a thousand muddy roads and kissed cool lips in a hundred rainy gardens. The people of the cold lands keep no slaves and have many laws, and their justice is the wonder of strangers; and so he found the bread of the cold lands hard and scant, and for a long time he cleaned boots for it, and for a long time dug ditches to drain their fields.

And each day the ship of Isid Iooo IoooE circled Zed, and when it had made several hundred such circles, Zed circled its lonely sun, and circled again, and yet again, so that Man's beard grew white, and the cunning that had won battles in the high, hot lands and burned the idol in the steaming lands was replaced with something better and less useful.

One day he plunged the blade of his shovel into the earth and turned his back to it. In a spinney he drew out Maser which he had not drawn for so long that he feared its magic was no more than a dream he had had when young) and cut a sapling. With that for a staff he took to the roads again, and when its leaves withered—which they did but slowly in that wet, cold country—he cut another and another, so that he taught always beneath a green tree.

In the marketplace he told of honor, and how it is a higher law than any law.

At the crossroads he talked of freedom, the freedom of the wind and clouds, the freedom that loves all things and is without guilt.

Beside city gates he told stories of the forgotten cities that were and of the forgotten cities that might be, if only men would forget them.

Often the people of the cold lands sought to imprison him according to their laws, but he vanished from their sight. Often they mocked him, but he smiled at their mockery, which knew no law. Many among the youth of the cold lands heard him, and many feigned to follow his teachings, and a few did follow them and lived strange lives.

Then a night came when the first flakes of snow were falling; and on that night the god Isid Iooo IoooE drew him up as the puppeteer lifts his doll. A few friends were in the lea of a wood with him, and it seemed to them that there came a sudden flurry of snow spangled with colors, and Man was gone.

But it seemed to him, as he stood once more in the presence of the god Isid Iooo IoooE, that he had waked from a long dream; his hands had their strength again, his beard was black, and his eyes had regained their clarity, though not their cunning.

"Now tell me," Isid Iooo IoooE commanded him, "all that you have seen and done," and when Man had told him, he asked. "Which of these three peoples loved you the best, and why did you love them?"

Man thought for a time, drawing the cloak Tarnung about his shoulders, for it seemed to him cold in the belly of the ship of Isid Iooo IoooE. "The people of the high, hot lands are unjust," he said. "Yet I came to love them, for there is no falsity in them. They feast their friends and flay their foes, and trusting no one, never weep that they are betrayed.

"The people of the cold lands are just, and yet I came to love them also, though that was much harder.

"The people of the steaming lands are innocent of justice and injustice alike. They follow their hearts, and while I dwelt among them I followed mine and loved them best of all."

"You yet have much to learn, Man," said the god Isid Iooo IoooE. "For the people of the cold lands are much the nearest to me. Do you not understand that in time the steaming lands, and all of the Land of Zed, must fall to one of its great peoples or the other?"

Then while Man watched through his eyes, certain good men in the cold lands died, which men called lightning. Certain evil men died also, and men spoke of disease. Dreams came to women and fancies to children; rain and wind and sun were no longer what they had been; and when the children were grown, the people of the cold lands went down into the steaming lands and built houses there, and taking no slaves drove the people of the steaming lands behind certain fences and walls, where they sat in the dust until they died.

"In the high, hot lands," commented Man, "the people of the steaming lands would have suffered much. Many of them I had, toiling under the whip to build my walls. Yet they sang when they could, and ran when they could, and stole my food when they could not. And some of them grew fat on it."

And the god Isid Iooo IoooE answered, "It is better that a man should die than that he should be a slave."

"Even so," Man replied, "you yourself have said it." And drawing Maser he smote the god, and Isid Iooo IoooE perished in smoke and blue fire.

Whether Man perished also, who can say? It is long since Man was seen in the Land of Zed, but then he was ever wont to vanish when the mood took him. Of the lost citadel in the mountains, overgrown with roses, who shall say who guards it? Of the little poisoned arrows, slaying in the twilight, who shall say who sends them? Of the rain-washed roads, wandering among forgotten towns, who shall say whose tracks are there?

But it may be that all these things now are passed, for they are things of long ago, when the Universe was old and there were more gods.

The Real Thing

by Larry Niven

If the IRS could see me now! Flying a light-sail craft, singlehanded, two million miles out from a bluish-white dwarf star. Fiddling frantically with the shrouds, guided less by the instruments than by the thrust against my web hammock and the ripples in the tremendous, near-weightless mirror sail. Glancing into the sun without blinking, then at the stars without being nightblind; dipping near the sun without being fried; all due to the quick-adjusting goggles and temp-controlled skin-tight pressure suit the chirpsithra had given me.

This entire trip was deductible, of course. The Draco Tavern had made me a good deal of money over the years, but I never could have paid for an interstellar voyage otherwise. As the owner of the Draco Tavern, Earth's only multi-species bar, I was quite legitimately touring the stars to find new products for my alien customers.

Would Internal Revenue object to my enjoying myself?

I couldn't make myself care. The trip out on the chirpsithra liner: that alone was something I'd remember the rest of my life. This too, if I lived. Best not to distract myself with memories.

Hroyd System was clustered tightly around its small, hot sun. Space was thick with asteroids and planets and other sailing ships. Every so often some massive piece of space junk bombed the sun, or a storm would bubble up from beneath the photosphere, and my boat would surge under the pressure of the flare. I had to fiddle constantly with the shrouds.

The pointer was aimed at black space. Where *was* that damned spaceport? Huge and massive it had seemed, too big to lose, when I spun out my frail silver sail and launched . . . how long ago? The clock told: twenty hours. It didn't feel that long.

The spaceport was coin-shaped, spun for varying gravities. Maybe I was trying to see it edge-on? I tilted the sail to lose some velocity. The fat sun expanded. My mind felt the heat. If my suit failed, it would fail all at once, and I wouldn't have long to curse my recklessness. Or—even chirpsithra-supplied equipment wouldn't help me if I fell into the sun.

I looked outward in time to see a silver coin pass over me. Good enough. Tilt the sail forward, pick up some speed . . . pull my orbit outward, slow down, *don't move the sail too fast or it'll fold up!* Wait a bit, then tilt the sail to spill the light; drop a bit, wait again. . . watch a black coin slide across the sun. tilt to slow, tilt again to catch up. It was another two hours before I could pull into the spaceport's shadow, fold the sail, and let a tractor beam pull me in.

My legs were shaky as I descended the escalator to Level 6.

There was Earth gravity on 6, minus a few kilos, and also a multi-species restaurant bar. I was too tired to wonder about the domed boxes I saw on some of the tables. I wobbled over to a table, turned on the privacy bubble, and tapped *tee tee hatch nex ool*, carefully. That code was my life. A wrong character could broil me, freeze me, flatten me, or have me drinking liquid methane or breathing prussic acid.

An Earthlike environment formed around me. I peeled off my equipment and sank into a web, sighing with relief. I still ached everywhere. What I really needed was sleep. But it had been glorious!

A warbling whistle caused me to look up. My translator said, "Sir or madam, what can I bring you?"

The bartender was a small, spindly Hroydan, and his environment suit glowed at dull red heat. I said, "Something alcoholic."

"Alcohol? What is your physiological type?"

"Tee tee hatch nex ool."

"Ah. May I recommend something? A liqueur, Opal Fire."

Considering the probable distance to the nearest gin-and-tonic
. . . "Fine. What proof is it?" I heard his translator skip a word, and
amplified: "What percent ethyl alcohol?"

"Thirty-four, with no other metabolic poisons."

About seventy proof. "Over water ice, please."

He brought a clear glass bottle. The fluid within did indeed glitter
like an opal. Its beauty was the first thing I noticed. Then the taste,
slightly tart, with an overtone that can't be described in any human
language. A crackling aftertaste, and a fire spreading through my
nervous system. I said, "That's *wonderful!* What about side effects?"

"There are additives to compensate: thiamine and the like. You
will feel no ugly aftereffects," the Hroydan assured me.

"They'd love it on Earth. Mmm . . . what's it cost?"

"Quite cheap. Twenty-nine chirp notes per flagon. Transport
costs would be up to the chirpsithra. But I'm sure Chignthil Interstellar would sell specs for manufacture."

"This could pay for my whole trip." I jotted the names: chirp
characters for *Opal Fire* and *Chignthil Interstellar*. The stuff was
still dancing through my nervous system. I drank again, so it could
dance on my taste buds too.

To hell with sleep; I was ready for another new experience.
"These boxes—I see them on all the tables. What are they?"

"Full-sensory entertainment devices. Cost is six chirp notes for
use." He tapped keys, and a list appeared: titles, I assumed, in alien
script. "If you can't read this, there is voice translation."

I dithered. Tempting, dangerous. But a couple of these might be
worth taking back. Some of my customers can't use anything I stock;
they pay only cover charges. "How versatile is it? Your customers
seem to have a lot of different sense organs. Hey, would this thing
actually give me alien senses?"

The bartender signalled negative. "The device acts on your
central nervous system; I assume you have one? There at the top?
Ah, good. It feeds you a story skeleton, but your own imagination

puts you in context and fills in the background details. You live a programmed story but largely in terms familiar to you. Mental damage is almost unheard of."

"Will I know it's only an entertainment?"

"You might know from the advertisements. Shall I show you?" The Hroydan raised the metal dome on a many-jointed arm and posed it over my head. I felt the heat emanating from him. "Perhaps you would like to walk through an active volcano?" He tapped two buttons with a black metal claw, and everything changed.

The Vollek merchant pulled the helmet away from my head. He had small, delicate-looking arms and a stance like a Tyranosaur: torso horizontal, swung from the hips. A feathery down covered him, signalling his origin as a flightless birds. "How did you like it?"

"Give me a minute." I looked about me. Afternoon sunlight spilled across the tables, illuminating alien shapes. The Draco Tavern was filling up. It was time I got back to tending bar. It had been nearly empty (I remembered) when I agreed to try this stunt.

I said, "That business at the end—?"

"We end all of the programs that way when we sell to Level Four civilizations. It prevents disorientation."

"Good idea." Whatever the reason, I didn't feel at all confused. Still, it was a hell of an experience. "I couldn't tell it from the real thing."

"The advertisement would have alerted an experienced user."

"You're actually manufacturing these things on Earth?"

"Guatemala has agreed to license us. The climate is so nice there. And so I can lower the price per unit to three thousand dollars each."

"Sell me two," I said. It'd be a few years before they paid for themselves. Maybe someday I really would have enough money to ride the chirpsithra liners . . . if I didn't get hooked myself on these full-sensory machines. "Now, about Opal Fire. I can't believe it's really that good—"

"I travel for Chignthil Interstellar too. I have sample bottles."

"Let's try it."

Grimes and the Great Race

by A. Bertram Chandler

"I didn't think that I'd be seeing you again," said Grimes.

"Or I you," Kitty Kelly told him. "But Station Yorick's customers liked that first interview. The grizzled old spacedog, pipe in mouth, glass in hand, spinning a yarn. . . . So when my bosses learned that you're stuck here until your engineers manage to fit a new rubber band to your inertial drive they said, in these very words, 'Get your arse down to the spaceport, Kitty, and try to wheedle another tall tale out of the old bastard!' "

"Mphm," grunted Grimes, acutely conscious that his prominent ears had reddened angrily.

Kitty smiled sweetly. She was an attractive girl, black Irish, wide-mouthed, creamy-skinned, with vivid blue eyes. Grimes would have thought her much more attractive had she not been making it obvious that she still nursed the resentment engendered by his first story, a tale of odd happenings at long-ago and far-away Glenrowan where, thanks to Grimes, an ancestral Kelly had met his downfall.

She said tartly, "And lay off the Irish this time, will you?"

Grimes looked at her, at her translucent, emerald green blouse that concealed little, at the long, shapely legs under the skirt that concealed even less. He thought, *There's one of the Irish, right here, that I'd like to lay on.*

With deliberate awkwardness he asked, "If I'm supposed to avoid giving offense to anybody—and you Elsinoreans must carry the blood of about every race and nation on Old Earth—what can I talk about?"

She made a great show of cogitation, frowning, staring down at the tips of her glossy green shoes. Then she smiled. "Racing, of course! On this world we're great followers of the horses." She frowned again. "But no. Somehow I just can't see you as a sporting man, Commodore."

"As a matter of fact," said Grimes stiffly, "I did once take part in a race. And for high stakes."

"I just can't imagine *you* on a horse."

"Who said anything about horses?"

"What were you riding, then?"

"Do you want the story or don't you? If I'm going to tell it, I'll tell it my way."

She sighed, muttered, "All right, all right." She opened her case, brought out the trivi recorder, set it up on the deck of the day cabin. She aimed one lens at the chair in which Grimes was sitting, the other at the one that she would occupy. She squinted into the viewfinder. "Pipe in mouth," she ordered. "Glass in hand . . . Where is the glass, Commodore? And aren't you going to offer *me* a drink?

He gestured towards the liquor cabinet. "You fix it. I'll have a pink gin, on the rocks."

"Then I'll have the same. It'll be better than the sickly muck you poured down me last time I was aboard your ship!"

Grimes's ears flushed again. The "sickly muck" had failed to have the desired effect.

My first command in the Survey Service [he began] was of a Serpent Class Courier, *Adder.* The captains of these little ships were lieutenants, their officers lieutenants and ensigns. There were no petty officers or ratings to worry about, no stewards or stewardesses to look after us. We made our own beds, cooked our own meals. We used to take turns playing with the rather primitive autochef. We didn't starve; in fact we lived quite well.

There was some passenger accommodation; the couriers were—and probably still are—sometimes used to get VIPs from Point A to Point B in a hurry. And they carried Service mail and despatches hither and yon. If there was any odd job to do we did it.

This particular job was a very odd one. You've heard of Darban? No? Well, it's an Earth-type planet in the Tauran Sector. Quite a pleasant world although the atmosphere's a bit too dense for some tastes. but if it were what we call Earth-normal I mightn't be sitting here talking to you now. Darvan's within the Terran sphere of influence with a Carlotti Beacon Station, a Survey Service Base, and all the rest of it. At the time of which I'm talking, though, it wasn't in anybody's sphere of influence, although Terran star tramps and Hallichek and Shaara ships had been calling there for quite some time. There was quite a demand for the so-called living opals—although how any woman could bear to have a slimy, squirming necklace of luminous worms strung about her neck beats me!

She interrupted him. "These Hallicheki and Shaara . . . non-human races, aren't they?

"Non-human and non-humanoid. The Hallicheki are avians, with a matriarchal society. The Shaara are winged arthropods, not un-like the Terran bees, although very much larger and with a some-what different internal structure."

"There'll be pictures of them in our library. We'll show them to our viewers. But go on, please."

The merchant captains [he continued] had been an unusually law-abiding crowd. They'd bartered for the living opals but had been careful not to give an exchange any artifacts that would unduly accelerate local industrial evolution. No advanced technology—if the Darbanese wanted spaceships they'd have to work out for themselves how to build them—and, above all, no sophisticated weaponry. Mind you, some of those skippers would have been quite capable of flogging a few hand lasers or the like to the natives but the Grand Governor of Barkara—the nation that, by its relatively early development of airships and firearms, had established *de facto* if not *de jure* sovereignty over the entire planet—made sure that nothing was imported that could be a threat to his rule. A situation rather analogous, perhaps, to that on Earth centuries ago when the Japanese Shoguns and their samurai took a dim view of the muskets and cannon that, in the wrong hands, would have meant their downfall.

Then the old Grand Governor died. His successor intimated that he would be willing to allow Darban to be drawn into the Federation of Worlds and to reap the benefits accruing therefrom. But whose Federation? Our Interstaller Federation? The Hallichek Hegemony? The Shaara Galactic Hive?

Our Intelligence people, just for once, started to earn their keep. According to them the Shaara had despatched a major warship to Darban, the captain of which had been given full authority to dicker with the Grand Governor. The Hallicheki had done likewise. And— not for the first time!—our lords and masters had been caught with their pants down. It was at the time of the Waverley Confrontation; and Lindisfarne Base, as a result, was right out of major warships. Even more fantastically the only spaceship available was my little *Adder*—and she was in the throes of a refit. Oh, there were ships at Scapa and Mikasa Bases but both of these were one helluva long way from Darban.

I was called before the Admiral and told that I must get off Lindisfarne as soon as possible, if not before, to make all possible speed for Darban, there to establish and maintain a Terran presence until such time as a senior officer could take over from me. I was to report on the actions of the Shaara and the Hallicheki. I was to avoid direct confrontation with either. And I was not, repeat not, to take any action at any time without direct authorisation from Base. I was told that a civilian linguistic expert would be travelling in *Adder*—a Miss Mary Marsden—and that she would be assisting me as required.

What rankled was the way in which the Admiral implied that he was being obliged to send a boy on a man's errand. And I wasn't at all happy about having Mary Marsden along. She was an attractive enough girl—what little one could see of her!—but she was a super wowser. She was a member of one of the more puritanical religious sects flourishing on Francisco—and Francisco, as you know, is a hotbed of freak religions. Mary took hers seriously. She had insisted on retaining her civilian status because she did not approve of the short-skirted uniforms in which the Survey Service clad its female personnel. She always wore long-skirted, long-sleeved, high-necked dresses and a bonnet over her auburn hair. She didn't smoke—not even tobacco—or drink anything stronger than milk.

And yet, as far as we could see, she was a very pretty girl. Eyes that were more green than any other colour. A pale—but not unhealthily so—skin. A straight nose that, a millimeter longer, would have been too big. A wide, full mouth that didn't need any artificial colouring. A firm, rather square chin. Good teeth—which she needed when it was the turn of Beadle, my first lieutenant, to do the cooking. Beadle had a passion for pies and his crusts always turned out like concrete. . . .

Well, we lifted off from Lindisfarne Base. We set trajectory for Darban. And before we were half-way there we suffered a complete communications black-out. Insofar as the Carlotti deep space radio was concerned I couldn't really blame Slovotny, my Sparks. The Base technicians, in their haste to get us off the premises, had botched the overhaul of the transceiver and, to make matters worse, hadn't replaced the spares they has used. When two circuit trays blew, that was that.

Spooky Deane, my psionic communications officer, I could and did blame for the shortcomings of *his* department. As you probably know, it's just not possible for even the most highly trained and talented telepath to transmit his thoughts across light years without an amplifier. The amplifier most commonly used is the brain of that highly telepathic animal, the Terran dog, removed from the skull of its hapless owner and kept alive in a tank of nutrient solution with all the necessary life-support systems. PCOs are lonely people; they're inclined to regard themselves as the only true humans in shiploads of sub-men. They make pets of their horrid amplifiers, to which they can talk telepathically. And—as lonely men do—they drink.

What happened aboard *Adder* was an all-too-frequent occurrence. The PCO would be going on a solitary bender and would get to the stage of wanting to share his bottle with his pet. When neat gin—or whatever—is poured into nutrient solution the results are invariably fatal to whatever it is that's being nourished.

So—no psionic amplifier. No Carlotti deep space radio. No contact with Base.

"And aren't you going to share your bottle with your pet, Commodore?"

"I didn't think that you were a pet of mine, Miss Kelly, or I of yours. But it's time we had a pause for refreshment."

We stood on for Darban [he continued]. Frankly, I was pleased rather than otherwise at being entirely on my own, knowing that now I would have to use my own initiative, that I would not have the Lord Commissioners of the Admiralty peering over my shoulder all the time, expecting me to ask their permission before I so much as blew my nose. Beadle, my first lieutenant, did try to persuade me to return to Lindisfarne—he was a very capable officer but far too inclined to regard Survey Service Regulations as Holy Writ. (I did find later that, given the right inducement, he was capable of bending those same regulations.) Nonetheless, he was, in many ways, rather a pain in the arse.

But Beadle was in the minority. The other young gentlemen were behind me, all in favour of carrying on. Mary Marsden, flaunting her civilian status, remained neutral.

We passed the time swotting up on Darban, watching and listening to the tapes that had been put on board prior to our departure from Lindisfarne. We gained the impression of a very pleasant, almost Earth type planet with flora and fauna not too outrageously different from what the likes of us are used to. Parallel evolution and all that. A humanoid—but not human—dominant race, furry bipeds that would have passed for cat-faced apes in a bad light. Civilized, with a level of technology roughly that of Earth during the late nineteenth century, old reckoning. Steam engines. Railways. Electricity, and the electric telegraph. Airships. Firearms. One nation—that with command of the air and a monopoly of telegraphic communications—*de facto* if not entirely *de jure* ruler of the entire planet.

The spaceport, such as it was, consisted of clearings in a big forest some kilometers south of Barkara, the capital city of Bandooran. Bandooran, of course, was the most highly developed nation, the one that imposed its will on all of Darban. Landing elsewhere was . . . discouraged. The Dog Star Line at one time tried to steal a march on the competition by instructing one of their captains to land near a city called Droobar, there to set up the Dog Star Line's own trading station. The news must have been telegraphed to Barkara almost immediately. A couple of dirigibles drifted over, laying H.E. and incendiary eggs on the city. The surviving city fathers begged the Dog Star line captain to take himself and his ship elsewhere. Also, according to our tapes, the Dog Star Line was heavily fined shortly thereafter by the High Council of the Interstellar Federation.

But the spaceport . . . just clearings, as I have said, in the forest. Local airships were used to pick up incoming cargo and to deliver the tanks of "living opals" to the spaceships. No Aerospace Control, of course, although there would be once a base and a Carlotti Beacon Station had been established. Incoming traffic just came in, unannounced. Unannounced officially, that is. As you know, the inertial drive is far from being the quietest machine ever devised by Man; everybody in Barkara and for kilometers around would know when a spaceship was dropping down.

And we dropped in, one fine, sunny morning. After one preliminary orbit we'd been able to identify Barkara without any difficulty. The forest was there, just where our charts said it should be. There were those odd, circular holes in the mass of greenery—the clearings. In two of them there was the glint of metal. As we lost altitude we were able to identify the Shaara vessel—it's odd (or is it?) how their ships always look like giant beehives—and a typical, Hallicheki oversized silver egg sitting in a sort of latticework eggcup.

We came in early; none of the Shaara or Hallicheki were yet out and about although the noise of our drive must have alerted them. I set *Adder* down as far as possible from the other two ships. From my control room I could just see the blunt bows of them above the treetops.

We went down to the wardroom for breakfast, leaving Slovotny to enjoy his meal in solitary state in the control room; he would let us know if anybody approached while we were eating. He buzzed down just as I'd reached the toast and marmalade stage. I went right up. But the local authorities hadn't yet condescended to take notice of us; the airship that came nosing over was a Shaara blimp, not a Darbanese rigid job. And then there was a flight of three Hallicheki, disdaining mechanical aids and using their own wings. One of the horrid things evacuated her bowels when she was almost overhead, making careful allowance for what little wind there was. It made a filthy splash all down one of my viewports.

At last the Darbanese came. Their ship was of the Zepplin type, the fabric of the envelope stretched taut over a framework of wood or metal. It hovered over the clearing, its engines turning over just sufficiently to offset the effect of the breeze. That airship captain, I thought, knew his job. A cage detached itself from the gondola, was lowered rapidly to the ground. A figure jumped out of it just before it touched and the airship went up like a rocket after the loss of weight. I wondered what would happen if that cage fouled anything before it was rehoisted, but I needn't have worried. As I've said, the airship captain was an expert.

We went down to the after airlock. We passed through it, making the transition from our own atmosphere into something that, at first, felt like warm soup. But it was quite breathable. Mary Marsden, as the linguist of the party, accompanied me down the ramp. I wondered how she could bear to go around muffled up to the eyebrows on such a beautiful morning as this; I was finding even shorts and shirt uniform too heavy for a warm day.

The native looked at us. We looked at him. He was dressed in a dull green smock that came down to mid-thigh and that left his arms bare. A fine collection of glittering brass badges was pinned to the breast and shoulders of his garment. He saluted, raising his three-fingered hands to shoulder level, palms out. His wide mouth opened in what I hoped was a smile, displaying pointed, yellow teeth that were in sharp contrast to the black fur covering his face.

He asked, in quite passable Standard English, "You the captain are?"

I said that I was.

He said, "Greetings I bring from the High Governor." Then, making a statement rather than asking a question, "You do not come in trade."

So we—or a Federation warship of some kind—had been expected. And *Adder*, little as she was, did not look like a merchantman—too many guns for too small a tonnage.

He went on, "So you are envoy. Same as—" He waved a hand in the general direction of where the other ships were berthed. "—the Shaara, the Hallicheki. Then you will please to attend the meeting that this morning has been arranged." He pulled a big, fat watch on a chain from one of his pockets. "In—in forty-five of your minutes from now."

While the exchange was taking place Mary was glowering a little. She was the linguistic expert and it was beginning to look as though her services would not be required. She listened quietly while arrangements were being made. We would proceed to the city in my boat, with the Governor's messenger acting as pilot—pilot in the marine sense of the word, that is, just giving me the benefit of his local knowledge.

We all went back on board *Adder*. The messenger assured me that there was no need for me to have internal pressure adjusted to his requirements; he had often been aboard outworld spaceships and, too, he was an airshipman.

I decided that there was no time for me to change into dress uniform so I compromised by pinning my miniatures—two good attendance medals and the Distinguished Conduct Star that I'd got after the Battle of Dartura—to the left breast of my shirt, buckling on my sword belt with the wedding cake cutter in its gold-braided sheath. While I was tarting myself up, Mary entertained the messenger to coffee and biscuits in the wardroom (his English, she admitted to me later, was better than her Darbanese) and Beadle, with Dalgleish, the engineer, got the boat out of its bay and down to the ground by the ramp.

Mary was coming with me to the city and so was Spookey Deane—a trained telepath is often more useful than a linguist. We got into the boat. It was obvious that our new friend was used to this means of transportation, must often have ridden in the auxiliary craft of visiting merchant vessels. He sat beside me to give directions. Mary and Spooky were in the back.

As we flew towards the city—red brick, grey-roofed houses on the outskirts, tall, cylindrical towers, also of red brick, in the centre—we saw the Shaara and the Hallicheki ahead of us, flying in from their ships. a Queen-Captain, I thought, using my binoculars, with a princess and an escort of drones. a Hallichek Nest Leader accompanied by two old hens as scrawny and ugly as herself. The Shaara weren't using their blimp and the Hallicheki consider it beneath their dignity to employ mechanical means of flight inside an atmosphere. Which made *us* the wingless wonders.

I reduced speed a little to allow the opposition to make their landings on the flat roof of one of the tallest towers first. After all, they were both very senior to me, holding ranks equivalent to at least that of a four-ring captain in the Survey Service, and I was a mere lieutenant, my command notwithstanding. I came in slowly over the streets of the city. There were people abroad—pedestrians mainly, although there were vehicles drawn by scaly, huge-footed draught animals and the occasional steam car—and they raised their black-furred faces to stare at us. One or two of them waved.

When we got to the roof of the tower the Shaara and the Hallicheki had gone down by there were a half-dozen blue-smocked guards to receive us. They saluted as we disembarked. One of them

led the way to a sort of penthouse which, as a matter of fact, merely
provided cover for the stairhead. The stairs themselves were . . .
wrong. They'd been designed, of course, to suit the length and
jointure of the average Darbanese leg, which wasn't anything like
ours. Luckily the Council Chamber was only two flights down.

It was a big room, oblong save for the curvature of the two end
walls, in which were high windows. There was a huge, long table, at
one end of which was a sort of ornate throne in which sat the High
Governor. He was of far slighter stature than the majority of his
compatriots but made up for it by the richness of his attire. His
smock was of a crimson, velvetlike material and festooned with gold
chains of office.

He remained seated but inclined his head in our direction. He
said—I learned afterwards that these were the only words of
English that he knew; he must have picked them up from some
visiting space captain—"Come in. This is Liberty Hall; you can spit
on the mat and call the cat a bastard!"

*I was wondering," said Kitty Kelly coldly, "just when you were going
to get around to saying that."*

*"He said it, not me. But I have to use that greeting once in every
story. It's one of my conditions of employment."*

And where was I [he went on] before I was interrupted? Oh, yes. The
Council chamber, with the High Governor all dressed up like a
Christmas tree. Various ministers and other notables, not as richly
attired as their boss. All male, I found out later, with the exception of
the Governor's lady, who was sitting on her husband's right. There
were secondary sexual characteristics, of course, but so light as to be
unrecognisable by an outworlder. To me she—and I didn't know that
she was "she"—was just another Darbanese.

But the fair sex was well represented. There was the Queen-
Captain, her iridescent wings folded on her back, the velvety brown
fur of her thorax almost concealed by the sparkling jewels that were

her badges of high rank. There was the Shaara princess, less decorated but more elegant than her mistress. There was the Nest
Leader; she was nowhere nearly as splendid as the Queen-Captain.
She wasn't splendid at all. Her plumage was dun and dusty, the
talons of the "hands" at the elbow joints of her wings unpolished.
She wore no glittering insignia, only a wide band of cheap-looking
yellow plastic about her scrawny neck. Yet she had her dignity, and
her cruel beak was that of a bird of prey rather than that of the
barnyard fowl she otherwise resembled. She was attended by two
he officers, equally drab.

And, of course, there was Mary, almost as drab as the Hallicheki.

The Governor launched into his spiel, speaking through an interpreter. I was pleased to discover that Standard English was to be the
language used. It made sense, of course. English is the common
language of Space just as it used to be the common language of the
sea, back on Earth. And as the majority of the merchant vessels
landing on Darban had been of Terran registry, the local merchants
and officials had learned English.

The Governor, through his mouthpiece, said that he welcomed
us all. He said that he was pleased that Imperial Earth had sent
her representative, albeit belatedly, to this meeting of culture.
Blah, blah, blah. He agreed with the representatives of the Great
Spacefaring Powers that it was desirable for some sort of permanent base to be established on Darban. But . . . but whichever
of us was given the privilege of taking up residence on his fair
planet would have to prove capability to conform, to mix. . . . (By
this time the interpreter was having trouble in getting the idea
across but he managed somehow.) The Darbanese, the Governor
told us, were a sporting people and in Barkara there was one sport
preferred to all others. This was racing. It would be in keeping with Darbanese tradition if the Treaty were made with whichever of us proved the most expert in a competition of this
nature. . . .

"*Racing?*" I whispered. In a foot race we'd probably be able to
beat the Shaara and the Hallicheki, but I didn't think that it was foot

racing that was implied. Horse racing or its local equivalent? That didn't seem right either.

"Balloon racing," muttered Spooky Deane, who had been flapping his psionic ears.

I just didn't see how balloon racing could be a spectator sport—but the tapes on Darban with which we had been supplied were far from comprehensive. As we soon found out.

"Balloon racing?" asked Kitty Kelly. "From the spectators' viewpoint it must have been like watching grass grow."

"This balloon racing certainly wasn't," Grimes told her.

The Darbanese racing balloons [he went on] were ingenious aircraft: dirigible, gravity-powered. Something very like them was, as a matter of fact, invented by a man called Adams back on Earth in the nineteenth century. Although it performed successfully, the Adams airship never got off the ground, commercially speaking. But it did work. The idea was that the thing would progress by soaring and swooping, soaring and swooping. The envelope containing the gas cells was a planing surface and the altitude of the contraption was controlled by the shifting of weights in the car—ballast, the bodies of the crew. Initially, positive buoyancy was obtained by the dumping of ballast and the thing would plane upwards. Then, when gas was valved, there would be negative buoyancy and a glide downwards. Sooner or later, of course, you'd be out of gas to valve or ballast to dump. That would be the end of the penny section.

I remembered about the Adams airship while the interpreter did him best to explain balloon racing to us. I though that it was a beautiful case of parallel mechanical evolution on two worlds many light years apart.

The Queen-Captain got the drift of it quite soon—after all, the Shaara *know* airships. Her agreement, even though it was made through her artificial voice box, sounded more enthusiastic than otherwise. The Nest Leader took her time making up her mind but finally squawked yes. I would have been out voted if I hadn't wanted to take part in the contest.

There was a party then, complete with drinks and sweet and savoury things to nibble. The Shaara made pigs of themselves on a sticky liqueur and candy. Spooky Deane got stuck into something rather like gin. I found a sort of beer that wasn't too bad—although it was served unchilled—with little, spicy sausages as blotting paper. Mary, although she seemed to enjoy the sweetmeats, would drink only water. Obviously our hosts thought that she was odd, almost as odd as the Hallicheki who, although drinking water, would eat nothing.

They're *nasty* people, those avians. They have no redeeming vices—and when it comes to *real* vices their main one is cruelty. *Their* idea of a banquet is a shrieking squabble over a table loaded with little mammals, alive but not kicking—They're hamstrung before the feast so that they can't fight or run away—which they tear to pieces with those beaks of theirs.

After quite a while the party broke up. The Nest Leader and her officers were the first to leave, anxious no doubt to fly back to their ship for a tasty dish of live worms. The Queen-Captain and her party were the next to go. They were in rather a bad way. They were still on the rooftop when Mary and I, supporting him between us, managed to get Spooky Deane up the stairs and to the boat. None of the locals offered to help us; it is considered bad manners on Darban to draw the attention of a guest to his insobriety.

We said our goodbyes to those officials, including the interpreter, who had come to see us off. We clambered into our boat and lifted. On our way back to *Adder* we saw the Shaara blimp coming to pick up the Queen-Captain. I wasn't surprised. If she'd tried to take off from the roof in the state that she was in she'd have made a nasty splash on the cobblestones under the tower.

And I wasn't at all sorry to get back to the ship to have a good snore. Spooky was fast asleep by the time that I landed by the after airlock and Mary was looking at both of us with great distaste.

* * *

"I'm *not a wowser*," *said Kitty Kelly.*
"*Help yourself, then. And freshen my glass while you're about it.*"

Bright and early the next morning [he went on, after a refreshing sip] two racing balloons and an instructor were delivered by a small rigid airship. Our trainer was a young native called Robiliyi. He spoke very good English; as a matter of fact he was a student at the University of Barkara and studying for a degree in Outworld Languages. He was also a famous amateur balloon jockey and had won several prizes. Under his supervision we assembled one of the balloons, inflating it from the cylinders of hydrogen that had been brought from the city. Imagine a huge air mattress with a flimsy, wickerwork car slung under it. That's what the thing looked like. The only control surface was a huge rudder at the after end of the car. There were two tillers—one forward and one aft.

Dalgleish inspected the aircraft, which was moored by lines secured to metal pegs driven into the ground. He said, "I'm not happy about all this valving of gas. You know how the Shaara control buoyancy in their blimps?"

I said that I did.

He said that it should be possible to modify one of the balloons— the one that we should use for the race itself—so as to obviate the necessity of valving gas for the downward glide. I prodded the envelope with a cautious finger and said that I didn't think that the fabric of the gas cells would stand the strain of being compressed in a net. He said that he didn't think so either. *So that was that, I thought. Too bad.* Then he went on to tell me that in the ship's stores was a bolt of plastic cloth that, a long time ago, had been part of an urgent shipment of supplies to the Survey Service base on Zephyria, a world notorious for its violent windstorms. (Whoever named that planet had a warped sense of humour!) The material was intended for making emergency repairs to the domes housing the base facilities. They were always being punctured by wind-borne boulders and the like. When *Adder* got to Zephyria it was found that somebody had experienced a long overdue rush of brains to the head and put everything underground. There had been the usual lack of liaison between departments and nobody had been told not to load the plastic.

Anyhow, Dalgleish thought that he'd be able to make gas cells from the stuff. He added that the Shaara would almost certainly be modifying their own racer, using the extremely tough silk from which the gas cells of their blimps were made.

I asked Robiliyi's opinion. He told me that it would be quite in order to use machinery as long as it was hand-powered.

Dalgleish went into a huddle with him. They decided that only the three central, sausage-like gas cells need be compressed to produce negative buoyancy; also that it would be advisable to re-place the wickerwork frame enclosing the "mattress" with one of light but rigid metal. Too, it would be necessary to put a sheet of the plastic over the assembly of gas cells so as to maintain a planing surface in all conditions.

Then it was time for my first lesson. Leaving Dalgleish and the others to putter around with the still unassembled balloon I fol-lowed Robiliyi into the flimsy car of the one that was ready for use. The wickerwork creaked under my weight. I sat down, very care-fully, amidships, and tried to keep out of the way. Robiliyi started scooping sand out of one of the ballast bags, dropping it overside. The bottom of the car lifted off the mossy ground but the balloon was still held down by the mooring lines, two forward and two aft. Robiliyi scampered, catlike, from one end of the car to the other, pulling the metal pegs clear of the soil with expert jerks. We lifted, rising vertically. I looked down at the faces of my shipmates. *Better him than us*, their expressions seemed to be saying.

Then we were at treetop height, then above the trees, still lifting. Robiliyi scrambled to the rear of the craft, calling me to follow. He grabbed the after tiller. The platform tilted and above us the raft of gas cells did likewise, presenting an inclined plane to the air. We were sliding through the atmosphere at a steep angle. I wasn't sure whether or not I was enjoying the experience. I'd always liked ballooning, back on Earth, but the gondolas of the hot air balloons in which I'd flown were far safer than this flimsy basket. There was nothing resembling an altimeter in the car; there were no instruments at all. I hoped that somewhere in the nested gas cells there was a relief valve that would function if we got too high. And how high was too high, anyhow? I noticed that the underskin of the balloon, which had been wrinkled when we lifted off, was now taut.

Robiliyi shouted shrilly, "Front end! Front end!" We scuttled forward. He pulled on a dangling lanyard; there was an audible hiss of escaping gas from above. He put the front-end tiller over and as we swooped downward we turned. The treetops, which had seemed far too distant, were now dangerously close. And there was the clearing from which we had lifted with *Adder* standing there, bright silver in the sunlight. but we weren't landing yet. We shifted weight aft, jettisoned ballast, soared. I was beginning to get the hang of it, starting to enjoy myself. Robiliyi let me take the tiller so that I could get the feel of the airship. She handled surprisingly well.

We did not return to earth until we had dumped all our ballast. I asked Robiliyi what we could do if, for some reason, we wanted to get upstairs again in a hurry after valving gas, He grinned, stripped off his tunic, made as though to throw it overboard. He grinned again, showing all his sharp, yellow teeth. "And if *that* is not enough," he said, "there is always your crew person. . . ."

We landed shortly after this. Robiliyi reinflated the depleted cells from one of the bottles while Beadle and Spooky collected ballast sand from the banks of a nearby brook.

Then it was Mary's turn to start her training.

"Mary? Was she your crew, your co-pilot, for the race?"

"Yes."

"But you've impressed me as being a male chauvinist pig."

"Have I ? Well, frankly, I'd sooner have had one of my officers. But Mary volunteered, and she was far better qualified than any of them. Apart from myself she was the only one in Adder with lighter-than-air experience. It seems that the sect of which she was a

member went in for ballooning quite a lot. It tied in somehow with their religion. Nearer my God to Thee, and all that."

Well [he went on], we trained, both in the balloon that Dalgleish had modified and in the one that was still as it had been when delivered to us. The modifications? On, quite simple. A coffee-mill hand winch, an arrangement of webbing that compressed the three central, longitudinal gas cells. The modified balloon we exercised secretly, flying it only over a circuit that was similar in many ways to the official, triangular race track. The unmodified balloon we flew over the actual course. The Shaara and the Hallicheki did likewise, in craft that did not appear to have had anything done to them. I strongly suspected that they were doing the same as we were, keeping their dark horses out of sight until the Big Day. The Shaara, I was certain, had done to theirs what we had done to ours—after all, it was a Shaara idea that we had borrowed. But the Hallicheki? We just couldn't guess.

And we trained, and we trained. At first it was Robiliyi with Mary or Robiliyi with myself. Then it was Mary and I. I'll say this for her—she made good balloon crew. And I kidded myself that she was becoming far less untouchable. In that narrow car we just couldn't help coming into physical contact quite frequently.

Then the time was upon us and we were as ready as ever we would be. On the eve of the Great Day the three contending balloons were taken to the airport. The Shaara towed theirs in behind one of their blimps; it was entirely concealed in a sort of gauzy cocoon. The Hallicheki towed theirs in, four hefty crew hens doing the work. There was no attempt at concealment. We towed ours in astern of our flier. It was completely swathed in a sheet of light plastic.

The racers were maneuvered into a big hangar to be inspected by the judges. I heard later, from Robiliyi, that the Nest Leader had insinuated that the Shaara and ourselves had installed miniature inertial drive units disguised as hand winches. (It was the sort of thing that *they* would have done if they'd thought that they could get away with it.)

We all returned to our ships. I don't know how the Shaara and the Hallicheki spent the night but we dined and turned in early. I took a stiff nightcap to help me to sleep. Mary had her usual warm milk.

The next morning we returned in the flier to the airport. It was already a warm day. I was wearing a shirt-and-shorts uniform but intended to discard cap, long socks, and shoes before clambering into the wickerwork car of the balloon. Mary was suitably— according to her odd lights—dressed but what she had on was very little more revealing than her usual high-necked, longsleeved, long-skirted dress; it did little more than establish the fact that she was, after all, a biped. It was a hooded, long-sleeved cover-all suit with its legs terminating in soft shoes. It was so padded that it was quite impossible to do more than guess at the shape of the body under it.

Young Robiliyi was waiting for us at the airport, standing guard over our green and gold racer. Close by was the Shaara entry, its envelope displaying orange polka dots on a blue ground. The Shaara crew stood by their balloon—the pilot, a bejewelled drone, and his crew, a husky worker. Then there were the Hallicheki—officers both, to judge from the yellow plastic bands about their scrawny necks. The envelope of their racer was a dull brown.

On a stand, some distance from the starting line, sat the Governor with his entourage. With him were the Queen-Captain and the Nest Leader with their senior officers. The judges were already aboard the small, rigid airship which, at its mooring mast, was ready to cast off as soon as the race started. It would fly over the course with us, its people alert for any infraction of the rules.

Two of the airport ground crew wheeled out a carriage on which was mounted a highly polished little brass cannon. The starting gun. I kicked off my shoes, peeled off my socks, left them, with my cap, in Robiliyi's charge. I climbed into the flimsy car, took my place at the after tiller. Mary followed me, stationed herself at the winch amidships. she released the brake. The gas cells rustled as they expanded; we were held down now only by the taut mooring lines fore and aft. I looked over at the others. The Shaara, too, were ready. The Hallicheki had just finished the initial dumping of sand ballast.

One of the gunners jerked a long lanyard. There was a bang and a great flash of orange flame, a cloud of dirty white smoke. I yanked the two after mooring lines, pulling free the iron pegs. Forward Mary did the same, a fraction of a second later. It wasn't a good start. The forward moorings should have been released first to get our leading edge starting to lift. Mary scrambled aft, redistributing weight, but the Shaara and the Hallicheki, planing upwards with slowly increasing speed, were already ahead.

Almost directly beneath us was Airport Road and in the middle distance was the railway to Brinn with the Brinn Highway running parallel to it. I can remember how the track was gleaming like silver in the morning sunlight. To the north, distant but already below the expanding horizon, was the Cardan Knoll, a remarkable dome-shaped hill with lesser domes grouped about it. We would have to pass to the west and north of this before steering a south-easterly course for the Porgidor Tower.

Shaara and Hallicheki were racing neck and neck, still climbing. I was still falling behind. I brought the dangling mooring lines inboard to reduce drag. I may have made a little difference, but not much. Ahead of us the Shaara balloon reached its ceiling, compressed gas and began the first downward glide. A second or so later the Hallicheki reduced buoyancy to follow suit. I looked up. The underskin of my gas cells was still slightly wrinkled; there was still climbing to do.

The last wrinkles vanished. I told Mary to compress. The pawls clicked loudly as she turned the winch handle. Then we scuttled to the front end of the car. I took hold of the forward tiller. We swooped down, gathering speed rapidly. The farm buildings and the grazing animals in the fields were less and less toylike as we lost altitude. I steered straight for an ungainly beast that looked like an armour-plated cow. It lifted its head to stare at us in stupid amazement.

I didn't want to hit the thing. I sort of half ran, half crawled aft as Mary released the winch brake. We lifted sweetly—no doubt to the great relief of the bewildered herbivore. I looked ahead. The opposition were well into their second upward beat, The Hallicheki soaring more steeply than the Shaara. But taking advantage of thermals is an art that every bird learns as soon as it is able to fly; there must be, I thought, a considerable updraught of warm air from the railroad and the black-surfaced Brinn Highway. But the higher the Hallicheki went the more gas they would have to valve, and if they were not careful they would lose all their reserve buoyancy before the circuit was completed.

The Shaara reached their ceiling and started their downward glide. The Hallicheki were still lifting, gaining altitude but losing ground. I couldn't understand why they were not gliding down their lift. And I was still lifting. Then I saw that, ahead, the Hallicheki had at last valved gas and were dropping. I pulled to starboard to avoid them. It meant putting on some distance but I daren't risk a mid-air collision. The Hallicheki had wings of their own and could bail out in safety. Mary and I hadn't and couldn't.

But there was no danger of our becoming entangled with the Hallicheki. They had put on considerable speed during their dive and were swooping down on the Shaara balloon like a hawk on its prey. They were directly above it—and then, although they were still well clear of the ground, were rising again. A failure of nerve? It didn't fit in with what I knew of their psychology. But ballast must have been dumped and it would mean an additional soar and swoop for them before rounding the Cardan Knoll.

And I was gaining on them.

But where were the Shaara?

Mary seemed to have read my thought. She said, "They're in trouble."

I looked down to where she was pointing. Yes, they were in trouble all right. They had lost considerable altitude and the car of their balloon was entangled with the topmost branches of a tall tree. The drone and the worker were tugging ineffectually with all their limbs, buzzing about it. But they would never get it clear. They'd lost all their lift. The sausage-like gas cells were limp, more than half deflated.

But that was their worry. We flew on. ahead, the Knoll was getting closer. I pulled over to port to pass to the west'ard of the brush-covered domes. The Hallicheki were already rounding the Knoll, lost briefly to sight as they passed to north of it. Then I was coming round to starboard in a tight, rising turn. I didn't realise until it was almost too late that the slight, northerly breeze was setting me down onto the hill; I had to put the tiller hard over to try to claw to wind'ard. The deck of our car just brushed the branches of a tree and there was a clattering, screeching explosion of small, flying reptiles from the foliage. Luckily they were more scared of us than we were of them.

Ahead, now, was the railway to Garardan and the Garardan Road. Beyond road and railway was the Blord River and, far to the southeast, I could see the crumbling stonework of the Porgidor Tower. Over road and railway, I reasoned, there would be thermals but over the river, which ran ice-cold from the high hills, there would be a downdraught. . . . Yes, there were thermals all right. The Hallicheki were taking full advantage of them, going up like a balloon. Literally. What were they playing at? Why weren't they gliding down the lift? And they were keeping well to starboard, to the south'ard of the track, putting on distance as they would have to come to port to pass to north and east of the tower.

I looked astern. The judges' airship was following, watching. If the Hallicheki tried to cut off a corner they'd be disqualified.

I kept the Porgidor Tower fine on my starboard bow; whatever the Hallicheki were playing at, *I* would run the minimum distance. And then, as I was lifting on the thermals over the railway, I saw that there was some method in the opposition's madness. There were more thermals over the power station on the west bank of the river and I had missed out on them.

Swoop and soar, swoop and soar. compress, decompress. Our muscles were aching with the stooped scrambles forward and aft in the cramped confines of the car. It must have been even worse for Mary than for me because of the absurdly bulky and heavy clothing that she was wearing. But we were holding our own, more than holding our own. that thermal-hunting had cost the Hallicheki their lead.

Then there was the Porgidor Tower close on our starboard hand, with quite a crowd of spectators waving from the battered battlements. and we were on the last leg of the course, over boulder-strewn bushland, with the twin ribbons of the Saarkaar Road and Railway ahead and beyond them the river again, and beyond that the mooring masts and hangars of the airport.

Swoop and soar, swoop and soar. . . .

I swooped into the thermals rising from the road and the railway so that I could manage a steep, fast glide with no loss of altitude. I began to feel smugly self-congratulatory.

But where were the Hallicheki?

Not ahead any longer. All that they had gained by their use of thermals was altitude. They were neither ahead nor to either side, and certainly not below, where the only artifact visible was a little sidewheel paddle steamer chugging fussily up river.

Then there was the anticipated downdraught that I countered with decompression.

Suddenly there was a sharp pattering noise from directly above and I saw a shower of glittering particles driving down on each side of the car. Rain? Hail? But neither fall from a clear sky.

Mary was quicker on the uptake than I was "The Hallicheki," she shouted. "They dumped their ballast on us!"

Not only had they dumped ballast on us, they'd holed the gas cells. Some of the viciously pointed steel darts had gone through every surface, dropping to the deck of the car. If we'd been in the way of them they'd have gone through us too. Razor-sharp, tungsten tipped (as I discovered later). So this was what had happened to the Shaara racer. . . .

"Ballast!" I yelled. "Dump ballast!"

But we didn't have any to dump. I thought briefly of the mooring lines with their metal pegs but the ropes were spliced to the pins and to the structure of the car. And I didn't have a knife. (All right, all right, I should have had one but I'd forgotten it.) Then I remembered my first flight with Robiliyi and what he had told me when I'd asked him what to do when there was no ballast left to dump. I stripped off my shirt, dropped it over the side. It didn't seem to make much difference. I sacrificed my shorts. I looked up. All the cells were punctured and three of them looked as though they were empty. But the planing surface above them must still be reasonably intact. I hoped. If only I could gain enough altitude I could glide home. Forgetting the company that I was in I took off my briefs, sent the scrap of fabric after the other garments.

I heard Mary make a noise half way between a scream and a gasp.

I looked at her. She looked at me. Her face was one huge blush. I felt my own ears burning in sympathy.

I said, "We're still dropping. We have to get upstairs. Fast."

She asked. "You mean . . . ?"

I said, "Yes."

She asked, her voice little more than a whisper, "Must I?"

I said that she must.

But you could have knocked me over with a feather when her hand went to the throat of her coveralls, when her finger ran down the sealseam She stepped out of the garment, kicked it overside. Her underwear was thick and revealed little; nonetheless I could see that that fantastic blush of hers suffused the skin of her neck and shoulders, even the narrow strip of belly that was visible. *That will do*, I was going to say, but she gave me no time to say it. Her expression had me baffled. Her halter came off and was jettisoned, then her remaining garment.

I'll be frank. She wouldn't have attracted a second glance on a nudist beach; her figure was good but not outstanding. But this was not a nudist beach. A naked woman in an incongruous situation is so much more naked than she would be in the right surroundings.

She looked at me steadily, defiantly. Her blush had faded. Her skin was smoothly creamy rather than white. I felt myself becoming interested.

She asked, "Do you like it?" I thought at first that she meant the strip show that she had put on for me. She went on, "*I* do! I've often thought about it but I had no idea what it would really be like! The feel of the sun and the air on my skin . . . "

I wanted to go on looking at her. I wanted to do more than that—but there's a time and a place for everything and this was neither. It could have been quite a good place in other circumstances but not with a race to be flown to a finish.

I tore my eyes away from her naked body—I heard a ripping noise, but it was only one of the rents in the envelope enlarging itself—and looked around and up and down to see what was happening. Mary's supreme sacrifice was bringing results. We were lifting—sluggishly, but lifting. And so, just ahead of us, were the Hallicheki. The gas cells of their balloon were flabby and wrinkled; they must have squandered buoyancy recklessly in their attacks on the Shaara and ourselves. And then I saw one of the great, ugly brutes clambering out of the car. They were abandoning ship, I thought. They were dropping out of the race. Then I realised what they were doing. The one who had gone outboard was gripping the forward rail of the car with her feet, was beating her wings powerfully, towing the balloon. Legal or illegal? I didn't know. That would be for the judges to decide, just as they would have to make a decision on the use of potentially lethal ballast. But as no machinery was being used, the Hallicheki might be declared the winners of the race.

What else did we have to dump? We would have to gain altitude, and fast, for the last swoop in. The hand winch? It was of no further use to us. It was held down to the deck of the car only by wing nuts and they loosened fairly easily. We unscrewed them, threw them out. We were rising a little faster. Then there were the shackles securing the downhaul to the compression webbing. Overboard they went. The winch itself I decided to keep as a last reserve of disposable ballast.

High enough?

I thought so.

I valved gas—for the first and only time during our flight—and Mary and I shifted our weight forward. We swooped, overtaking the crawling, under tow, Hallicheki balloon. We were making headway all right but losing too much altitude. The wince would have to go.

It was insinuated that my jettisoning it when we were directly

above the Hallicheki was an act of spite. I said in my report that it
was accidental, that the Hallicheki just happened to be in the wrong
place at the wrong time. Or the right time. I'll not deny that we
cheered when we saw the hunk of machinery hit that great, flabby
mattress almost dead centre. It tore through it, rupturing at least
four of the gas cells. The envelope crumpled, fell in about itself. The
two hen officers struggled to keep the crippled racer in the air,
ripping the balloon fabric to shreds with their clawed feet as their
wings flapped frenziedly. Meanwhile *we* were going up like a
rocket.

The Hallicheki gave up the attempt to keep their craft airborne.
They let it flutter earthwards, trailing streamers of ragged cloth.
They started to come after us, climbing powerfully. I could sense
somehow that they were in a vile temper. I imagined those sharp
claws and beaks ripping into the fabric of our balloon and didn't feel
at all happy. *We* didn't have wings of our own. We didn't even have
parachutes.

It was time for the final swoop—if only those blasted birds let us
make it. There was no need to valve any more gas; the rents in the
fabric of the gas cells had enlarged themselves. We shifted our
weight forward. Astern, and overhead I heard the throbbing of
engines; it was the judges; airship escorting us to the finish line. The
Hallicheki wouldn't dare to try anything now. I hoped. My hope was
realized. They squawked loudly and viciously, sheered off.

Overhead, as I've said, there was the throbbing of airship
engines—and, fainter, the irregular beat of an inertial drive unit.
Adder's atmosphere flier, I thought at first, standing by in case of
accidents. But it didn't sound quite right, somehow. Too deep a
note. But I'd too much on my plate to be able to devote any thought
to matters of no immediate importance.

We swept into the airport, steering for the red flag on the apron
that marked the finish. We were more of a hang glider now than a
balloon but *knew* somehow that we'd make it. The underside of the
car brushed the branches of a tree—to have made a detour would
have been out of the question—and a large section of decking was
torn away. That gave us just the little extra buoyancy that we

needed. We cleared the spiky hedge that marked the airport boundary. We actually hit the flagpole before we hit the ground, knocking it over. Before the tattered, deflated envelope collapsed over us completely we heard the cries of applause, the thunder of flat hands on thighs.

It was quite a job getting out from under that smothering fabric. During the struggle we came into contact, very close contact. At least once I almost . . . Well, I didn't. I'm not boasting about it, my alleged self-control, I mean. There comes a time in life when you fell more remorse for the uncommitted sins—if sins they are—than for the committed ones.

At last we crawled out of the wreckage. The first thing we noticed was that the applause had ceased. My first thought was that the natives were shocked by our nudity and then, as I looked around, saw that they were all staring upwards. The clangour of the strange inertial drive was sounding louder and louder.

We looked up too. There was a pinnace—a big pinnace, such as are carried by major warships—coming down. It displayed Survey Service markings. I could read the name, in large letters, ARIES II. *Aries*' number-two pinnace . . . *Aries*—a Constellation Class cruiser—I knew quite well. I'd once served in her as a junior watchkeeper. She must still be in orbit, I thought. This would be the preliminary landing party.

The pinnace grounded not far from where Mary and I were standing. Or where *I* was standing; Mary was on her hands and knees desperately trying to tear off a strip of fabric from the ruined envelope to cover herself. The outer airlock door opened. A group of officers in full dress blues disembarked. Captain Daintree was in the lead. I knew him. He was a strict disciplinarian, a martinet. he was one of the reasons why I had not been sorry to leave *Aries*.

He glared at us. He recognised me in spite of my non-regulation attire. He stood there, stiff as a ramrod, his right hand on the pommel of his dress sword. I still think that he'd have loved to use that weapon on me. His face registered shock, disbelief, horror, you name it.

He spoke at last, his voice low but carrying easily over the distance between us.

"Mr. Grimes, correct me if I am wrong, but your instructions, I believe, were merely to maintain a Terran presence on this planet until such time as an officer of higher rank could take over."

I admitted that this was so.

"You were not, I am certain, authorised to start a nudist club. Or is this, perhaps, some sort of love-in?"

"But, sir," I blurted, "I won the race!" Even he could not take that triumph from me. "I won the race!"

"And did you win the prize, Commodore?" asked Kitty Kelly.

"Oh, yes. A very nice trophy. a model, in solid gold, of a racing balloon, suitably inscribed. I have it still, at home in Port Forlorn."

"Not that prize. It's the body beautiful I mean. The inhibition-and-clothing-shedding Miss Marsden."

"Yes," said Grimes. "She shed her inhibitions all right. But I muffed it. I should have struck while the iron was hot, before she had time to decide that it was really Beadle—of all people!—whom she fancied. He reaped what I'd sown—all the way back to Lindisfarne Base!

"When you get to my age you'll realise that there's no justice in the Universe."

"Isn't there?" she asked, rather too sweetly.

If You Can Fill the Unforgiving Minute

by David Andreissen & D. C. Poyer

"And yes, I know," Gerald Corcoran continued after the pause that always followed his favorite poem. "It's sexist, racist, and terracentric. Kipling. But in his day, kid, Earth was all there was, though you're a little young to remember."

"I've heard that piece before, sir," said Ayid Hafouz, hanging the last of his clothing in his locker. Po-xiang, the Cantonese trainer, moved silently about the athletes' ready room. "In my English classes. You know that I will run as well as I can, coach. It is just that I am not a sprinter."

"Neither is he . . . it . . . whatever." The American, red-faced, tall but getting heavy, stalked nervously around the ready room, punching his fist into his hand. "I know you'll do your best, kid. You didn't get to Olympia from that godforsaken watering hole of yours—"

"Al Jarzhireh," the boy murmured, extending his right leg to the trainer. He winced a little as Po-xiang knelt and began to rub an emollient into the long stringy muscles; his right knee had been giving him trouble, a vague ache deep within. Corcoran, ignoring the interruption, talked on.

Ayid stared down at his thin, brown legs. Po-xiang, his round face intent, worked silently and steadily, moving from the thighs to the hard, resilient calf muscles, his short powerful fingers digging deep, loosening the pre-race tension.

Five years, Ayid was thinking. Five years from the bare sun-scorched hills of PanArabic Algeria. Years of steadily harder train-ing, first at the national camp at Tarabulus, later at the Olympic camp itself in Ireland. Then, after his upset victory over the Atlantic Union and Soviet Federation distance champions in the 2084 games, to the special camp in Colorado.

Where he had met Corcoran and his team, and learned, really, how to run.

A long trip. *How many kilometers have you run in your life, Ayid?* The coach's voice went on unheard as he drank the glucose-and-water solution the trainer poured for him. *How many miles?* Running the hills barefoot, for shoes were still scarce in his village. Running since before he could remember to herd the family's four camels, six goats, and to pick up their valuable dung before the other children could pounce. The M'zab, the 'puritans of the Des-ert,' still clung to the old ways—tradition, the Qu'uran; even irriga-tion was mistrusted as desecrating the land Allah had willed to be desert. Ayid had grown up in the faith, wanting no other life, running for pleasure along the long sun-shimmering ridges of sand that dragged· at his feet and made his heart pound and breath wheeze in his throat. And then one day the Minister for Arab Sport had come to Al Jarzhireh to see the wind whipping at the burnous of a figure that ran, ran, almost keeping pace with the aged khaki Rolls-Hover. . . .

A hand fell on his shoulder, and he glanced up. The American looked angry. "Look, kid, I know it's close to race time, but how can I coach you if you won't listen to me?"

"I am sorry, Mr. Corcoran. What were you saying, sir?"

"I want you to lead all the way. A fast start's a fast finish, so I want you off the beam fast and give it all you've got right up to the end. It's a hell of a long sprint, but that's got to be our strategy."

Ayid nodded, got up, and stretched. His naked body, loose now from the massage, felt strong and supple. He bounced on his toes, feeling the Achilles tendons taut as drawn bowstrings.

"How do you feel, Ayid?" said Po-xiang.

"Very good, Wang. I feel light, somehow."

"About a kilo," said Corcoran. "Olympia's point-eight-five Earth normal. Should help your times a bit . . . but it might help *them*, too."

"How far is it this first time, again, coach?"

Corcoran pulled out a black notebook and flipped pages. "The Chircurgi just came out with the schedule . . . wait a minute, they measure everything in these damn Mediational units . . . yeah. First race, today, one hundred Mediational standards. Comes out to 270 meters."

"A dash?"

"Push it all the way, like I said. We're really depending more on Southern and Kwarafa in this first race, but I want you up front. Second race, tomorrow, five thousand standards, a little over thirteen thousand meters—seven-plus miles; that'll be a good race for you."

Ayid felt fear in his stomach, but did not allow it on his face. It was an old companion before a race. The M'zab did not believe in showing fear or any emotion, and he had learned how to bottle it up inside himself until the final second when he poised toppling at the starting line and the crack of the pistol converted all fear to desperate energy. He spread thin brown fingers on the bench and said quietly, "And the third race, sir? Do the Dhelians have an event as long as our marathon?"

The American hesitated. "Longer," he said at last. Po-xiang looked up in surprise from Ayid's feet, which he was massaging, bending them far back to stretch and warm the tendons.

"Longer than a marathon? *Bism'Allah*—I mean, how much longer, sir?"

"Eighteen thousand standards," said Corcoran slowly. "Forty-eight kilometers. A little over thirty miles."

* * *

Olympia, as the Terrans called it, was a beautiful world. Ayid stood in the center of the field in a warmup suit, jogging in place, and looked about him.

The track, where the first two events would take place, lay in the center of a (natural?) bowl of low hills. Across from him, built up along the sides of the bowl, were seating areas, already filling up with spectators from the spaceports and hotel areas to the east. Teams of officials, holo personnel, and police were busy around the edges of the track.

The track. This was the first time he had seen it in daylight. Dhelian-style, it was longer than standard Earth tracks, and laid out in a figure-8 rather than an oval. Under the bluish-white, tiny, hot sun, the close-cropped 'grass' around the track lay all in one direction, as if combed. It sparkled oddly, as if diamonds were scattered about in it. The running surface itself, some ten meters wide, was natural; it seemed to be of a mosslike plant, moderately hard, but feeling good to his bare feet as he stepped out on it to begin his stretching routine.

He moved slowly into the warmup. Designed for him by Corcoran's bioengineers on Earth, it stretched and warmed every running muscle and every joint and tendon. The warmup suit itself was electrically heated at calf, thigh, arm, and neck. As he moved out for a slow lap he was already sweating despite the thin, cool air.

He took it slowly, testing the surface and the effect of the loop. Better for the longer races, he saw, since the curves were taken in opposite directions. The moss was soft under his bare feet, yet gave good traction. He rounded the first turn, which was banked to the right, and found himself face to face with the Dhelian spectators.

His first thought was, how human they look; his second, a feeling of devout Moslem shock at their lack of clothing. Stacked up the sides of the hills, their faces seemed like those of any human crowd. There was a low murmur as he jogged past them, then a burst of sound. Ayid could not tell if they were applauding, or jeering. Did Dhelians jeer?

A strange people, he thought, leaving the turn and entering the second straight. Lifting his head, he accelerated smoothly to about three-quarters of his full sprint speed, knees high, legs reaching out for distance, arms pumping smoothly, every muscle that was not working relaxed. Through his mind ran what little he knew of this oddly humanoid race.

Earth had been discovered in the early 21st century. Not by Dhelians, but by another Mediational race of scales and many arms and quick reptilian movements—and a capability of calculating profit instantly to the thousandth of a per cent: the Chircurgi. Mankind could have fought several of the wars it so much enjoyed for the price the Chircurgi asked for their stardrive; but in the end, the UN had paid.

Ten years later, when the first Earthbuilt starship had triumphantly docked at a Dhelian planet, mechanics at the port offered the crew a complete set of blueprints for the equivalent of $12.95. To add to their fury, the humans learned that the plant derivatives they had bartered away were far more valuable in a galaxy-wide market than they had ever been on Earth.

How the Dheils must have laughed, Ayid thought, feeling a rush of shame. Not for himself . . . but for all human beings.

The Dhelians, the Dheils. The dominant race, if there was one, of the sixty races of the Mediation. Reassuringly humanoid, after the Chircurgi; but so far superior to humans in everything human that to the natural Terran resentment at being bilked by aliens was soon added a racial inferiority complex. Naked, tall, beautiful, intuitively intelligent, the sexless Dhelians were humanity as it might be in another million years. Every human envied them, wondered about them . . . and hated them.

Ayid slowed after three laps, evaluating his body. He felt good. The bothersome pain in his lower legs was nothing and would not even be felt during the race. His lungs felt good and his head clear. He felt full of energy; the four days' rest on the ship from Earth had done him good, as had Po-xiang's massages and diet supplements. Though it was wearying, Ayid thought, to have to fend off some of the things—forbidden things, by the severe M'zab laws—that Corcoran wanted him to take.

He was ready for this race.

Sunlight glinted blue from multiple lenses as he swung off the track in front of the Terran stands. The holo teams were set up to transmit. The Working Press had arrived.

"There he is. Hey, Hafouz!"

"Abe Berenson, UBC," said a fat man, a gyroed stereo mini-camera perched on his shoulder like a pet owl. "Your impression of the Dhelian runner, what's his name, Tseil Laol. Over-refined? Can human go-getiveness—"

"People's Network," a dark woman broke in. "Brother Hafouz, can you make a statement about the—"

"Clear out!" Corcoran's bull-roar made Ayid jump. "You there! Get away from him!" Reporters scattered as the American charged through them, but quickly recovered, clustering around the coach as Ayid stammered and blushed.

"Coach Corcoran—statement for the press?"

"Damn vultures. Okay. But get back a little." He stuck his hands in his pockets as silent cameras focused on him and on the gray-suited runner, sending the flat red face of the American and the thin dark visage of the Algerian bolting out over hundreds of light-years . . . via Dhelian equipment that Earth engineers did not begin to understand. "Here's your statement. Ayid, don't stand there, keep warming up. Okay.

"As you know, today is the first running event of the 15,614th Mediational Sports Convention. Sort of an interstellar Olympics, held roughly every eleven years. This is the first Convention that Earth has been invited to. We have entries in a few other events— zero-gee-dancing, long jump, a weight-throw, skiing, personal combat. Think we have a K-ball team though it's not ready for the majors yet in my opinion. But we're not favored in those. There are other species in the Mediation that can swim like barracuda, put a hundred-kilo shot over a mile, high-jump ten meters under three gee's.

"But mankind—we're a running animal. Have been ever since we grew up out on the African savannah.

"So I think we've got a good chance in this event."

"Are the xogs good runners?" asked the woman who had called Hafouz 'brother.' Corcoran looked at her. She was very pretty but suddenly he felt that if he got to know her he would not like her.

"They're not 'xogs'—I don't like that word. Yeah, they're good runners. Their skeletons and muscle structure seem almost like ours. Major differences are sexual organs . . . and maybe the brain. Maybe."

"Coach Corcoran. One last one. Can Ayid win?"

"Well, in the longer distances, he's the best we've got. But remember, it's a team effort. Kwarafa and Southern have to do their jobs in the dash and middle distance to give us a win overall." He took his hands from his pockets and glanced after Ayid. "Got to go now."

"RUNNERS FOR FIRST EVENT ASSEMBLE AT STARTING POINT," echoed between the hills. The announcing system paused, then repeated itself in several other languages. One of them—smooth, softly voweled, rapid—was Dhelian.

"Five minutes, kid," said Corcoran, stopping just inside the door of the ready room.

Ayid looked up, nodded, then placed his head to the floor again. He would finish the long Sura, the 72nd, always one of his favorites and one he had learned by heart:

> . . . the gods whom they call upon beside Him, they shall not be able to intercede; they only shall be able to intercede who bore witness to the truth.
>
> If thou ask them who created them, they will be sure to say "God." How then can they hold false opinions?
>
> And it is said, "Oh Lord! Verily these are a people who believe not."
>
> Then shalt thou turn from them, saying "Peace." For in the end they shall know their folly.

He salaamed three times—not in the direction of Mecca, for who could know the true direction of Mecca here, but toward the east, toward the morning sun—got up, rolled up the prayer rug, and placed it carefully in his locker. He held out his arms and Po-xiang slipped off the warmup suit. Underneath it he was naked. His brown skin, paler around midriff and thighs, gleamed with oil, and the long dark hair of the M'zabite male was tied back. He looked at the floor and not at the other two men, but his voice was low and fairly steady as he said, "I'm ready."

"Chemistry?" said Corcoran.

"Number one," said the trainer. "Took them just before he started to pray."

"Sugars?"

"Final stage was at minus ten. Hundred CC's straight G. Decay starts in fifteen minutes. Race'll be over long before then."

"You give him anything else?"

"He didn't want it," said the trainer, eyes expressionless.

"Maybe he'd better," said Corcoran tentatively. "The rules here are different than on Earth. Anything goes, implants, drugs—"

"No drugs," said Ayid. "Sir."

"Well, it's just a sprint; we're really counting on Terry and Kebe." Corcoran thumbed him toward the door. "But I'd like to be surprised, Ayid."

Applause swelled around him as Ayid jogged out into the open air. Blushing—he felt his nakedness keenly, though Dhelian rules demanded it and the Kharidjite elders had approved it.

"Big crowd, Ayid." Beside him, a short, stocky runner, dark as ebony; Kebe Kwarafa, the PanAfrican who had startled the world by running a hundred meters in 9.2 seconds in 2084. "Going to win this one?"

"I will try hard. But you're the one who will win. It's your distance."

"Maybe." The African put out a hand, stopping Ayid in mid-trot. They walked together toward the starting line. Ayid felt nervous perspiration chill on his skin. "Listen, Ayid. You must save yourself a little. This is only the first race, you know."

Ayid slowly turned his head and stared at him. Kwarafa's broad features were contorted with strong emotion. "What do you mean, Kebe? Only the first race? These are the Mediationals!"

Kwarafa's muscular arm chopped into the air, pointing. "Yes . . . but how can we defeat *that*?"

"Allah," said Ayid softly.

An angel stood at the starting line, shifting easily from foot to foot, looking up toward the Dhelian stands.

Tseil Laol Laia. Ayid recognized the proud line of the back, the tawny hair, from numberless training holos. But the reality was breathtaking. The long, spare, graceful legs, hairless and golden brown. Tawny reddish hair flowing back from a massive forehead and down the slim neck. Terry Southren, the Australian middle distance champion, looked squat and animalistic beside Laol as he walked by him to his own lane. With horror Ayid saw his own number, four, on the lane to Laol's right.

Two other Dhelians walked rapidly toward the line as the one minute call sounded. A murmur from the crowd filled the valley. Ayid winced as something hard struck his shoulder. It was Kwarafa's solidly muscled fist. "Remember, Ayid . . . save a little for the next two races."

"Good luck, Kebe."

An odd thing to say to a runner, thought Ayid, stepping into his lane. Then he glanced to his left, and the conversation with the PanAfrican was wiped from his mind.

He was looking into Tseil Laol's eyes. Vast, golden, godlike eyes . . . the eyes of a *djinn*, almost of Allah himself. Wise, compassionate, strong. . . . "Hello, Ayid Hafouz," said the Dheil.

"Ah—" he stammered, ducking his head. Blood rushed to his face. He was as tall as the other runner but felt like falling to the ground before him, felt like prostrating himself before this godlike man—

Man? Ayid stared speechless at the other's groin. He had read of it, of course, but it was different *seeing* that smooth tuck of skin, hairless, devoid of any sex at all . . . he wrenched his eyes up to see a slight smile on the Dheil's lips. "Run hard," he heard him say softly, in near-perfect Standard English. "And let the best between us have the victory." He extended a slim golden hand. Ayid stared, unable to believe it was for him.

"RUNNERS, TAKE YOUR MARKS."

Reflex snapped him down, to the blocks. They weren't there. Belatedly he remembered Dhelian abhorrence of all artificial aid to sport, even though Mediational rules permitted it; apparently that included blocks. He decided on a bunch start and dug his bare toes into the soft surface. Hunkering down, he glanced quickly to left and right. Alone now in their lanes, the three Terran and three Dhelian runners were withdrawing into themselves, readying their minds and bodies for the few explosive seconds that would determine the outcome of the sprint. Ayid looked down at his hands. The mossy surface of the track smelled like crushed cinnamon, and this close to it he could see the weblike interlocking of the rough flat leaves. He breathed harder, feeling the surge of energy in his legs and in his blood as he called on Allah a last time and fixed his eyes on the starting beam.

"SET."

The crowd saw and the holo cameras sent the line of six backs rising at once, six heads drawn up, six muscled bodies tensed for the start. A soft sound rolled across the valley; the indrawn breaths of thousands of spectators, both human and Dheil.

The glowing beam snapped off. Ayid, his body already in flight as his mind recorded it, exploded like a breaking spring. His toes drove thudding into the soft soil of Olympia. With shock, he realized that he was looking at four rapidly departing backs, two of them human, two Dhelian. He was still bent far forward, still accelerating, but they were already in full sprint. The ten-standard line flashed past almost unseen, and then he hit his stride and put all he had into shoving with the long hard muscles of his thighs and calves.

"Push it!" said Corcoran in his ear, the command tinny and distant through the transplant mike and mastoid. *"You can still catch up. Push. That's it!"*

Not used to this. Ayid bent forward farther and concentrated on reaching for distance. Head up now. Were the backs a little closer? The tall form of Tseil Laol was just ahead. Beyond him, Southren. Kwarafa and the remaining Dheil were in the lead, and seemed now to be drawing ahead.

Another line. Thirty standards. Seventy to go. *At full speed like this, how long can you last, Ayid?*

But he could see the distance closing between himself and Laol, who was running smoothly, gracefully, heels flashing alternately and rapidly in the sun as Ayid closed from behind. The roar of the crowd seemed deafening. The track flashed by, blurred with speed. Laol just ahead now, on his left, the runners still in their marked lanes. Ayid stuck to him stubbornly, wondering where the third Dhelian was. Behind him. But how far?

Fifty standards. The midpoint. *"Thirteen even,"* came Corcoran's voice, excited. *"Good, but—lengthen your stride. Get that head up!"*

He jerked up his head, feeling weariness suddenly grip his driving thighs. Ahead, Southren had moved up, was now between Kwarafa and the leading Dheil, and the three were running neck and neck as if glued together. The roar of the crowd grew louder, grew frenzied, demanding speed; and Ayid responded to it, the hot air sawing into his throat, arms milling desperately as if he could reach out and claw the leading runners back to him.

Centimeter by centimeter, he suddenly saw, he was gaining on the Dheil. Tseil Laol was now only a stride ahead, and the realization gave Ayid a burst of strength that carried him level with the red-haired runner.

Seventy standards, and he was straining to stay with his man when a movement ahead broke the pounding rhythm, attracting his instant attention. Kwarafa, running like a berserk machine, was drifting out of his carefully-marked lane . . . to the right. The blue glare of sky between him and the Australian runner narrowed. Southren, unaware of anything outside of his straining body, did not notice the African's slow drift into his lane. Running full out, there was nothing Ayid could do save stay with Laol, who had now seen him and was threatening to pull ahead again.

It happened. Kwarafa's arms merged with the blur of Southren's. At the speed they were travelling the merest contact was disaster. Southren faltered, leaning instinctively to the right to escape Kwarafa. The African, realizing his error, tried to recover his lane, stumbled, and fell. An outstretched arm brushed Southren's legs. Then Ayid was past and there remained only

"Ten left! Pour it on, kid!"

He prayed, and tried. But the sprint was too long. He was running as fast as his body would take him. His legs dragged as though through hot sand and there was no oxygen in the thin air of Olympia any more. Desperate, he spent his last reserves—he could see the scarlet beam of the finish—Tseil Laol, his twin, his shadow, had to be tiring too—a last effort, *Allah*, though his legs were leaden and the air a red shaft in his throat—

The sound became deafening as he and Laol broke the beam together two strides behind Southren and the lead Dhelian sprinter. Ayid turned it off and coasted to a slow jog, sobbing deep breaths to replace the oxygen his muscles had sucked from his blood. *"Nice running, kid,"* came Corcoran's voice. *"I think you took him there at the finish. We may have a first and a third. I saw twenty-six five for your time."*

Ayid left the track and jogged in a little circle on the turf. He could hear cheers from the Terran stands, but he kept his eyes on the ground. Though the cheering was good, a Kharidjite from the M'zab did not show emotion either in triumph or defeat. He did a few quick stretches and then jogged back toward the finish.

Kwarafa, limping slightly and supported by two PanAfrican trainers, was just reaching it. As Ayid came up he heard him apologizing to Southren. "Terry, I was at fault. Drifted out of my lane. It wasn't deliberate—"

"I know, Kebe. Don't apologize." The Australian draped a freckled arm around Kwarafa. "I'm pretty sure I had him anyway. Man, can that Maior sprint."

"RESULTS, 100-STANDARD DASH," boomed the excited tones of the Terran announcer. The field grew quiet. "FIRST PLACE: SOUTHREN, TERRY. TIME, TWENTY-FIVE POINT TWO EIGHT SECONDS BY BEAM."

Southren's face kindled in a wide Outback grin, and he held his arms aloft as Ayid and the Dhelian who had come in second—Maior, Southren had called him—slapped him and hugged him. Kwarafa hesitated for a second, then joined in, smiling broadly.

"SECOND PLACE: AIA MAIOR LAIA. TIME, TWENTY-FIVE POINT FOUR ONE SECONDS BY BEAM."

Southren and the Dhelian, still smiling, shook hands. "I congratulate you. You are quite a runner," said Maior.

"You too," said Southren. The two looked into each other's eyes for a moment, and Ayid saw surprise come into Southren's face. "You—"

"Bear you no envy," said the Dheil. "That surprises you, does it? Then we have much to learn about each other."

The stands were emptying rapidly as the remaining times were announced; Humans and Dhelians were streaming back to Olympia Port for an afternoon of carefully segregated enjoyment. Ayid, feeling the air chilling him, said his so-longs and jogged off toward the Terran stands, where he could see Corcoran and Po-xiang waiting for him. He felt good, though as it turned out Tseil Laol had beaten him by two hundredths of a second, leaving Ayid fourth in the dash. Probably his arm happened to be up, breaking the beam first, he thought, waving to the two waiting figures. But a human, after all, had taken first. He was smiling as he reached the stands. But then he stopped.

Corcoran's face was icy, and he barely looked at Ayid. He turned to the trainer, whose round face betrayed no elation at all at the win. "Wang, I need to talk to Hafouz. Could you—"

"Sure, Jerry—but say, he ran well—" the Cantonese caught Corcoran's look and fell silent. "Sure." He walked away, toward the ready building. Corcoran watched him until he was out of earshot, then swung on Ayid, fists balled, eyes frozen mad.

"What kind of a frigging performance was that?"

"Coach—ah—ah—" Ayid stammered, amazed.

"Shut up. I'm disgusted. Fourth! You should have taken a second at least."

"S-Second? Mr. Corcoran, I'm not—"

"Don't hand me that 'ay yoom noot a spreen-tar' crap, Hafouz. If you could run a 26:42 you could have done 26:40. Hell! Two hundredths of a frigging second! You *let* that red-haired pansy beat you!"

"I was doing my best, sir." Ayid felt the blush slide down over his face, felt it burning on his naked shoulders. His hands moved self-consciously to cover his groin. He cursed himself silently, his shyness, his inability to speak out. This big red-faced Yankee, this unbeliever, made him want to—

"You don't catch on too quick, do you, Hafouz. Maybe you believe all this buddy-buddy crap I saw them laying on you at the finish. But this was the psych race for you and Laol. By winning this one he's achieved dominance over you." Corcoran seemed to be losing the hot edge of his temper, but his face was still fiery. "Will, kid, will. That's what wins long distance races. And you've handed him the advantage on a plate."

He turned away, looking up at the by now nearly empty stands. "They're happy because Terry Southren won. A human took first place. Great. But that's only for one out of the three races—and with Dhelians in second and third, and Kwarafa fouling out, *they're ahead in total points.*"

Ayid nodded silently. Now he understood. He had failed. Had he been giving it his best effort? Hadn't the African's warning had some effect, even if only subconsciously? Hadn't he been holding something back, leaving it to the sprinters to win, saving himself for the long, grueling trials of the last two races? "I'm sorry, coach," he said humbly.

"Here's your workout for this afternoon." Corcoran tore a page from his notebook and handed it to Ayid without looking at him or acknowledging his apology. "Finish by five. Light dinner, class five, high carbos. The team will watch holo replays in the ready room at seven. Bed at nine."

"Yes, sir," said Ayid miserably. Corcoran stared at him for a moment, then turned and walked rapidly away.

"No, it wasn't a good first race," said the pale woman, tapping the rim of her glass against her teeth. She took a sip of the violet liquid and lowered the glass to the table. Blue Scandinavian eyes examined Corcoran and the other coldly. "But if we all pull together, the situation can still be retrieved. There are still two races to be run."

The pale woman, the American coach, and two other men were

sitting in one of the anonymously dim nightspots in Olympia Port. It was very late, after midnight, but around them Terran spectators in loud clothing were still discussing the races, the evening's entertainment, the strange Dhelian liqueurs, Southren's victory. There were smiles and toasts and laughter at every table but this. Here the expressions were grim and though there were glasses in front of each person there were no toasts.

Corcoran looked around at the other men as she talked; Clyde Matthews, the British ex-hurdler who coached and represented Southren, and an extremely tall and taciturn Masai, whose name was i-Zalai. He was a PanAfrican. Together with the pale woman, who wore at her breast the blue riband of the UN Mediational Relations Committee, they were Earth's non-judging delegates to Olympia. Corcoran took a deep swallow of iced milk and looked back at the woman as Matthews asked her, "You still think the athletes themselves ought not to be told?"

"No." A sharp Swedish-accented voice. "Young people form relationships easily, they trust easily. A locker-room friendship with one of the Dhelians could develop. The Dhelians have no idea, we feel sure, that a relationship exists. We'd much rather keep it that way for the time being."

"It's been confirmed?" said Corcoran. "About the ship?"

"Yes. The excavations are complete. It was a primitive ship compared to what they fly today . . . but it's definite.

"We are the descendants of a lost Dhelian expedition."

The tall Masai sighed wordlessly.

"This is bloody beautiful," said Matthews. "This can wipe out all the nasty feelings. Humans and Dheils—brothers under the skin. When will you announce it?"

"That depends on you gentlemen . . . and, of course, on the boys."

"Why not now?"

"We can't, Mr. Matthews. Too many Terrans hate out-worlders—'xogs' they're calling them now. We've run psych extrapolations and we feel that with this prejudice—really a feeling of inferiority like all prejudice—the mass of our people would simply reject the truth, and show it by voting against joining the Mediation in the plebiscite next year."

"But with this news—"

"Wait; there's another objection. The Dhelians. You know their traits. Pride, distaste for what they see as Human pushiness, our preoccupation with technique, our general backwardness and lack of *dalanai*—their concept of honor, morality—"

"I haven't felt very much of that," said Matthews.

"You're in sports. To some extent our traditions of fair play are compatible. But our business people, scientists, political leaders . . . there's been friction, gentlemen. It's been hushed up, but believe me, it's there.

"And this could rip the lid off the whole thing."

"But if we're really Dhelians—"

"It's not that simple, Mr. Matthews. Five million years on Earth has done things to the parent stock, and I strongly suspect that the Dheils have changed too in that period of time—the merging of the sexes when they went to external reproduction, for example, where we've kept the old system. The few hundred people in that ship were only the starting point. In time, as they reverted to nature, adaptive radiation and isolation produced sub-races, what we used to call australopithecus, erectus, neanderthal. *Homo sapiens* was the branch that survived, but we're not Dhelians any more. To them, right now, we're a different, primitive, rather inferior race. Perhaps it's best to keep it that way."

"Why?" said Corcoran.

"Because our other choice, as things stand now, is to be regarded as degenerates. The Jukes and the Kallikaks of the galaxy, a textbook case of isolation, inbreeding, and abnormality. Of the two choices, which do you think would be better received by the Mediation? Which would the people of Terra prefer?"

With the explanation it fell into place for Corcoran and he nodded, impressed. "Yeah, I see that. Okay. But why did you tell us, then? Frankly, I'd have been just as happy not knowing."

"Now we come to the important part." The woman glanced

around the noisy room without seeming to. An outburst of drunken singing from near the bar forced the men to lean forward to hear her. "These games. Sport is an extremely important part of Dhelian culture. The Mediationals are viewed on every Dheil planet; and of these games, running is by far their favorite. It sums up their values for them: individuality, fair play, natural ability, courage—and *dalanai*. Tseil Laol Laia is a hero to every Dhelian alive. If he can be beaten by a human, our status in their eyes will undergo a quantum leap. From inferiors we can become equals, physically, at least. If in time we can impress them in other ways, artistic, scientific, perhaps someday we can reveal our discovery of the ship."

She searched their faces. Loud shouts came from the bar, then the sound of breaking glass. "And if we can do that, and be accepted as a subspecies of Dheils—"

"We inherit," said Matthews softly.

"That's right." She tapped her empty glass for emphasis. "We inherit—with our cousins—the leadership of the Galaxy."

"And if we lose in these games?" said the Masai, speaking for the first time.

"We will remain as we are. A backwater." She stared at him. "A possibility, i-Zalai, that the PanAfrican government would deplore—would it not?"

But the Masai had gathered his cloak of silence about him again, and only stared back at her as the drunken singing welled up again around them in the dark.

One, Two, Three, Four.

One, Two, Three, Four.

On his back on the prickly short grass of Olympia, studying the hard metallic sky. His left leg doubled under him, Ayid forced his knee down again and again, loosening and stretching the groin and upper thigh. Forty reps, till all pain was gone and the action smooth as warm oiled metal. Then the other leg, a little more carefully because of the odd feeling in the knee.

One, Two, Three, Four.

He bounced to his feet and sprang up and down, feeling the good tautness in his thin ankles and long knitted calves at the limit of their stretch. A fine sheen of sweat gleamed on his dark skin where neck and wrists and feet emerged from the gray warmup suit. "Squats now," said Po-xiang, who was holding the workout clipboard. Ayid began jackknifing to the ground and up again rapidly. "Slow down," said the trainer. "These are stretches, not calisthenics. Take them slow and concentrate on the muscles. Feel the blood flowing to them. Feel them warm in your mind."

"How's he look, Wang?"

Ayid went on with the stretch, not wanting to meet his coach's eyes. He still felt guilty from the day before and was resolved to redeem himself today.

"Good, Jerry. He took five thousand calories last night and a balanced two thousand this morning."

"Tests?"

"Half an hour ago. CPK back to normal. Urine protein a little elevated but within normal limits. BUN low normal, electrolytes all in balance. Sympathetics: epinephrine high end, norepinephrine ditto, ACTH and A-steroids normal. Kirlian is hot and red."

"I'm concerned about sugar."

"One-thirty-five."

"Good. Think we need to worry about water?"

"I don't think so, not over thirteen and a half kilometers," said Po-xiang. "He's carrying 20% over. At this air temperature that should leave him at only minus five at the finish." He flipped sheets on the clipboard and held out a computer-generated table. Corcoran took it, traced a curve with his finger. He grunted and handed the clipboard back and looked down at Ayid.

"Hafouz," he said.

"Yes, sir?"

"Don't stop—I want you limber as a hot snake. Hafouz, I'm satisfied with your physical condition. We've got six specialists monitoring you here and more back in Colorado. They all tell me that you're in the best shape, physically, that you can be without danger. But I'm worried about something else."

"High kicks," murmured Po-xiang. Ayid straightened up and began swinging his long legs skyward.

"I'm talking about your mind," said Corcoran. "Your will. Your mental preparation for this race. Are you determined to win this one, Ayid? Or is there some reservation I should know about?"

"I'm . . . I am determined to win, yes, sir," said Ayid.

"Then why did you refuse the supplement this morning?"

"Coach . . . I do want to win. But the M'zab . . . my people believe that Allah abhors all forms of intoxication. Those drugs you wish me to use . . . the Malikite school of rabbins has interpreted the Qu'uran to mean—"

"Excuse me," said the trainer. "I'm going in. Ayid, forty minutes till the start. Jog a lap if you want, but be in the ready room at the twenty-minute call." He walked away, leaving Ayid and Corcoran alone near the center of the field.

Corcoran looked around them at the stands. Already they were almost full. "I've heard you say that before," he said quietly. "I respect your beliefs, kid, but these are *not* the sort of drugs that make you high, as your elders seem to think. Not the ones that were in this morning's supplement. And you already know that *any* drug, any supplement, is legal under Mediational rules, since it's impossible to distinguish unfair advantage among sixty races."

"Do the Dhelians use these 'supplements,' coach?"

"Oh, probably not," said Corcoran. "They're such purists about their running sports they've lost sight of the main thing—to win. Damn it, kid, can't you see it's stupid not to take advantage of any loophole when the stakes are so big?"

"Stakes, sir?"

"Ah—yeah. What I mean is, Earth has spent millions to train you and get you here. Now, it's your right to refuse something you think unsafe. But don't you see that you owe Terra a duty . . . to take advantage of anything, *anything*, that could make the difference between winning and losing? That's the realistic attitude to take."

Ayid stared at his bare feet. He felt torn in two. He could see Corcoran's point, and he did, he felt, sincerely desire to win. Why wouldn't he? But to take such things . . . "I'm not sure, sir," he said miserably. "I don't like to . . . take advantage. . . ."

Corcoran glared, then shook his head. "I just don't get you, Hafouz. Any American kid would understand in a second. Well." He glanced at his watch. "Take a lap. Meeting in the ready room in ten minutes."

When the coach left Ayid stared at the ground for several seconds, then remembered the time and looked upward. The sun, little larger than a star but intensely blue-bright, was, he estimated, almost at its peak. To try to coordinate the five daily prayers with his home would have been impossible, so he had simply observed the rise and climb and set of this strange sun and prayed in accordance with it. Allah, after all, was everywhere. He knelt and turned his face to the east.

A few minutes later he rose, jogged two laps, and swung easily off the track as the twenty-minute call came over the loudspeakers. Jogging in to the ready room, he passed Aia Maior Laia, the Dheil who'd come in second the day before. Before he could think, he raised his hand to him in a casual runner's wave. The Dheil, nude as usual, smiled slightly and flipped his wrist in return. Ayid, embarrassed, ran by him. *Should I have done that?* he wondered.

He felt something different as he opened the door to the Earth team's ready room. Southren and Kwarafa were already there, working easily on two toning machines, sweat showing dark at the waists and armpits of their warmup suits. Corcoran and the other coaches, whom Ayid knew slightly, looked up from around a table. Po-xiang, face expressionless, nodded to him from his place at the trainer's desk. "Good, you're here," said Corcoran, not unkindly. "How do you feel, kid?"

And suddenly Ayid felt wonderful. A current of energy surged up from his lungs, a buoyant feeling that made him want to jump up to touch the ceiling. "I feel very good," he said, grinning widely.

"On to the toner, then. It's set for thirty per cent, just enough to keep you warm."

Ayid fitted himself into the toner, a spidery framework of tubular struts, stirrups, small servos. Po-xiang checked the straps and set it to gently flexing and kneading his legs, arms, and lower body as he pedaled against moderate opposition.

Why do I feel so good? he wondered. The lightness and joy increased from second to second. It felt like a taste of the Paradise the prophet promised, a taste such as he occasionally had on the track, an unexpected and omnipotent joy amid weary kilometers. But it had never happened before off the track. His nervousness was dissolving, drifting away as he gulped in great draughts of the warm air of the ready room.

"All right, listen up," Corcoran began. "After Run One we're trailing by four points. Not so much that we can't regain it in this race and go on to win.

"Terry, Ayid—this is your race. Especially yours, Southren. The 5000-standard is only three and a half kilometers longer than the 10,000-meter you've both run in the Olympics on Earth. Now remember, we want you both in front early. I think we found out yesterday that we can't count on retrieving a lead when we've got Maior or Tseil Laol in front of us."

Ayid was nodding, bobbing his head as the toner began to buck, loosening his torso and diaphragm. He felt silly and almost broke out laughing.

"To help you with your pacing, we'll be giving you individual times over the coach-runner circuits. On this track 5000-standards is ten complete laps. Let's aim for under 3 minutes 36 seconds per lap. It'll be tough, but you're the best old Terra's got."

"Too right," said Matthews, thumping the table. The Masai said nothing.

"Maintaining three-thirty-six a lap would give you a course time of about thirty-six minutes. We've checked Dhelian records and that's a damned good time. Neither Tseil Laol nor Aia Maior has done that well, although Laol has come close. Maybe you can't either. But it would be nice if you did—open with not only a victory, but a new record.

"So." Corcoran stared at the three runners. "You've all tested out

4.0, you're tanked up with water, sugars, your chemistry's been checked, and you've all had supplements—except, of course, Hafouz." He looked at Ayid questioningly.

"No, thank you, sir. I feel . . . wonderful! . . . even without it."

"Right." A picture flashed silently on the holo monitor near the ceiling. "There's the call. Let's get out there . . . and win!" The runners tumbled from the toners and jostled for the door. Corcoran exhaled and looked after them.

So much depends on them, he thought. So much. Would it help them to know what a victory could mean?

But it was not up to him to tell them. He got up. "Okay," he said to Matthews and the inscrutable PanAfric. "Let's get on up to the remotes. Wang—let's get this room aired out before some dummy tries to smoke and blows his face off."

At least we got some O_2 into him, Corcoran was thinking as he rode the lifter to the top of the stands. *That may help. Though it would help a lot more if he were free of all that ancient brainwash.* Superstitions and rituals the modern PanArabs had left behind almost a century before. . . .

He walked past the news and holo people into the suddenly quieter air of the soundproofed room where coaches, officials, and the accredited holo commentators overlooked the track from two hundred meters up. He stopped by the window, looking down the hill. To his right and below a blanket of multicolored humanity was spread across the hills. To his left the Dheils were seated, less colorful than the Terrans since unclothed, but equally numerous. Above them all the sun, blue and hot, glared down. Again today there was not a cloud in the sky. Corcoran remembered reading somewhere that Olympia had been a designed planet, that it had been moved to this star from a system doomed by its own sun's instability. Could clouds, he wondered idly, have been left out of the Dhelians' grand design?

He walked quickly to his own seat, to his own console, and sat down. The clocks, the lap computer, the telemetry, the one-way radio linking him to Hafouz, all were already on. Corcoran taped the mike to his throat and subvocalized as he caught sight of Ayid's thin figure far below.

"Hey, kid. Nod if you can hear me."

At the same time he pressed a switch and a holo cube leaped on, the camera locking automatically on Hafouz. His image, magnified twenty times, turned to look upwards, and nodded slightly.

"Admirably organized, Mr. Corcoran."

Corcoran turned at the interruption, then smiled and rose, extending a hand. "Denda Lai Anyo. Nice to see you. Ready to race?"

"You make me wonder." The Dhelian, taller and thinner than Corcoran, had a gentle lined face and streaks of silver in his flowing gold hair. He was, Corcoran knew, well over two hundred years old and had been as famous a runner as Tseil Laol in his youth. Now, like Corcoran, he was a coach. Laol's coach. The Dheil nodded at the panels in front of the American. "So much mechanism. Like piloting a spaceship, is it not?"

Corcoran kept his smile fixed, though the Dhelian's words touched a hidden spring of resentment in him. *They have to keep laughing at us,* he thought. *Well, after these games we'll be laughing too. Because we poor benighted mechanically-minded human beings with the anachronisms between our legs are going to win.* But aloud all he said was, "I wouldn't know. I don't suppose you use it."

"No. We see sport differently than your culture does, I think. Though in many other ways we may be more alike than we think at present."

"Could be," said Corcoran. *What is he getting at? Or is this just the polite pre-race conversation it appears to be?*

"Don't you feel that all this technique, this planning, takes away the . . . exhilaration?"

"Well, we're here to win," said Corcoran, still smiling. "We're not here for the 'exhilaration'."

"I see."

"And if you'll excuse me, the race is about to start."

"I understand," said the old Dheil, smiling too, but a bit sadly. "I hope that your methods result in the success you desire."

"Good luck to you too, sir." Corcoran shook hands again and then turned back to the panel angrily. *The patronizing old bastard,* he thought, and picked up the earphones to hear the holo network commentary.

"Hello from the UBC Sports Network. It's 14:28:11 Greenwich Mean Time back on Earth, and at this moment, here on Olympia, you're watching the runners prepare for the second race of the Mediational running events. A five thousand standard race—that's 13,500 meters. Favored in this event are the Dhelians, on their track, their distance, and with the psychological advantage of a four-point lead. Our UBC sportscomp has given us a prediction of how the race will go, based on the physiques and times of the six runners—"

The sportscomp began speaking in its annoyingly hyped-up manner (holo people always referred to it, for some obscure reason, as a 'cozelle'), but Corcoran's mind tuned it out as he watched the six runners take their marks. Like all the Dhelian events the 5000-standard started on the long straight of the infinity-shaped track and the first turn would be clockwise. Corcoran was too far away to see the results of the choice-ritual but smiled as he saw Ayid given the right hand lane for the start. That would put him on the inside for the first turn, making it necessary for anyone wanting to grab the lead to pass him on the outside. A small advantage . . . but races were often won with small advantages. The human commentator was speaking again and Corcoran heard:

". . . A nice turn of luck at the start favors Hafouz of Earth, but later things will even out. A lot can happen in thirteen thousand meters, a race that will take about thirty-six minutes to run. The weather today is fine, clear, and cloudless. Temperature is a crisp but comfortable 10.5°, with perhaps five kph of wind across the track. It's a fine day for running.

"The athletes are digging in. That white beam you see a few

centimeters in front of them is the start beam. When it goes off a snapping sound is heard and the race begins. Our Dhelian sources say that at one time, long ago, that was a high-power laser beam. Tended to discourage false starts . . . when all the runners have passed it, it goes on again and becomes a lap marker, changing color each time until the last, when it's a deep pulsating ruby."

"Ready, kid? Get that ass down, they haven't given 'set' yet. Breathe deep, stay ahead on oxygen. You'll need it." Gerald Corcoran's eyes swept the telemetry, transmitted from a network of microimplants in Hafouz's major muscles and arteries. They looked good, trembling at levels that except for pulse rate would be panic reaction in a normal human but that in a long distance runner meant that he was ready to efficiently convert a sizeable percentage of his body weight to kinetic energy. The thin Algerian was at the fine peak of conditioning, youth, nutrition, and physiological readiness.

Corcoran hoped that he wanted to win as much as his coach did.

"Set!"

Snap! The beam winked out, and Corcoran half-rose in his chair as the six runners lunged forward. Kwarafa was ahead in the first five strides, then seemed to remember that he had a long way to go this time and throttled back. Corcoran zoomed the camera. Hafouz was showing his teeth—probably had his jaw clenched, a waste of energy that could also tighten his neck and back in time.

"Relax, kid," Corcoran transmitted.

Ayid felt for the tension and found it in his neck and jaw. Running was very easy, and he felt good. The first turn was ahead, and he went into it smoothly. Someone was at his left but he increased his speed enough to discourage them and they fell into step behind him. There was no one in front of him, and he felt joy and at the same time caution for there was a long way to run yet and much yet to happen.

The off-white beam winked as six bodies occulted it; second lap. Corcoran formed words in his throat as he stared at the clock.

"Three forty-one, kid. A little slow but a good first lap." He checked the screen. *"You're leading Laol by two steps. Southren, Maior, and Sene Dior are in a cluster on his tail. Kwarafa's hanging back, looks like he'll be happy just to finish. Hold that pace, pick it up if you feel comfortable."*

Comfortable . . . Corcoran bit at his lip as he watched the tiny figures rounding the turn again on the far side of the valley, passing in front of the Dhelian stands. His own gut was tight and he felt his palms sweating as they rested against the cool surface of the panel. Comfortable.

By now, he knew the first fresh burst had gone and Ayid and the others were running through the point where the body realizes what is happening and tries to rebel. He had known some of his runners to say that this and not the finish was the hardest part of a race, or at any rate the point where they felt closest to quitting, to jogging to a stop and saying shove it and walking off the track and out of running forever.

Thinking about it took him back to his own running days at USC. Running in the conditioned air under the big dome at Brown Field. Class of 2058. Yes, that had been a long time ago. Before the Chircurgi had come and then the Dhelians; before things had changed so much he sometimes felt out of place on Earth. His own AAU championship, then the try at the Olympics in '60 . . . in Beijing they had been, that year . . . how he had wanted to win. . . .

Strange, he thought, *how a loss can shape your entire life.* Before Beijing he'd expected to follow his parents into government service. Running had been only a game. But with the sense of his own decline had come a fierce determination. If he could not win himself then Gerald Corcoran would build winners. He had studied and worked single-mindedly to produce Klepner; then Abell, the 'Black Streak' from Richmond, who had astounded the pre-Contact world with an 8.9 hundred-meter dash, a record that still stood . . . probably always would, now that Terran sports were all switching to the Dhelian distances and rules.

Corcoran stared down at the track, not quite seeing it. With Contact, and with the invitation to compete in the Mediationals, he had been set. Corcoran, the UN had reasoned, had produced winners for the U.S. He would produce them still—but now, for Earth.

This, he knew, would be his last effort. The lancing pain that had stopped him suddenly three hundred yards from the finish line in Beijing came often now in the night when he lay sweating quietly. Nothing they could do, though some talked vaguely of a transplant. (When they saw his face they stopped. Gerald Corcoran Senior had died, blue, swollen, with a borrowed heart ticking like a bomb inside his stapled chest). No, this was his last contest, his last and his biggest. Corcoran, Ayid, Terra *had* to win.

Gerald Corcoran stared down at the track, eyes dilated, breathing fast and shallow.

They had to win.

"Third lap now—the beam is yellow. Unofficial elapsed time for the first fifteen hundred standards is ten minutes fifty-three point three seconds. Seven laps to go. Rounding the far turn at this moment, Hafouz of Terra leads, Aia Maior moved up to second not far behind and slowly gaining right now. Dhelia's best, the legendary Tseil Laol Laia, is running smoothly in a dead heat for third with Terry Southren. The two sprinters, Sene Dior and Kebe Kwarafa, are dropping back. Hard for them to keep up this pace lap after lap.

"And it will keep getting harder.

"You're watching the second race of the Mediational Games Olympia, brought to you by the UPC Sports Network, holo at its best, Human and Dhelians locked in a grueling five thousand standard run.

"By special arrangement we have the Dhelian, ah, chairperson for the team here, and would like to welcome him to UBC holo. Is it—Denda Lai Anyo, sir?"

"Denda Lai, or Lai, will do. The last name is an honorary, descriptive term applied to individuals after they've achieved some success. Such as Tseil Laol; the last element, 'Laia,' means simply 'the runner.' "

"I see. I was about to ask you about, ah, him?"

"To spare you difficulty, 'him' will do."

"Yes. Well, Laol *is* a fine runner, as we can see down on the track right now."

(CLOSE UP: Laol striding, head high, blue light glistening from sweat-wet planes of face)

"How old is he? Where is he from? Can you fill us in on some of his background, sir?"

(INSERT: databoard: fourth lap, elapsed time for leading runner 14:32:51)

(CUT TO: head of D.L., lit from left to emphasize age.

"I'll be happy to tell you about him, but some of the answers may not translate too well; there are many things for which your languages have no words as yet. Laol is 1730 time-standards old, which I think is about 73 Terran years. Is that correct?" (turns to off-camera) "Seventy-seven, my aide informs me. He has been running in competition since he was seventeen."

"Standards?"

"No, of course not. Years."

"I see. The subject of Dhelian life-span is fascinating to us, but let's stay with Tseil Laol for the present. He's been running in events for sixty years, then? Fascinating. Is he a professional athlete?"

"Oh, no. We have no professional athletes."

"I see." A hint of anger in the interviewer's voice, but carefully masked. "Then what does he do?"

"He is a researcher," said Denda Lai.

"Researching . . . ?"

"Difficult to state in your terms. It's a field your science hasn't yet investigated. He studies certain aspects of movement—"

"Physics? We know quite a lot about motion." The dislike is now evident in the interviewer's voice. "Kinetics—"

"You misunderstand. It is biological movement, and its relation to what you call the 'mind.' We study certain lower races—"

"Such as humans?"

"No. I'm sorry. I meant species, not races. For example—"

"*Would* you call humans a lower race, sir?"

"I'm afraid you are deliberately misinterpreting my words. I see no reason to prolong this interview."

At the seventh lap Ayid heard a pounding behind him and to his right, and a moment later Tseil Laol was beside him and then had slipped into position just ahead as they entered the turn. It was quickly and neatly done, and Ayid had not had time to react.

"*That lap was slow, kid. Three forty-four. He's not kicking, he's just keeping up the pace. Stay on his heels for now.*"

The tinny voice in his ear brought Corcoran and the rest of the world back with it. Three minutes forty-four seconds! He had thought he was running strong. Now he realized that he had slowed and that was how Laol had passed him. He lifted his head a fraction, feeling the wind carry cold sweat past his eyes, and ran harder, staying with the red-haired Dheil just ahead. It was always a little easier to follow; but later he would have to battle again for the lead.

His mind clicked from point to point in his body. Left foot going to sleep, as it always did near kilo nine. It would free up later. Knees and legs good, better than they had felt at the start. Tired, but good; hours on the toner at 100% were paying off. Back loose, gut fine now that he was into the race, shoulders and jaw too tight again. He relaxed them and reached out, pumping his arms, transmitting more of the sway of them with each stride to his shoulders to loosen them. This picked his pace up too, and he began to close on Laol, now three strides ahead.

Lungs, good so far; but the deep ache was well advanced. He felt his running headache beginning, but that he ignored. He was sweating well, and as yet there was no chafing of his privates or thighs. Toes OK.

But he was getting tired. Seven and a half. *That's about 1400 meters a lap, or over ten thousand already,* he told himself, calculating through the sound of the crowd and the pounding of feet and the harsh rasp of breath. *The last time I got, at the end of the sixth lap, was 21:56. That was for 6 x 500, no, 6 x 1400, eighty-four hundred*

*meters, okay. For each thousand meters I'm taking about 2 minutes,
36 seconds. . . . Is that right? Anyway it's way too slow.* No wonder
Laol had passed him. Before he could act the orange-red beam
whipped past him and he was into the eighth lap.

"*Better,*" Corcoran's voice crackled. "*Three thirty nine. This is the
lap to start to burn. Pull rods, Ayid! Let's pass this shmuck!*"

They moved into the turn. His lungs were hurting but he was
ready to move. He was going to move, now, around the Dhelian.
Now.

But he couldn't. At that last instant Maior had moved up, on his
outside. The two Dhelians had him boxed in. The three of them
swept along, fixed together as by invisible struts. Maior did not
move by him but stayed at his elbow, blocking any move to retake
the lead.

Was it deliberate? In the pain that rose in his head it was hard to
think.

The Terran stands were a maelstrom; people below were standing,
shouting, throwing things. A few left the lowest benches and ran on
to the field. "Boxed in! They're boxing him!" said Corcoran, gripping the panel. "Damn them! Ayid—"

But on the zoomed holo he saw it happen. Saw the way Ayid's
head turned to the side, just for a fraction of a second. The way his
eyes met Maior's. And the way the Dhelian, sheering a meter to the
outside, opened a gap for the Terran. If he could take it.

He did. Corcoran could hear even through the soundproofed
walls how the ugly sounds from the crowd changed suddenly to
cheering as the Algerian, arms flailing, moved slowly through the
gap and drew abreast of Tseil Laol. And how it turned to surprise as
Terry Southren, finding a burst of energy somewhere, moved up too
to pace Aia Maior, stride for stride, centimeters apart.

The straight again. They pounded down it, holding their positions through it and through the next turn and then they passed the
beam that flashed red and it was the

"Last lap! Laol and Hafouz are neck and neck for first. One step behind are Maior and Southren, with the two sprinters, Kwarafa and Dior, lagging far back; they've lost the pace, and now less than three hundred standards to go!" (CUT FROM: sportscaster to panning closeup of lead runners. Laol's face is calm, Ayid's flushed and fierce as they battle for the lead.) "And two hundred! Wait! *Southren is breaking loose!* This is his distance and it looks like he's been saving it up for a sprint right up to the beam! Will he try it on the turn—no—drops back—*here he comes!* The other runners can't match this—Laol has the inside on this turn—Southren going to the outside—that's Southren, Australia, 5000-meter world champion—into the last straight, the home stretch, *Southren's on Ayid and Maior and passing*—Kwarafa and Dior still falling back but grimly fighting for a fifth place—"

"Run, run, Ayid," murmured Corcoran. The transmitter was off; talk would only distract him now. He gripped the panel with white fingers. He could feel the pain coming but could not spare the time to reach for the injector he carried in his wallet. *One more race, I've got to see him through one more race.* "Run, run, run. Bring it home. Run, damn you, kid—"

"They're halfway down the straight   "

There was no pain. He had outrun it. It would catch up as soon as he crossed the beam but now he had no time for it. There was only himself and the track and another runner on either side. Someone was ahead. It didn't matter who. He was flying. It didn't matter even if he died afterward so long as he crossed that beam, flaring, pulsating ruby, that swept toward them as they ran locked together—

Corcoran stabbed the 'freeze' button and the image locked motionless in his cube.

"RESULTS, FIVE THOUSAND STANDARD RUN," said the announcing system, then paused. The crowd shifted, but was generally quiet, waiting. The speakers crackled twice as if someone had turned them on and then off again and then continued

"JUDGE'S CALL. FIRST PLACE: AIA MAIOR LAIA, WITH A TIME OF THIRTY-SIX MINUTES, SIXTEEN POINT OH TWO SECONDS. SECOND PLACE: TERRY SOUTHREN, THIRTY-

SIX MINUTES, SEVENTEEN POINT TWO FOUR SECONDS.
THIRD PLACE: A TIE, TSEIL LAOL LAIA AND AYID
HAFOUZ, WITH TIMES OF THIRTY-SIX MINUTES, NINE-
TEEN POINT FIVE FIVE SECONDS. FOURTH PLACE: KEBE
KWARAFA, THIRTY-SEVEN MINUTES TWO POINT THREE
SECONDS. FIFTH PLACE: SENE DIOR, THIRTY-SEVEN
MINUTES ELEVEN POINT NINE NINE SECONDS."

"You have just heard the results of the five thousand standard
race." The professionally excited tones of the UBC announcer
squirted out among the stars. "And the score between Dheils and
Earthmen is even.

"With one race—the longest—still to be run."

The quick night of Olympia had come, and with it, the end of his
day. Ayid, pleasantly rotund with the high-carbohydrate meal Po-
xiang had prepared, walked alone through the clicking night. Clicking, with the singing of thousands of . . . insects? . . . in the darkness
of the low, deserted hills. Above them, to the eastward, glowed the
reddish loom of the Port's lights. Ahead of him, over the track, a
single reddish-white ball hung burning in midair. Beyond it he
could see the windows of the small building where the Terran
athletes slept.

He stopped on the soft combed grass and looked upward, smell-
ing cinnamon. The stars were different, more crowded together
then they had been above Al Jarzhireh. The night looked, smelled,
even sounded different from a Terran night; and he was suddenly
homesick for the silent desert of home.

Standing there, he gradually became aware that he was being
watched. His eyes drifted slowly down from the stars and he found
himself looking at a patch of darkness at the side of the trail. There,
the strange Olympian insects were silent.

"Who is there?"

"Ayid?" A familiar voice, but one he did not immediately recognize.

"Yes. Who is that?"

Against the dark of the hills he could now make out, dimly, a human figure. It grew larger. Ayid wondered if there was a reason for his sudden desire to run. But he was a M'zab. . . .

"'*Issalaamu alleichum*," said the shadow.

"Peace be upon you, the mercy of Allah, and his blessings," replied Ayid automatically in Arabic. His eyes widened as the dark suddenly resolved itself into the stocky figure of the PanAfrican sprinter. "Kebe. What are you doing out in the dark?"

"A late meal. And you?"

"The same."

Kwarafa extended a leg gingerly, then high-kicked, wincing. "Sore. I can't take these long races."

"An even longer one the day after tomorrow. Thank Allah they gave us a rest day."

"True. Ayid . . . can we talk together, you and I?"

"Talk? Well . . . sure. Let's go on back to the—"

"No. Not in the apartments. Nor the ready room. You and I, we are Africans, are we not? Let's sit here, on the grass. Under the sky."

Africans? Ayid glanced at the other's face, hidden by the night. True, they were both from the same continent . . . but he had not known the PanAfric was a Believer. This far from home that had to make a difference. "All right," he said.

They squatted in the cool grass under the stars. A moment passed. "What was it you wished to say?" said Ayid.

He heard the scratch of Kwarafa's finger in the dust. "Ayid. Brother. It is hard for me to say the thing that is in my heart."

His Arabic is good, thought Ayid. Classic, the kind the wandering marabouts took into West Africa long ago. "If it is a hard thing, says my tribe, it is best said quickly. Then it is out for all to see and judge of its rightness."

"But all may not see the truth. Nor *can* see it."

"What is this truth that demands such delicacy in its revelation?" Beyond his growing curiosity Ayid also discovered a simple pleasure just in speaking Arabic again. "Tell me of this truth, Kebe."

"That you must not win on the day after tomorrow. There, it is out, as short and quickly as you suggested."

Ayid felt unreal. The darkness hid the African's face from him but not his tone and from this he could tell that the other was not joking.

"Yes, that is short and direct. But I do not understand it. Why must I not win?"

"For the good of our people."

"The PanAfricans?"

"All Humans."

"I do not like this talk," said Ayid.

"Sit, brother, please. I will explain. I know how much I am asking; I too am a runner, though not as good as you. But sit quietly and listen and I will explain."

"Do so, then."

"First," Kwarafa stated, "you must not win because to do so would cause the *djinn* to become angry."

"*Djinn?*"

"Devils. You must see them so too. Don't you?"

'I don't think they are devils. The Dheils? They are not like us but once one is over that one sees that they are not *djinn*. And why should they become angry?"

"Because they are proud. To lose to us here in their own sport, the first time we meet with them, would be intolerable."

"I don't believe that. But continue."

"Second, you must not win because it would make Humans feel that they are the equals of Dheils."

"Why would that be bad? They feel inferior now."

"Yes. And they should continue to feel that way."

"You surprise me," said Ayid. "You think that humans are inferior to—"

"No, no," said Kwarafa, sounding horrified. "I don't think so. We are different, yes, but just as good."

"Then I do not understand why it should be bad for us to feel that way."

"Because of the third reason. This you *must* understand because it is the most important. *You must not win because Earth must not join the Mediation.*"

Surprised before, Ayid was speechless now. Not join the Mediation! Not join that loose but glorious confederation of star-traveling races? Not join the godlike Dheils, the tricky but clever Chircurgi, the even more exotic races that Terrans had so far only heard of? "Why not?" he said, amazed.

The African scratched in the dirt again. "I had hoped that I would not have to explain to *you*," he murmured. "Your people, too, saw the whites come two centuries ago. With their guns and religions and then their roads and machines and medicines and politics. And how long did it take your people to regain themselves?"

"It's not the same. The Dhelians are not colonialists."

"Not quite. They don't want our land. But that's not what we PanAfrics fear, Ayid.

"You see, Earth's civilization was at a crossroads. In another century we would have reached the stars ourselves, without the Chircurgi. Instead, star travel was given to us—no, worse, *bartered* to us, a cheap set of beads for our gold and ivory. Do you not see how they regard us as savages?"

"That was not the fault of the Dheils."

"Have they acted to correct the wrong? No. So they share it. And now worse things are happening. You've been insulated in your training, insulated by the Americans. But we PanAfrics see, we know what to look for. The Dheils are trying to give us new sciences, new technologies, whole new philosophies and social systems so far in advance of ours that they are like magic, like holo to a savage. We don't understand how they work, and we can't adapt to them.

"The consequence? Culture shock. A loss of faith in ourselves. Do you know what the suicide rate among scientists is now? Among priests and psychologists? It's frightening, Ayid. Before the knowledge of the Dheils our greatest minds are like medicine men before a locomotive. And if we join the Mediation, open ourselves to trade and visitation, it will be even worse—then it will be every human who is bewildered, lost, and doomed to live with his own inferiority before the gods from the stars. Earth is in great danger, Ayid, and her only defense is to *shut the Mediation out*."

Ayid was silent.

"So do you see why you must lose, brother? If enough resentment exists, enough hate, the people will vote no to joining the Mediation. Your loss—your sacrifice—can help that happen."

"Is this your feeling, Kebe, or—"

"It's my government's feeling, but it's mine too. Africa has been through all of this before. Now we wish to mold our own lives for a time. Is that so unreasonable?" Kwarafa waited for a moment and then leaned forward to place a broad, surprisingly warm hand on Ayid's shoulder. "You need time to think. All right. But, brother, promise one thing—that you will consider well my words."

"I will do that."

"Good."

The 'grass' rustled and when Ayid looked up the African was gone. He squatted there, thinking, for perhaps half an hour as the insect drone faded into the final silence of the deep night, and then he rose to his feet and jogged slowly back to the apartments, and to his bed.

"Get the hopping hell off that track," said Corcoran.

"Coach, I am—"

"I don't give a rat's ass what you're doing. Get off that track. I said no workout today."

"I—"

"No workout." The American whirled and started away.

"Can't I just jog, sir?" Ayid called after him. Corcoran turned and glared, and then his face slowly relaxed into a half-smile.

"Okay. A little, no more than half an hour at 25%. But you've got to be fresh for tomorrow." A thought occurred to him and he motioned Ayid closer. "By the way—there are some rumors floating around concerning this last race tomorrow. Someone heard from someone else—that sort of thing. Have you heard anything?"

"Just what you told me, sir, that it's a thirty-mile course over rough country. What kind of rumors?"

"Well, don't waste time worrying about it—but supposedly there's more to the last event than an eighteen-thousand-standard cross-country run."

"What else could there be, coach?"

"That's the problem—I don't know, and can't find out. I called the judging staff, and all they'll say is that they can't discuss the final race in advance. That seems to be kosher; I looked it up in the rule book they passed out; but the nasty thing is that most of the judges for this event are Chircurgi, since they're non-runners and presumably neutral. But I just don't trust those shifty bastards."

"No," said Ayid.

"Well—jog if you want. Stop by the ready room when you're done."

"Yes, sir."

I wish they'd let us see the course, Corcoran was thinking as he watched Hafouz jog away. *But what the hell—we know the distance, and I'll be giving him times and monitoring him all the way. He'll do okay.* He was filled with a sudden cheerfulness, a presentiment of victory. Whistling, he headed for the coaches' dining room, pancakes, hamburger, and coffee on his mind.

Ayid looked over his shoulder as his coach walked away. He had been tempted to confide in Corcoran, to talk about Kwarafa's request . . . but he could not. Not to the American, with his blind need for victory at any price, his overbearing manner, the ready profanity that grated on a Believer's ears. A Kharidjite guarded his tongue, for Allah recorded every word. . . .

The thought of Allah brought the memory of a pair of eyes to him as he jogged slowly around the empty track. A pair of immense, calm, understanding eyes. Perhaps he could talk to the Dheil. Not with complete openness; but still, to talk would be good.

Where could he find Tseil Laol this time of day?

That's easy, he thought. He'll be readying himself for tomorrow's race. Easily, very easily, for everything must be saved and no bit of energy wasted. Forty-eight kilometers! There was no need of anything else. Maybe Corcoran's story about the rumors was only the American's way of keeping him nervous. He rounded another turn, and saw that his guess about Tseil Laol had been right. The tawny-haired Dheil was stretched out by the track, flexing his limbs in the same exercises the Terrans used. A moment later he rose and began swinging easily along the track, lifting his knees high and pumping his arms. Ayid did not wish to startle him, so he called as he came up from behind. "Tseil Laol!"

The Dheil turned his head, and once again Ayid was struck by the immensity of the golden eyes that seemed to see more than one wanted to reveal. "Ayid. Greetings. Come on up and run with me."

Ayid moved up. They ran easily together, floating, stretching their legs. Around them spread the bare hills, empty stands, deserted buildings, and the blue sun glared down. *Now that I'm with him, what do I ask him?* Ayid thought. He glanced sideways at the Dheil.

"You ran well yesterday, Ayid," said Tseil Laol.

"Ah . . . thank you. You ran well, too." They entered the straight leading past the empty Terran stands and Ayid searched nervously for Corcoran. He wasn't in sight.

"It is a fine day for running. Just for pleasure," said the Dheil.

"Yes," said Ayid miserably. He knew now that it had been a mistake to think that he could talk with the Dheil. The gulf was too great.

"You wished to ask me something?"

"What?"

"That is why you came after me. Isn't it?"

"Ah—"

"It's all right. You are doing nothing wrong. It was Earth's idea to keep us separated, even eating and sleeping apart, you know. Not ours."

"I didn't know that," said Ayid.

"You thought we Dheils wanted that? That we wanted even the audiences to be in separate stands? Of course not. The races of the Mediation mix at pleasure, subject to atmosphere and gravity preferences. These games are meant to promote friendship, not segregation and mistrust."

"Then why did you agree to it?"

"This is your race's first appearance among us. You are uncomfortable with other species. In time you will become more civilized, but for now we can afford to be accommodating."

In time you will become more civilized. Ayid heard Kwarafa's

words inside his head: *Do you see how they regard us as savages?*
"How do your people see us?" he blurted out.

The wide golden eyes, looking amused, swung to examine him,
then moved back to the track. "Shall we pick up the pace
a bit?"

"Why not?" said Ayid, recklessly. They moved faster, still together. He noted that the Dheil's strides were the same length as
his and that they were moving in step, like soldiers double-timing.

"How do we see Humans? As a youthful race." Laol breathed for a
few strides, then resumed, "One that has developed well in isolation, but which still has much immaturity. It was very unfortunate
that you met the Chircurgi first. That has complicated the whole
business."

"What business?"

"Of getting you into the Mediation. And then of helping you
develop with as little permanent damage as possible."

Youthful. Immature. *Well, perhaps they have good reason for
calling us that,* thought Ayid. *Though we have the wisdom of the
Prophet to guide us.* That brought another question to his mind and
he said, "Do you have a religion? A prophet?"

"We've had several hundred of both," said Laol, though without
sarcasm or mockery.

"How old are the Dheils?"

"That's hard to say. Our recorded history goes back about six
million Earth years. But even when those records began we had a
star drive—a clumsy, undependable kind; many ships were lost—
and we had long forgotten our home planet. Most think we came
from somewhere in Quadrant Two, perhaps from a now-vanished
planet called Dhela or Dhelia."

"Quadrant Two?"

"The Galaxy is shaped like a disc—that you know. We divide it
into quadrants, radioids, distants, and longitudes in order to navi-
gate." Laol stopped to breathe for a few meters, then resumed,
"Quadrant Two is across the galactic center from Earth."

"I don't understand," said Ayid

"That's all right. You will learn, and as you live longer you will learn how to learn more. When your eldest men have lived as long as the oldest Dheil you will be as wise as we. But that will take you many centuries."

Ayid sensed himself at the hard part. He decided to chance it; so far, the Dheil had seemed to hold nothing back. "Many centuries. But tell me, Tseil Laol, will there not be great suffering before we become like you?"

"Like us? Humans won't become like us. You'll become more than you are, but not like us. Unless, as some think, all races will someday outgrow the need for bodies. But to answer you, yes, there will be much suffering with change. Is it worth it? That has to be your people's decision when they vote whether or not to join us."

Ayid could think of nothing to say and so they ran on side by side for awhile.

"*Ayid.*" It was Corcoran, in his head. "*Where are you? Report in to me at the ready room.*"

"It's time for me to stop," he said to Laol. "It was good to run with you."

"And to talk. I've a little farther to run. See you tomorrow."

Ayid looked after him. The Dheil's figure grew slowly smaller, graceful, thin in the blue-white sun, until the Terran turned away.

"Ah, there you are, kid. Didn't go too far, did you?"

"Just a couple of laps, sir."

"Good. Eat a heavy lunch today." Corcoran leaned against the door of the ready room, where they were, for the moment, alone. "But wait a sec; they'll hold your meal. I want to talk about tomorrow."

Ayid nodded.

"Sit down." The American pushed the doors closed and looked at Ayid with an odd expression, half fond, half concerned. "It seems like I'm always asking this question, I know—but tell me again that you *do* want to win tomorrow."

Hide the confusion, Ayid thought. "Yes, sir, I do. Sure."

"I want to be sure. Because I'm going to ask you a favor."

Corcoran hesitated, then reached into a pocket and brought out a flat plastic package. He tore it open and shook out a small tubular capsule. He held it up. "I'm going to ask you to take this with you."

"Take it with me?"

"That's all."

"What is it?"

"Cocaine."

Ayid knew what that was. He had seen it sold furtively in the souks of the coastal cities, though he would never use it himself— nor would any M'zab. "Why? I don't wish pleasure."

"It's not for pleasure, kid. It's for running."

"I don't understand."

"Then listen. Coke is a pain killer. It's more: it's a stimulant. Incan messengers used it centuries ago to banish fatigue when they ran. Now, you've run in marathons before."

"Yes." Images of the prestigious Boston Marathon, which he had won the year before, twenty-six miles in an hour and forty-seven minutes, rose in his mind; time had blunted the memory, but he still remembered the agony of the finish. "They are very painful."

"Right. To run thirty miles, now—you can't do that unaided."

"The Dhelians do."

"That's beside the point, Ayid. Look. You *have* to win tomorrow. And this could be just the thing to get you the last klick to win. And best of all, it's legal."

Have to, have to, Ayid was thinking. This was the price of being first, the end of the road he had begun to run long ago along the camel trails of Algeria. To take orders, to be treated like a tool by Kwarafa, by Corcoran, to *have to.* His head was lowered but something in him was beginning to revolt at last.

"Why do I have to?"

Corcoran stared at him. There was a moment of absolute silence as they stared at each other; then the older man's eyes slid aside. "All right," he said. "I suppose you have a right to know. So I'll tell you.

"Ayid—we are Dhelians."

At first he did not understand. Corcoran, glancing nervously at the door, explained about the discovery of the old ship, the subsequent history of Man as he diverged from the parent stock. "No one knows this yet, Ayid. Not the public, not the other runners, and especially not the Dhelians. And they must not be told. You know why?"

He thought for a moment, then had it. "To let us earn their respect first. So that they see us as equals, and not as . . ."

"Degenerates."

"Thank you." He had known the word in Arabic but not in English. "Thank you for telling me this, coach."

"Yeah. Well, keep it to yourself, kid."

"I will."

"Then, I guess—you can go on to lunch." He stepped away from the door, then paused. "Oh, yeah. The coke. I'll give it to you tomorrow. I've got a skin patch the injector will fit under."

"I can't take it."

Corcoran frowned. "Now wait. I just explained why you had to."

"No, sir. You explained why I had to win. Not why I had to take a drug to do it."

"But drugs are legal."

"They are legal by Mediational rules. But I am a Believer."

"Oh, Chr—sorry. Or whatever. Look, Hafouz, don't you think all that's a little irrelevant here? Do you have any idea how far we are from Mecca?"

"It does not matter how far we are from Mecca. Drunkenness is still forbidden. Drugs that steal the reason are still forbidden. To purchase a victory at that price is a sin. And for a M'zab sin is sin in Mecca or on Olympia. Sir."

Corcoran stared at the thin boy. He looked on the ragged edge of that insane self-control of his. *An American*, he said to himself again, *would understand. A Russian would understand. It's winning that counts, not abiding by some inane rules a bunch of senile old men in smelly robes made up a thousand years ago.*

"I don't understand you, Hafouz," he said.

"I do not understand myself," said the boy gravely. "That is why I live by the rules of my people."

"Go eat your lunch," said Corcoran. When the boy was gone he looked down at the object in his hand. *He'll take it*, he thought. *I'll find some way to make him take it. And he'll win.*

Then he thought of a way.

"Hello, Terry, Kebe," said Ayid, pulling out a chair to sit down. "Well, this is the day." The African smiled up at him; the Australian, engaged in his breakfast and looking glum, barely nodded.

Ayid looked out the window of the team dining room as he waited for his food. It was very early; and the sun, looking oddly yellow, had just cleared the rim of hills. Mecca . . . who knew where it lay? But one could face the sun. And he had, just before breakfast, kneeling on his prayer rug on the sparkling grass.

Po-xiang brought in two trays and left without speaking. Ayid dug in heartily; the race would not begin till early afternoon, and he was hungry. There was rice, a small cut of lamb, much fresh bread, all the coffee he liked, rich, thick, and powerful; orange juice; the flat date cakes he loved, a strange Chinese fish cake that the trainer had introduced him to. He had to force himself, toward the end, to stuff down the last few morsels on the second tray, but he knew that every calorie had been calculated in advance and he had to eat it all. Southren watched him unsmilingly over a half-eaten plate of kippers, waffles, oatmeal, and marmalade. "You have a good appetite," he said, when Ayid finally wiped his fingers with a napkin and settled back in his chair.

"You should eat, too, Terry. We'll need it all to run thirty miles."

"I've never run that far."

"Neither have I."

Kwarafa had already finished. "Listen to him," he said to Southren. "Eat it all."

Southren stared at Kwarafa. "You planning to run today?"

"Of course. Though I'm a sprinter, and I'll take it very slow—"

"You seem to take all the races very slow."

Ayid glanced at Kwarafa. Anger clouded the African's face, but he said levelly, "I haven't done so well, no."

Southren stared at him for a moment more, then looked at Ayid.

"I wish to bloody hell I knew what was going on around here," he said. "Something smells."

"I'm . . . not sure myself," said Ayid. He looked after Southren as the Australian left. "He seems angry."

Kwarafa shrugged. "Perhaps he's afraid of what will happen today. I've heard there may be something different about this event." He leaned forward and his dark eyes bored into Ayid. "You've thought about our conversation?" he said in Arabic.

"Yes."

"You'll do as we suggest?"

"I don't know. Other . . . something else has come to my attention. It may be best that I win, Kebe, for other reasons than those you know."

"But perhaps I do know. You mean the Dhelians—and us. Yes, the PanAfrican government knows about that. My coach told me."

Ayid nodded, relieved. Now there would be no more uncertainty. "Then you understand," he said.

"I understand that it's a lie," said Kwarafa. "There is no ship. We are not descended from Dhelians. It is merely propaganda, a trick to make sure you run to win."

"They would trick us like that? I don't believe it. Mr. Corcoran would not—"

"Trust me," said Kwarafa. "By the bowels of the Prophet I swear to you it is false. And as for your American coach—is there anything he would stop at to win?"

Ayid stood up, feeling dizzy. "I've got to think," he said, and left, not hearing Kwarafa's farewell.

Corcoran picked him up at eleven and walked him over to the coach's lounge. He would not be drawn into discussing the race. "We'll be in it soon enough," he said, showing Ayid into the meeting room, a low-ceilinged, homey place with deep chairs and even a bar in one corner. "I'll be on the circuit, giving you times and monitoring the medical stuff. I've got confidence in you—any Chircurgi tricks, we'll come through."

Ayid stopped just inside the doorway. A woman was waiting, tall, pale-skinned, yellow-haired, dressed in a severe green suit decorated only with the UN Mediational Relations Committee emblem.

"Ayid. Come in." She extended a cool hand. "This won't take long." He lowered his eyes under her icy-blue stare. "Coach Corcoran says you have an objection to performance-enhancing substances, based on the religious beliefs of your tribe. Is that essentially correct?"

"Uh . . . yes," he faltered. He always felt uncomfortable looking at a woman's naked face.

"Please read this." She held out a sheet of plastron.

It was short, concise, the sweeping Arabic characters looking out of place on a translight message form:

> *Ayid Hafouz of the M'zab of Al Jarzhireh: Peace. The Council sitting in Ghardaia has granted you dispensation from such rules of the faithful as you deem necessary to excel in your final race. Bring honor to Earth, to PanArabia, and to your tribe.*

He read it twice, then raised his eyes. "Do you have any further objections to following Mr. Corcoran's advice this afternoon?" the woman asked, taking back the form.

Wordless, he shook his head.

"Good," said Corcoran briskly. "In that case, let's go into warmup. We've about an hour to start time." He held out a small package, and Ayid took it numbly. "You can go on now. Po-xiang will be waiting in the ready room."

When the boy had left Corcoran and the woman exchanged looks. "I hated to do it," he began.

"You were right; they have instant respect for anything in writing. He didn't question its authenticity at all."

"But a lie?" Corcoran looked unhappy. "I've never lied to one of my runners before."

"Don't weaken now," said the woman. "Lies are sometimes necessary, for purposes of the greater good. Don't you agree?"

"I guess I just did," said Corcoran, reaching for his pocket as the pain became acute. "After all . . . it's a long way from Mecca."

What shall I do?

Shall I do my best to win? Or lose, on purpose? Perhaps Tseil Laol will leave me so far behind that it will be out of my hands.

As he walked toward the starting line, Ayid Hafouz hoped desperately that someone would decide for him.

On this fourth and last day of the Mediational running events, the crowds had far outstripped the seating capacities of the stands. Dark masses of Humans and Dheils covered the grassy areas of the hills. The sun sparkled on thousands of binoculars, cameras, personal holos, making the whole vast bowl glitter. By Dhelian rules, they would see only the start and the finish of the race; the rest would be run cross-country, out of sight, though of course the judges would be watching the course through remote holos.

He felt his legs trembling, the large muscles of his thighs quivering. His bladder was tight, both with nervousness and the two liters of sweet fluid Po-xiang had poured into him. He reached the start line and bounced on his toes as the other runners fell into place around him. They exchanged short words— "Good luck"—"Good running." Kwarafa squeezed his shoulder and said in a low voice, "Remember, brother." Tseil Laol, in the lane farthest from Ayid for the start, did not look toward him but seemed involved in himself alone.

"RUNNERS FOR THE 18,000-STANDARD RACE, TAKE YOUR MARKS. THIS RACE WILL BE RUN ON SEPARATE COURSES MARKED BY GREEN SIGNALS. IN THE COURSE OF THE RACE THREE OBSTACLES OR TRIALS WILL BE PRESENTED INDIVIDUALLY TO EACH RUNNER."

Ayid felt a sudden thrill of excitement, not unmixed with fear. The rumors were right; this would involve something more than a forty-eight kilometer run, though Allah knew that alone would be bad enough. He hoped that he could face up to the 'obstacles,' whatever they were.

"—AND THE FIRST RUNNER TO NEGOTIATE ALL TRIALS AND FINISH THE COURSE WILL BE THE WINNER.

"SET!"

He crouched slightly. No need of a particularly fast start in a race this long. The outside world, Corcoran, Kwarafa, all his uncertainties and doubts, dropped away as he raised his head to watch the beam.

Snap. He uncoiled forward in an easy, fast, distance-eating lope. The six runners, roughly abreast, moved in a ragged line down the long straight. Beyond it a narrow lane had been roped off, leading over the hills to the northwest. In the distance, over the hills, a brilliant green light burned some meters in the air. The crowds, Dhelian on one side, Human on the other, reached out to touch the runners as they passed between them. Ayid hardly noticed the outstretched hands, hardly heard the surf-sound of applause, thinking to himself: *a slow start even in marathon terms. Well, we're all apprehensive, I suppose.*

The line began to stretch out as each runner settled into his own pace. Aia Maior settled in front of Ayid, who decided to let him set the pace for the first kilometer and see what his times were like. The grass was rougher than the smooth turf of the track, with the irregularities of a natural surface, and felt good to his toughened, bare feet. He reached the top of the low hill and followed Maior down the other side, toward a forest. As they descended he looked out over the terrain ahead. Fairly flat for as far as he could see; some mist far away on the horizon; low hills in the distance that disappeared behind strangely blue trees as they approached the woods line.

"*Slow start,*" said Corcoran. "*But let's save it for now, stick with the Dheils. I'll feed you times. We're going to win this one, Ayid!*"

The green star, moving ahead of them, gleamed above a path leading in. Maior, now some twenty meters ahead, plunged after it. Ayid followed, hearing footsteps close behind him. The forest closed in around him, long flexible frondlike brachiations interlocking overhead, making the path they followed gloomy with a deep blue underwater light. The trail turned and twisted, and soon he lost sight of Maior.

There, the green signal—over a side path. Fronds whipped at him as he turned off the main trail. The footfalls behind him grew fainter and disappeared. He emerged onto a broad, bare, sand-surfaced road and went swinging along it.

He suddenly realized that he was alone. The sand of the road was unmarked by Maior's feet, and when he risked a glance back he saw that there was no one behind him. Was he lost? No, the green light still led him on. *We're running separate courses,* he thought. Probably rated and measured to make sure they all run the same distance. It made sense, in a way . . . but he had to admit to himself that he missed the presence of the others.

"One kilometer, kid. Three minutes fifteen. Slow but okay."

Though perfectly audible, Corcoran's voice seemed fainter. *It will improve,* Ayid thought, *when I come up on the hills beyond.*

And now he had to concentrate on running. So far to go, farther even than a marathon, those contests of pain. But he felt good, felt tremendous with omnipotent energy. *I'll do it,* he thought. *I'll finish, and I'll win, too.*

But *should* he?

He glanced at his left arm. The squarish lump of Ayid-colored tape in his armpit contained the injector. No, he decided, he would not think of that now, nor ponder the strange ruling of a Council that had never before evinced the slightest tendency to bend the age-old Kharidjite dogma.

The sandy trail began to slant upwards, and it grew lighter. Abruptly he left the forest behind and was headed uphill on a bare dirt path. He looked around as he ran, but save for the green spark ahead he was alone. The hill was low and the top quickly reached, and he started down again. *Must be two kilos by now,* he thought, wondering where Corcoran was with his times. More forest ahead, but whitish shapes among the trees . . . what could those be?

The path now was straight, and Ayid allowed himself to increase speed. Now, early, was the time to stretch his legs. He tended to run faster in the last half of a marathon, and Corcoran had told him numberless times that a stronger run early would put him in a better position for the final kick to the finish.

The trail curved left at a tortured-looking wall of natural stone. Ayid leaned easily into the turn. The wall flashed by. Hollowed, convoluted, it bulged from the sandy ground in tall finlike ridges higher than the trees, with narrow channels between. Ayid was curious, but not curious enough to stop.

Another wall, to his left this time. The trail curved right and forked. He looked for the signal but it had gone on ahead of him, or so he thought, and he took the wider branch.

Thirty seconds later he was hopelessly lost. Only the bright sky, hemmed in by towering walls of the twisted rock, was familiar. And the green light, his guide, had disappeared.

Was this a test? Or was he simply lost? He jogged reluctantly to a stop and stared around. Three paths led off into the maze of rock. He jogged in place, wondering which to take. He examined the walls for marks. There were none. He bent to the ground but there were no footprints there but his own.

Which way?

Okay, let's think. We've been heading northwest ever since we left the track. Northwest? He was confused for a moment as he realized he might be in Olympia's southern hemisphere, then he shook his head in annoyance. Didn't matter what you *called* it. He looked up again and was relieved to see the blue sun. Praying by its position five times a day he had become thoroughly familiar with its daily course. If the correct direction continued to be northwest, then he should take the left-hand trail, he decided. That led to another crossroads, which he navigated in the same manner, and then to a long, narrow defile down which he loped at three-quarter speed, hoping. The canyon narrowed. Ahead of him he could see that it zigged sharply, then seemed to end. Ayid ran on, feeling rock brush his shoulders. He felt despair. He'd been wrong. There, ahead, the trail ended.

Or did it? He slowed. No, it was a corner. He turned it, scrambled up through a niche—and saw the trail widening ahead, sloping downward. And ahead of him, almost due northwest by the sun, shone the green star.

"Praise Allah, Who gives men minds to see Him," murmured

Ayid. He sailed downward, letting out the muscles that had unconsciously become cramped in the rocky maze. He could, he realized,
have been delayed there for hours. Except that he had remembered
and reasoned. *The first problem,* he thought, *was one to be solved
by the mind. What will the second one be?*

He lost the thread of that thought as the slope carried him into a
wide valley. It was misty on its far side, though he caught some
impression of a dark mass far away before the drifting white closed
over it. Below and before him, drawing closer at each long heel-
jarring downhill stride, was another forest.

But different from the first. An odd hard glitter ran across its
surface as the wind moved its millions of leaves, making it look like a
dark sea. As he followed the trail down into it he could make out
individual trees at its edge, looking strangely pyramidal, or like men
with legs astraddle. Another moment and he saw why: the trunks
emerged from the ground at several points, uniting in a sort of
flying-buttress way to form the main trunk. The trail led winding
among them and soon he was leaping to clear the roots that occasionally encroached on the path.

The silence behind his ear was beginning to worry him. Where
was Corcoran? Had something gone wrong? He would need his
times to run at his best now that there were no other runners to pace
himself against.

Silent. Yes, it was . . . no sound but the thud, thud of his own feet,
the in-in-out rhythm of his breathing. It was cool in the shadows and
with the sweating he was already doing it felt like a shower of cold
water; good, but . . . it left him shivering. He had a sense of something vaguely wrong. He risked another look back. No, none of the
other runners were visible.

His feet thudded in harsh syncopation. The trees seemed closer
together now. Their foliage, reflective from above, was impenetra-
ble from below, and the gloom swiftly deepened until he could
barely make out the trail under his feet. At times he came close to
colliding with the reaching roots of the trees.

There! He caught his breath even as he swerved abruptly to one
side. There, he'd cleared it, but—*the tree had moved!*

No, he thought, *it couldn't have.* But he glanced back and saw its roots square astride the trail. He couldn't have run under it.

Worse than that, he felt it now, felt the air of menace that surrounded him in the lightless wood. He began to run in earnest, fear spurring him on, making his breath come ragged and his heart begin to pound. *No*, he thought, *I've got to keep to the pace. I can't exhaust myself now. Not with so many kilometers to go.* He forced himself to slow down.

Another tree moved suddenly, right in his path; and he ducked. This time it had been a branch. The movement had been slow, though; and he'd seen it coming as the trunk began to lean.

"They're too slow," he sobbed, twisting away from another blindly groping root. Ahead in the dimness the green light burned, blotted out from time to time by moving forms, limbs, slow deliberate trunks. He ran, weaving between shadows. Turn back? He couldn't—he'd never make it back through the alerted trees behind, and without the signal he might lose the path. But more than that he *had* to go forward, had to do it to finish the race. Even if the trees trapped him, caught him. And then . . . ? A smooth, hard, oddly warm limb poked into his side, knocking the breath from him, and with the nausea came sudden anger. They wouldn't stop him. With his hands he would tear them apart, these creaking, swaying, unnatural—

He struck straight into a solid trunk, rebounded, and fell. He lay there dazed and gasping. A crackling and swaying of branches came from above, and he rolled over and scrambled on hands and knees. Around him he felt the slow writhe of the roots. The anger was all he felt now; and when something coiled around him, he stamped and tore savagely and heard, somewhere above him, a harsh rasp of pain.

Then, quite suddenly, he was out and pounding all out down a dim forest lane, the green light gleaming far ahead. There were still trees to either side, but they were straight-trunked, and their only movement came from the wind. Ayid gradually regained control, slowed a little, and felt at his side as he ran. Bruised, but he couldn't feel anything broken. His mind? Not so simple. He was all right, he would finish the race, but he would never forget those long minutes of darkness and utter terror. *That, the second trial? Allah,* he thought, *they might have killed me.* He had no idea how he had escaped; all he could remember was the terrible anger.

He asked himself how far he had to go.

You've gone about fifteen kilometers, Ayid, he answered himself. How do you know?

Just by the feel. As a runner learns to do.

Then we're a third of the way to the finish.

Yes, he said to himself. About a third. And one more trial yet to come.

The canopy of foliage above him opened gradually as he ran on, maintaining what he felt was about a 3:10 per kilometer pace. The sky became visible; and harsh blue light streamed down in long, glowing, laserlike rays. At last he came out of the trees entirely and climbed a series of short hills to a reddish, dry-looking plain. The white mist he had seen from far away now obscured his vision ahead, but he could see well for at least five hundred meters ahead, and he drove on relentlessly, stepping up his pace despite the pain from his bruised side. Kilometer after kilometer sped by on the dead level, without feature or tree or even a large rock to break the monotony. Ayid began to feel that he was on an endless treadmill of red plain and hard-packed trail. He kept glancing back. The fog was rolling in behind him, but there did seem to be a tiny black dot far back there. He couldn't even tell whether it was Human or Dhelian.

In the monotony—he felt that he could crank out five-minute miles for hours on end, the nervous reaction after leaving the forest made him so buoyant—he began to think about Kwarafa, and what he had said about the Dhelian impact on Earth.

The PanAfrican was right. That was obvious; Tseil Laol had admitted it without qualification. There would be suffering, the Dheil had said. Hadn't even softened it by calling it friction or unpleasantness. Had said, suffering.

And the colonial analogy was sound. Holo was frowned on by the M'zab; but Ayid had seen, in the government schools, the old documentaries on the Wars of Liberation in the twentieth century, then the Moslem reaction that had in turn given way to the unified PanArab state. All of it violent, a history full of hatred and murder. And all of it due to the shock of facing and losing to a different, Western culture.

Was it worth it?

Dimly he suspected that if he had grown up a city dweller he might not think so. If he had grown up with holo, plenteous food, education, all the privileges of the PanArab upper classes. But he hadn't. He'd grown up a M'zab, ignorant and dirt-poor; and that made him appreciate the Western-derived medicine that had cured his sister once, the Western-derived engineering that had brought a meter-wide pipeline of fresh water in from the sea and given the M'zab, for the first time in their history, enough to eat. No, the European culture was not superior; but a wise nation could select what it wanted over the years and reject what was harmful. It had taken the Arabs two centuries to do it. But it could be done.

Which leaves you where, Ayid Hafouz?

It left him against Kwarafa. He knew the stocky African was sincere. He'd given up a sure first in the sprint to try to foul Southren. No athlete, and that Kebe Kwarafa was, could make a greater sacrifice. But Ayid did not agree with him. Algerians could not have stayed forever in the twelfth century, lopping off hands and dying of hunger and the plague. And now Earth could not immure herself in the twenty-first, not without turning inward and, finally, dying.

I will not lose this race if I can help it, Ayid thought. *Corcoran is right. I must win it and with Allah's help I will.*

And the M'zab, his tribe, with their stubborn denial of progress? Ayid decided he did not want to think about that just then.

He had been glancing upward for the last few minutes, puzzled by a huge shadow looming above him. The mist, thinning as he drove on, gradually allowed him to make out what it was.

It was a mountain. It reared up from the plain like a strong man standing with arms outspread. It was so tall that he had to tilt his head back to see the top of it. For a moment he hoped that the trail might lead around it. Then he saw the green signal glimmering, far ahead, already a quarter of the way up the huge greenish-gray flank.

Not a mountain, Ayid. You can't take a mountain, my friend. Not after thirty kilometers and a scare and a poke in the *butuun*.

But he ignored himself. He was running well: better, probably, than he'd ever run before. The fear, the anger, the clear resolve now to win, combined to flood him with energy, breaking the fatigue he had begun to feel. A second wind.

He began the climb, slowing only a little at first, then more as the grade steepened.

It grew hotter as he climbed. The glare of the sun bounced up from the grayish sand surface of the trail, seeping into his face and melting into the sweaty heat of his long legs and arms. He felt the prickle of sweat break out again and pulled an arm across his forehead in mid-stride. Sweat was good—it cooled a runner; but it could be bad—could make him chafe at armpits and groin and thighs, rubbing the skin right off. So far, though, he felt all right.

The path narrowed and changed to a smooth rock surface. It seemed to have been sliced out of the living stone of the mountain, leading upward in a series of switchbacks. He couldn't imagine how the Chircurgis, or the Dheils, or whoever had planned the course, had done this to solid rock. The hardness of it jarred right up to his eyes with every step, and his right knee gave a warning pang. He came up off his heels, running with toes and calves. Still he could feel a shock in his legs at each stride.

It grew still hotter. The sun, high in the sky, flooded the narrow cut with blue-hot light. He shortened his stride, slowing down. He felt that he was barely inching up the mountain, like a fly climbing the side of the starship that had taken him outward from Earth. All that distance, all that energy . . . and here he was, straining to put one bare foot in front of the other. He almost smiled.

He turned at a switchback and the way up became steeper. He leaned into the slope, digging at the rock with his toes. The trail seemed to end just above at blue sky and he labored up to it gratefully but it was only another switchback. Far above him he glimpsed a green spark. He bent his head down and leaned stubbornly into the mountain.

His calves and thighs, fatigued already down on the plain, began to hurt in earnest. He swung his arms but that failed to move him any faster. His breathing, loud between rock walls, afforded no relief in this hot, thin air. A leaden feeling invaded his chest.

Another switchback. He turned grimly. How far? How high? He couldn't guess; the plain, white-shrouded below him, seemed as far away as if he were leaving the planet. And he hurt. He felt pain at the bottom of his chest, like a bar of heavy hot metal; in his mouth, parching, thick with ropy saliva; in his legs. Each step sent a shaft of pain upwards into his skull until the dull running headache ignited. His mind returned from his body to himself with data:

You won't make it. Have to stop, rest.

I'll make it.

You can't. Your knee is going.

Can't be much farther. Hold on. No isolated mountain can be very high.

On Earth, maybe. This is not Earth. In the Prophet's name let us stop and rest for a moment. There is no one behind.

There is someone behind. We saw him back on the plain, remember? Even now he is behind us on the mountain. Tseil Laol? Aia Maior? Or Southren? In any case it doesn't matter. We have to keep on. You shut up now and just help me run.

Another switchback, disappointing him terribly. Now he had to lift his foot at each step, and sometimes he slid, scraping skin from his toes and the soft side of his foot. He barely felt it. Up, up. His breath rasped. The trail suddenly became too steep to run straight and he was forced to plant his bruised feet sideways. The pace was agonizingly slow. With each step he had to pull himself up the mountain.

The red lights came on in his lungs and head and legs all at once. He was still moving, but it was almost a walk. Each step was a triumph of will. The pains in his legs and head and back were gone, lost in the screaming from his whole body. He was numb, leaden. But he still moved. Upward. Another turn ahead.

Blood supply to his stomach had been cut off long before; it had shut down, contracting like a fist, squeezing blood from itself to the straining muscles. Now his body began to cut off other demands. He blanked out for a moment but snapped back as he blundered against the face of the mountain. He took another step. The world was a mass of pain and he felt it all. He took another step. He took another step.

The grade ended and like a clown he tangled his legs and fell. He lay there hugging the cool and lovely horizontal as red-hot shafts of air sawed in and out of his lungs. After some time he was able to stagger up.

It was not a mountain after all; it was, or had been, a volcano. To his left lay the crater, a pit of grayish rock with trees lower down and between them the tantalizing sheen of water. To his right, to the east, lay all the land he had crossed. The mist still lay like lamb's wool over the red plain; far off he could see the sparkle of dark forest; beyond that, slightly indistinct in the shimmer of heat-haze, the low hills behind which lay the track. For a moment he saw a gleam in the sky even beyond that—a ship, lifting from Olympia Port on its way to Terra or to one of the Dhelian planets.

The thought of Terra brought him back to himself. He was Ayid Hafouz, running the last race of the Mediationals, and as far as he knew, he was in the lead. He must not lose it. He launched himself gingerly into the down-slope.

Much easier. The grade on this side was shallow, the trail drifting downward without need of switchbacks along a gentle ridge of harsh-looking volcanic rock that had been smoothed somehow and paved with a narrow trail of sand. He felt weak as water, and all his joints had stiffened in the brief stop, but he stretched his legs and tried to pick up speed on the straight sections. *I can't have more than twelve kilos left*, he thought. A good forty-five minutes' run. The mountain had to have been the third challenge. Purely physical. There should be nothing now but a straight run on in to the finish.

He wondered again why he hadn't heard from Corcoran. Out here, high up, he was almost in line-of-sight of the track. But there was only silence from behind his left ear . . . such silence that he could hear, transmitted through his bones, an ominous clicking noise from the faulty right knee.

Somewhat cooler now, a slight breeze in his face as he descended. He was panting. All the reserve water in his system was long gone. His mouth was dry and his head ached. He forced himself along the trail, letting gravity pull him down, flowing with it. When it reached level ground again he slowed and almost stopped, then shook himself and moved into a sort of dragging jog.

Ten more?

The trail was darker sand now, blending with an almost black, rough-looking sand that layered the plain on this side of the volcano. The slight breeze disappeared and soon he was running, panting, through a limpid shimmer of dry heat. The green star danced in the rippling air ahead of him, at times doubling and tripling itself, a mirage. He found it hard to keep his eyes on it. The horizon seemed to be spinning slowly around him. . . .

He crumpled softly into the sand. It was burning hot and he wondered vaguely why it had not hurt his feet when he was running on it. He lay there for several minutes, then tried to get up. On the fifth or sixth try he succeeded and tottered forward again. Bright white trails, like slowly-moving falling stars, moved at the edges of his vision. On and on. He had no more idea of what his pace was, or of the passage of time. The blue-white sun had always been over-head, his tongue, swollen, had always filled his dry mouth. But ahead, slowly, the green hills began to rise above the horizon.

There . . . a dark line, between him and the hills, low on the ground. It expanded quickly as he ran on. It ran from his left to his right straight across the trail and as he came up to it a human figure stood up and suddenly reached out to grab at his legs and pull him down at the very edge. "Sorry," said Tseil Laol. "But I thought you were going to run right in."

Ayid lay flat, his chin over the edge, and looked down into the gorge. A mighty river must have run there once, perhaps even before the Dheils had wrenched Olympia from its doomed sun and spun it across space to here. But now it was almost dry, and fifty meters below them smooth boulders gleamed. He rolled over painfully and looked up at the tall Dheil.

Laol's face was bloody; a long cut had laid his scalp open across the forehead. He looked far past exhaustion; his fingertips were bloody; his feet were bruised blue and swollen. He tried to smile at Ayid's unspoken question. "Yes, about as bad as you look. This has not been an easy race."

"How—" It was hard to speak aloud. "How long have you been waiting here?"

"Not long. I saw you behind me, going up the mountain. You didn't look up."

"No," said Ayid. He looked into the gorge. "This is another trial?"

"It shouldn't be." Ayid's face hardened. "Not by the conventional rules. There were to be three, and they all have to be negotiable. This isn't. It's the Chircurgi. Their aim's clear enough—they want neither of us back before dark, to make both humanoid races look bad . . . especially us. Ayid, my poor Human friend, there are jealousies even within the Mediation."

Ayid sat up and examined the obstacle. A nearly straight cut through the black desert, its banks, humped and lined with water-rounded boulders larger than a man, dropped precipitously to the nearly-dry bed. Neither to north nor south could he see any way around, short of climbing the mountain again.

"Couldn't we make a bridge?"

"Too far across. And I've looked up and down the banks. No trees, no vines, nothing but rock."

They looked at each other. Ayid waited, then saw that the Dhelian wanted him to speak first.

"I'll let you down," he said.

"Do you want to rest for a minute first?"

"Yes. Okay."

When he regained his breath they started down. Ayid, stretched out flat, locked his hand on the Dheil's fragile wrist as Tseil Laol wriggled over the edge. He felt himself being slowly dragged into the gorge as the other runner searched for a purchase. "Let go," said Laol at last. He opened his hand and the wrist disappeared over the edge.

"Are you all right?"

"Yes. Come on. Step onto my hands, then slide down; I'll break your fall."

He lost some skin from his upper arms, but found himself on a ledge about three meters down. He looked at Laol, who was panting. The Dhelian looked bad, but his eyes were calm. "You're next," he said, holding out his hand.

They worked their way downward from ledge to ledge, boulder to boulder. Tseil Laol opened the cut on his head again on a projecting point, sending blood pouring into his eyes. He wiped it out with the back of one hand and Ayid let him down and they were almost at the bottom and it was Ayid's turn to go down first. They rested for a few moments, breathing hard; then Ayid nodded. "Almost there."

Laol held out the hand, and Ayid took it and went over the edge. He dangled helplessly, pressed flat against the rock, and groped with his feet. Nothing . . . not a rock, not a ledge, not a crevice. He could see the riverbed but it was too far to drop and the rocks looked cruel down there. No, they couldn't get down there. His arm was being pulled out of joint. "Get me up," he called.

There was a pull on his arm, but he only came up a few centimeters. He felt the hand begin to slip from around his wrist. It felt sticky. The blood was making the Dheil's hand slip. "Laol, pull me up," he croaked, looking down into the gorge.

"Ayid—"

Something slipped. Ayid turned briefly in the air as he fell. He felt his right leg buckle outward at the knee, heard a terrible tearing crunch as ligament and cartilage gave way. Someone screamed, the sound echoing.

"Ayid! Are you hurt? My hand slipped!"

He lay there, looking at his leg. It did not hurt at all. He looked up, saw the anxious look on Laol's face. "I don't know. Think I hurt my leg . . . move over to your right about five meters and you'll be able to hang by your hands and drop."

The Dheil let himself down cautiously, hanging by both arms, and let go. He dropped about two meters and hit, rolling. Ayid got up and put weight on the leg. Odd. That terrible sound and though it felt weak he could stand on it. Laol came over. "I'm sorry I dropped you. Are you all right?"

"I guess," said Ayid. A low trickle caught his ear and he and Laol both looked toward the center of the bed. A tiny stream of fluid meandered down it. He limped over to it and bent to sniff it. It was water. He picked up a handful and sniffed it, then drank. Water in the desert was one thing he knew. Sand grated in his teeth. "It is good to drink," he said. "Here. Let me wash that cut of yours out."

Tenderly he trickled the murky water over the Dheil's face. "That does not hurt?"

"One does not have to show it."

Ayid nodded, pleased. "So my tribe feels too."

"You're sure this water is safe?"

"Yes."

Laol sucked in a few mouthfuls and spat. Ayid followed suit and splashed some on his head and chest. It evaporated quickly, refreshingly cool.

"Shall we climb up now?" said Tseil Laol.

"Yes. Now."

There was one point on the way up—when Ayid was only a few meters from the top, and thought he saw a foothold that he could use alone—that he was tempted not to turn around and help the Dheil up. *For Earth, Ayid? Leave him here, and go on alone—for Earth?*

It took no time at all to make that decision. Ayid knelt, fixed his knees firmly, and lowered his shaking hand. "Come on up," he said.

They looked at each other at the top for a long moment. Ahead of them only the low hill lay between them and the track.

Without another word, they turned and began to run.

Now it is between us again, thought Ayid. *As it should be. The only way the race could end.*

The green beacon was poised now at the crown of the low hill.

Beyond that, he knew, was the downhill, the final kilometer in full view of the stands. The holo cameras. The crowd. In view of Corcoran. And as if his thought of him had called him back, he heard him again, faint, but rapidly growing stronger:

"Don't know if you can hear me but . . . blood sugar way below critical . . . lot of disturbance in blood chemistry . . . Po-xiang thinks you're injured . . . way overdue but heart rate shows you're still running . . . nobody else has finished yet . . . we're still cheering you on, kid."

It was only a gentle uphill, only a knoll, but the pain was worse than on the mountain. No feeling in his legs. The headache a red haze with darts of fire. The chafe in the groin. The sickening sound loud now in his right knee.

And Laol slowly, slowly drawing ahead.

The Dhelian, he saw, was running as hard as he could, but it was little better than a fast walk. He was only ten meters ahead. Couldn't he go faster? Couldn't he force himself to overtake?

They reached the crest, and the sight of the track and the stands burst over him. A tremendous roll of sound came drumming up the hill as they headed together down, down toward the green flicker that was now stationary a kilometer away.

"Kid!"

"You made it. God—you look—what happened out there? Never mind. You made it. You stayed with him!"

Right, Coach, he thought.

"He's only a few meters ahead of you. You can catch him easy. Now's the time to kick it in!"

There's no kick left, coach. I don't even know if this knee, the grating sound louder now at each step, will get me to the finish.

"You're dead. I know you're dead beat, kid. You look bad. But you can catch him. Ayid, kid. The injector. Take it off."

He ran, without thought.

"Ayid, the injector!" Corcoran's voice, inside his head, pleading. It finally penetrated. *"Take it out!"*

Eyes on the finish beam, now redly visible under the green at the end of the straight, he obeyed. The tape came off his arm easily. The injector was hot from his skin, wet.

"Use it! Press it to your arm!"

Blind with pain, he saw only the finish. Not Laol's weaving form just ahead. Not the staring holos. Not even the blue-white sun. Only the finish. Only when he glanced down to guide the injector to his arm did he realize what it was. He threw it away weakly. It bounced once on the grass, rolled, and then he was by it. No more energy. There was no more in his entire body. He sagged.

"Ayid, Ayid, you didn't—"

But he had, and now he could run no more. He stopped, stood uncertainly, and began to fold.

"Walk, anyway. Walk, damn you, you stupid Arab."

A last vague ripple of anger came to his rescue. He converted the fall to a stagger, the stagger to a hopping movement forward. Step at a time. Hatred for the red-faced American. Little faster. Stupid Arab. Knee hurts now. A hundred meters ahead he saw Tseil Laol break the beam, saw the Dhelian stands go wild. The red-haired runner raised an arm, and then fell. Ayid staggered on. Only a few now. The sun was red, not blue. Only a little.

He passed the beam, turned round once, and crumpled beside Tseil Laol. He sank down, inside himself, into the nothing behind his mind; and then he felt cold over his entire body and the sting of an injector on the side of his neck. He gasped and came up again, and strong arms were hoisting him up and forcing him to walk. By degrees, as the injection took hold, he regained control of his breathing and began to sob.

"Good," said a vaguely familiar Oriental face that wavered in front of him. "You stopped breathing there for a second. How do you feel?"

"Knee," he panted. "Rest . . . okay. See Laol." He gulped at something sweet held to his lips.

"He's got his own medics." A rough loud voice: Corcoran. "How is he?"

"He says okay, except for his knee." Po-xiang stooped down to manipulate the right leg. "It's shot, Jerry. He's torn the ligaments on the inside and the patella's displaced. I don't see how he made it except for the shock."

Ayid looked down, and felt fear. His thighs were bloody from the chafed groin, but the knee looked worse, swollen and bruised purple.

"Keep those holo people back," snapped Corcoran to someone. "He's hurt." He looked at Ayid for the first time. "Well. At least you finished. But throwing it away like that. . . ."

"Yes." Ayid rubbed sweat and involuntary tears from his face. Po-xiang's hands were gentle, but now the pain from the shattered knee was beginning to come through shock and adrenaline. "Guess I'm through. Done."

Corcoran didn't answer. He looked old suddenly, old and beaten. "Yeah," he said at last. "We're both through. This was the last one."

"Mr. Corcoran."

They looked up. It was Tseil Laol, a thin line of red showing on his forehead where the wound had been. His hair was wet. "Good race," said Corcoran after a moment.

Laol nodded, but he was looking at Ayid. "I understand that he is hurt."

"The knee's gone. He'll run again, given time, but never this far," said Po-xiang. "Are you all right?"

"Just tired. I came to see if I could help."

"We can take care of him," said Corcoran.

"Maybe there is one thing I can do," said Laol. He bent toward Ayid. "You won't be back to Olympia?"

"No." Ayid swallowed. A voice from his past, his father: A M'zab does not show emotion. Even at the moment of his greatest loss.

"Except to watch. And I am poor . . . perhaps only by holo.

"But I will be back."

Laol straightened. He looked at Corcoran. "Denda Lai saw what he did, at the end. We know about drugs, of course. And how eager Earthmen are to win. He probably could have beaten me, but he chose to lose, because that was the way of the sport. The way of *dalanai.*"

Corcoran narrowed his eyes.

"So—" Laol turned to face cameras, and newsmen, that had somehow magically appeared. "—I exercise an ancient Dhelian custom—and resign the victory to one that showed the greater *dalanai.* Will you honor me, my brother, by accepting?"

"Ah—"

"He accepts," said Corcoran.

There was little to see outside the port once the blue-brown circle of Olympia, an opal on velvet, had dwindled to a distant light moving with parallax against the stars. The ship was gaining speed. Ayid leaned back and shifted his leg, propping the cast on a convenient table, and went back to his musing.

Had Tseil Laol known? He'd called him 'brother,' there at the end. But sexless, artificially reproduced, the word would be meaningless to Dheils. Laol knew English, true. But how had he understood the word? Which of its deep and enduring human connotations had he meant?

Did he, did the Dhelians, know about the relationship between their two races?

It was useless to think. He was out of the running now, in any sense of the term. But he would not be going back to the M'zab; he knew that. Corcoran could teach him coaching; there would be new runners coming up, inspired by the Mediational coverage. They would need his experience.

In a way, Ayid thought, it had all worked out well. Almost suspiciously well. If it had been done purposely it was very clever. Earth, proud now of both runners, showed every sign of approving the Mediation. From envy and suspicion, most Humans had turned to wholesale admiration and acceptance of the Dhelians, who in their turn were lavish with their praise of Human prowess. If it had all been planned, it couldn't have been done more neatly. Had Laol planned it? Had the Dheils?

Again, there was no answer. But in spite of the uncertainty he felt at peace. He had done his best in a fair race. He had—what was that old thing Corcoran liked to quote—oh, yes—

If you can fill the unforgiving minute
With sixty seconds' worth of distance, run;
Yours is the Earth, and everything that's in it;
And, what is more, you'll be a man, my Son.

reprinted by permission of Scott Meredith Literary Agency; **THE GOD AND HIS MAN** by Gene Wolfe, copyright © 1979 by Gene Wolfe, reprinted by permission of Virginia Kidd, literary agent; all stories previously appeared in *Asimov's Science Fiction* published by Dell Magazines, a division of Bantam Doubleday Dell Magazines.

463